THE LAST
TIME
SHE DIED

BOOKS BY ZOË SHARP

ZOË SHARP

BLAKE & BYRON THRILLERS: BOOK 1

THE LAST TIME SHE DIED

Bookouture

Published by Bookouture in 2021

An imprint of Storyfire Ltd.
Carmelite House
50 Victoria Embankment
London EC4Y 0DZ

www.bookouture.com

ISBN: 978-1-80019-743-5
eBook ISBN: 978-1-80019-742-8

This book is a work of fiction. Names, characters, businesses,
organizations, places and events other than those clearly in the
public domain, are either the product of the author's imagination
or are used fictitiously. Any resemblance to actual persons, living or
dead, events or locales is entirely coincidental.

For Daisy Clementine Mary
Welcome, and good luck!

PROLOGUE

Ten Years Ago

Three go into the forest.

Two squint against the lash of rain, grunt with the effort it takes to half carry, half drag the third through the claw of branches and brambles. Mud already slick beneath their boots. Feet already sodden.

One of them wishing to be anywhere but here.

The other just wishing it done.

Their burden is not yet sixteen. Easier to haul than a full-grown adult but…

Dead weight.

Dead.

If not quite yet, then she soon will be.

Doesn't matter much, either way.

Long dark hair, matted with dirt and blood, hides the ruin of her face.

Long dark night hides the ruin they hope to avoid.

Long dark rain keeps the poachers in their beds.

Torch beams hit falling water, slicing down. Illuminating little. Nothing to see but trees and night. And the eyes of hidden watchers, lurking just beyond.

No condemnation there. Only hunger. They'll scavenge what you bring, if you don't bury it deep.

'He better be here,' mutters the first. The rain bites through the band of his hat, crawls beneath his collar, swamps his gloves. His hands are numb.

'He will be,' says the second, waits a beat. 'He has the most to lose.'

The implication penetrates faster than a blade.

The first man shivers, trudges on.

In a clearing ahead, the sudden flare of headlights blinds them, catches them in a frozen tableau that has no extenuation.

This can only be what it is.

A body dump.

A diesel engine turns and catches, belching out smoke that mists against the lights, against the rain.

Clanking, the machine lurches forward. The arm drops and the bucket rakes the shifting ground. It lifts and swings aside. Water gushes down, gushes in, trying to fill the void. But even on this night, the storm cannot compete.

In minutes, the makeshift grave is dug. The operator shifts the arm to one side and lowers it, almost gently, to rest the bucket nose down. An elephant folding its trunk and taking a bow.

At no time does the operator leave the shelter of the cab.

Sighing, the two who brought the body position it closer. The first man takes the feet, keeps his gaze averted.

But the second clears the tangled hair from the features, as if trying to match the living to the dead, one last time. Reaches for the slender neck. Sees the silver locket on the narrow chain.

'Bit late to check for a pulse, isn't it?' snaps the first. He glances, then quickly away.

The second does not answer. He grips her jacket, jerks her up and over.

It is a long drop to the bottom of the hole.

Afterwards, he is never sure if the sound he hears is merely air impacted from the lungs, or some kind of final cry.

They do not wait to see the digger's arm rise again. They are already turning, heads slanted into the rain as they retrace their steps.

Three went into the forest.

Only two came back.

ONE

Now

Over the years, Byron had been to more than his share of funerals.

He'd buried both parents, an older brother, friends, colleagues…

A wife.

That was quite apart from services he'd attended for those met only *after* their deaths – the murder victims, whom he came to know in ways more intimate than family.

Those were the ones who called to him in the night and strolled through his dreams.

But the man being lowered into the ground in the elaborate casket – for which, Byron swore, an entire oak might have been sacrificed – was almost a stranger.

A week ago, Byron was barely aware of Gideon Fitzroy, let alone prepared to drive a hundred and forty miles to reach this little churchyard in the Derbyshire Dales, in time to see the man buried.

Officially, no crime had been committed.

He had to remind himself that crime, of any sort, was not currently his business.

And yet, here he was, standing a respectful distance back from the graveside of a man he didn't know, surrounded by people who had, thus far, largely ignored him. In truth, that was partly his own fault. He'd misjudged the traffic leaving north London, and finally arrived just as the service itself was starting. He slipped into the back of the Norman church unnoticed, then out again while the coffin was being hoisted for its final journey.

PC Jane Hudson, formal in her No1 dress uniform, caught sight of Byron. She gave a restrained nod but followed it with a wink. He inclined his head by way of response.

She looked well, he considered. Trading her urban beat for the wilds of Derbyshire clearly suited her. Jane had come to policing via the Royal Navy, the experience lending her an air of self-assurance. A transplanted Scot, she had a fair Celtic complexion scattered with freckles. Her pale red hair, normally a riot of tight curls, was firmly pinned beneath her cap.

The man standing alongside the young officer noted the exchange and followed her gaze. He was older, broader, with a stocky build that would easily run to fat if he didn't keep a grip on it. Even now, Byron noted the altered stance to compensate – feet apart, leaning back slightly. The man turned and studied Byron with narrowed eyes, not troubling to hide his scrutiny. With years of practice, Byron hardened his features and stared back. The other man looked away first.

Nice to know I haven't entirely lost the knack.

The vicar droned through the familiar liturgy in a tone that was half sorrowful, half smug. A kind of 'I told you so' inflection, as if the deceased was, right about now, discovering all that might have been.

Byron tuned it out.

Instead, he watched the reactions of those who'd gathered to see Gideon Fitzroy into the grave. A blonde woman in a designer dress, face hidden behind an old-fashioned brimmed hat and veil. Was the fine black mesh to conceal her grief, or lack of it?

She was flanked by a boy and a girl, both fair like their mother. The boy was maybe fifteen or sixteen, gawky, not yet grown into his limbs. His face was peppered with acne that did not quite hide the livid mesh of recent scarring along his jaw.

The girl was perhaps three or four years younger – Byron found it hard to put an age on children between toddler and teen. The sleeve of her jacket had been tailored to fit over the cast on her right arm. From the set of her mouth, the way she kept blinking, he suspected only pride kept her from weeping.

It was interesting to know that one person, at least, mourned Fitzroy's passing.

A man hovered next to the trio, close but somehow excluded from their circle. His dark hair, no matter how carefully arranged, was thinning. The breeze occasionally ruffling across the church-yard had him nervously smoothing it down.

There was something similar about the shape of the man's face, the bridge of his nose, the line of his mouth, that was echoed in the teenage boy. An ex-husband, perhaps?

On the other side of the grave an older man, tall but slightly stooped, stood behind a woman in a wheelchair. As Byron's gaze rested on the pair, he saw the man's hand move to her shoulder. She reached up and squeezed it with her own, not hiding her distress. Byron judged them married by their matching rings but wondered idly at their relationship to the deceased.

The only other person to catch his eye was a thin woman whose worn coat marked her out from the other mourners. Perhaps it was her discomfort at this difference that made her scurry for the gateway before the service was finished. It was hard to tell.

For Byron, playing this game was a habit not easily discarded.

A small movement on the other side of the churchyard pulled his eyes from the others. At first, he took the figure there as male. Slim-hipped and slender, in skinny black jeans, ripped at the knees, and a dark hoodie beneath a short jacket. Then the figure shifted and he changed his mind.

A young woman – anywhere from late teens to late twenties. At this distance, that was as close as he could guess.

Her clothing might be dark but it was hardly traditional funeral garb. He could tell by the way she watched the coffin into the ground with such intent that she was no chance bystander. She'd come to see this done.

As if feeling his gaze, she threw him a quick, furtive glance and turned away abruptly, ducking her head as if to avoid recognition. Byron's memory for faces, names, was renowned. But, in that brief moment, he was certain he'd never set eyes on her before.

So, who are you?

Almost without conscious thought, Byron's feet shifted as if to follow, but a voice at his shoulder diverted his attention.

'Mr Byron, sir?'

His eyes flicked to where the figure stood, but she was gone. He pulled his focus back. The vicar had finished his spiel and Jane Hudson now hurried towards him, hand outstretched. The stocky man was at her side.

Byron took the woman's proffered hand. 'Jane. Good to see you.'

'Thank you, sir. You, too. Wasn't sure you'd made it.'

'Traffic.' He shrugged apologetically.

Hudson turned to her companion. 'Sarge, this is Detective Superintendent John Byron – my old mentor.'

Her appreciation sounded genuine.

'I think you better put aside the rank, Jane,' Byron said. 'I've yet to get back on the job…'

Sometimes, Byron had to remind himself that he'd been signed off for almost a year. There were times when he didn't feel remotely ready to return to any kind of duties. And others when he fought the utter frustration of doing nothing.

They can tell you to 'take your time' as much as they like.
What they don't tell you is how.

'This is Ed Underhill – my predecessor on this patch,' Hudson was saying. 'He's been showing me the ropes.'

'I don't think there's much need for that,' Underhill said. 'The lass's picked things up pretty quickly.' He sounded friendly but Byron knew he was being weighed up, that the other man was gauging the gap between Byron and himself – in age and appearance as well as prosperity. The job had taken its toll on Byron but he was still only in his mid-thirties and looked it. Underhill was probably twenty years older and had left the force considerably further down the career ladder. For a moment, something tightened in his face, then he gave a rueful smile.

'It might take me a while to stop calling you "sir", sir.' Hudson dimpled. 'Not sure I'm quite ready to start calling you "John".'

'Please don't.' Byron had always disliked his first name, partly for exactly the emphasis the woman had just placed upon it. A John was a toilet, a mug punter on a used-car lot, the client of a prostitute. 'Just Byron will do.'

Whatever response Hudson might have made was pre-empted by the arrival of the man Byron had dubbed the ex-husband. He tapped Underhill on the arm and leaned in.

'Sorry to interrupt, Ed. Do you have a moment?'

'Of course,' Underhill said. He nodded to Byron. 'Good to meet you, Mr Byron. I hope we'll get a chance to chat before you head home?'

Byron gave a noncommittal smile and watched him leave. He did not enjoy talking shop, rarely seeking out the opportunity. He hoped to avoid being cornered by Underhill and peppered with well-meaning reminiscences.

There are some things I'd really rather forget.

'Ed's been great while I've been settling in.' Hudson pulled a wry face. 'I get the feeling he regrets retiring.'

'So why did he?'

'Bad back. And he'd done thirty years, so no one can say he hasn't earned it…'

Hudson's voice trailed off awkwardly and Byron hid a smile. The ongoing repercussions from his own injuries looked like they might force him out early, albeit at a level that came with a very healthy pension. Not to mention compensation and insurance. He knew there had been plenty of rumours about that.

'As long as he's doing right by you, that's all that matters. Who was the other chap, by the way?'

'Oh, Roger Flint – Mr Fitzroy's brother-in-law.'

'The sister being…?'

'Fitzroy's wife – well, widow – Virginia.' Hudson indicated the woman in the veil. 'The kids are hers from a previous marriage.'

'Ah.' Byron nodded. 'So, how are you liking it up here?'

'Oh, fine, I think. Rustic Derbyshire is a far cry from the Met, though. Not much goes on around here.'

'Sudden death of a local bigwig notwithstanding, you mean?'

Byron hadn't missed the pair of journalists hovering by the gate – a local man and a stringer for the nationals, if he was any judge. No doubt they'd hoped – in vain – for celebrity attendance. To his mind, the fact there were only two of them spoke volumes.

Gideon Fitzroy was yesterday's man.

'Aye, well, apart from that.' Hudson tried to offset the twitch of her shoulders with a smile that didn't quite make it to wry. 'Not that it isn't lovely to see you, Mr Byron, but I have to ask – why are you *really* here?'

TWO

Fifteen minutes later, the young woman Byron had observed in the churchyard dropped down on the inside of the high brick wall surrounding a manor house just outside the village, and dusted the grit from her hands.

She pushed back her hood, revealing long blonde hair, almost white, tied into a loose plait at the nape of her neck. For a moment she stood silent amid the ancient spruce and rhododendron, head cocked, listening.

There had never been dogs loose here in the past but that didn't mean she had to take chances. She heard nothing but the susurrus of leaves as the wind rolled through the branches.

Staying within the cover of the trees, she skirted the house, picking her way with care through nettles that came up to her chin. Not much about Claremont had changed. The boxy Georgian pile had been added onto over the years, until the classical symmetry of its lines began to sprawl. At some point, the original pale cream render had been painted a shade of yellow that, to her eyes, vaguely resembled pus from an infected wound. It was stained and peeling in some places, swamped in others by ivy and Virginia creeper.

It might look more unkempt since her last time here, but security had been upgraded. That was no surprise – it had been upgraded everywhere. She spotted the cameras mounted up near the parapet in the obvious places. They were small, wireless, and no doubt motion-operated and infrared as well as daylight. But on the west side, she was able to get within fifty or sixty metres of the outside wall of the property. Close enough to read the manufacturer's name on the alarm box near the upper cornice and, using the zoom lens on her phone camera, even the model number.

Going to one knee, she shrugged out of her small backpack and dug inside for a handheld amateur radio transmitter, the size of a walkie-talkie. It only took a moment to search the licensing database for the correct frequency and dial it in. She keyed Transmit and held it down with a strip of duct tape. With the unit in her hand, she slung the backpack over one shoulder, and stepped out onto the expanse of lawn.

She had few doubts about the effectiveness of the kit she was using. But still, by the time she reached the wall near the rear entrance, she was aware of a thudding in her chest that echoed in her ears. With her back to the building, she stared out across the flagged terrace and waited for her pulse to settle.

So far, all she had done was trespass in the grounds. What came next would be far harder to excuse.

When her hands had steadied, she turned, crouched, and studied the old mortise lock on the door. It was a standard curtained five-lever – one she could pick in a few minutes without too much difficulty. Instead, she let her eye drift over the tubs and planters of herbs that surrounded the rear step. One had several rings around the base of it, denoting movement. She tilted the tub to one side and, sure enough, a spare key lay on the stone beneath.

'Ah, will they ever learn…?'

The key was a slack fit in the lock, turning loosely. She checked one more time that the duct tape was still pressing the Transmit button down fully on the radio, then pushed the door open. A chill seemed to emanate from within.

Inside, the black-and-white tiled hallway led away into the gloom. At the far end, above the doorway, she saw the red motion sensor start to blink as it activated. But as she passed the alarm control unit on the wall, it remained oblivious to the intrusion.

She checked the time and hurried through to the study. Second door on the right from the main hallway, past the stairs. Inside, the décor hadn't changed. It didn't even look like the place had seen a fresh coat of paint.

The same hunting print hung behind the desk. She lifted it down to reveal the wall safe with her fingers mentally crossed for no change there either. Her luck held. It was still the old strongbox, secured by a key rather than a combination.

She moved to the three-drawer filing cabinet in the far corner, walked it forward enough to heave it onto its back edge. Balancing it there, she reached underneath the front and flipped the lever bar holding the drawers shut. When she set it down again, the top drawer pulled out without resistance beyond the screech of metal runners. It sounded horribly loud in the empty house.

The key to the safe was, as ever, lurking beneath the file hangers at the front of the drawer.

Because, of course, nobody would ever *think to look there...*

The safe door swung open easily. Inside were several folders of paperwork, a jewellery box, and a wad of cash held by an elastic band. She riffled through the banknotes. All twenties – probably about a grand. Pulling a face, she dropped the money behind her onto the desktop.

The jewellery box bore the name of a diamond merchant with a Hatton Garden address. She ran her thumb across the name embossed on the lid with eyebrow raised.

'Looks like *somebody's* been splashing out.'

Flicking the catch revealed a sapphire necklace – a decent piece, if not top drawer. The stones were good-sized, evenly weighted and interlaced with tiny diamonds, but too dark to be the highest quality Cornflower Blues. She dangled it between finger and thumb, up against the light, pursed her lips at the visible imperfections.

'He might even have loved you,' she said, her voice dry. 'But not *that* much…'

Setting the box aside, she reached for the folders. The second one down was marked: 'Wills'.

She nudged the chair back from the desk with the toe of her boot and sat, opening the folder.

'Well, *this* ought to be good…'

*

Outside, ten minutes after the interloper sat down to read, the activation light on the exterior alarm box began, silently, to flash.

THREE

'What did you make of Gideon Fitzroy?' Byron asked.

Jane Hudson could glean little from the detective superintendent's voice. She glanced sideways at him before replying. The neutral expression on his face told her even less.

They'd first met four years previously, when she was fresh out of the Royal Navy and training to be a copper. Byron came to deliver a guest lecture at Hendon. He had been around thirty, and one of the youngest detective chief inspectors in the Met back then. His dark good looks had caused hearts to flutter in many of the female trainees – and a few of the males, too. Hudson had set out determined not to be impressed by the man, convinced he would be far too full of himself.

Besides, he was an inch or two shorter than she was. At five-ten Hudson knew she was tall for a woman, but some men seemed to take this as either a personal affront, or a challenge. Within the first five minutes, listening to him speak, she'd been forced to revise her opinion. His rank and reputation, she decided, had been well earned.

After she began as a probationer with the Met, their paths had crossed again during the first major investigation she was part of.

A very small, insignificant part, she reminded herself – initially just keeping the log of official comings and goings at the entry to the crime scene. As she'd handed the clipboard to Byron for his signature at the cordon, shivering in the pre-dawn darkness and the rain, she hadn't expected for a moment that he'd remember her.

In fact, she was a tiny bit suspicious when he'd called her by name and asked, with a faint smile, if the reality of the job was living up to her expectations. It sounded too much like the start of a chat-up. But she'd never got that creepy vibe from him. Not like some of the male officers she'd worked with, regardless of their marital status.

'Well, I only met the man a couple of times,' she said now. 'Once when I first arrived here – Ed Underhill took me round and introduced me to all the local worthies.'

'And the second occasion?'

'About a week before he died. Mr Fitzroy was involved in a minor traffic incident in Wirksworth – er, the nearest small town, sir. It's about three miles from here,' she added before he could ask. 'I happened to be passing. It wasn't really an official shout.'

That caused a raised eyebrow. Shadows around his eyes made them seem almost black. He was thinner, too, the hollows below his cheekbones more pronounced.

Hardly surprising, after what he's been through.

'Who was at fault?'

'Hard to tell. At the time, I suggested they took equal blame and let the insurance companies sort it out.'

'But?'

Hudson blinked. She thought her tone was entirely matter-of-fact. Obviously not.

'*But*, with hindsight… maybe it was more his fault than the other driver's. And, I mean, it was only a week before his fatal crash. I hate that I might have let his social standing – former Member of Parliament, local lord of the manor, that sort of thing – influence my judgement, you know?'

Byron nodded. 'As long as you recognise that fact, then you've learned something valuable from the experience. Move on.'

They were walking slowly around the churchyard now, along a gravel path that crunched underfoot. Hudson saw the same family names repeated on clusters of gravestones. Some dated back to the 1700s.

'Even so, in light of what happened,' Hudson admitted, 'well, I wish I'd done things differently.'

'Did you take a look into Fitzroy's background? Just for curiosity's sake…'

Hudson reddened. Blushing easily was a disadvantage of her colouring. And it was no becoming rose tint to her cheeks. More a ruddy flush that blotched her neck and the tips of her ears beneath her hat. 'Well…'

'Oh, spit it out, Jane. If you hadn't bothered, I'd think less of you.'

'It feels like gossip, that's all,' she protested, still pink. 'After Fitzroy's first wife died – nothing untoward there,' she added hastily, seeing the question already forming on Byron's lips. 'Cancer, so I'm told, and not quick. But… they had a daughter. She was only nine or ten when her mum passed and she went off the rails a bit.'

'Is this the gossip part?'

'No. She did a runner when she was fifteen – just disappeared one day and never came back.'

Byron glanced at her. '"Never" as in…?'

'She's still missing.' Hudson nodded. 'And *that's* where the gossip comes in. Rumours started that Fitzroy must be a proper tyrant if his own daughter ran away at that age.'

'Was there any kind of investigation into her disappearance?'

'Apparently not. Of course, he was still an MP back then, so he was probably keen to keep it low-key.' She hesitated. 'I know you – the Met, I mean – investigated quite a few MPs during that whole Westminster paedophile case—'

'The one that all fell apart?'

She nodded. 'Anyway, Fitzroy was never even remotely implicated in that, was he?'

'No. Although, murder was always my speciality rather than vice.'

'Aye, that's what I thought. And round here… Well, from what I've heard, he helped keep the village shop and the pub open, sponsored the community bus, and last year he made a major contribution towards resurfacing the kiddies' playground.'

Byron paused, hands in pockets. They had circled to the far side of the churchyard, where a hedge bordered a garden of remembrance. The markers were smaller here, laid flat into the grass.

Back towards the church itself, Hudson could see the fresh grave into which Gideon Fitzroy had been lowered. The mourners had already walked across the road to the village hall. Tea and sandwiches and awkward conversation. Hudson had no desire to join them. Two men had cleared away the matting around the grave and were shovelling earth on top of the coffin with practised speed.

Byron turned back, levelling a rut in the gravel path with the toe of his polished shoe. 'What about Fitzroy's accident? Anything suspicious there at all?'

She glanced at him sharply. 'Not as far as we know. He veered onto the wrong side of the road, went through a low wall and down the banking. His two stepchildren were in the car with him at the time.'

'It's lucky they weren't all killed.'

'Aye, well, you can say one thing for Mercedes – they know how to build a good solid motor.'

'Why do you think I drive one myself?'

'If he'd been wearing his seat belt, they reckon he might have survived,' Hudson said as they walked on. She hesitated. 'Fitzroy's driving record was a bit… spotty. He'd built up nine points for speeding, and there was that bump. Nothing serious, but all the same…'

'Possibly indicative of careless habits.'

'Aye. That was my take on it.'

'And the inquest verdict?'

'Accidental death. The post-mortem exam revealed he was pre-diabetic, could have given his liver a helping hand if he'd cut back on the booze, lost some weight, done a bit more exercise, but nothing conclusive.'

'You're describing most men over sixty in the entire country.'

Hudson snorted. 'Most men over thirty, more like.'

He gave her the side-eye. 'Watch yourself. It comes to us all, sooner or later.'

She recalled he was only thirty-five himself and flashed a quick grin. 'I'll try to remember that, sir.'

'And please, stop "sirring" me.'

'Yes, si—' She managed to stop herself just in time. 'OK, yes, sorry.'

The path had turned back. They were nearing the gateway where the cars waited. The pressmen, Hudson noticed, had finally given up and gone. She took a deep breath, picked her words with care.

'If I can ask… why the interest in Fitzroy? He was never a suspect, as far as I know, and he stepped down as an MP eighteen months ago, so… what changed?'

Byron eyed her for a moment. She fought the urge to fidget under his gaze. 'This goes no further, yes?'

'Aye, no, of course not.'

'Fitzroy recently got in touch with the lead officer in the investigation we mentioned, and said he had certain information about some of the people involved that might be… illuminating.'

'Ah. And the next thing you know, he's dead.'

'Precisely. I've been asked simply to look over the ground, as it were. Unofficially, of course.'

'Understood.'

'We used to walk in the Derbyshire Dales and the Peak District when I was… Well, a few years ago. I thought I'd take the opportunity to reacquaint myself with the area, so I've booked a room at the pub here. I understand they do a decent pint and a home-made pie, if you'd care to join me?'

Before Hudson could answer, a buzzing in her pocket had her fumbling for her phone.

'Work,' she muttered apologetically. 'That's the trouble with being the local copper – you're never completely off duty… Yes, hello?'

She was aware of Byron watching anger form in her face as she asked a couple of brusque questions, ending the call with, 'OK. I'm on my way now.'

'Trouble?'

'Aye. That was the alarm company who monitor the system at the Fitzroys' place.' Her voice was tight. 'Some little toerag has waited until they knew everyone would be out at the funeral, and broken in.'

FOUR

When he left London that morning, the last place Byron had expected to find himself on this trip was in the passenger seat of a police car, driving fast along narrow, winding roads.

Thought I'd left all this behind me.

In spite of that, his first instinct had been to volunteer to go with Hudson to the Fitzroy property. She was still green and he knew that backup in a rural area could be a long time coming. Byron had stuck his hands in the pockets of his coat as if to prevent them acting of their own accord.

As Hudson hurried away to collect keys and the alarm code from Virginia Fitzroy, Underhill nudged his arm.

'Think we ought to go with her?' When Byron glanced at him, Underhill was frowning. 'Never know what she might be walking into. It's a big old place. And if some professional crew has been keeping their eye on the obituaries, looking for an opportunity… Well, it wouldn't be the first time, eh?'

'Indeed.'

Underhill nodded. He was silent for a moment, then said, 'It's hard, isn't it?'

'What's that?'

'Letting go of your responsibilities.'

'Old habits?'

'Yeah. Tell Jane I'm just fetching my car, would you? If needs be, I'll see you there. It's not like I don't know the way.'

It was Byron's turn to nod. He watched the other man head for the gates, something purposeful now in his stride.

A moment or two later, Hudson came out of the village hall and made for the patrol car parked on the lane that bordered the cemetery. Byron moved to intercept her. When he got there, she was at the boot of the vehicle, laying her tunic and white gloves carefully inside and pulling on her stab vest.

'I'll come along, Jane, if you've no objections?'

Hudson looked at him sharply. Byron kept his expression bland. If she was searching for lack of confidence in her abilities, she didn't find it.

'With all due respect, Mr Byron, you are technically a civilian.'

'So is Underhill, but he said he'll meet us there.'

And if Hudson scowled at that news, Byron suspected it was partly to hide her relief. She jerked her chin towards the passenger door.

'All right, then. Buckle up.'

Byron spent the journey braced in his seat, trying to keep his face impassive. He couldn't help releasing a long, pent-up breath when the patrol car finally slithered between two impressive stone gateposts onto a gravel drive. He just had time to catch the name 'Claremont', the letters carved into the stone and picked out in white paint.

When they cleared the rhododendron bushes and the house came into view, the first thing Byron noted was Underhill, climbing out of an old Ford saloon on the gravel forecourt.

The second thing was the flashing light on the alarm box.

'No bell or siren, or have they cut it?' he wondered aloud. His gaze automatically skimmed every door and window.

'Around here, with a property as isolated as this, people tend to go for a silent alarm and off-site monitoring,' Hudson said, offhand. 'There aren't any neighbours close enough to hear it except the Hardings, and they're in no fit state to respond.'

'Oh?'

'You would have seen them at the funeral – older gentleman and his wife. She was the lady in the wheelchair.'

She pulled up next to Underhill's car, braking hard enough to throw up a flurry of gravel. Byron found the move irritated him. Not only because it lacked discretion, but also because it reflected badly on him. He recalled that Hudson had been a little impetuous in training – he suspected she had something to prove. He'd rather hoped it had been drummed out of her as a probationer.

Hudson tried the front door, found it firmly locked. For a moment, she hesitated. Byron saw the way her eyes flicked from himself to Underhill and realised Hudson's dilemma. They might be civilians, but both he and Underhill had far more experience.

'You're the only one here with a valid warrant card, lass,' Underhill said then, his tone measured. 'Consider us yours to command.'

'Oh, right, yes. Well, in that case, if you wouldn't mind staying here?' she said to Byron. 'Ed and I will circle the property – see if we can spot the point of entry.'

'Of course.'

Underhill fetched a bulky torch from his vehicle, hefting it as he returned. He eyed Byron's empty hands dubiously.

'What's he supposed to do if they come charging out the front?'

'I shall engage them in polite conversation.'

'Oh, that's what you call it.' Hudson flashed him a quick grin. 'Well, try to leave at least one of them conscious, would you?'

She nudged Underhill's arm and jerked her head. They moved off in opposite directions, reached the corners of the house and were gone.

Byron, for all his apparent nonchalance, moved to the far side of the patrol car, just in case. He knew how his reputation had been earned, even if he felt it was mostly undeserved. The declarations of heroism embarrassed him. He'd been reckless rather than brave, and things had turned to tragedy. He still woke in the night sweating, crying, screaming.

Still had to cope with the nagging pain of injuries not yet entirely healed.

Determinedly closing off that avenue of thought, he leaned on the roof of the car and studied the front façade.

For a man who had spread his largesse around the local community, he considered, Gideon Fitzroy had not taken particular care with the upkeep of his main residence.

And who chose that God-awful colour?

Byron let his gaze linger on each blank window in turn, trying to pierce the image of sky thrown back by the glass. In truth, he did not expect any kind of bid for freedom from whoever had triggered the alarm.

If you've any sense, you're long gone by now.

The house felt empty. The flash he caught from an upstairs window could so easily have been the reflection of a bird, swooping past…

The light on the external alarm box suddenly stopped flashing. Byron straightened. He heard the locks turning on the front door and it swung inwards. Underhill appeared in the gap, beckoning him in.

'Nobody at home,' he announced cheerfully. 'Looks like they scarpered when they realised there really was an alarm and not just a dummy box on the outside wall.'

Byron said nothing.

The entrance hall was grand. A wide central staircase, tiled floor, and an impressive oil painting of some distant ancestor high on the wall at the half landing, from where he peered down at all comers with equal disdain.

Hudson stuck her head out of a doorway further back.

'In here, sir,' she said, and had disappeared again before Byron could remind her once more about the 'sir' business.

The room, when he and Underhill reached it, was a study, decorated in a style that was almost self-consciously drab. There were two sash windows looking out over the rear garden. The lower casement of one had been thrown wide open, breaking the contacts between the frame and the wireless alarm sensor on the bottom edge.

'Well, that explains how they gained entry – exit, probably, too,' Hudson said. 'Kids, most likely. Bit of a dare.'

'Hm. Do you have any gloves on you?' Byron took the disposable pair he was offered and pulled them on before moving around the desk.

'This picture is crooked,' he remarked, studying the print – not one of Munnings' best. 'Nothing else in this room seems out of place, so… Ah, yes, a safe. I think it might be a good idea – before we proceed any further – if you asked Mrs Fitzroy to come and confirm that nothing of value is missing, perhaps?'

Byron was aware that he'd almost slipped up, managing to change his order into a question only at the last minute. Underhill had been right – stepping away *was* hard. More so, in the circumstances.

Hudson nodded and was reaching for her phone when they heard a faint noise from somewhere above them in the house. A noise that might have been the closing of a door.

'Did you clear the upstairs?'

'Well, no.' Hudson's face flushed. 'We didn't think—'

This time, Byron made no attempt to soften his command. 'Then do it now!'

FIVE

By the young woman's reckoning, it took twenty minutes from her deliberate activation of the alarm sensor on the study window, for the cops to arrive.

Which is none too shabby, all things considered.

She had expected it to take longer when she'd climbed the stairs to the upper floor and made her way to a bedroom at the far eastern end of the house.

As she pushed open the door, she was aware of a momentary feeling of trepidation. She wasn't sure what she would have done if the room had been utterly repurposed – turned into a home gym, or a painter's studio. Or even if one of the step-kids had claimed it.

She needn't have worried.

The room was on the small side, with an awkward cut out to allow for the door to the hallway, and no walk-in wardrobe or en-suite bathroom.

Of course they wouldn't want it – quite apart from its provenance.

Inside, the looming effect of the freestanding wardrobe was exaggerated by its dark oak finish and the slight downward cant of the old floor joists towards the middle of the room. The dressing table was still there, empty but for a layer of dust. And the single narrow bed, the mattress deflated by time rather than use.

No bedding was in evidence, not even a bare pillow. She took off her hoodie and stuffed it behind her, then sank down and let the memory take her.

The memory of two teenage girls, perched together on the edge of the bed, their hands gripped tight, as if letting go would mean falling, falling…

She remembered the fear coiled low, of seeing that same fear reflected back. The sense of running in every direction at once, but all the while being frozen in one place. Waiting for the inevitable. Different fates, each as bad as the other.

Of there being no respite and no escape – for either one of them.

Most of all, she remembered the moment when they first realised that, perhaps, there might be a chance for both.

A car pulled up hard and fast on the gravel outside. For a second the fear of who might be arriving made her heart punch in her chest.

Whoever it is, it won't be him.

She took a breath, but didn't stand and move to the window until she realised there were three distinct voices outside. Not loud enough for her to hear the words, but she caught the differing tones easily enough. Two men and a woman.

That was sufficient to intrigue her. She kept well back from the glass and peered down to see two vehicles on the forecourt – only one of which was a police car. As she looked, a figure appeared, moving back to stand behind the patrol car. A defensive position, she recognised. But he wasn't in uniform, so who was he?

Just then, he glanced up. Instinct had her ducking back out of sight. She cursed under her breath, knowing that her best option would have been complete stillness.

Ah well, too late to worry about that now…

A second later, it registered that the man was the same one who'd spotted her at the churchyard. Something about him there had made her wary. He wasn't a big man, and had all the trappings of civilisation – that suit, for instance, had been tailored to fit – but he had a certain look about him. One that riffled the hairs at the back of her neck.

She had spent too long as a shark swimming through shoals of unsuspecting prey not to recognise another hunter when she encountered one.

So, what was he doing here?

And why now?

Returning to the mattress, she heard the faint beep of the alarm code being punched in, far below. She forced herself to sit back, swing her legs up and cross her feet at the ankles. A determined show of nonchalance.

You can do this. Just remember that.

But in all her planning, the man in the bespoke suit was an unknown and un-bargained-for factor.

It took another minute or so before she realised they weren't going to check the house thoroughly. Rolling her eyes, she got up and moved to the door. Opening it a few inches, she closed it with a firm shove. It made a satisfying hollow clatter – not too obvious, but just enough.

Then she sat down again, and tried to keep both the anxiety and the anticipation away from her face while she waited for them to come and get her.

SIX

Gideon Fitzroy's widow arrived back at Claremont by chauffeur-driven Daimler limousine – the same car, presumably, that had taken her to the funeral service. Byron could only assume, since she had paid for a return trip, that she was determined to enjoy it.

But she did not wait for the driver to nip round and open her door. She was out of the car and hurrying across the gravel almost before the wheels had stopped rolling. Byron observed her speed with no small measure of concern, considering the height of her heels and the uneven ground.

During the journey, Mrs Virginia Fitzroy had removed her hat and veil, so he was able to get a proper look at her face for the first time. It was striking, he realised, in a rather haughty kind of way. Some people went for the icy society princess type. Byron was not one of them.

If he were being candid, she reminded him too much of his mother.

'Well?' she demanded as soon as she was within calling distance of the portico, where Byron waited by the open front door. 'What have the little bastards taken?'

Yes, she reminded him *precisely* of his mother…

'We were rather hoping *you* could tell *us*, Mrs Fitzroy,' he said, his voice neutral.

'"We"?' It was only as she drew level that she paused and looked down her implausibly straight nose at him. '"Us"?' Excuse me, but who exactly are *you?*'

'My name is Byron, ma'am. I came down from London this morning to see how Jane – PC Hudson – was settling in. We met at Hendon, while she was training.'

She swept her gaze up and down, little more than a flicker. 'A little *old* to be a newly turned-out police constable, aren't you?'

'Oh, no, ma'am. I was the one *delivering* the training.' And, knowing it would silence her scorn, he added, 'I'm a detective superintendent with the Met but, in this instance, I'm here purely to offer assistance to PC Hudson,' without explaining his current medical leave.

Virginia Fitzroy said nothing. Giving a brisk nod, as if he'd just about passed muster, she swept past him into the hallway. It was so smoothly done that Byron almost missed the fleeting moment of disquiet that bled through her shiny carapace. Natural in the circumstances, perhaps, but what interested him was the fact it had not appeared until after he'd introduced himself. He'd enough experience with the Fitzroys of this world to know they expected to be taken seriously, and took the presence of a higher-ranking officer as their due.

But not in this case.

Hudson was waiting for her inside the house. Byron noted the respectful stance. Perhaps she had not entirely learned her lesson about undue deference.

'Try not to worry too much, Mrs Fitzroy. Nothing appears to be missing and we got here fast enough to prevent any vandalism or damage,' Hudson said. 'We laid hands on the culprit, hiding in one of the upstairs bedrooms, before they had a chance to make an escape.'

'Not *mine*, I hope,' she shot back. Her face twisted. 'Or the children's!'

'Oh, no, one of the empty rooms at the far end.' Hudson gestured vaguely towards the staircase. 'Ed Underhill's keeping an eye on her in the study and—'

'"Her"?' You don't mean to tell me that a *girl* tried to rob us? And the *study*? Really? Why on earth have you put her in there? Surely the cellars would be a more suitable place?'

Hudson gave an uneasy laugh, as if Virginia had been joking, and quickly drew her along the hallway. Byron followed the pair. He was glad that the local village green did not boast old wooden stocks, or no doubt the woman would be advocating their use, too.

'Well, after we'd, ah, examined the study—' here Hudson had the grace to look slightly abashed '—we were of the opinion that the safe might have been tampered with. Need you to open it – verify nothing's missing.'

'If you really think that's necessary…'

Byron took advantage of the hesitation to move ahead on the pretence of good manners, opening the study door and stepping through to hold it wide.

In reality, he wanted the opportunity to observe Virginia Fitzroy's face the moment she laid eyes on the would-be burglar.

All he saw as she entered was incomprehension, perhaps a trace of anger that this person had dared to violate her home. But there was no hint of recognition.

His gaze flipped to the intruder and something he couldn't quite identify flashed through her eyes, quickly hidden. Silently, he berated himself for not watching *her* instead. If anyone knew why this house, why now, it was the young woman rather than Virginia.

She was of medium height, slim-hipped and wide-shouldered like a swimmer. Hardly surprising that he'd taken her at first sight for a boy. The concealing hoodie from the churchyard was thrown back to reveal pale hair, tied into a plait, and a pale-lipped face devoid of make-up. Even close to, it was still hard to judge her age.

They had set a dining chair in the centre of the room, as if for an interrogation, and handcuffed her wrists through the arm of it. She sat in a negligent sprawl with her hands pulled to one side.

'Are you *quite* mad?' Virginia demanded. 'That chair's mahogany, and an antique—'

'Hepplewhite, actually.' The intruder tapped the chair arm with one finger. 'And it's not mahogany, it's elm. Look at that grain.'

Virginia stiffened and said in a frozen voice, 'I do *not* need a lecture on my own furniture from the likes of *you*, thank you *very* much!'

'Ah, *your* furniture, is it? And here was me thinking this stately pile belonged to Gideon Fitzroy.'

Virginia paled even further, if that was possible.

'So *that's* your game,' Hudson said tightly. 'Quick recce before your mates come in, mob-handed, and strip the place, is that it?'

The intruder turned her head, slow enough to be insulting. 'Just because I can probably name that cheap perfume you're wearing,' she said, 'doesn't mean I plan to steal it.'

Hudson took a step forwards, almost involuntary, but the intruder didn't move a muscle. If anything, that was further provocation.

Byron saw the officer's fists clench and said quickly, 'Perhaps if you would open the safe for us now, Mrs Fitzroy? Then we can remove your... uninvited guest from the premises.'

The intruder's eyes trailed over him, almost lazily. They were grey. Amusement lurked in their depths.

Why are you enjoying this? he wondered. *Is it all a game to you, win or lose?*

And he couldn't quite prevent a twitch of anger himself, at what was clearly a good brain put to bad use. After everything he'd encountered in his career, he was mildly surprised to feel anything at all.

SEVEN

In the rear of the second funeral car, twelve-year-old Lily tried to ignore the way her forearm itched mercilessly beneath the cast by staring fixedly out of the side window at the familiar scenery blurring past. She told herself this was partly to avoid succumbing to motion sickness, which she'd suffered from since she was a baby. And partly so she didn't have to meet the gaze of her brother, who was squashed into the jump seat opposite.

She had called dibs on the rear bench seat before they left the churchyard, sealed the deal by threatening to be *sure* to vomit over Tom if, or – as was more likely – *when* she threw up. Everyone knew she couldn't sit facing backwards, even on trains.

But now she regretted her insistence.

For one thing, Tom had shot up during the previous year at boarding school. At twelve, he'd been one of the smallest boys in his class, a fact which had led to a string of bloodied noses – mostly his own.

But Lily recalled her amazement when he came home for the last May break. He unfolded himself from their mother's car and just kept unfolding until he towered over her, grinning his lopsided smile, in a scuffed uniform too short all round. How had she missed the way he'd grown over the last three years?

He'd started referring to her as his 'little' sister with far more emphasis than was needed.

Flicking her eyes sideways at him now, Lily saw that her brother was perched on the edge of the low seat, back too straight and bony knees sticking up too high. Not only uncomfortable, she recognised with remorse, but undignified, too.

When she thought about it, he'd put up only a token resistance when she'd staked her claim. *Humouring me.*

In a way, he'd been humouring her ever since the accident. Lily didn't remember much about it, if she was honest. Tom had grabbed the front seat, relegating her to the back. He and Gideon had been talking about some politician on the news – someone Gideon had known on the opposition benches. Bored, and able to catch only one word in five because of the noise of engine, tyres, and radio, Lily had leaned back in her seat and dozed.

The next thing she knew, the car smashed through the dry stone wall and began to plummet. It left her stomach behind, that dreadful feeling she hated about roller coasters. It had never occurred to her that falling for real would seem exactly the same.

Then the car had hit and rolled and started to come apart around them. The nausea overwhelmed her first, followed by the frantic urge to pee. The pain seemed to come a long way down the line. She didn't even remember hitting her arm, much less breaking it.

Tom had stayed in hospital for more than a week, because of the concussion and the surgery to his face. Lily, somewhat to her chagrin, was not even kept in overnight. They'd simply reset her wrist and pronounced her fit to go home.

It was only then, when she was delivered into her mother's care, that she found out her stepfather had died in the crash. She'd been too numb to cry.

Today, watching the coffin go into the grave, was the first time it seemed real. She had not been called at the inquest. Tom was, of course. He'd refused to talk about it with anyone beforehand, so when he stood there in the coroner's court, so tense it made her

ache just to look at him, it was the first time she'd heard his side of
the story. He recounted the lead-up to the accident in words that
were spare and stilted. His voice had been wavering as it broke,
but the day of the inquest it finally settled somewhere at the top
end of baritone. It had all combined to make him seem suddenly
very adult, very distant. And to make Lily feel rather alone.

In the seat alongside her, Roger Flint – their mother's younger
brother – let out a short, annoyed huff of breath. Lily hardly
needed to turn her head to know the cause. He had been glued
to the screen of his smartphone for the entire journey, and she
was well aware what *that* meant.

'Are you winning or losing today, Uncle Roger?' Tom asked,
his tone just the right side of insolent.

Lily turned away from the car window just in time to see her
uncle, face flushed, fumbling to shut down the gambling app.
Even so, she caught the mind-bending amount displayed on it.

'Well, they hardly run these things to make the punters rich,
do they?' Roger tried to keep his voice light but a sulky undertone
bled through.

Definitely losing then.

'If it's a mug's game, why take part?' Tom asked.

'It's just a bit of fun, you know? I mean, you both have games
on your phones, don't you?'

'So you're just playing at it?'

Tom kept his expression bland, pretended he didn't see Lily's
pleading glance. Uncle Roger might be a figure of fun but that
didn't mean poking him with a stick was a good idea. Even before
Gideon's demise, their uncle had been twitchy whenever money
was mentioned. Since, he had reeked of desperation.

The big car swung off the road and into the driveway, rolling
through the potholes in the gravel like a ferry in a heavy swell.
Lily felt an echoing wallow in her stomach. For once, it was not
caused only by motion.

As they emerged from the shadows of the rhododendron bushes, Roger edged forwards in his seat. From her side of the car, Lily had a clearer view of the activity in front of the house. She had been given no reason for her mother's hurried departure from the village hall – no change there. The sight of the patrol car gave her a jolt.

'What's happened?' she demanded. 'Why are the police here?'

Tom twisted in his seat so fast she thought he'd hurt his neck. It was nice to know he wasn't *quite* as blasé as he pretended, sometimes.

'Somebody tried to break in, so your mother said.' Roger gave a jerky nod, cleared his throat. 'Paying our property taxes still gets us something, then.'

'Since when do *you* pay any of that?' Tom muttered under his breath. She scowled at her brother in silent warning but he folded his arms and glared back. Uncle Roger either wasn't listening or pretended not to hear.

Roger jumped out as soon as the Daimler limo glided to a halt beside the other funeral car. He threw, 'Stay there, you two!' over his shoulder, then he was off at a trot to join their mother under the front portico.

'What are we… dogs?' Tom unclipped his seat belt and flopped into the vacated seat, buzzing down the rear window. 'Do they honestly think we're little kids who don't need to know? That we have to be protected from anything scary?'

Lily didn't think he was *trying* to speak loudly but he still wasn't used to his adult voice, the way it carried. She noted the man who'd been at the funeral – some friend or relative of PC Hudson, she thought – standing by the patrol car, close enough to hear every word. He was looking into the limo and their eyes met. The man had the kind of gaze that looked into you as much as at you. One of her schoolmistresses was like that – impossible to lie to. She ducked her head.

'Tom, for heaven's sake, keep your voice down.'

'What for?'

Lily risked another peek but the man's attention had shifted away, over the top of the Daimler. She twisted in the seat to glance out of the back window. Her view was partially obscured by a dusty posy of silk flowers on the parcel shelf.

Behind them, the Hardings' converted minivan was just pulling up. Lily climbed out, leaving the door open for Tom. He leaned over and pulled it pointedly closed behind her.

Be like that, then!

With the side door of the minivan open, the ramp cranked out on hydraulics at the press of a button. Anne was able to remotely release the braking system that kept the chair locked down during transport, and buzz down the ramp without outside assistance.

When she was younger, Lily had regarded Anne Harding's state-of-the-art motorised wheelchair with awed fascination. The fat tyres coped with gravel, garden paths and lawns, even mud, with relative ease. Now she saw only all the places it *couldn't* go. All the things Anne could no longer do. It made Lily's broken arm, the inconvenience of the temporary cast, insignificant by comparison.

Anne trundled across to the front portico. Her husband walked beside her to where Tom's mother stood, still unmoving. Uncle Roger had a consoling arm around her shoulders. Tom must have got out of the car at some point, because he followed, with Lily behind him. They all converged on her mother, even the quiet man from the funeral, the one Lily didn't know. He didn't intrude but he still got close enough to be intrusive.

'Virginia, my dear,' Anne said. 'How perfectly bloody for you. I do hope nothing has been taken?'

Lily saw her mother flinch minutely at the question.

'Yes, yes, we really ought to do a full inventory,' Roger said. 'And call the insurance people, just to be on the safe—'

'I am not an imbecile, Roger,' her mother snapped, shrugging herself out from under his arm. 'Don't *fuss.*'

Lily blinked. Her mother could be sharp with her brother – and who could blame her for that? – but she usually hid it better in company.

What does that *mean?*

She recalled Tom's friends from school recounting stories – urban myths, perhaps, but always sworn as true – about what some burglars did once they got inside your home. Spitting in your food, weeing in your bed, wiping their bums with your toothbrush – or worse.

She opened her mouth to ask but got no further.

Behind her mother, the front door opened and PC Hudson came out, propelling a slim young woman in a hoodie ahead of her. Sergeant Underhill – she still thought of him by his former rank – was on the far side of their prisoner, as if she might make a break for freedom. The young woman's wrists were cuffed in front, one hand stacked above the other. She saw them all standing there and slowed, regarding them without expression, one after another.

Lily couldn't help staring. Whatever she'd expected a burglar to look like, she wasn't quite sure, but it wasn't this. She was not... pretty, exactly, but not ugly either. There was *something* about her face – Lily would have said *arresting* if it wouldn't have been the most awful pun, in the circumstances.

'Come on.' PC Hudson tugged her arm, not altogether gently. 'You don't belong here.'

The prisoner smiled. It was unsettling, that smile. Too knowing. Like she was in on a big practical joke that was going to burst open on the rest of them at any moment. And they'd all come off looking stupid and only she would be prepared, and she was already laughing at them all.

'Wait!'

For a moment, Lily thought it was her mother who'd spoken. When she looked, it was Anne Harding who was wheeling herself closer to the interloper, a look of shocked confusion on her face. 'Who are you? I would swear I know you…'

'Mrs Harding—' It was PC Hudson who protested.

And the prisoner who cut her off.

'I think you'll find I *do* belong here,' she said, letting her eyes range across them, one more time, before settling on Anne. 'And you ought to know me… I'm Blake.'

EIGHT

'*Well*,' Anne Harding said, letting out a long huff of breath like a racehorse first past the post, 'I can't say I was expecting *that*. Blake – after all this time.'

She spoke from the rear of the modified people carrier, where her motorised chair was locked into position for travel.

Byron twisted in the front passenger seat to look back at her as they pulled away from the front of the house.

'What made you think that young woman might be Gideon Fitzroy's missing daughter?' he asked.

Harding, his long form hunched over the steering wheel, glanced sideways. 'He's right, darling. There's a faint resemblance, but…'

Hudson had taken her prisoner to the nearest police station, and Byron had not asked to accompany her. When – or indeed, if – the case came to court, he had no desire to cause any procedural irregularities that might rebound on Hudson.

So, with his own vehicle still back in the lane bordering the churchyard, he'd found himself stuck at the Fitzroy residence, for the moment at least. Which was both a minor inconvenience and an opportunity.

Byron took advantage of it, slipping upstairs while Virginia was occupied carrying out a survey of the more valuable contents, at her brother's urging, and the others were milling around in the kitchen. He sought out the bedroom where the intruder had been found. It wasn't until he was on his way down again that Roger Flint accosted him, bristling with suspicion and questions.

Flint didn't quite throw him out – he wasn't brave enough for that – but it was a close-run thing. The Hardings offered him a lift back into the village.

Oliver Harding drove slowly and carefully, no doubt conscious of his cargo. Byron assessed the man's age, putting him anywhere from worn early-sixties to well-preserved late-seventies. He was over six feet, with wide bony shoulders that made the formal jacket of his funeral suit hang loose on his frame. At least, Byron noted, he had given in to baldness gracefully, choosing to keep what was left of his hair – a narrow band that stretched, pure white, from ear to ear at the back of his skull – ruthlessly clipped.

'Of course it was Blake,' Anne said now, blinking at them both in surprise. 'Couldn't you tell?' Without waiting for an answer, she waved a dismissive hand towards Byron. 'Sorry, forgetting – you've never met her before, have you?'

'I regret that no, I have not.'

'She could be a moody girl,' Harding said, his voice reflective. 'And she was a little more... plump. On the whole, very little resemblance to—'

Anne gave his shoulder a nudge with the back of her hand. 'Oh, come on, darling. Blake was fifteen when she disappeared – still a child. That was no more than puppy fat. And you recall what she was like that last summer? Hid her spotty face behind a curtain of hair and hardly said two words to anybody, poor kid. Desperately self-conscious.'

'You sound as if you knew her well,' Byron said.

Anne flushed a little as she turned back to him. She had a square face, deeply lined, that showed strength of character rather than the more conventional charms. He noticed that she tended to fix her gaze on the person she was speaking to and imagined most people might find that unnerving. Byron was not most people.

'I did. We watched her grow up.' Her smile was wry. 'We always felt very close to her.'

'Fitzroy didn't marry his second wife until after Blake had gone, I understand?' Byron asked. 'How did they meet?'

'Oh, that would be through her brother. Roger was something to do with Gideon's constituency office, wasn't he?' Anne said, and Harding nodded. 'They must have got on, because after Gideon stood down, he offered Roger a job as his general assistant, running the estate and looking after the holiday cottages – that kind of thing.'

'Actually, that was something I've wondered,' Byron said, pushing a slightly puzzled I'm-only-a-simple-copper note into his voice. 'Why *did* he resign, do you know? I would have thought he had it all to play for.'

It was surprising how often it worked, that vague and apparently guileless air.

'I think he and Virginia went through a sticky patch,' Anne said, lowering her voice as if they might be overheard. 'I got the impression he knew if he didn't pay her more attention, things might end badly.'

'Really? I thought he'd had a health scare – heart problem or some such.' Harding made it sound like a character defect. 'He certainly fussed about it enough. I expect that's why he got on so well with Roger.'

'Oh?'

'Roger was good at sweating the small stuff, and Gideon did like things done a certain way.'

Anne snorted. 'He was a martinet, you mean. I think that's why he and Blake became so distant. We never met Catherine – Gideon's first wife. She died just before we moved here. But it was obvious that Blake took losing her mother hard. For a while it seemed she was turning into a daddy's girl. But… it wasn't to be.' She gave an uneven shrug. 'She grew into a bitter, angry teenager, as they often do.'

Harding reached a hand back and Anne gripped it in her own. A replay of the gesture Byron had observed by the graveside.

It was rare he encountered a husband and wife who seemed so well suited, two halves of a matched whole. More often than not, there was tension between them. Niggling strife. If teased out, carefully, it often told him more than straightforward questions ever did.

He glanced out of the window, forcing his mind along a strictly analytical path. From what he could remember, they were almost back at the outskirts of the village.

'I understand from Jane – PC Hudson – that when Blake disappeared it was very sudden. She didn't leave a note of any kind,' he said casually, noting Anne's eyes flick towards her husband's face. 'Was there anything in particular that caused it, do you recall?'

'You've no idea how often we've talked about this over the last ten years,' she said. 'I just wish she'd come to us…'

'You can't blame yourself, darling,' Harding said, meeting her gaze in the rear-view mirror. 'She and her father were like chalk and oranges – just too different on too many levels.'

She flicked Byron a quick smile. 'Well, I still think Gideon took the wrong approach with Blake. I think she would have responded better to a discussion – a negotiation rather than outright orders. It was almost inevitable that they clashed.'

Byron straightened his shirt cuff. 'I don't suppose you know why Mr Fitzroy didn't report his daughter missing at the time?'

'Surely, he did?' Anne said, frowning. 'I mean, I always assumed so…'

Harding cleared his throat. 'It was difficult for Gideon, you know – a man in his position. And he never thought it would take. He said she was a spoilt child who didn't know when she was onto a good thing, and predicted she'd be home within six weeks.'

'And was she?'

'I'm sorry?'

'Spoilt.'

'Ah, no, I wouldn't have said so. Strong-willed, perhaps, but generally thoughtful. Bright, too. Very bright.'

Harding trundled down the main street and pulled up at the entrance to the church. Byron thanked them both for the lift as he undid his seat belt. Then he paused.

'Were you surprised, by the way, when Blake left home?'

'When she ran away, you mean?' Anne shook her head. 'Shocked? Disappointed? Certainly. But surprised, no.'

NINE

Just to one side of the gavel forecourt at Claremont stood an ivy-covered brick building that housed a large double garage – added after pony and trap was no longer the conventional form of transport. Above the garage was a storage loft, reached via an open-tread wooden staircase just inside the personnel door. The loft tended to be used as a general junk room, filled with garden furniture, a chaise longue from the drawing room awaiting eventual refurbishment, Christmas decorations, trunks of old clothes, cobwebs and dust.

It was one of Lily's favourite places.

Well, not the cobwebs part – at least, not if there were spiders to go with them – but she didn't mind the dust.

Her mother, on the other hand, would throw a fit if she knew Lily was up here still in her best clothes from the funeral. She should have changed before she came out, but the need to get away from the family bickering had seemed not only important, but urgent, too.

Something that had to be done right away, before her head exploded.

Things had been… weird since she and her brother and Uncle Roger got back to the house just as the woman who'd broken in was being taken away in handcuffs. Lily had heard mention of Blake, of course she had. Her disappearing like that – so suddenly and completely – was still a cause of village gossip, even ten years after the event.

Back then, Lily had been little more than a baby. Her father – her *real* father – was still alive, although Lily barely remembered him. A blurry impression of a big man with a gruff voice and that was about it. She could pick him out of photographs but only by learned habit rather than genuine recall.

They had apparently lived in some London suburb at the time. She remembered little of that, either. Her mother worked as a parliamentary researcher because Uncle Roger had 'put in a good word for her' as he was fond of recounting. That was how she'd first met Gideon Fitzroy.

Lily didn't really recall her mother getting together with the man who was her boss. In the hazy pattern of recollections, it seemed that he had simply appeared, almost overnight, like sleight of hand. *Not* there one minute, and *there* the next. Hey presto!

Friends had told her she was lucky to have a stepfather like Gideon. That step-parents were either distant and resentful, or tried excruciatingly hard to ingratiate themselves.

Gideon wasn't like that. He'd seemed to take a genuine interest in her and Tom.

The loft had standing headroom only along the centre line, below the peak of the roof, tapering down to less than a metre at the eaves. The only natural light came from a circular window in the gable end facing the house. Lily lay on the chaise beneath the window. If she craned her neck, she could see down onto the forecourt and catch all the comings and goings.

Not that there was much going on at the moment. Bored, she checked her phone, scrolling through her social media feeds and messaging apps. Most of her friends were in lessons, though, so posts and replies were sporadic enough for *that* to be boring, too.

She sighed.

Normally, if she was up here, she would be using the stock of old clothes as costumes for her acting ambitions. She'd been trying out for the end-of-year school play, rehearsing up here where there was nobody to mock her efforts. Her mother and uncle and brother all thought she was wasting her time.

Strangely, only Gideon had encouraged her. She bit her lip.

I'll miss him.

Below her, she heard the crunch of footsteps on the gravel. She rolled onto her stomach and stared down.

Uncle Roger had just left the house by the front door, turning his coat collar up against the drizzle that had begun to fall. As she watched, he hurried for the shelter of the garage, head down and mobile phone clamped to his ear.

She heard the side door open and the sound of Uncle Roger's voice echoed up the bare steps.

'*Fine*? How can you say that? Am I the only one who seems to realise the gravity of the situation here?'

Lily sat up straight, latching onto the irritated desperation in his tone as much as the words.

There was a pause, then he said, 'Yes, of course I understand how "dead and buried" works, but—'

A pause.

'Yes, but what if—?'

The pause was longer this time, as if whoever was at the other end of the line was talking fast – trying to calm him down, by the sound of it. It was impossible to tell if it was working.

Especially when his next words were: 'Virginia,' in a kind of hollow voice. 'She has the most to lose.'

That shook Lily. She slipped off the chaise to her feet. Uncle Roger was pacing as he spoke, and she heard his footsteps fading now as he moved away towards the other side of the garage. Lily tiptoed for the stairwell, straining to hear what else he said.

She was concentrating on that too much to be as careful as she should have been. The weight of her cast caught her out constantly. It scuffed against the edge of a storage box, making it begin to topple. Heart in her mouth, she lurched to catch it, but knew from the sudden silence below that he must have heard.

There was a muttered, 'Wait a moment,' and then she heard the outer door slam.

She rushed back to the window, in time to see him scurry away, phone still in place. Just before he reached the portico, he glanced suddenly over his shoulder, up and back.

Lily ducked down out of sight at once. But she couldn't be sure, even so, if he'd seen her.

TEN

The young woman sat alone in an interview room. PC Hudson had removed the handcuffs, given her a plastic cup containing water – which she had not touched – and left her to wait.

She did not mind waiting.

She had already waited a long time for this.

The only furniture in the room was four chairs grouped around a scuffed table. Their design was not intended to be comfortable but she sat without fidgeting, her forearms resting on the veneer surface in front of her. Her hands were loosely clasped, so she would not leave prints anywhere they could be easily lifted. They had, of course, taken her fingerprints on arrival, and were no doubt running them through whatever systems they had access to. Still, it was force of habit.

And anyway, she was confident they would not find her details listed.

Since she turned eighteen, she'd managed to stay out of trouble. Well, that was not quite true. But she'd managed to avoid being caught for anything, at least.

She comforted herself that they hadn't truly caught her, even now.

After maybe half an hour of dull immobility, the door opened and PC Hudson entered with a sheaf of paperwork in a manila folder.

'Sorry to keep you waiting,' she said, tucking her mobile phone into a pocket as she spoke. The young woman judged lack of contrition in her tone.

Hudson took the chair opposite, set the folder on the table, and jerked her head towards the video camera mounted high on the wall behind her.

'We are, of course, recording this. OK?'

She shrugged. Not much she could do even if it wasn't OK, so why argue?

'Could you start by telling me your name?'

'Blake Claremont.'

'I thought the *house* was called Claremont.' The copper's mouth twisted as if she'd just flunked her first question. 'Shouldn't you have said Fitzroy?'

'Fitzroy was my father's name. That doesn't make it mine. My mother's name was Claremont.'

She could have added to that, of course – told her that the house had been in Catherine Claremont's family for generations – but she resisted. Most people had a tendency to over-explain under interrogation. To reinforce the impression of honesty by being open. Even with someone as obviously inexperienced as Hudson, she knew that wasn't likely to work. Not to mention with anyone else who might watch the recording afterwards. Or be watching it now...

Hudson picked up the folder, settling back in her chair so the contents weren't visible as she opened it. She asked a few standard ID questions – date of birth, the name of her doctor and dentist when she was a child, which schools she'd attended, names of various teachers. It was all the kind of stuff anyone could glean from a cursory Google search. Little more than what they called Out-of-Wallet info. The kind that could be gleaned from a stolen handbag or lifted wallet. She'd expected better.

Or, at the very least, she'd expected more.

Eventually, Hudson closed the folder and almost threw it onto the table. 'Do you really expect me to believe that on the very day of your supposed father's funeral, you just turn up out of the blue, and presume to be welcomed back into the family fold?'

'No. The last thing I'd banked on was to be welcomed,' she said calmly. 'Nevertheless, I do have a right to be here.'

'Hm, a bit convenient that the one person who could confirm that is dead, isn't it?'

'You mean you thought I'd come back while the old bastard was still alive?'

That earned her a look of reproach. 'How did you know he was dead?'

'News report. The death of a former MP – even one as undistinguished as Gideon Fitzroy – tends to make the papers.'

It was a weak point in her narrative. She had to force herself not to tense, to keep her breathing steady. Staring was almost as bad as breaking eye contact but she couldn't seem to look away, watching for the first signs of narrowed suspicion to form on the other's face.

'So, you read about Mr Fitzroy's demise and were suddenly overcome with homesickness, is that it?' Hudson demanded instead. 'Nothing to do with the possibility of an inheritance up for grabs, then?'

'If you think there's a chance in hell my father left any provision for me in his will, you clearly did not know him very well,' she said flatly, covering her relief. 'And if you don't believe me, ask the current Mrs Fitzroy. I'm sure you'll find he's named her as his sole beneficiary.'

If Hudson noticed her careful wording, she did not comment on it. 'Supposing for a moment that I believe you *are* Mr Fitzroy's daughter. In that case, and if your assumption is correct that there's nothing to inherit, why come back at all? I mean, what's in it for you?'

'Look at it from another angle – why should I stay away any longer?'

Hudson tilted her head, considering. 'How long is it since you… went?'

'Ten years – or it would have been on the eighteenth of next month.'

'What were you wearing?'

She raised an eyebrow. 'Can you remember what *you* wore on any given date ten years ago?'

'Not necessarily.'

'Well, there you are then.'

'But this wasn't just *any* old day, was it?'

She shrugged. If she said that she'd given great thought to how she'd dressed, had considered and discarded numerous options before making a final decision on her running-away gear, Hudson would probably have believed her. And why not, when it was close to the truth?

Still, she said nothing.

'So, you don't know.' A statement, not a question.

She waited until Hudson's gaze dropped.

'Jeans. Levi's 501s – thirty-three long. A black T-shirt – extra large. And Doc Martens – size six.' When she noted Hudson's eyes flicking over her, she conjured a mocking smile. 'As you can see, I've dropped a bit of weight since I was fifteen.'

Travelling light – constantly being on the move or ready to run – did that to a body.

Hudson opened the file again, leafed through the pages without looking at her. 'What design was on the T-shirt?'

'There was no design – it was plain black.' She paused. 'Nice try, though.'

The copper shifted in her chair, as if becoming more uncomfortable the more answers she got right. 'What actually made you do a runner in the end?' Hudson asked, both the tone and the change of subject abrupt. 'I mean, was there some… trigger for it?'

The young woman covered the lump in her throat by sitting back in her chair, almost a sprawl. Just until she could be sure she had control of her voice. 'Teenage angst?'

'That's too glib.' Hudson shook her head. 'I mean, I suffered from teenage angst. Never made me disappear for almost a decade without a word to anyone, though.'

'How about Daddy issues? Bet you didn't have those. Oh… you *did*. My mistake. What was it – never quite good enough to meet his expectations?' She caught the faint flush about the woman's ears and nodded. 'In my case, the opposite was true. He rated my prospects at a big fat zero and took great delight in telling me so at every available opportunity. By the end, I couldn't wait to get away.'

'I don't suppose you have any proof of anything you've claimed so far?'

She laughed without humour. 'When I finally made my escape, the last thing I wanted, after going to all that trouble, was to have them pick me up, find ID on me, and then to be Returned to Sender like a misplaced parcel.'

'So, not a shred of proof,' Hudson said, with enough relish that she knew her crack about Daddy issues had hit home. 'What about where you've been living and what you've been doing between then and now?'

'Ask me any questions you like about my life here ten years ago and I'll give you answers,' she said. 'But the rest of it is my business.'

Hudson shook her head. 'I daresay we'll come back to that. As for what you got up to back then, I wouldn't know if anything you said was correct or not.'

'Then get someone who *does* know.'

Her vehemence seemed to take the copper aback, but she had not expected such apathy in response to her arrival. That they would ask a few desultory questions and dismiss her, not because she got things wrong but because they didn't know either way. And they cared even less.

Well, if it doesn't seem important right now, it will do soon…

'How have you been getting by?' Hudson asked. 'Employers tend to ask for things like National Insurance numbers and tax codes. And you don't *look* like you've been on the streets. You know as well as I do that you can't rent anywhere these days without proof of your right to remain in the UK, at the very least, never mind a bank account and references.'

'You *have* led a sheltered life, haven't you?' She let her voice drawl. She'd learned to tailor her speech patterns to the company she was in and the effect she wanted to have – either to fit in or stand out. Now, she knew, it played to some deep-rooted sense of inferiority in the other woman. And any weapon that knocked her off her game was fair play.

'What about work – money?' Hudson asked. 'Or have I led a sheltered life there, too?'

'There are still plenty of people who are willing to pay cash in hand and ask no questions.'

'For doing what?'

She gave a slow smile. 'Whatever I had to, in order to survive.'

'Such as?'

'I don't believe I'm obliged to incriminate myself,' she said, knowing that the copper's no-doubt sordid best guess was not likely to be correct. Indeed, there was an edge of disdain to her features that she was not yet skilful enough to conceal. Clearly, the assumption was she'd been selling her body, without consideration that her brain might be a far more valuable asset.

She kept her expression bland, resisting the urge to put Hudson right on that score. It was not worth losing the war for the sake of one battle, however satisfying a victory it might be.

'A refusal to answer is usually taken as an admission of guilt,' Hudson said then. 'But who said anything about incriminating yourself? I was thinking more along the lines of mitigating circumstances. After all, there is the small matter of the breaking and entering charge.'

'There was no "breaking" involved.'

Hudson shook her head. 'If you had no permission to enter, then in the eyes of the law the charge still holds.'

'Why would I need permission to enter? I believe you'll find it's still my official address.' She raised an eyebrow at the other's silence. 'My father might be dead but the whole question of the will is yet to be settled.'

'How would you know that?'

'There hasn't been enough time. The law of probate may be many things, but quick is not one of them,' she said. 'So, until a legitimate will has been recognised and read, the house is as much my home as it is Lavinia's.'

'It's Virginia.'

'Whatever,' she dismissed. 'Either way, under the circumstances I fail to see what laws I'm supposed to have broken.'

ELEVEN

Her mother told her to stay in the car but no way was Lily going to do that.

And since everyone treated her like a kid, she wasn't above using it to get her own way. After all, it had got her this far, hadn't it?

She'd crept back in from the loft above the garage, hoping to find out what Uncle Roger's secretive phone conversation had been all about. Instead, she found her mother in the hallway, car keys in hand.

'I'm going to the police station at Ashbourne to sort things out about this girl,' Virginia had announced.

Lily decided immediately that this was a far more interesting proposition. Her mother was apparently determined to go alone, but Lily managed to successfully wind herself into tears at the prospect of being left behind.

'F-first D-Daddy, then G-Gideon, and now *you're* leaving us, t-too!' she'd wailed, burrowing tight to her mother's side.

It had, as she'd intended, pressed all the right buttons.

'Oh, *darling*!'

Virginia had wrapped her into a tight hug. Behind her mother's back, Tom had rolled his eyes and mimed shoving fingers down his throat. Lily had stuck out her tongue at him.

Still, Tom was currently skulking at home while *she* – Lily – trotted into the police station at Ashbourne, close on her mother's heels. And to make the triumph even sweeter, her mother had ordered Uncle Roger to stay at home, too.

Her mother swept up to the front desk and announced her name in a tone that dared them to argue or delay. Indeed, it only seemed to take a few minutes before a door opened into the reception area and a uniformed Asian man appeared in the gap.

'Mrs Fitzroy?' he asked. His voice held the usual note of deference that name provoked. 'My name is Khan. If you'd come this way, ma'am?'

Lily stayed close. The man, she noticed, was badged an inspector. They'd just done a project at school on official ranks. The two pips on his epaulettes were actually bath stars, she'd discovered, not after the city but something to do with the ritual of bathing before being knighted. She couldn't quite remember the details but wondered if the pair on each shoulder meant he'd had to bathe twice.

'I'm afraid we don't have much for you, at this stage,' Inspector Khan said. 'So far, she hasn't made any obvious slips with anything she's told us. We haven't yet made a positive identification but it's only a matter of time, I expect.'

'That's quite all right,' her mother said, giving him one of the not-quite-real smiles Lily had come to recognise from social events attended under sufferance. 'Actually, that's why I'm here... Oh dear, this is all rather embarrassing...'

The inspector frowned, led them to an office and ushered them both into chairs. 'Please, I'm sure you have nothing to be embarrassed about,' he said. 'I do understand that even without this... unexpected interruption, it must have been a most difficult day for you – and your family, of course.' This last comment was directed, gravely, to Lily. She decided at once that she rather liked Inspector Khan.

'Thank you. You're very kind,' her mother said graciously. 'But to save any further use of police resources... Well, it would rather appear that she – the girl – is, well... who she claims to be...'

The inspector's mouth hung open for a second too long. He closed it again with a snap, then said quickly, 'Mrs Fitzroy, I really must urge caution. Until her identity has been verified, she could have any number of ulterior motives for masquerading as your late husband's daughter—'

Virginia held up her hand and he stopped talking. 'I *so* appreciate your concern, Inspector. And, truthfully, I'm as sceptical as you are. But, my brother worked for my late husband for years and was well-acquainted with Blake as a child, and I'm partly here at his urging.'

Lily blinked at this, but said nothing.

'Only "partly"?' the inspector asked, frowning.

Her mother gave that social-obligation smile again, Lily noted. 'Our neighbours – Mr and Mrs Harding – have known the family for years. Mrs Harding, in particular, is convinced this girl is indeed Blake.'

'Nevertheless, I must—' he began.

Virginia leaned forwards, her expression earnest. 'If it *is* her… I couldn't live with myself, if I thought I'd been responsible for the poor girl being thrown in prison, when all she was trying to do was come home.'

For a few moments, the inspector regarded her without speaking, then he sighed. 'As you wish, Mrs Fitzroy. We'll release her without charge.'

'That's excellent news. Thank you,' Virginia said brightly. She sat back in her chair and folded her hands in her lap. 'We'll wait.'

TWELVE

The door to the interview room opened with no preliminary knock. As Blake looked up, a uniformed Asian inspector came in, his face expressionless.

'Wrap this up, Jane,' the man said.

'Boss?' Hudson managed to inject both confusion and disbelief into the single word.

The inspector stared at her for long enough to ensure there would be no further objections, then subjected Blake to brief study. 'Mrs Fitzroy is here. I believe she would like to speak with you.'

A raised eyebrow was her only response. The inspector made a harrumph of sound and turned away. As he pulled the door open, he glanced back, frowning when she hadn't moved from her chair.

'Well, come on then. I haven't got all day and we've wasted quite enough time on you already.'

'Meaning…?'

'*Meaning*, you're free to go.' And he jerked his head towards the corridor outside.

She flicked her eyes to PC Hudson, who appeared stunned into silence, then got to her feet. She walked out without looking back, followed the inspector towards the front desk where her details had been recorded on arrival. As they reached the door to the reception, the inspector paused to give her the hard eye.

'Mr Fitzroy was well-respected around here,' he murmured. 'People won't take kindly to anyone trying to… take advantage of his widow.'

'Oh, "well-respected", was he?' she said, voice cool. 'So why did nobody wonder why he gave up such a safe parliamentary seat?'

She left him scowling after her as she stepped out into the reception area. Virginia Fitzroy was standing poised near the main door, with the little girl from the funeral hovering nearby. Virginia's smile looked forced.

'So you're Blake. Of course you are. I'm so sorry for… everything. But, I assure you, I'd no *idea*.' Her words were rushed, the tone breathless and there was a faint possibility she might even be sincere. 'I never met Catherine – your mother – although I heard *so* much about her, naturally.'

'Oh, naturally.' Blake felt her eyebrows climbing. 'But not from my father, I bet?'

Colour leached up the sides of Virginia's neck and lit the tips of her ears. 'Gideon never spoke much about his first wife – I think he didn't wish to upset me. But I understood that losing her must have been very painful for him – for you both – of course.'

'Of course,' Blake echoed. The contradiction between Virginia's placatory words and the stiffness of her body language was fascinating.

What are you up to? What do you hope to gain by accepting me with such apparent candour when surely you, *of all people, have the most to lose…?*

Virginia turned to the inspector, who was still in attendance. He was watching the exchange, like a passer-by at a particularly slow-moving but brutal train wreck. She thanked him profusely for his help in sorting out 'the situation' and praised PC Hudson's prompt action. It might have been coincidence that the officer in question followed them into reception as she was doing so, but Blake suspected not.

When she put her mind to it, Virginia Fitzroy could play the consummate politician's wife. Anybody, watching her now, could be forgiven for believing she had offered her supposed burglar tea and biscuits rather than suggesting they be thrown in the cellar.

Maybe that's *it…*

Movement in her peripheral vision caught her attention. She looked down to find Virginia's daughter – it was easy to spot the likeness – had edged closer. She was a serious-looking child, who stared at her now with frank curiosity.

'Hello,' Blake said. 'What happened to your arm?'

The child blinked. 'I fractured my wrist in the accident when Gideon was killed,' she said, entirely matter-of-fact. 'The car rolled *all* the way over and *all* the windows broke.'

'Wow. That must have been dramatic. I bet you were scared.' When the child shrugged, she leaned in and added, '*I* would have been terrified,' with the air of someone sharing a great secret.

The child giggled, looking suddenly far younger. 'Are you *really* Blake?'

She took a quiet breath, aware of standing on the edge of something – the point of no return. 'Yes, I *really* am. What's your name?'

'I'm Lily. Does this mean you're sort of my sister? I've always wanted a sister. Well, I really wanted a kitten, but a sister would be *nearly* as good.'

Blake grinned in response. As she straightened, she saw Virginia shake hands briskly with the two officers.

'Come along,' she said, touching her daughter's shoulder. 'Time to go.'

Blake watched them head towards the obligatory Range Rover parked near the station. Virginia paused after a few strides and looked back at her. 'You too, my dear.'

'Oh? Where are we going?'

'Home, of course – back to Claremont. You're family, after all. Where else would you stay?'

Virginia's voice was pitched to be heard by their audience but she had her back to them so her face was hidden. Lily had gone on ahead and was pulling open the passenger door of the Range Rover. It was only Blake who saw Virginia's expression.

Just for a second, she read in it the anger, dislike, disdain and, underneath everything else, a thread of something that might have been fear.

And she realised then the lengths to which the woman was prepared to go in order to protect what she saw as hers.

Blake forced a smile as she allowed herself to be shepherded into the passenger seat. Virginia handed her the seat belt buckle and shut the door, as if not giving her the chance to change her mind. In the rear seat, Lily was humming to herself, oblivious.

As Virginia strode around the front of the car to the driver's side, Blake saw her jaw clamp tight shut, her face momentarily thunderous. It was clear that, however certain the Hardings might be that Blake was, indeed, who she claimed to be, Virginia was not at all convinced. It made her motives for apparently coming to Blake's 'aid' interesting, to say the least.

'Keep your friends close and your enemies closer, perhaps?' Blake muttered under her breath. 'Oh, that is *very* clever…'

THIRTEEN

Byron woke suddenly from the depths of a bad dream. Of late, this was an all too familiar occurrence. Gone were mornings when he had the luxury of surfacing refreshed through a warm haze.

He lay blinking up at a beamed ceiling he didn't recognise, waiting for his heart to stop punching against his breastbone. Finally, he felt able to sit up. The waft of air from the open window stirred the curtains and chilled his sweating skin.

He shivered. The bedclothes were a tangled snarl around his limbs and, just for a second, he was almost overwhelmed by the panicked urge to struggle free. He rubbed grit from his eyes with fingers that still trembled.

Byron despised his own weakness. He'd tried to fight it alone, then admitted defeat and let the Met-appointed shrinks poke about inside his head. Neither course of action had proved successful.

So here I am – halfway through my thirties and headed for the scrapheap.

Sighing, he leaned across for his wristwatch on the bedside table. It was a little after six in the morning. He swung his legs out of bed and rose, trying to massage the aching stiffness out of his hands as he moved across to the window.

The view, filtered through thin muslin curtains, was of a quiet main street bordered by sandstone houses. No traffic, no sirens, nobody stirring except a scruffy black and white cat that was washing itself in the middle of the road.

In the pub the night before, the conversation among the regulars had been almost entirely taken up with the appearance of Blake Claremont – or her doppelgänger – on the day of Gideon Fitzroy's funeral. Even the landlord joined in. Byron had listened more than he spoke – just a nudge here and there to keep the conversation rolling. One or two people hinted at her possible involvement in Fitzroy's death but could not produce any facts to support this view.

Byron was interested to note that the wilder theories petered out once Jane Hudson arrived, even if she was out of uniform by then. Ed Underhill joined them soon after, and any local gossip died away entirely. Aware of the keen ears all around them, Hudson knew enough not to discuss police business in public, so the conversation took a more mundane, if less informative slant. Still, at least it seemed to deter Underhill from talking shop.

It was only at closing time, when the bar had almost emptied out, that Hudson leaned across and said quietly, 'I don't suppose you had a chance to take another look at the room where we found the lassie, after I'd taken her down the station?'

'I stuck my head round the door – purely for interest's sake.'

'Did you… find anything?'

Byron had looked her straight in the eye and shrugged. 'There was nothing to find.'

Now, in the early light of morning, he reached for his mobile phone, hesitated only for a moment, then fired off a quick text:

Pls call me when convenient. B

Less than a minute later, the phone began to buzz. Byron didn't need to glance at the screen to know who was on the other end.

'Good morning, Commander,' he said. 'I trust you're well, ma'am.'

He received a grunt by way of reply. Then: 'How is it that you abbreviate "please" to "P-L-S" but go to the trouble of typing out "convenient" in full?'

'The joys of predictive text,' Byron said. 'Not too early, is it?'

'Yes,' Commander Daud said bluntly. 'But I'm now both awake and intrigued, so stop prevaricating, and just get on with it.'

He smiled. 'You will be pleased to hear that the funeral went off as well as these things ever do.'

'Just as long as the bloody man really did die accidentally, then frankly they could've danced the tango on his coffin for all I care.'

He refrained from comment. Before Byron's enforced period of leave, Commander Shamshi Daud had been two steps above him in the Met hierarchy. The rumours had her destined for the very top.

She was the only child of Somali immigrants who'd arrived in the East End of London when she was a babe in arms. They had remained with one foot forever in their African homeland. She had grown up East London through and through, with an accent to match. Her parents were initially disappointed when their ferociously bright and ambitious daughter had joined the Metropolitan Police, only to see her begin a meteoric rise.

Then Daud had been put in charge of the investigation into an alleged paedophile ring active at the heart of government. Numerous MPs, as well as high-ranking civil servants were rumoured to be involved. Daud had eaten, slept and breathed the operation for nearly two years before it blew up in her face. There were some who believed her career had stalled – permanently – as a direct result.

'Nobody appeared to be quite *that* pleased at his departure,' Byron said. 'The widow even shed a few tears.'

'Well, there's quite a bit of property, isn't there? Perhaps she was heartbroken, worrying about how she's going to spend it all.'

'I talked to the previous beat copper – recently retired – and to Jane Hudson, who's taken over his patch, both at the funeral yesterday and again last night. There's no indication they think Fitzroy's death was anything other than an accident.'

'What about a pro job? Plenty of contractors out there who specialise in very convincing "accidents".'

'Perhaps, but I can't see a professional sending his car off the road when his stepchildren were with him. It's too… messy.'

'Damn. I was hoping… Now I don't know whether to be relieved or disappointed.'

'I wouldn't give up hope just yet,' Byron said. 'When I introduced myself to Mrs Fitzroy, her reaction was… interesting.'

'Don't be cryptic. My brain won't stand it at this time in the morning. In what way "interesting"?'

'She seemed slightly alarmed to discover I was a detective with the Met.'

'Like she had something to hide, you mean?'

'Possibly, yes.'

'You didn't mention your current non-operational status, I take it?'

'No, ma'am.'

'Ah, now that *is* interesting.'

'I thought so.'

'Don't be smug, either. It doesn't suit you,' Daud said but he could hear the smile in her voice. 'I assume that, so far, nobody has queried your reason for being there?'

'Hudson sniffed out an ulterior motive right away, but I always had her marked down as a bright cookie, right from Hendon.'

'What did you tell her?'

'I spouted the company line – that Fitzroy contacted us with possible information about the Westminster debacle, thus making his untimely death worthy of further – albeit unofficial – investigation.' He kept his tone neutral. 'I also spoke to an older couple, name of Harding, who have been friends and neighbours of

Fitzroy's since the death of his first wife. So, naturally, I asked if they had any idea why he stood down from parliament.'

'Oh, I love it when you do your butter-wouldn't-melt act. What did they say?'

'Mrs Harding suggested marital troubles with wife number two, while Mr Harding had been told it was some health problem. Make of that what you will.'

Daud swore under her breath. 'His name never came up during the original investigation – not a whisper. We looked at him – hell, we looked at everyone. Not a sausage. That, and his resignation, it made him perfect… But if I started a rumour that got him killed, I'll be up to my neck in an IOPC investigation faster than you can spit—'

'Shamshi,' Byron said. The quiet reproach in his voice was enough to cut her off before she let the fear overwhelm her.

'I know, I know, but they've given the buggers bigger teeth of late, and once they get them into you…'

The Independent Office for Police Conduct had been granted wider-ranging powers in the light of recent police corruption scandals. Any officer who bent the rules – never mind broke them – was in the habit of checking over their shoulder these days.

'There's been an unforeseen development here, though,' Byron said.

'Which is?' Any jokiness in the commander's voice instantly switched off.

'Fitzroy had a daughter by his first marriage. A girl called Blake. She disappeared – ran away, so it was reckoned – ten years ago, when she was fifteen.'

'I think that was noted in his file. We made unsuccessful attempts to locate her, I seem to recall, just in case she had anything to add… So?'

'Hm, well. A young woman turned up yesterday, claiming to be the missing daughter.'

Daud let out a low whistle. 'How'd the family react?'

'As you'd expect – to begin with, at least.'

'Hostile?'

'Oh yes. But Virginia Fitzroy had something of a change of heart and welcomed her into the fold.'

The commander was silent for a moment. Byron let her ponder.

'You think she wants this would-be daughter where she can keep an eye on her?' Daud said then. 'It's not a bad strategy.'

'It's probably what I would have done.'

'Ah, but not everybody has a mind quite as nastily devious as yours.'

'I'll take that as a compliment – I think.'

'As you should.' She paused. 'What's your opinion of her, by the way?'

Byron turned away from the window, frowning. 'Well, she's not your average returning runaway, that's for sure. Intelligent, composed, and… calculated. She definitely has an agenda. I just haven't quite worked out what it is yet.'

'And is she who she claims to be?'

'Well, that's where complications come up,' Byron said. 'According to PC Hudson, who interviewed her, she denied she was likely to benefit under the terms of her father's will, which makes both her and her reason for returning seem more authentic.'

'I assume Hudson will be making every attempt to establish her identity one way or the other?'

'Of course. She was printed and photographed when they first took her in, as a matter of course, although apparently nothing has popped up on the system so far.'

'I'll do some digging at this end,' Daud said.

'Ah, well.' Byron cleared his throat. 'In that case, I may have an additional lead, if you wouldn't mind checking it out for me?'

'Uh-oh. I know that tone,' she said sharply. 'What have you done?'

'Nothing you need to worry about—'

'It's a bit late for that!'

He sighed. 'Do you want this or not?'

'Oh, go on then. What is it?'

He lifted the phone away from his ear, called up a couple of digital images and attached them to an email. When he'd fired it off, he said, 'On its way to you now. Should be fairly self-explanatory. Let me know what you find out.'

'Very good, my lord,' Daud mocked. 'You know I *live* to act as your unofficial secretary.' She was silent for a moment. He could almost hear her struggling not to ask for details. With obvious effort, she changed the subject. 'What about a DNA match?'

'No charges were brought – it's a moot point if she actually broke any laws. We have no cause to compel a sample.'

'And you can't find a way around that?' she asked in a dry voice. 'Anyway, surely the family will demand one.'

'Possibly – providing they can obtain DNA from Fitzroy's effects. I doubt they'll want to go to the trouble of an exhumation.'

'Oh God, let's hope not – the press will have a field day.' She paused. 'If this woman *does* turn out to be Fitzroy's daughter, though, she may be able to provide a unique… perspective.'

'Indeed, ma'am.'

'And if she's a fake?'

'Ah. Then, relying on anything she had to say could mean we come out of this with a significant amount of egg on our faces.'

Daud gave a soft laugh. He heard the bitter thread running through it. 'Nicely put, Byron. What you mean is, *I* could come out of this with a faceful of egg – and rotten egg at that. It's all right for—'

She broke off, no doubt realising how close she'd come to rubbing salt into an open wound.

Into the awkward silence that followed, Byron said drily, 'They could still take away my benefits, you know.'

'I *very* much doubt that. But I'm sorry. That was crass of me. And I *do* appreciate what you're doing – especially when you've no need to get involved.'

'If I don't keep pushing myself, I'll never know if I'm ready to come back.' He kept his voice light enough to belie the truth in his words. 'Besides, you've probably saved my sanity.'

'Hm. Either that or become the focus for your madness.'

'Yes, ma'am,' he agreed. 'There is *that* possibility, also.'

FOURTEEN

'I must be going mad,' Blake muttered under her breath.

She was kneeling in front of the open wardrobe in the little upstairs bedroom at Claremont. The base of the wardrobe itself, and the two loosened floorboards beneath it, were stacked to the side of her. Yesterday, while she'd waited for the police to arrive, she'd stashed her backpack into the cavity now revealed between the bedroom floor joists.

She was fairly certain that, when she'd pushed the backpack inside, the straps had been nearest the outside wall.

Now they faced into the room.

She glanced over her shoulder. It was early morning and, as far as she could tell, nobody else in the house was stirring. In any case, before she'd climbed into bed last night, she'd taken the upright chair from the dressing table and wedged the back firmly under the door handle.

Rather than reach inside the backpack, she eased it out from its place of concealment and unzipped it fully, so it lay spread open on the floor. She wasn't sure if she should be relieved or disappointed to find nothing had been added or taken away.

Shrugging, she picked up her smartphone. She got as far as opening the leather case to power it up when she hesitated, tilting the phone this way and that to catch the light sneaking in between the curtains. There was something amiss about the phone that she couldn't quite put her finger on…

Then it struck her – there were no fingerprints on the touchscreen. She had turned the phone off before tucking it away in the pack, of that she was quite sure. No point in having it on her for the police to confiscate. But she hadn't wiped it down. She was sure about that, too.

Which can only mean…

Heart in her mouth, she pressed the power button. The phone went through its start-up routine as normal, asking her to key in her security code and scan her thumbprint. Slightly reassured that the odds were against her security having been compromised, she sat back on her heels.

But why go to all the trouble of searching, only to leave it where you found it?

She put down the phone and ran a close eye over the contents of the backpack.

That confirmed it.

Experience had taught her to always pack methodically, adding items in the order she'd most likely need to access them. That order had been disrupted. Not by much, but enough – enough that she could tell.

An involuntary twitch rippled across her shoulders. In the past, she'd stayed in places where the concept of personal property did not exist. If it could be found and taken from you by someone bigger, stronger, meaner, or simply further up the food chain, then it was as good as gone.

But she'd never before had somebody look for and look *at* her stuff, but then leave it behind.

Somehow, that was worse than having it stolen.

FIFTEEN

Breakfast at the village pub was a hearty affair. The landlord seemed disappointed in Byron's meagre request for scrambled egg on wholewheat toast, with black coffee. The only other guests were a retired couple in walking gear and a young, slightly scruffy-looking family of four.

The walkers pored over large-scale Ordnance Survey maps while they ate, and discussed the merits of the route options available to them with all the gravity of planning an ascent from base camp. The young family were too focused on their phones and tablets to engage in conversation – with each other or anyone else.

Byron lingered over yesterday's paper and waited for them all to leave. He was interested to note that only the young family pushed in their chairs neatly and thanked the staff as they went.

A woman began clearing the tables. Byron took in the expensive watch, well-cut blouse and hair, and the fact she was in full make-up at eight o'clock in the morning, and pegged her as management rather than labour. He folded his paper and waited. When she glanced across, he smiled encouragingly and hoped she was the chatty type.

'Good morning,' she said. 'Can I get you more coffee?'

'Thank you, no. I think I'm about done, although I've enjoyed my lazy start to the day – breakfast was excellent.'

'Oh, good. I'm glad you enjoyed it.' She moved the placemats and wiped down the table's slate surface as if considering her next words with care. 'You came up for Mr Fitzroy's funeral yesterday, didn't you?'

'I did.'

'It was such a shock to all of us. I'd only seen him a couple of days before the accident. He was a lovely gentleman. Did wonders for the village.' She gave him a look of sympathy. 'Were you... close?'

Byron didn't think the truth would be in his favour. He gestured vaguely and said, 'We had a... London connection.'

'Oh, I see,' she said blankly. 'So were you there – when that lass turned up, making out she was his daughter?'

'It certainly seemed to take everyone rather by surprise.'

If she noticed his sidestep, she didn't comment on it. 'Well, it would! Ten years, she's been gone, with not a word. I mean, who *does* something like that? Although, from everything I've heard, she was a proper tearaway, that one.'

The front door opened and another woman hurried in. She wore jeans and cheap trainers. Her dark hair was longish, greying, and she was small and intense, with quick, nervy movements. Byron got an impression of worn-down middle age as she skirted his table without looking directly at either of them. Her hunched shoulders spoke of someone whose mission in life was to escape notice. Even so, he remembered her from the churchyard the day before.

'Morning, Pauline,' the landlady said, glancing pointedly at her watch. Her tone was more brisk than when she spoke to the guests. 'Could you make a start with the loos and the other bar?'

Pauline nodded as she stepped round her employer.

'I'm not sure I was aware Fitzroy *had* a daughter until yesterday,' Byron said, a gentle nudge which didn't stray far from the truth, just in case the landlady was distracted by the interruption.

And because she was still in his eyeline, he saw the sudden tensing of the small woman's shoulders. Only momentary, then she darted through a doorway leading towards the kitchen at the back of the pub.

'Oh, he never mentioned her,' the landlady went on, oblivious. 'It must have been painful for him, though. Just imagine – losing his first wife, and then his daughter just *disappearing* like that.'

'Did you know them? His wife or his daughter?'

'Sadly, no. Me and Kenneth, we've only been here five years. We know Virginia – Mrs Fitzroy – of course. A lovely lady. I feel for her, I really do – what she must be going through.'

'Indeed.' Byron kept his expression bland. 'And now there will undoubtedly be a lot of fuss over whether this young woman is who she claims to be.'

The landlady blinked at him, then laughed. 'Oh, you don't think there's any chance the girl really *is* Blake, do you?'

Behind her, Pauline came back into view in the doorway, now wearing a floral tabard with a tin of furniture polish sticking out of the front pocket. She carried a mop and a tin bucket and froze when she caught the landlady's words. Just for a second, Byron caught a mix of anguish and anger flicker across the woman's face.

'Really?' he murmured.

'Oh no,' the landlady went on. 'She'll be some hoaxer hoping to make a quick buck, that's who *she'll* be, you mark my words.' She hoisted the tray stacked with dirty plates and cups, pausing only to deliver her parting shot. 'Wouldn't be the first time somebody's tried a trick like that, and I'm sure it won't be the last!'

SIXTEEN

Lily crouched in the cupboard under the stairs, in the dark.

Hiding.

She had been sent up to bed ridiculously early the night before. Nine o'clock! It was outrageous. Especially as she and Tom were home from school at the moment, what with the accident and the funeral and everything. Her mother had described it as 'compassionate leave', which sounded so grown up.

And which also made it doubly annoying that she was sent to bed at her usual time, like a little kid, when her mother, and Uncle Roger, and Mr and Mrs Harding, must have spent the rest of the evening asking Blake all kinds of fascinating questions, trying to see if she really *was* Blake. Her mother *knew* Lily had wanted to stay up and hear everything that her newly discovered stepsister had to say.

It was *so* unfair.

Lily had seen pictures of Blake – well, one, anyway – of a shy-looking slightly plump girl who used her long dark hair to hide behind, so it was hard to really see her face. But the Blake who'd returned had really got herself in shape, like one of those reality TV shows where they put people through diet and exercise regimes so they emerge transformed.

So, this morning, she woke especially early, threw on her clothes and crept downstairs before anyone else was about. She slipped into the cupboard beneath the main staircase, not even switching on the light because she knew it would show through the gap under the door to anyone walking past.

She sat with her back against the wall, arms wrapped round her knees, trying not to think *too* much about mice, or spiders, or any other creepy-crawlies that might be scuttering about in there.

Instead, she mulled over the fractured conversation she'd heard Uncle Roger having, after the funeral yesterday.

He may understand what 'dead and buried' means, but I don't.

She'd tried since to get a peek at his phone, but for once he'd kept it close to hand.

From somewhere above her, she heard footsteps cross the landing.

Her mother was first down. Lily knew that quick tread. A confident march that did not go out of its way to be either quiet or noisy. Her brother was next, slothful and heavy-footed. At one time he was so funny and easy-going. This year he'd been nothing but grumpy – and that was *before* the accident. Her mother said it was his hormones and all to do with him growing up, but she wasn't so sure. She missed the brother he used to be.

Then Uncle Roger came down. He must have been half asleep still, because he tripped part of the way. Lily heard him swear as he recovered his balance.

It seemed to take forever for the unknown footsteps to start on their way down. Lily held her breath. She stared upwards at the underside of each stair as it was reached, unable to see much of anything in the gloom. Saw it all inside her head anyway.

There were twelve steps in the last flight from the half-landing to the hallway.

She counted only ten footfalls.

When she heard the tap of boots on the tiles, Lily bounced out of her hiding place, throwing the door open. She screwed her eyes up against the sudden brightness of the hall. When she blinked her vision clear, the stranger stood frozen, one hand still on the banister.

'So you *are* her,' Lily said.

'Oh?' The young woman eyed her, unsmiling. 'And how do you work that out?'

'Because you stepped *over* the squeaky treads, of course,' Lily said, and there was a hint of scorn in her voice. It was obvious. 'Third from the top and second from the bottom.'

The young woman frowned. Her gaze flicked sideways to the staircase, as if she hadn't given it any thought until that moment.

'Yes,' she said at last. 'But don't forget all that time I was alone in the house yesterday. I *might* have discovered the noisy treads then, and decided to avoid them – better for stealth.'

'Oh.' Lily felt her face heat, as if she were being mocked. 'Oh. Did you?'

The other gave a slight smile and said nothing.

Suddenly self-conscious, Lily studied the hem of her jumper as she said, offhand, 'I thought you might like to come and see my dressing-up box. I have lots of lovely costumes in there, for doing plays, and Tom doesn't take *any* interest so—'

'I have things I need to do this morning,' the young woman said. And, no doubt seeing her crestfallen expression, gave her the standard adult brush-off: 'Maybe later.'

Lily sighed, head jerking up as she realised the other had moved and was now standing right in front of her. She took an involuntary step back, bumping into the open door with a gasp.

'Come on,' the young woman said. She winked. 'Don't want to miss breakfast, do we…?'

SEVENTEEN

Blake heard voices inside the kitchen, engaged in indistinct but vigorous debate. As she pushed open the door, they stopped as if someone had hit the mute button.

She ambled in, doing her best to behave as if nothing strange had just happened. After a pause, she sensed Lily follow suit. Virginia was sitting in state at the head of the table. She was made-up and styled as if for public display and she eyed the pair of them over the rim of her coffee cup. Looking, Blake suspected, for signs of collusion.

Roger Flint hovered near the range cooker in its tiled alcove, leaning his hip against the polished rail that ran across the front of it. Wearing yesterday's suit with his shirt collar open and no tie, he was doing his best to look casual. The rigid set of his shoulders gave him away.

Only Tom paid no attention to their arrival. He was hunched in a chair at the far end of the table from his mother, apparently engrossed in the pattern of milk and cereal in his bowl.

'Good morning,' Virginia said, placing her cup down very precisely in its saucer. 'I trust you slept well?'

'Fine, thanks,' Blake said. She began opening cupboards, deliberately without being invited, until she found one containing mugs. 'You?'

Virginia blinked at her.

Roger lurched upright.

'We buried my sister's husband yesterday,' he said stiffly. 'You might want to show some respect.'

'In case it escaped your notice, the man you buried yesterday also happened to be my father,' Blake replied. 'So… I will if you will.'

Roger took in a breath to start a tirade but Virginia stayed him with a single glance. 'Don't, Roger. She's quite right, of course.' She managed a tight smile. 'I'm sorry. That was… thoughtless of me.' She nodded to the mug in Blake's hand. 'There's coffee in the pot. Do help yourself.'

'Thanks.'

Blake took her time pouring coffee, then stood leaning against the countertop as she took her first sip. Virginia's attitude was interesting. She'd expected more hostility but the woman was made of sterner stuff.

I guess she had to be, if she married the old bastard…

Lily was fussing around with a packet of breakfast cereal, shaking it very carefully into a bowl as if counting it out flake by flake. All the while, the tilt of her head showed she was taking in every word. Tom still stared morosely into his food.

'So – *Blake*,' Virginia said, with all the enthusiasm of someone who's just found a slug in their salad but still feels obliged to compliment the chef, 'what are your plans for today?'

'Oh, I thought I'd reacquaint myself with the area. Take a look around, you know – see what's changed since I was last here.'

It was Roger who asked, his tone still belligerent, 'And what do you intend to use for transport, hm? Didn't get here by car, did you?'

'I thought I'd use my father's car.'

'What?'

It was Roger who spoke but it might have been any of them. Tom's spoon landed in his bowl with a clatter, splashing milk onto the tabletop. Lily added to the mess with spilt cereal as her hand twitched over her own bowl. Only Virginia seemed to retain her poise.

'As you should be only too aware, my husband's car was all-but destroyed in the accident,' she said, her voice brittle. 'I believe the police still have it.'

'That's beside the point,' Roger broke in. 'Because what makes you think we'd just let you loose in an expensive vehicle—'

Blake eyed him calmly. 'Well, I seem to remember *you* being trusted with that big Lexus my father used to have, even *after* you tried to drive it home from the pub one evening and stuck it nose-first in a ditch on the way back from Hognaston.'

'It was sheet ice—' Roger began, then stopped, mouth moving but no words coming out, as the significance of what she'd said – of what she *knew* – hit him. He looked away, his voice sulky, 'I think you'll find it was a BMW, on the road to Wirksworth. Not the same thing at all.'

She shrugged, as if the discrepancies were of no account.

'Actually, when I said my father's car, I was thinking of his old Land Rover,' Blake said, noting the tiny flinch Roger failed to hide. 'He always swore he'd never get rid of it, so I assume it's still about the place somewhere?'

'It's in the old carriage house. Tom and I used to play in it,' Lily offered when nobody else answered, causing her brother to scowl in her direction. 'We would pretend we were on a trans-Saharan expedition or something. I don't remember it going anywhere *real*, though – not for *ages*.'

Blake, content to have scattered a few seeds of general anxiety around her, smiled at Lily. 'Well, perhaps it's time it did, then.'

Lily put down her spoon. 'I could show you, if you like?'

Blake was on the verge of refusing – it wasn't as if she didn't know the way, after all – but something in Lily's pleading expression stopped her. She moved towards the scullery, throwing a brief smile over her shoulder.

'Come on, then. Why not?'

They left by the back door, taking a diagonal path across the rear lawn towards the woods. It was a cold, crisp morning, the dead leaves dry enough to crunch underfoot as they wound beneath the trees. Blake shoved her hands into the pockets of her hoodie and breathed deep. Autumn had always been one of her favourite times of year.

A distant, sharp crack echoed through the wood, making her start, wary. Several more reports quickly followed.

'It's just the local shoot,' Lily said, with the straightforwardness of someone used to living in the country.

Of course – it's pheasant season.

Blake identified shotguns, half a dozen different varieties, fired at close intervals as, no doubt, the hapless birds were driven into flight towards the guns. She had no particular objection to game shooting – providing those taking part were prepared to dress and eat what they killed.

She ducked her head and hurried on, with Lily chattering alongside her.

It wasn't far to the old stables. They were positioned out of sight of the main house, just far enough for the smell of manure not to carry, and long disused for their original purpose. A small cobbled yard with old-fashioned stalls, a harness room and a caged run – presumably once intended for outdoor dogs. To one side was the carriage house, three arched doorways for the family's horse-drawn vehicles, from dogcart to grand six-in-hand coach. A hayloft stretched right round the upper floor.

Blake dragged open one of the sagging doors to the carriage house, the bottoms of the planks scraping the ground. Inside smelt of cobwebs and rust. The only vehicle was the old Land Rover, the side walls of its knobbly tyres cracked with age. Its paintwork, a dull mid blue, was oxidised to grey in some places and had flaked away to reveal bare aluminium in others.

Frowning at the neglect, Blake circled the old workhorse. The front bumper was bent downwards at the passenger side and that headlight was broken, too. When she rubbed away the dirt at the bottom corner of the windscreen, she saw the last tax disc expired nine years previously.

'I remember this was his pride and joy,' she murmured. 'So, what happened…?'

The question was at least half rhetorical, but Lily shrugged. 'Tom taught himself to drive it. Then he taught me. We used to go all over the estate. But then Mummy caught us, and we're not allowed any longer.'

'How on earth did your brother teach *himself* to drive?'

'YouTube,' Lily said airily.

Blake frowned, looked about her. Leaning in a corner, almost hidden by dusty cobwebs, was a long pole with a brass hook on the end of it.

'Have you ever been up into the hayloft?' she asked. And when Lily shook her head, 'Would you like to?'

'Ooh, yeah.'

Blake used the pole to open the loft hatch in the boarded ceiling. It swung down on rusted hinges, revealing the end of a ladder. The same hook fitted over the last rung, and Blake pulled the ladder out through the hatchway at an angle, bringing a cloud of musty straw fragments with it, until it tilted down close enough to grab the end.

The floor was polished brick and tended to be slippery. The original builders had foreseen this, and laid one line of floor bricks higher than those on either side, just where the foot of the ladder needed to rest. Blake tucked the foot of the ladder carefully behind the bricks and gave it a tug, just to be sure.

Lily watched her closely enough that Blake knew she was planning a repeat visit at some point, on her own. 'That's clever.'

'It is. The floor slopes down slightly towards the doors, so they could wash the mud off the carriages and it would all run into that gutter at the front. Apparently, they used to rest the front carriage wheels against the raised bricks, too, to stop them rolling away.'

'Can we go up now?'

'I'll go first, just in case. I don't think anyone's used this ladder in a while, and if it will take my weight, it will certainly take yours.'

'You're not heavy.' Lily giggled. 'You used to be *much* chubbier than you are now. I've seen photos.'

Blake had already begun to climb and raised her eyebrows at the question, but heard only curiosity rather than malice. 'Yes, I did.'

'What happened?'

'I started burning more calories than I ate.' She reached the top of the ladder and stepped sideways onto the floor of the loft, testing the boards for undue give. They still seemed solid enough. 'OK, up you come.'

Lily scrambled up and onto the hayloft floor beside her. She looked, Blake thought, a little disappointed by what she found, which was basically just crumbling bales of hay and straw, the remains of rotting shutters at the open windows, and lumps of mortar from the underside of the slate roof. Swallows had built a whole housing estate of nests attached to the beams. The piles of droppings beneath each one showed they probably came back year after year. Lily wrinkled her nose at the smell.

'What else is up here?' she asked.

'Not much. The hayloft runs over the stables on the other two sides, too. There are wooden chutes into the hay racks in every stable, so you could come up here and feed all the horses, one after another.'

Lily shrugged, unimpressed. She wandered over to the shutters and peered out through a gap.

Blake turned a slow circle, looking across at the stack of straw taking up half the space, stacked up to the beams. And she remembered being there with another girl – one her own age.

The two of them lying nestled into the bales, hidden from view, planning a future in hushed voices.

We had such dreams.

Suddenly, Lily stilled, tense.

Blake turned. 'What is it?'

'Um, nothing… I think. I thought I saw someone, down there in the courtyard, but…'

Blake moved across, stared out, pressing tight to the wall so she could look down almost directly below them. She saw no one.

'Are you sure?'

'N-o…' Lily said. 'Do you mind if we go now? This place is creepy.'

Even as she uttered the words, they heard a muffled clatter from the carriage house below. Something banged against the bottom of the ladder. It jumped, juddering against the frame.

Lily dashed forwards as if her means of escape was about to be snatched away from her.

'Lily, wait!'

But before Blake could reach her, Lily had scrambled onto the ladder and was already on her way down, her movements awkward because of the cast on her wrist.

She'd barely made two rungs when the ladder lurched abruptly as the foot of it began to slide, unchecked now, along the brick floor. The side rails scraped against the frame of the hatch, disappearing rapidly. Lily let out a terrified shriek.

Blake threw herself at the hatchway, just as the ends of the ladder slipped from the inside of the beam and dropped from sight. She dived her head and shoulders through the gap, made a wild grab for the ladder as it fell. The palm of her right hand slapped against the top rung, hard enough to sting. She locked her fingers around it and held on for grim death.

For a second, she thought the weight of ladder and child would drag her head first out of the hayloft and send them both crashing to the bricks below. She teetered on the very edge of balance, fingers of her left hand clawed into the wooden boards alongside her.

She dug in with the toes of her boots, trying to hutch backwards and heave the ladder back onto the frame at the same time. After two attempts, she gave up. Not only did she simply not have the upper body strength, but the action jolted the ladder. Lily, both arms wrapped around the rungs in a death grip, gave a squeal each time.

'Lily… I don't know how long I can hold this, sweetheart. You're going to have to climb down.'

Lily glanced up at her, face tight with fear, and gave a mute headshake. It sent a tremor up through Blake's hand and arm, both rapidly turning numb. Her shoulder felt as if it was being yanked from its socket in slow motion.

'Lily, please…'

Oh, for… What the hell are you supposed *to say a twelve-year-old to reassure them?*

'*Lily*!' It came out harsher than she intended, but the girl's eyes flew to hers in conditioned response. Blake thought about Virginia, and the style of parenting she was likely to have employed.

'LILY!' she roared. 'Stop being such a baby and get your arse down this bloody ladder, right now!'

There was a moment's shocked silence. Then, at last, very carefully, Lily began to move.

EIGHTEEN

Not for the first time that morning, PC Jane Hudson was on hold. She rubbed her fingers across her forehead and pressed them into the side of her temple. It did not help relieve the headache that was brewing, nor her sense of growing frustration.

With a huff of breath, she let the receiver drop onto her shoulder. She could still hear the distorted squawk of the phone system playing local radio, but it was no longer quite as painful on the ear.

A tap on the open door of the office made her glance up, to find Ed Underhill lounging in the gap.

'Now then, lass,' Underhill said by way of greeting.

'You're really struggling with this concept of retirement, aren't you?'

Underhill grinned. 'I was passing. Thought I'd drop in and see how you're getting on with identifying that lass from the Fitzroys' place. Vested interest and all that.'

'Idle curiosity, more like.'

'Aye, well – that, too.' Underhill moved further into the office, hands in his pockets. After the formality of the funeral the day before he was back in his usual garb of moleskin trousers and a quilted jacket. 'How are you getting on with her?'

Hudson held up a finger and snatched the receiver back to her ear but it was still the radio station rather than a real person. She slumped back in her chair again.

'I'm not,' she said. 'Fingerprints aren't in the system and nothing popped on the photo. Nor does anything come up for the name Blake Claremont – or Fitzroy, for that matter.'

Underhill took one of the chairs on the other side of the desk, rocking it so the frame flexed. He pursed his lips.

'Not even a driver's licence or a passport?'

'If she has either, they're not under the name Fitzroy or Claremont.'

'Medical records?'

'Tried that. Her GP at the local health centre retired six years ago. The practice manager tells me that, quite apart from needing patient consent or a court order, they have a policy of getting rid of old records eight years after last attendance.'

'Ah. What about dental, then?'

Hudson pulled a face and pointed to the phone she was still cradling. 'They're checking, although judging by how long I've been hanging on, they must keep their records in Outer Mongolia—'

'Not quite *that* far, Constable Hudson,' said the woman she'd been dealing with, coming back on the line in time to catch that last remark. Her tone was justifiably tart. 'But I assumed you would prefer diligence over haste, yes?'

'Absolutely, yes,' Hudson said quickly, ignoring Underhill's silent laughter.

'As it is, I'm afraid we can't help you,' the woman continued. 'Part of the reason for the delay was because I wanted to double-check our archive. The Data Protection regulations dictate that we keep sensitive personal information no longer than is absolutely necessary.'

'And how long is that, usually?'

'Sadly, there's no definition of "necessary" – it depends on individual circumstances. Our normal procedure would be to invite the patient to come for their usual check-ups – in writing to the address on file. If they fail to respond, we delete both paper and digital records after two years.'

'That soon?' Hudson murmured, mentally trying to calculate when she'd last been to her own dentist.

'We have a waiting list,' the woman said primly. 'If some people are desperate to receive treatment, it wouldn't be fair to deny them for the sake of those who, for whatever reason, no longer attend.'

'Might the records have been transferred to a new practice – if someone moved away?'

'It varies. Unlike a doctor, any work by a dentist is usually self-evident as soon as the patient opens their mouth. It's useful to have previous records, but not always necessary in order to treat them satisfactorily.'

'A wash-out, then?' Underhill surmised as Hudson dropped the receiver back onto its cradle.

'Aye. Whoever this lassie is, she had no documentation or ID on her when we picked her up and she doesn't appear to be on record anywhere, either.' She raked her fingernails through her hair. 'It's like she's a ghost.'

NINETEEN

'Blake! How lovely. Do come in.' Anne Harding wheeled back a little from the front door, leaning to peer past Blake out into the driveway. 'I didn't hear a car.'

'I cycled – it's not far,' Blake said, indicating the rusting bicycle propped against one of the garden walls, next to the old Toyota Hilux pickup that Oliver Harding used as a general workhorse.

'I never even thought to ask… Do you have a driving licence?'

'I can drive,' Blake said and if Anne realised the evasion in the answer, she didn't query it. 'But I found my old bike in the back of the carriage house. It was surprisingly intact after all this time – and easier to make road legal than the Landie.' She had already decided not to mention what had befallen her and Lily while they were there.

Anne frowned. 'Landie?'

'You remember that old blue Land Rover? My father kept it as a sort of local runabout.'

'Oh, gosh, yes. Do you know, it's been so long I'd forgotten all about it. But cars were never my thing, darling.'

As Blake stepped over the threshold, Anne caught her hand in both her own and squeezed it. Her grip was a mixture of hard and soft, fingers tight but the thumb hardly exerting any pressure at all. For a moment, neither of them spoke.

Then Anne cleared her throat. 'Come through to the conservatory. Oliver's out being terribly industrious, raking leaves out of the pond, but I confess I'm still drinking coffee and reading the paper. Would you like a cup? Or I have some of that South African tea you used to enjoy?'

Blake thought of her unfinished coffee back at Claremont. 'Coffee would be lovely, thank you.'

Anne spun neatly and drove the chair at a fast walking pace deeper into the house. Blake fell into step alongside her, looking about.

'You've redecorated,' she said.

Anne glanced at her in surprise. 'Well, yes – did you think we wouldn't have, after ten years?' She frowned. 'Although, the colour scheme hasn't changed…'

'I wish I could say the same for Claremont.'

Anne gave a bark of laughter. 'No, it is an acquired taste, isn't it?'

The old kitchen opened out into an ultra-modern glass and steel extension that wrapped around the back of the house. The polished wood-burning stove in the centre of the rear wall was already lit, filling the space with warmth. Anne had scattered clippings on top of it from the bay tree in the garden. The oil in the herb released a comforting smell into the air. A large ginger cat was curled up on a discarded newspaper, tail tucked neatly around his nose.

Anne nodded to one of the oversize sofas looking out on the rear lawn. Over by the large pond, Blake saw the tall, stooped figure of Oliver, in old corduroys, a padded waistcoat with a rip in the side, and a shapeless hat. He was dragging leaf debris out of the water with a long-handled wooden rake.

Anne rolled into the kitchen. Half the units between the sitting area and the kitchen were low enough for her to use from her chair. Blake watched her reach into a drawer for a mug and pour coffee from the cafetière.

'How do you take it these days – still milk and two sugars?'

'Just black.'

'Ah, yes. Amazing how we lose our childhood sweet tooth.'

Blake took the mug with a nod of thanks, turned away and sank into the cushions of the nearest sofa. She stroked the top of the ginger cat's head. He uncoiled into a twanging stretch, splaying an impressive set of claws, and began to purr.

'When did the Land Rover come off the road?' Blake asked. 'It looks as if it hasn't been taxed since—'

'*Blake.*' Anne's voice was sharp as she cut across her. She smiled, immediately contrite, but Blake caught the tremor of her chin. 'Blake,' Anne repeated, more quietly. 'Darling, you've been gone *ten years.* There are so many things I want to know – about what you've been doing all that time. About where you've been. About *how* you've been.' She made a helpless gesture with her hands. 'Honestly, I don't know where to start. You were like a daughter to me and I feel I've missed *so* much of the most significant time in your life…'

She pressed her lips together, eyes suddenly too bright. 'The last thing I'm interested in is Gideon's old truck!'

Blake swallowed and said nothing. Still absently stroking the cat, she looked away, watching Oliver raking the leaves up onto the edge of the pond, steady and untiring, utterly absorbed. She heard rather than saw Anne's sigh.

'When you left you were still a child and look at you now – a lovely young woman.'

'I'm sorry.'

'You don't have to be sorry for being lovely.'

Blake smiled, felt some of the tension lift. 'Hardly lovely, but at least I'm fitter – healthier.'

'Happier?'

'That, too.'

Anne gestured to Blake's hair. 'You look so different… blonde. It suits you, though.'

'I like it.'

'So… is there anyone important in your life?' Anne gave a shaky laugh. 'For all I know you could have a husband hidden away and half a dozen children by now.'

Blake shook her head. 'No children. No husband – no wife, either,' she said, looking away. 'No one important.'

Anne moved in closer. The sofa was low enough that Blake had to tilt her head up slightly to meet her eyes. Anne reached out and took her free hand. Blake set down her coffee on the side table and gave her both. The older woman clutched them fiercely.

'My turn to say "I'm sorry" – for all those lost opportunities.'

'I'm OK. I survived,' Blake said. 'That's all any of us can say, isn't it?'

'Yes, I suppose it is.'

Silence fell between them. A log settled in the wood burner. The cat continued to purr.

Blake reached for her coffee mug again and took a sip. It was lukewarm but strong as sin. Just the way she'd learned to like it.

'You've changed,' Anne said. 'You're… harder. You've lost that sense of wonder.'

'I was too naïve for my own good.'

'Do you think that, one day, you'll be able to tell me your story?' Anne asked, her voice tentative. 'Of where you've been, and who with…?'

'Why is it so important that you know?'

'Because… well, you were here one minute and simply gone the next. We were all devastated.'

'Not all of you.'

'Oh, Blake, how can you say—?'

'So why didn't any of you bother to report me missing?' she demanded. 'I mean, my father, I could understand, but… you? Oliver? Did you forget about me so easily?'

Anne reared back, a mixture of hurt and shock in her face. 'I thought Gideon had done!' she said, almost as a reflex. 'I knew he didn't want a big fuss made, but still, I was certain he had people looking for you. He must have done, surely?' But the lack of conviction in her voice was obvious.

Blake bowed her head, staring into the half-empty mug gripped tight in her fingers. She bit her lip.

Anne said softly, 'Oh, *darling*…'

In a rush, Blake thrust the mug onto the side table and slid off the sofa onto her knees. She reached for Anne, who wrapped her arms around her and held on while she vibrated with emotions to which she could not – *would* not – give in. One of Anne's hands went up to Blake's head to cradle it, brushing a tangle of hair back from her face.

Blake flinched away.

Anne froze. 'Blake, stop. *Please*, darling, let me see.' She pushed the hair back, tracing the ragged scar that weaved into her hairline at the temple. 'My God,' she murmured. 'What happened to you?'

Blake shrugged her hands away, struggled back onto the sofa and sat there, hunched in on herself. The cat, as if sensing inner torment, climbed onto her lap and butted his head against the underside of her chin. She wrapped her arms around his warm body. But when she looked up, her eyes were bleak.

'I don't know,' she said, her voice hollow. 'I don't remember…'

TWENTY

After breakfast, Byron strolled down to the church to collect his car. The main street was busier but still not congested. People walking their dogs gave him a smile and a friendly greeting. A woman was working on a dry stone wall that bordered a narrow lane. In the distance, he could hear shotguns. In London that would have been cause for alarm. Here, people's first thoughts ran to game-bird pie rather than armed robbery.

At the bottom of the hill, he cut through the churchyard. He was almost at the side gate into the lane where the Merc sat, its roof dotted with fallen leaves, when his steps slowed.

Abruptly, he altered course, retracing the path he'd taken with Jane Hudson around the edges of the graves. He reached the hedged garden of remembrance where he'd first seen the figure at the far side of the churchyard.

Opening the small wrought-iron gate, he stepped inside. The small grave markers were all laid flat here, some of them almost overrun by the surrounding grass. Others were clearly cared for, neatly trimmed and adorned with urns of fresh flowers. He wondered what had drawn the young woman here, other than the concealment of the hedge that bordered the garden.

He had already begun to turn back for the gate when a single white lily draped across one neglected marker caught his eye, its petals wilted into the damp grass. Byron crouched, lifting the wilting bloom to reveal the name carved into the stone:

Catherine Claremont.

He rose slowly, wiping his hands. You would have to know whose grave this was, he reflected. It was not something easily stumbled upon. Was it the young woman who'd left the single bloom here?

In the pocket of his overcoat, his phone began to buzz. Byron pulled it out, still distracted, and answered in a clipped tone. 'Byron.'

'It would be nice if you sounded *slightly* happier to hear from me,' Commander Daud said drily, 'considering I bring news.'

'What news, oh wise one?'

'All right, Byron. Don't overdo it.' Her voice turned brisk. 'Those serial numbers you sent me – for the mobile phone and the SIM card. We have partial hits.'

'How do you define "partial"?'

'Well, they're both registered to a Pay-As-You-Go burner, which would normally be a dead end.'

'Indeed, ma'am.'

'Hm, have you ever noticed that the more interested you get, the politer you get?'

'I believe it has been mentioned once or twice.'

'Yeah, and the more you sound like your arse is stuffed with tweed. If this is what comes of taking on fast-track detectives, straight from uni…'

'I believe *that* has been mentioned a few times, too.' Byron headed for the side gate, pressing the alarm fob to unlock the doors of the Mercedes as he reached it. 'So – the phone, ma'am?'

'Hm. We were able to track the wholesaler and retailer who sold the batch containing our target phone. Two others were bought at the same time, by the same buyer. One is also a burner, but the third was put on contract.'

'By whom?'

'An art and antiques dealer from Chiswick called Alexander Vaganov, known to his mates as Lex.'

'*Vaganov.*' Byron stilled halfway through buckling his seat belt, eyes narrowing. 'Why do I know that name?'

'I'd be surprised if you did,' Daud said. 'He's respectable enough on the surface but dig a little deeper and it's rumoured he was quite a scam artist – an expert in the long con. Not that we've ever been able to get anything to stick. But, as far as I know, he's never killed anyone, so that would have kept him out of your particular orbit.'

'A point in his favour, then.'

'Yeah. Word is that Vaganov also collects and trades information – he acts as a broker. So—'

'Give me a moment, ma'am.' Byron started the car. After a second or two, the hands-free facility kicked in. He slid the handset into its holder on the dash and Daud's voice came at him from the Merc's speakers.

'I would suggest that if your party crasher is closely associated with someone like Lex Vaganov – close enough for him to supply her with a smartphone and who-knows-what background information, anyway – then she's almost undoubtedly as dodgy as he is. Although, what she might hope to achieve by impersonating Fitzroy's missing daughter is anybody's guess.'

Byron recalled Jane Hudson's assumption back at the house – that the young woman was some kind of advance party for a specialist burglary team, after Claremont's antiques. At the time it had seemed pure speculation. Now he wasn't quite so sure.

'I don't want to alert anyone that I'm here on anything other than an unofficial basis. So, I won't tell Hudson but I'll keep an eye on her, just in case I can throw a spanner in her plans – whatever they turn out to be.'

TWENTY-ONE

'I'm telling you, Vee, you ought to send that damn girl packing. Or, at the very least, keep her away from your daughter,' Roger Flint spluttered. 'My God, Lily could have been killed.'

Virginia listened in silence to her brother rant as he paced the drawing room. He'd been going on and on about it ever since the two girls got back to the house, and Blake – or the person *claiming* to be Blake – admitted what had happened. Virginia had her suspicions that the only reason anything was said at all was because Lily was in too much of a state for it to be hushed up.

It was an excuse, of course – some wild story about a mystery intruder who had shifted the end of the ladder. Virginia had no doubts that Blake simply hadn't seated the bottom of it properly and was attempting to explain away her own carelessness with such nonsense.

It *had* to be that.

Because the alternative was almost unthinkable.

Or is it?

Her mind went back to a week before Gideon died. The two of them had gone into Wirksworth. He'd had a silly bump in traffic. Oh, he'd blamed the other driver but to Virginia's mind it was the result of his own lack of attention. She had caught him staring at a figure on the pavement outside shops on the other side of the road. A girl, which wouldn't usually have meant much – Gideon always had an eye for a pretty girl. But this one was different, if only because she seemed to be as transfixed by the sight of Gideon as he was by her.

Then a delivery truck had paused between them, blocking her from view.

When it moved away, she was gone.

Now, looking back, Virginia was sure it had been Blake standing there.

That raised all kinds of questions – like was it merely a coincidence that she turned up in the vicinity shortly before Gideon died? She still worried about Tom's rather hazy explanation of what caused her husband's car to leave the road in the first place. And now Lily had been put in jeopardy…

'Where's Tom?' she asked suddenly, cutting Roger off in midsentence.

He gaped at her for a moment, then said, 'In the kitchen, when I last saw him – glued to his phone, as usual. Why?'

Virginia favoured him with an icy stare. 'My husband is dead and my daughter's life has just been endangered. Is it any surprise that I might be concerned as to the whereabouts of my son?'

There was a moment's pause, then Roger nodded. 'Quite right. Until we've found out what this girl is playing at, we should all be careful. You don't honestly believe she *is* Blake, do you?'

Virginia shrugged. 'I thought it prudent to have her where we can keep an eye on her until we find that out. Incidentally, you knew Blake when you first started working for Gideon, didn't you?'

'Well, not really. I mean, she was about the place, of course, but I didn't really *know* her. She wasn't exactly what you'd call outgoing.'

'Did she have any… distinguishing marks, do you know?'

That seemed to mystify him. 'Such as?'

'Well, Anne phoned. Apparently, Blake went to see her and she noticed… The girl has a scar, quite a noticeable one, in her hairline above her left eye. I don't suppose you recall anything like…?' She glanced up, caught her brother's expression. 'Roger, are you all right?'

'Of course. I'm fine.' He straightened, tried a smile that barely made it past his lips. 'And no, there was nothing like that. I-I think this whole business with the girl – turning up out of the blue like this – has me a little shaken up. The timing stinks. Gideon wanted his estate to go to you, as is only right. I don't want to see anything get in the way of that, for your sake. You deserve to be kept in comfort.'

'I'm still not sure why Gideon didn't make provision for you in his will – after all the years you've worked for him.'

Roger made a dismissive gesture, as if it was of no importance. 'Oh, he knew you'd take care of me, Vee. We're family, after all. That's what families do.'

TWENTY-TWO

Byron had programmed his destination into the Merc's navigation. It immediately told him to do a U-turn and head for Wirksworth. He left the speed restrictions for the village, and the road began to twist and undulate through a dark tunnel of hedges and trees.

As he started to drop down a steep hill, he spotted a thin figure plodding along the side of the road, shoulders hunched as if into driving rain. It took Byron a moment to recognise her as Pauline – the cleaner from the pub. She walked slowly, as if her feet hurt and she was pacing herself for a long slog.

He pulled up alongside and lowered the passenger window, making her dodge sideways onto the verge like a shying horse.

'Pauline, isn't it?' he said, leaning across the centre console and speaking gently, reassuringly. 'My name is John Byron. I'm staying at the pub in the village. I don't know if you recall seeing me there – at breakfast, this morning? Can I offer you a lift?'

She blinked in surprise, then said doubtfully, 'Erm, well, I'm going all the way to Wirksworth…'

It was about three miles. A couple of minutes by car but the best part of an hour on foot. He gave her a reassuring smile. 'That's all right. I'm going through there.'

'Oh.' She hesitated, torn, then gave him a quick nod. 'Well, in that case… Thank you.'

She climbed into the passenger seat and fumbled with her seat belt. As he set off again, he noticed she slid down in her seat as if to avoid being seen. Now he was able to study her, he realised she was younger than he'd first suspected – in her early forties, maybe, rather than her fifties. The way she moved, it was hard to tell.

'Do you live locally?' he asked.

'In the village. I've got another cleaning job to go to, though, and my car's, erm… Well, it's off the road at the moment.'

Something about the hurried way she said it made Byron suspect the cost of repairs was the issue. He made a mental note to leave a generous tip for the chambermaid – undoubtedly Pauline – before he checked out.

'Have you always lived here?'

'Oh, I was born here. Me mum and dad had a farm – tenanted, like.'

'Ah, I see.' He paused, slowing for a blind corner. 'So, you knew Mr and Mrs Fitzroy – the *first* Mrs Fitzroy, I mean?'

She tensed, hands suddenly tight in her lap. 'I used to help out a bit at Claremont, if they was having a bit of a do, you know?'

'Then you'd remember Blake – before she went missing?'

She nodded. Glancing sideways briefly, he saw her throat work as she swallowed. 'Yeah, she was a nice kid. Loved animals, but she was right shy, like. Took losing her mum really hard. Well, you would, wouldn't you? Especially at that age.'

'Losing a parent is tough at any age. Still, at least she had her father… Were they close?'

Pauline squirmed in her seat. She was looking down, so her hair hung lank around her face. It looked as though she took scissors to it herself. Her ears stuck through at the sides.

'I dunno. Didn't know her or the family *that* well. And, after her mum died, the parties… well, things weren't the same.'

She grew fidgety, as if realising she'd said more than she ought and Byron switched to safer topics. He asked about her work at the pub, changes in the village, the age of the church. Despite his attempts to put her more at ease, when he pulled up at the junction leading to the main road through Wirksworth, she had her belt off and the door half open before he could ask where exactly she'd like to go.

'This'll do right here. Thanks very much,' she said quickly, and almost leapt from the car. But just as she was about to slam the door, she wavered, stooping to meet his gaze for the first time. 'Don't believe all the good things you hear about Mr Fitzroy. He had his dark side, that one.' And she was gone.

Byron watched her scurry away. Just for a second, he considered going after her, then dismissed the idea. He glanced at her as he drove past, but Pauline had her chin tucked in as if deliberately avoiding his gaze. He kept one eye on her in the rear-view mirror until he crested the next hill and she was lost from view.

'Parting shot aside, if you didn't know Blake very well,' he wondered aloud, 'how come you're the only person who's mentioned that she loved animals…?'

TWENTY-THREE

Jane Hudson perched on a corner of the sofa in the conservatory of the Hardings' place, her notebook out on her knee.

'I'm not really sure how we can help,' Oliver Harding said. 'We've no more idea than anyone else if this girl truly is Blake.'

Harding had been apologetic about being in his gardening scruffs when Hudson first arrived, had insisted on tidying himself up. Hudson had kicked her heels for the time it took Harding to change and return in cavalry twill trousers and a check shirt under an expensive looking sweater.

Hudson wondered if it was an attempt to intimidate her with status, or just the man's natural orderliness. On the previous occasions they'd met, Harding had always struck her as one of those organised types. He'd been in some Guards regiment or another, Hudson recalled, so she supposed it went with the territory.

Harding's wife looked as classy as always. There was an attractive delicacy about Anne. Some women seemed to have that quality about them, without trying. She made Hudson feel galumphing by comparison.

She shifted in her seat and kept her eyes on her notebook. It didn't help that she was dressed for the outdoors with stab vest and full kit. The wood-burning stove just to her left was chucking out enough heat to smelt iron.

She'd already had to fend off the attentions of their ginger tom. The animal recognised at first glance that Hudson was not a cat person, and had gone out of its way to waft itself in her face. Her eyeballs were beginning to itch. She'd read up on allergies, and discovered it was not cats' fur that irritated the sinuses but their saliva. All that constant licking themselves…

She closed her mind to the troubling mental images that thought created and soldiered on.

'I understand you and your wife were particularly close to Blake, after her mother passed away. I'm just after anything you can tell me about her – who her friends were, any problems or worries she had. Well… anything at all, really.'

Not that I'm clutching at straws here, but…

Harding frowned in concentration. 'I'm not sure that anything springs immediately to mind—'

'The farm girls!' his wife said suddenly. She glanced at her husband, who'd perched on the arm of the sofa opposite, alongside Anne's chair. 'Don't you remember, Oliver? At the Allbrights' place, just the other side of Carsington Water?'

His frown deepened. 'Are you sure, darling? I can't say I really recall any particular friendships Blake might have had—'

'Oh, of *course* you do,' Anne said, laughing. She nudged him with her elbow and wrinkled her nose as she smiled at Hudson, as if her husband's forgetfulness was a secret shared just between the two of them.

Hudson raised an enquiring eyebrow, pen poised over her pad. 'What can you tell me about these lassies?'

'Not a great deal, I'm afraid. It was all to do with some charity scheme Gideon was involved in – I don't remember the name. They took teenagers who were in care or foster homes, and sent them to spend the summer on Will Allbright's farm. I think they hoped that working on the land and with the animals might do them some good. The theory was that it would develop their self-esteem and give a sense of responsibility – something like that.'

'Did it work?'

'I suppose it must have done – there've been dozens of them over the years.'

'Lassies only, was it?' Hudson queried, half-expecting the worst. She tried not to pre-judge, but so often in cases like that, the first assumption was the correct one.

'The Allbrights had three young daughters,' Anne said, a little stiffly. 'They didn't really want teenage boys hanging about the place, leading them astray.'

'Allbright…' Harding said reflectively, apparently oblivious to any change in atmosphere. 'Nice chap. Very dependable. His wife's from Vietnam, I believe. Delightful woman.'

Hudson glanced down at her scribbled notes and wondered if she'd be able to make any sense of them later. 'So, these lassies… You say Blake was friendly with them?'

'Not all of them,' Anne said. 'But that last summer there was one girl in particular. The two of them seemed quite inseparable. Now, what was her name…? Still, I daresay the Allbrights will be able to help you there.'

Hudson rose, light-headed from the heat. The urge to make her escape was becoming overwhelming. The cat immediately slunk into the seat she'd just vacated, sat down and began chewing its own toenails.

TWENTY-FOUR

Byron stood by the side of the road staring down at a scene of destruction.

The place where Gideon Fitzroy died.

After dropping off Pauline, he'd continued on through the town of Wirksworth, up a steep main street bordered by individual shops and cafés without a national chain in sight. The road passed through a deep cutting, chiselled from the rock on either side, then the satnav told him to bear left towards Middleton and Ashbourne.

The road climbed again. As he'd neared his destination, Byron spotted a suitable place to pull over and park. He took a last glance at the Fitzroy file before sliding it down the side of the passenger seat.

The air was sharp with the bite of autumn and approaching winter. Byron had forsaken yesterday's dark suit for tactical trousers, hiking boots and wax-cotton Belstaff jacket. Practical, for what he was about to do.

According to the report, Fitzroy's Mercedes saloon car had been travelling from the direction of Middleton, returning from Buxton. As he walked uphill on the narrow pavement, Byron could see a freshly repaired section of low wall up ahead to his right. The skid marks were clearly visible, too. They would be for some time. Dark impressions left when oily substances in the asphalt were suddenly overheated by friction from the locked-up tyres. A semi-permanent reminder.

He tracked the progress of the skid, watching the accident unfold in his mind's eye from the evidence on the road. First the heavy braking – interrupted marks as Fitzroy must have stamped on the pedal hard enough for the car's anti-lock system to operate.

Then the crescent-shaped solid curve as the car yawed abruptly sideways, mounted the kerb, and punched through the wall into the trees beyond.

Byron leaned over and looked at the drop. His jaw tightened.

It was the devil of a long way down.

He took a breath and swung his legs over the wall. The ground sloped away so sharply he had to hang onto the vegetation to stay on his feet on the other side. For a second or two, he worried that his grip wouldn't be enough to hold him.

It wasn't hard to follow the path of the Mercedes through the flattened bracken and snapped-off trees, their broken limbs pale gashes of bone against the darker foliage.

Broken glass and plastic fragments crunched underfoot. A huge divot had been gouged out where the front end of the car dug in as it bounced down for the first time and began to barrel roll.

At the bottom of the gully, the Mercedes had come up against a more substantial tree that withstood the impact to bring the car to a slamming halt, upside down. It was at this point, the accident investigators calculated, Gideon Fitzroy had been ejected from the vehicle.

When will people learn to wear their damned seat belts?

In the pathologist's considered opinion, had the broken neck not killed Fitzroy instantly, then the head injuries would have ensured he was unlikely to survive or recover.

Everybody reckoned it was a miracle that neither of his step-children were more seriously hurt.

Byron studied the final tree, a sturdy ash. Its bark was scarred and one large branch had clearly been recently removed with a chainsaw – perhaps by the emergency services or recovery people. He glanced back towards the road. It seemed a long way above his head.

He gave the ash a last consoling pat and clambered back up the incline. At the top, he hauled himself over the wall again, breathing harder than he would have liked.

Retracing his steps down the hill, Byron wiped his gloved hands and frowned. He still had questions about the crash but, now he'd examined the scene, he felt certain it could not have been a professional hit. There were too many variables, not least of which was what had caused Fitzroy's initial, violent manoeuvre.

Maybe it really *had* been an accident…

Although help had been quickly on the scene, the only actual witnesses were Tom and Lily. But Lily claimed to have been asleep at the time, waking only as the car launched through the wall. It was her screaming from the upturned vehicle that alerted the occupants of nearby houses.

Tom had been cut from the wreckage unconscious. He'd come round briefly as they loaded him into an ambulance. Byron noted that the person he'd immediately asked after was his stepfather rather than his sister.

In his official statement, Tom blamed an oncoming car for causing Fitzroy to swerve, although no additional skid marks were recovered. Because of the dark, and the glare of the headlights, he was unable to give any details of the other vehicle. Byron didn't read too much into that. He wouldn't put it past the unknown driver not to have braked.

As he neared the place where he'd left his own Mercedes, Byron slipped a hand into his pocket for his keys.

And froze.

There was movement inside the car.

Someone was sitting in the passenger side, head bent as if looking down at something. As if they might be reading something…

He didn't run, but he certainly lengthened his stride, moving onto the balls of his feet so his boots made little noise as he approached. He skirted the back of the car and reached for the passenger door handle, noting it was unlocked. Yanking it open, he stared down at the intruder.

She looked remarkably calm, considering he'd just caught her red-handed. Only her quick indrawn breath gave any indication of surprise.

'Hello, Blake.'

TWENTY-FIVE

Inwardly, Blake cursed herself for not paying more attention to her surroundings. She knew better than that.

Recognising Byron's car from his arrival at the funeral, she'd intended only to have a quick nosy inside. The contents of someone's glovebox, coin tray, or back seat could tell you much about them. But as soon as she'd lifted that folder and caught the name "Fitzroy" on the outside of it… Well, she wouldn't have been human if she hadn't taken a look.

Byron's sudden appearance genuinely shocked her. It took serious effort to contain her instinctive fight or flight response. To favour the man with a sunny smile as if situations like these were everyday occurrences, and to return his greeting.

'Hello, Byron.'

For a moment, he stood there, one hand on the car roof and the other on the door frame, caging in her escape route. His eyes, she noticed for the first time, were a deep mossy brown, flecked with green. They stared down at her without blinking.

Then, at last, he said, 'Care to comment?'

The question threw her. She'd been expecting anger or accusations – or at least that he'd be patronising. That she could handle. She was used to it.

He seemed determined to keep surprising her.

'Excuse me?'

He nodded to the file lying open across her knees. 'I assume you've picked up the gist of that, so I'm asking for your opinion. Do you think Gideon Fitzroy's death was an accident?'

'Why?'

His eyebrow lifted slightly. 'Why do I think so? Or why am I asking you?'

'Both.'

He didn't answer, letting go of her door instead and moving around to the driver's side to climb in.

'Trusting, aren't you? I could have done a runner just then.'

'You still might,' he agreed. 'But I think that, right now, you're more interested in this.' He tapped the file.

She smiled. 'OK, you got me there. And if you'd been another five or ten minutes, I might just have read enough of it to tell you what I made of it.' She lifted the papers, riffled her thumb across the edges. 'There's a lot to get through.'

'Take your time. Although, at some point we really must have a talk about your attitude towards locked doors.'

'Really? I would have sworn it was unlocked when I got here,' she said blithely. 'Do you mind if we have some heat? I'd forgotten how cold my hands get, cycling at this time of year, even with gloves.'

Her gaze dropped to his own hands as she spoke. He wore leather gloves that he hadn't removed, a fact which started a tickle of unease at the back of her neck. But he started the engine without comment, adjusting the air con. She found his reticence unnerving, too.

She tried to concentrate on the crash report and the statements, but all the while she could see him out of the corner of her eye. He was smaller than he'd first appeared, sharp featured and inscrutable. Younger, too. She wasn't sure if he hadn't bothered to shave that morning, or if the dark stubble on his face was intentional. If so, it was probably the first indication of personal vanity she'd picked up from him. Everything else about him, she realised, was a form of mask – a disguise.

He sat without fidgeting, the kind of stillness that comes from the inside. But the more relaxed he appeared, the more tense she became.

After a minute or so, she admitted defeat.

'Look, we'll be here all day at this rate. I'd rather just ask questions, if you're prepared to answer them?'

'If I am able to – of course.'

'Do you always speak like you're giving evidence in court?'

'Force of habit, perhaps?' His tone was dry.

'It makes you seem…' *Older,* she'd been about to say, then realised that was probably the point, and instead settled for, 'It adds a certain gravitas.'

A smile threatened to break out at the corner of his mouth. 'Thank you – I think.'

'You're welcome.'

'Was that really what you wanted to ask?'

She took a deep breath. 'Why all this interest in my father's accident?' She was careful to refer to Fitzroy that way, to reinforce her identity in Byron's mind. 'Unless you suspect it wasn't accidental?'

'That was a possibility.'

'"Was", or still is?'

'I don't know.' He inclined his head slightly. 'Maybe.'

She let her head drop back against the seat, let the sarcasm curl through her voice. 'Thanks. That's very… enlightening.'

The corner of his mouth twitched again. 'Well, Fitzroy's driving record wasn't exactly spotless, was it? His previous accident was only a week before the fatal crash.'

Blake indicated the report. 'You can hardly compare a minor bump, in crawling traffic, to something like this.'

His eyes narrowed. 'How do you know?'

A mistake – one she covered with a smile. 'Gossip is one of the perils of a small village. Besides, the car he hit was owned by… one of the people from the pub.'

'You mean Pauline?'

That threw her. 'Yes… My turn to ask "How do you know?"'

'I gave her a lift into Wirksworth earlier. She happened to mention her car was off the road.'

Damn, so that was a guess – one I've just confirmed for you.

To her relief, he didn't pursue that line of enquiry, switching back to her father instead.

'If his last crash *wasn't* accidental, it begs the question of who would have deliberately run him off the road when there were two children in the car at the time?'

'Someone who doesn't know they're going to be there?' she mused. 'Or someone who knows but doesn't care.'

'According to the statements, it could have been either Mr or Mrs Fitzroy who collected the children that evening. It was only decided at the last minute.'

Blake absorbed that for a moment. 'Perhaps you'd better tell me what caused doubt in the first place.'

'The… convenience of it. When a man ostensibly in good health, suddenly veers off a comparatively straight piece of dry road, at night but in clear weather, it's always going to raise eyebrows.'

'No heart attack, stroke, embolism?'

He shook his head. 'His death was as a result of the crash, not the cause of it.'

'And no obvious mechanical tampering – that would have been brought up at the inquest.'

'The vehicle yielded nothing, forensically speaking.'

'The boy, Tom – I still can't think of him as my stepbrother – he was in the front seat at the time, wasn't he? What does he say happened?'

'That there was an oncoming car on the wrong side of the road with its lights on high beam. Fitzroy swerved to avoid it and lost control. Needless to say, nobody came forwards.'

'Did you honestly expect them to?'

'Hm, probably not. And, by all accounts, Tom got on reasonably well with his stepfather. Fitzroy was the first person he asked about when he came to, anyway.'

'Really? Not his sister?'

'That question was put to him. He was fairly confused. Said he thought he'd asked about her already.'

'He and Lily don't seem all that close, from what I've seen of the two of them together. She's a bright little chatterbox, and he's a morose teen who communicates mostly in grunts. Hard to tell if he was any happier or more articulate *before* the accident.'

'Quite.'

Silence descended. The only sounds the underlying buzz of the car's engine and the whirr of the heater fan. She leafed further through the paperwork contained in the folder, taking in the breadth of information that had been so comprehensively gathered. The more she read, the more excessive it seemed.

'Tell me, apart from him being a former MP, why is a high-ranking detective with the Met – on active duty or not – so interested in anything that happens up here in Derbyshire?'

He flicked at a smear of lichen on his trousers. 'You remember there was a major investigation several years ago into a possible paedophile ring operating in Westminster?'

'Which came to nothing, I seem to recall.'

He ignored her tart comment. 'There was a rumour that Fitzroy knew more about it than he admitted at the time, and that he might have been about to... break ranks, as it were – make a statement.'

For a moment she was flattered by his apparent candour, then her brain caught up. 'Bollocks.'

He glanced at her in amused surprise. 'Oh?'

'That would imply either that he had integrity, or perhaps that he was losing his nerve, afraid of getting caught. If you'd ever met my father, you'd know he was arrogant in the extreme. He would have bluffed it out to the bitter end. No... that rumour was started by someone else, wasn't it?'

Again, Byron said nothing.

Her mind quickened. 'Not only started by someone else, but... it was started by you, wasn't it?'

More silence greeted her, but she'd learned to read micro expressions a long time ago. The fractional widening of his eyes, the constriction of his pupils, told her all she needed to know.

'Oh, probably not you personally, but by the cops, without doubt. And that could only be to flush out somebody else. So *that's* what this is all about.' She tapped the file on her lap. 'Somebody further up the food chain is afraid they got him killed, and they've sent you out on an arse-covering exercise.'

'I've always been better at covering the arses of those below me in the pecking order,' he said. 'It's my experience that those above me are more than capable of looking after their own.'

TWENTY-SIX

Jane Hudson bumped along the rutted track that led to the Allbrights' farm. As she jolted through yet another mud-filled pothole, she wondered which would give way first – the patrol car's suspension or her own constitution. As it was, her teeth and her eyeballs felt loose in their sockets.

It was otherwise a hell of a view, though, looking out across the reservoir through a gap in the trees. Carsington Water was man-made, planned and dug over the course of thirty years between the sixties and the nineties. Hudson had a mind to windsurf there next summer, if she got around to it.

She needed to do *something* to get rid of the extra weight she was starting to carry. She'd kept fit when she was in the Navy – never had any trouble passing her annual fitness test. But that was the trouble with a rural beat – everywhere had to be reached by car.

And, she admitted privately, much as she enjoyed the company of Ed Underhill, she didn't want to end up the same shape.

At the bottom of the driveway she pulled up near the back door to the farmhouse. A couple of working dogs lurked in a pen. When she arrived, they went into a barking frenzy. Hudson checked carefully that the pen was latched before she climbed out.

The main farmhouse and some of the outbuildings were local sandstone, the individual stones worn concave in places by wind and weather, so the mortar bands stood proud. The rest were modern steel constructions in the almost-but-not-quite-finished style.

A precarious lean-to storm porch had been added to the doorway of the house, cluttered with dirty rain jackets, walking sticks and hats. Hudson had to step over a pair of large wellington boots just inside, abandoned with the waterproof trousers bunched up around the ankles, as if the whole lot had been removed as one piece. The smell of manure was enough to make her eyes water.

'Hang on!' called a woman's voice when she rapped her knuckles on the peeling paintwork of the door itself.

She'd radioed-in the names she'd been given, just to check if the Allbrights were in the system. They were but not in a negative way – they'd had the usual checks carried out on them by what was once the Criminal Records Bureau. It was now the catchily titled Disclosure and Barring Service. DBS checks had to be passed before anyone was allowed to work with minors, and the Allbrights were no exception.

Suddenly, the door was pulled inwards by a woman wearing an apron over jeans and a polo-necked jersey. With hardly a glance, she beckoned Hudson inside with a Sylvester the Cat glove puppet, and shot back towards the kitchen, calling over her shoulder, 'Sorry, bread's just coming out of the oven so it's all hands on deck. Come in, come in, and shut the door behind you.' And she was gone. Hudson followed.

She had chance to take in the woman while she deftly shifted half a dozen bread tins onto cooling racks spread across the kitchen table. The glove puppet turned out to be an oven mitt.

Hudson wasn't quite sure what she'd been expecting of Xuan Allbright, but when she straightened, turned to face her visitor, the reality took Hudson a little by surprise. The other woman was almost as tall as she was, and not many women were. There was an olive tint to Xuan's skin, and she wore her dark hair cut in a short and spiky style that made her age hard to judge. But crow's feet were just beginning to radiate out from the corners of her eyes, putting her around forty.

'Now then, hon, who's done what to who?'

Xuan's smile was wide, her teeth very bright and straight. And her accent was pure Black Country, to the west of Birmingham.

Hudson found herself off-balance enough to hedge. 'What makes you think anyone has done anything to anyone else?'

She received a flinty look that almost had her shuffling her feet. 'Experience,' Xuan said succinctly. 'Tea and cake?'

'Just tea, please – Mrs Allbright, I assume?'

'Oh, call me Xuan.' She turned to lift a large brown teapot that had been keeping warm on top of the Aga, pausing to glance at the wall clock. 'And if you're after our Will, he'll be in for a cuppa himself in about five minutes.'

In fact, by the time she'd dug out mugs, sugar, a jug of milk thick as cream, and slabs of fruit cake, Hudson heard the back door open again and a deep voice call, ''Lo.'

A moment or so later, Will Allbright padded through in his stockinged feet. He was tall enough to duck to clear the door frame. A big-boned man with little fat on him, cheeks gaunt above a close-cropped beard with a lot of ginger in it. He nodded in general greeting on his way to scrub his hands at the sink.

'Now then, Constable, what brings you out our way?'

'Nothing sinister. I'm hoping you might be able to give me a bit of information, that's all.'

'Oh aye?' he said warily.

Xuan grinned. 'Ooh, does this mean we're "assisting with police enquiries", then?'

'Well… it's nothing official at the moment—'

'Don't worry, flower. I'm only pulling your leg. What d'you need?'

She topped up Hudson's mug with tea, pouring two others for herself and her husband, then put away plates from the drainer on her way to sit down. Watching her, Hudson realised she was like a human time-and-motion study, extracting the maximum effect for the most efficient amount of effort.

Allbright dried his hands on a towel hanging over the front rail of the Aga and took a seat himself.

'I understand you used to take in problem teenagers to work on the farm,' Hudson began.

'Still do,' Allbright said. He picked up a wicked-looking bread knife and sawed a wedge off one end of a new loaf. It was still so hot from the oven that steam rose from it. 'Usually have one or two about the place, come summer.'

'Do you keep a record of who they are, and when they come and go?'

It was his wife who answered. 'Of course. Social services need to keep a check on them, and the charity pays something towards bed and board, so we make a careful note of everything. Not to mention the hoops we have to jump through for the Inland Revenue.'

Allbright slathered his cut crust with butter, bit, chewed and swallowed, then said, 'What's this all about?'

Hudson sighed. 'You'll have heard about Gideon Fitzroy's daughter?'

'Of course,' Xuan said immediately but Hudson noticed a slight hesitation before her husband nodded.

'We're trying to establish her bona fides.'

'Oh, aye? Police matter, is it?'

'Well, if she isn't Blake Claremont, then aye, it is,' Hudson said. *Fraud and identity theft, for starters.* 'I've been told that, the summer she disappeared, Blake was very friendly with one of the lassies who was staying here. Do you have any thoughts who that might have been?'

'That's going back a bit.' Xuan got to her feet. 'I'll get the diary for that year and we'll take a look, shall we?' She paused to remove her apron, hanging it on the back of the door on her way out. There was a bounce in her step that spoke of boundless energy.

Allbright, by comparison, did everything at a far slower pace. He was in no rush to fill with chatter the silence that followed his wife's departure. Instead, his jaw continued to work steadily through the chunk of bread while he stared through the kitchen wall opposite.

Xuan returned quickly with an old hardcover diary in her hands. She laid it open at the Notes section in front of Hudson. In a neat hand was a list of ten girls' first names in two columns of five.

'That many?' she murmured and her heart sank a little. She'd been hoping for maybe one or two names to chase down, not an entire field lacrosse team.

'Two girls per month, for a month, from mid-April to mid-September.'

'So, which—?' she began.

Xuan beat her to it. She tapped the page beside the last set of names – Karen and Hope.

'Hope. She and Blake were thick as thieves, right from the moment they met.'

Hudson thought of the way the intruder had broken into Claremont and how apt that description might turn out to be.

'What was her last name? And where was she from?'

Allbright shrugged. 'Don't know. They never tell us.'

Hudson glanced between the two of them, eyebrows raised. 'What?'

'The charity is all about giving them a fresh perspective, without preconceptions,' Xuan said. 'So, they come to us with no… baggage attached.'

'OK, so what *can* you tell me about her?'

'After ten years? Not very much. Blake happened to call round not long after Hope arrived, I remember that, and they hit it off right away. Hope was withdrawn otherwise – she could be moody. But then again, what teen isn't? I don't think she talked about her life at the home or her family situation and we don't pry.'

'But she and Blake were pally. Did Hope ever go over to Claremont, do you know?'

'Oh yes – all the time. As long as they do their daily tasks and are back here at a reasonable hour, we don't keep the girls under curfew.'

'And if Hope was one of the last pair that year, she would have left in mid-September, yes?'

Xuan nodded. 'The eighteenth – I checked.'

Hudson frowned. Blake had gone missing a month later. On the surface, there was no connection, but…

More in hope than expectation, she asked, 'I don't suppose you have any photographs or anything like that…?'

'Oh, yes,' Xuan said serenely. She lifted the pages to slide a photograph out from inside the front cover. 'She's not on her own, I'm afraid. It's one of Hope and Blake together. Is that any use to you?'

TWENTY-SEVEN

'How long have you known Alexander Vaganov?'

This time, Byron waited until his passenger had no opportunity to bail out before he asked the question – no build-up, straight out of left field. Even so, he didn't miss the way her eyes flicked instinctively towards the side window, at the hedgerow blurring past, before she spoke.

'Well, well, Mr Byron, you're full of surprises, aren't you?'

'In that regard, it would seem that I'm not the only one.'

It had begun to rain. Not hard, but enough to make the prospect of cycling back to the village less appealing than the outward journey. He'd offered to drive her, and – after taking in the ever-darkening sky – she accepted. By quick-releasing the front wheel, the bicycle fitted easily inside the Merc's cavernous boot.

Now, she rode in silence for a few seconds, then said, 'Lex is… He's been a good friend.'

'So I gathered.'

'Oh?'

'The phone.'

'Ah.'

She nodded slowly to herself, as though something that had been bothering her was suddenly clear. He waited for her to ask more about that, but either she didn't feel the need, or didn't want to know.

'So, how long have you and Mr Vaganov been such good friends?'

She said nothing.

After a moment, he spoke without taking his eyes off the road ahead, his voice level. 'At the moment, I have not passed on this… connection to PC Hudson. Would you rather I did so, and let her ferret about for herself?'

'The alternative being…?'

He sighed. 'Either you are Blake Claremont, or you aren't. It follows, therefore, that either you know all about Fitzroy because you really are his daughter, *or* you've carried out an enormous amount of research to stand any chance of pulling off such a deception.'

He allowed his gaze to flick sideways briefly, caught an expression on her face he couldn't immediately identify. 'You may be able to fill in some blanks for us about Fitzroy. So, answer the question, and – if I deem the information to be unrelated – it goes no further.'

'You're asking me to trust you.' Her amused tone made his request sound outlandish.

'You don't have much of a choice.' He let his voice drawl, just to provoke her.

Sure enough, she scowled. 'And what do I get out of this?'

'Besides my discretion, you mean?'

'Yes – besides that,' she agreed gravely.

'Possibly… my assistance.'

It was only as Byron made his offer that he realised it was entirely genuine. The very fact of it surprised him into silent self-analysis. In his career, he had persuaded, bluffed, or cajoled confessions out of more criminals than he could count. When he had to, he'd promised things in return – protection, or leniency.

But he'd never volunteered it up front, without any idea exactly what he might be buying, or if it was worth the price.

He might tell himself that he was merely utilising every available resource, but he was not convinced. Depending on the nature of her association with Vaganov, she might be as good a con artist as he was supposed to be. It was hard to know for certain when none of the man's rumoured victims were ever willing to talk. Oh, they might give initial squawks of outrage, but – when they'd had time for more sober reflection – they inevitably retracted their statements, along with any willingness to press charges.

If it was the case – that she was here at Vaganov's direction – then this whole thing could turn out to be nothing more than an elaborate charade – although, to what end?

They had almost reached the village before she spoke again. Her voice was halting. It was the first time Byron had heard her sound unsure. 'When I initially got to London, Lex was… one of the first people I ran into. He offered me a kind of… sanctuary – looked after me when he didn't have to – without any… expectations. I've never forgotten it.'

The threads of sincerity, of loyalty, wove through the words. He had no doubts that she believed them to be true.

Even if they didn't answer any of his questions.

'Does Vaganov know you're here?'

'He does.'

'O-K.' He drew out the word. So, this was a guessing game with no clues. 'Did you come at his instigation?'

Her lips quirked, just a fraction.

'I'm here with Lex's knowledge but not his blessing – and certainly not at his behest. Does that satisfy your curiosity?'

'No,' he said, finding himself torn between frustration and humour. 'Not in the least.'

They were driving up the main street now.

'You're staying at the pub, I assume? In which case, drop me here and I'll cycle the rest of the way back. It's not far.' She leaned forwards, staring up at the sky. 'I think the rain's given over for a bit.'

With reluctance, Byron pulled into an empty space near the pub. He switched off the engine but made no immediate move to get out. Residual droplets of rain ran down the slope of the windscreen like tears.

'You need to give me *something* to work with.' He tried hard not to make it either a plea or a threat.

'I wish… I've told you as much as I can – for the moment,' she said. 'It's really not my secret to share…'

TWENTY-EIGHT

'Well, that proves it, then,' Ed Underhill said.

'So, that's definitely her?' Hudson took the copy photo she'd borrowed from the Allbrights and studied it again. 'The real question is, though – is the Blake who turned up yesterday the same Blake in the picture from ten years ago. To be honest, I thought it could be either of them.'

The photograph showed two girls sitting against a backdrop of baled hay or straw. Hudson was not countrified enough to tell the difference. And, in this case, it didn't matter much anyway. Apart from the haystack, there was nothing else in the background. Just the two girls.

'That's Blake on the left,' Underhill said. 'Unusual that she's got her face to camera for once. From what I remember, she was always moping about, hiding behind all that hair.'

'Well, she looks happy enough there. They're both of them having a laugh about something.'

Hudson studied the picture again. The girl Underhill indicated had her head thrown back, revealing a hint of good bone structure beneath the unformed features. Unfortunately, it had the effect of foreshortening her face, making it harder to analyse. Certain aspects didn't change, she knew – the mouth and chin, the area between the eyes, the end of the nose. Not without surgery, anyway, and she doubted the girl claiming to be Fitzroy's daughter would have gone to those lengths…

'So, the other one is this farm girl, is she?'

'Hope, her name was, aye.'

Hudson took another look at the photo herself. Where Blake was dark, Hope was fair, with long ashy blonde hair. She was turned slightly towards the other girl, more in profile to the camera, her eyes on Blake's face. It was hard to fully interpret her expression – enjoying the joke, certainly, but somehow there was more to it than that…

'Hm. I don't remember her at all.' Underhill peered at the picture more closely, lifting it up towards the nearest lamp and tilting it this way and that.

He handed the photo back. 'Mind you, there's no reason why I should remember her – not unless there was any trouble.'

They were in the small front room at the pub. It was a convenient place to meet and rarely crowded except for high days and holidays. Today, they had it to themselves. The other patrons had ordered at the tiny bar – little more than a serving hatch – and taken their drinks through to the rear parlour, where the wood-burning stove was already ablaze.

'And was there?'

'Was there what?'

'Ever any trouble – at the Allbrights' place? After all, the kids sent there by that charity were all from care homes or fostered. You'd think there were bound to be a few wrong 'uns among that lot.'

Underhill took a swig of his pint – one of the parade of weekly guest beers – and wiped his mouth.

'Not that I recall. Kept to themselves, mostly. And, from what I gathered, each of them were only on the farm for a month. Not much time for them to get bored and start causing bother.'

The door to the pub opened and John Byron stepped through. As he pulled the door closed behind him, he seemed to pause for a split-second, as if taking a mental inventory. He was as casually dressed as Hudson had ever seen him, but there was nothing casual about that quick, all-encompassing glance.

How long do you have to be a copper before it becomes habit like that to check every room you enter?

'Afternoon, Mr Byron,' Underhill said, sitting back and saluting him with the last of his beer. 'You been out for a stroll, enjoying our Derbyshire weather?'

'I have. It certainly clears the cobwebs,' Byron said equably. 'Can I get either of you something to drink?'

'I've got to be getting back, unfortunately,' Underhill said. He grinned. 'Next time, though, I'll take you up on that.'

Hudson gestured to her empty glass. 'I wouldn't mind another – a Diet Coke, if that's OK? I'm just waiting for a pie and then I'm away back to work.'

Byron nodded and went to the bar. Underhill drained his glass, plonking it down on the tabletop, and gestured to the blonde girl in the photo. 'Good luck tracing this Hope.'

'I'm keeping an open mind about where – and who – she might be, for the moment.'

Underhill grinned again, as if Hudson had confirmed his suspicion.

Byron returned from the bar with her Coke and what looked like a gin and tonic for himself. Underhill said his goodbyes, turned up the collar of his coat, and left.

Byron sat opposite Hudson. He took a sip of his drink and raised an enquiring eyebrow.

Hudson spun the photo round and pushed it across the table towards Byron, who leaned forwards to study the picture.

'Ah, Blake and...?'

'Aye, but which of those two would you say is Blake?'

Before Byron could answer, the landlady bustled out of the back with Hudson's lunch. Before she reached the table, Hudson noted that Byron picked up the photo, without haste, and slid it out of sight.

'There you go, Jane. That should keep you going for a bit.' She collected the empty glasses. 'Can I interest you in today's pie, Mr Byron? Steak and ale – it's always a favourite.'

'That sounds excellent, thank you. I'll have another just like that, please.'

When the woman had gone, he put the photo back on the table.

Hudson was already tucking in to her pie. Maybe she'd start that diet tomorrow. She gestured to the picture with her fork. 'So, which d'you reckon?'

Byron slowly tapped the image of the dark-haired girl with his forefinger. 'But only because I know Blake at fifteen was dark haired and carried an extra pound or two. Otherwise, they both have a very similar underlying look that makes it hard to choose between them.'

Hudson nodded around a mouthful of scalding steak and gravy. 'The other girl is called Hope Glennie. She was staying on a local farm for a month, just before Blake went missing. The two spent a lot of time together, apparently.'

Byron's gaze was still on the photo, his face expressionless. 'Important to trace her, I think. Although... do I get the impression you think she's impersonating our present-day Blake?'

'Aye. It might explain how this lassie seems to know so much about Blake's family – and the house, of course.' Hudson managed to pick up the edge of her pie dish, using her napkin, and tip the contents out onto her plate, where it steamed gently. She glanced up and caught the frown on Byron's face. 'You don't agree?'

'Oh, certainly, it's one explanation. But, unless Hope wrote everything down at the time, how – or why, for that matter – would she remember it all, in such detail, ten years later?'

TWENTY-NINE

From the window of her bedroom at the front of the house, Lily spotted Blake cycling back up the driveway. She recognised the ancient bicycle as one that had been propped at the back of the carriage house, behind the old Land Rover, for as long as she could remember. It had never occurred to her that it might still be useable.

Besides, who'd want to be seen out on a rusty old relic like that?

Lily had been up in her room since she and Blake got back from the stables and reported their near-miss. Her mother had gone into full meltdown – no surprises there. Blake had stayed entirely calm, which only seemed to infuriate her mother still further. It was hard to tell if Virginia was angry, or scared – or angry because she was scared.

And then Uncle Roger had joined in, too. Blake let them spew out all their accusations and threats. Then she turned on her heel and walked out without saying another word, leaving both adults open-mouthed and spluttering with outrage behind her.

Lily couldn't help but admire this strategy for dealing with her mother when she went totally off on one. Somehow, though, she didn't think *she'd* be able to get away with it.

If she'd been hoping for any support from her brother, Tom was conspicuous by his absence when they got back. Lily assumed he was in his room, until he came in through the back door about twenty minutes later, shrugging the rain off his jacket. He'd taken in the atmosphere at once, Lily's tears, and the tumbler of scotch in Uncle Roger's hand.

'What's happened?'

Their mother gave him *her* version of the story – how it was all Blake's fault that Lily was almost killed or badly injured.

'Steady on, Mother. Lily's clearly OK, and it could have been just an accident.'

'An *accident*?' Virginia repeated, her voice taking on that shrill note that set Lily's teeth on edge. 'This family's having far too many "accidents" of late!'

Tom let out a fast audible breath, almost a snort, and stomped towards the door again, ignoring his mother calling him back.

After that, Lily was sent up to her room. Officially she was told to 'rest'.

Lily protested, but in truth she still felt very shaky. She kept reliving that moment when the ladder first started to slip, leaving her stomach behind and her heart in her throat. It had suddenly seemed a long way down, with all kinds of old tools and other junk waiting underneath to impale her.

And then she'd felt the judder through the boards as Blake threw herself across the room and grabbed the ladder just as it began to plunge downwards. She'd moved so fast...

Now, Lily watched from the window as Blake dismounted the bicycle by the garage, then continued on foot across to the house. Only a few minutes later, there was a tap at Lily's door, and Blake stuck her head round the leading edge.

'Hi. How are you feeling?'

Lily shrugged, playing it cool. ''K, I s'pose.'

'So why are you skulking up here?'

'Staying out of the way – Mummy and Uncle Roger are just going on and on about the hayloft and the ladder and everything. They even had a go at Tom when he got back.'

'Got back?' Blake stilled. 'I didn't realise he'd gone out after we did… I don't suppose you know where he went?'

'Probably just off for a walk somewhere in the woods. He actually *enjoys* walking in the rain. He's weird that way.' Her glance was considering. 'Why do you ask?'

Blake flashed a quick smile. 'Oh, no reason. Is he in his room? I think I'll just go and have a quick chat with him – time I got to know him a bit better.'

'You can't,' Lily said, which was greeted by a raised eyebrow, until she added, 'He went out again. Well, stormed off in a huff, really. But he's been really grumpy for weeks now.'

'Ah, well, brothers are like that, so I'm told.'

'They *so* are.' Lily rolled her eyes and gave a loud sigh. 'I mean, I know I can be the annoying little sister some of the time, but not *all* of it. You'd think Tom would be a bit more grateful, wouldn't you? I mean, honestly, who'd have a brother?'

Blake regarded her gravely but there was a hint of a sparkle in her eyes. 'Hm, I'd stick with sisters, if I were you.'

Lily grinned. 'OK.'

Blake's eyes shifted, seeming to take in the rest of the room for the first time. A designer had come up from London and created 'the perfect little girl's bedroom' when Lily was eight. All frills and pink tulle. She'd hated it on sight, but Gideon – who'd paid for everything – seemed so delighted with the end result that she'd said nothing.

'This is… interesting,' Blake said.

'I know,' Lily moaned. 'Why do you think I'm trying to cover up as much of that wallpaper as I can?'

'Well that's a cool way to do it.' Blake moved over to inspect the pictures of actors that formed a centrepiece on one wall. Virginia refused to let Lily put up posters, but she'd allowed a few framed photos. Some of them were even signed.

Lily had chosen people she admired for their talent rather than their outright fame. She waited for the usual comments, but instead Blake only nodded, as if she understood.

'I want to be an actress,' Lily confessed, suddenly shy.

'That's a tough business to break into.'

'I know, but I practise all the time. I have costumes and everything.'

'Really? What sort of costumes?'

'Oh, all sorts. Well, they're just old clothes nobody uses any more – hats, and wigs, and dresses I found in one of the trunks in the loft over the garage. That's where I do my rehearsing.' Lily sat up. 'We could go there now, if you like? I could show you—'

'Perhaps it would be a good idea if we stayed away from lofts – at least for today.' Blake's tone was dry. 'I don't think your mother's nerves would stand it.'

'No,' Lily agreed. 'And anyway, I try to stay out of Uncle Roger's way when he's in one of his moods.'

She thought Blake tensed momentarily before she asked, 'What kind of moods?'

'The kind that make him drink too much. I hate it when he does that,' Lily said. She lowered her voice. 'He's not very good at it.'

'Ah, well,' Blake leaned in, conspiratorial, 'maybe that's why he practises so much.'

Lily giggled. She picked at a loose thread on her pink duvet cover. Having a sister – albeit a stepsister – would be fun, if only…

'Do you really think someone moved the bottom of the ladder – when we were up in the hayloft?' She was aware of the anxiety in her own voice, like she was asking a question to which she did not actually want the answer. 'I mean, it *could* just have… bounced out of place, or something, couldn't it…?'

Blake didn't answer immediately, just continued to study the photos on Lily's wall of fame. Then she headed for the door, tossing another of those quick smiles over her shoulder.

'You know what? I think you're right. That's what must have happened.'

THIRTY

Late into the evening, Ed Underhill sat in front of the TV in his cottage on one of the narrow yards leading off the main street. He was not watching the programme that blared across the screen – would have been hard-pressed to name the topic, if he was honest.

Instead, he stared at the digital image of two teenage girls sitting smiling in front of a haystack.

He'd stolen a quick snap of it with his phone when young Jane had gone up to the bar. Not that he thought his successor would object to him making a copy. It was just… caution – not wanting to seem *too* interested.

Nothing wrong with that.

Just as she had not pointed out, or commented on, the feature visible in the picture – the one conclusive piece of evidence, as far as he was concerned, that the girl claiming to be Blake Claremont was a fraud.

He was still frowning as he went through his usual nightly routine, clearing away his supper plate and locking up before climbing the narrow staircase.

As he brushed his teeth over the bathroom sink, he woke the screen on his phone and looked again at the image of the two teens. He zoomed in until the picture blurred and pixelated.

Even so, he could tell it was a match.

Underhill dropped his toothbrush back into the water glass on the glass shelf below the mirror and shuffled through to the bedroom. He was just unbuttoning his shirt when he thought he heard a sharp rattle of noise, and froze.

A few seconds later, the noise came again. This time, ready for it, he was able to glean the direction – the window. It sounded like a handful of gravel had been thrown against the glass.

'Damn kids!'

He strode across, reaching up to yank the curtains aside. But, at the last moment, he hesitated, suddenly unwilling to expose himself against the light. Instead, he stepped to the side and lifted the very edge of the curtain fabric to peer down into the lane.

Underhill's cottage was almost the last house before the village turned into open countryside. The streetlights were few and far between, even on the main street, and mostly he preferred it that way. Meant he didn't need thick curtains to be able to sleep – even back when he was working shifts.

Now, he wished for floodlights outside.

Initially, he could see nothing out in the gloom besides the stone wall on the other side of the lane, the snicket running between two cottages further up, the corner of a tumbledown barn.

He only saw the figure when it stepped out further from the shadows.

Deliberately showing itself.

He let out a startled curse, then scowled at his own reaction. He told himself it was surprise that made his heart thump, made the air seem short in his lungs, and not the way this intruder was dressed.

Jeans, boots, and a rain jacket in a dark red material. The colour brought a jolt of memory. He didn't need to see more to know the figure was female, even with the coat covering her to mid thigh and the hood pulled up so her face merged with the darkness. Somehow, though, he could tell she was looking up at the window.

Looking up at him.

Underhill fought the urge to recoil, to let the curtain fall back into place, as if the flimsy barrier might protect him. He stood his ground, watching, waiting.

After a moment longer, the figure below took one hand out of her pocket and raised it, forefinger extended, to point at him directly.

Then she drew it, as if a blade, sharply across the top button of the jacket, where her throat would be.

Underhill lurched away from the window and bolted for the stairs. He struggled for precious seconds getting the bolt open on the front door, and dashed outside, still in his slippers.

With the light from the hallway spilling out around him, he swivelled frantically in all directions.

He saw nothing.

Holding his breath to keep the gasp out of his ears, he listened for retreating footsteps.

He heard nothing, either.

The figure had gone like she'd never existed.

THIRTY-ONE

Virginia went to bed late and tired, but sleep did not come easily.

She lay staring up into the darkness of her bedroom. Gideon's own room had been next along, with an adjoining door. At the beginning of their marriage, she had been surprised to be allocated separate bedrooms. By the end of it, she had been privately relieved to be left undisturbed more often than not.

Now, she found herself unable to rest. She was equally unwilling to switch on the lamp and pick up the half-read biography on her bedside table, or channel-hop through late-night TV. It felt like giving in to defeat.

In her mind's eye, she kept picturing what must have happened – and what *might* have happened – in the hayloft above the carriage house. She didn't want to imagine it, but couldn't switch off her brain. Logically, she knew Lily had survived relatively unscathed, but that didn't seem to help.

She had never liked the stables, which were run-down and becoming an eyesore. It didn't matter that they were out of sight of the main house. She had tried several times to persuade her husband to redevelop the whole courtyard of buildings – they would have made very desirable holiday cottages – before they deteriorated to the extent that demolishing them was the only option.

It infuriated her that Gideon had always refused to consider it.

Since his death, Virginia had already been in touch with an architect who specialised in such work. She was just waiting for the will to be read – until it was all official. Meanwhile, she had made it clear to both Tom and Lily, over dinner, that the stables were now completely out of bounds.

Earlier, Virginia had dismissed Blake's assertions that someone had tampered with the ladder, but now she could admit – to herself, at least – it was a feasible explanation. And the only reason anyone would do such a thing was to deliberately cause injury.

Or worse.

Her only question was, who was the intended victim – Lily, or Blake?

If her daughter had been the target, that raised all kinds of questions, not least about the crash that killed Gideon. Was this part of an orchestrated campaign? Would Tom, or Virginia herself, be next in line?

Or Roger?

And if they'd been after Blake, was this danger something she'd brought with her – into their lives, into their home – from an outside source? Or was her return here reason in itself for somebody wanting her out of the way?

Virginia shifted restlessly under the bedclothes, then stilled.

What was that?

She strained her senses in the dark, listening, and heard it again – the creak of a floorboard out in the corridor. Turning her head, she saw a faint glow slide into the room underneath the bedroom door. It was not bright enough to be the main lights.

Quietly, Virginia slipped out of bed and pulled on a silk robe that hung from the back of the door. She reached for the handle, hesitated a moment, then yanked the door open and strode out, flicking on the lights as she did so.

'Roger! What on *earth* are you doing creeping about in the middle of the night?'

Right at the far end of the corridor, her brother spun to face her. He was wearing pyjamas under his rather tatty towelling dressing gown. One hand was raised to knock timidly on the door to Blake's room, while the other clutched his mobile phone to his ear. At the sight of her, his mouth dropped open and he ducked instinctively, as if to avoid a blow.

'Um, it's... Well, I...'

She plucked the phone out of his hands as she marched past. 'Who *is* this?'

'Oh, Virginia? It's Ed – Ed Underhill.'

'Edmund? What's going on? Do you have *any* idea what time it is?'

'It's that damn girl, Blake. She's just been throwing stones at my cottage – trying to put the wind up me.'

'Really?' Virginia frowned. 'And why would she want to do that?'

She listened to him splutter for a moment, then he let out an irritated breath and said, 'Look, before we get into all that, would you just check where she is? Please?' he added, as an afterthought.

Against her better judgement, Virginia complied. She knocked on the door with far less subtlety than her brother had employed. After a second or two, she knocked again, hard enough to make the panel rattle in its frame. At the same time, she twisted the handle and shoved the door wide.

The light from the corridor shone across the empty bed with its rumpled duvet.

She lifted the phone to her mouth again. 'She's not here.'

'I knew it,' Underhill said with dark satisfaction. 'Well, she's over-reached herself. It will take her a good fifteen minutes or so to get back from the village, so—'

'What are you doing in my room?'

The voice behind them made Virginia start so badly she dropped the phone. As Roger scurried to retrieve it, Virginia saw

Blake approaching along the corridor, wearing an old dressing gown that was both too short in the arm and too large in the body. She carried a glass of water.

'We thought…' Roger began. 'That is, we were told that you were, um…'

'Where have you *been*?' Virginia asked, her voice testy. For years, her motto had always been, "when under attack, attack back".

Blake raised an eyebrow and her water glass at the same time.

'I was thirsty. Why, is there a problem?'

'No, there's no problem,' Virginia said, sending her brother a daggered glance. 'A… misunderstanding, no doubt.'

But she heard the studied innocence in the girl's voice. With a sense of foreboding, she realised that, however impossible it was for Blake to have got back from the village so fast, she knew *exactly* why they were checking her room. And not only that – she had planned on it.

THIRTY-TWO

The following morning, Byron sat at the same table for his breakfast, and ordered the same meal. This time, although three other nearby tables were set with crockery and condiments, he had the room to himself.

The pub landlady – whose name, Byron had learned, was Vera – came bustling out of the kitchen to set a fresh pot of coffee in front of him.

'I hear you ran into little Miss Claremont yesterday, Mr Byron,' she said, raising her well-plucked eyebrows.

Byron was glad of the necessity to chew and swallow before he felt obliged to reply. 'Ah, it seems that the village rumour mill is in full working order.'

If she was aware of a stiffness in his tone, Vera took no offence. She laughed.

'Oh, you can't blame them. It's the most exciting thing to happen round here for years. Besides, they say you dropped her off right in the middle of Main Street, so I presume you weren't trying to be secretive about it…?'

Byron, aware that such a provocative statement was designed to prod him into an ill-considered response, smiled politely and poured himself coffee. After a moment's hopeful anticipation, Vera returned, disappointed, to the kitchen.

Byron went back to his breakfast and the morning paper. He'd already spoken to Commander Daud, giving her his opinion on the accident. She appeared to agree with his assessment – not happily, it must be said.

The snick of the outer door latch caught his attention. He looked up in time to see the inner door open and Blake walk in. Her hair was loose today, but otherwise she was wearing the same ripped jeans and hoodie as previously. Vaguely, he wondered if she possessed any other clothes.

She crossed to his table with purpose and paused with one hand on the back of the chair opposite. Her expression was calm but he didn't miss the slight bunching of her knuckles.

Ingrained manners compelled him to rise from his seat, to greet her with a noncommittal, 'Blake.'

'Byron.' She smiled slightly, the moment of tension buried. 'Do you mind if I join you?'

'Please do.' He regained his seat. 'Have you eaten?'

'I'm fine – although I won't turn down coffee if there's any more in that pot?'

Byron leaned across to one of the other tables and snagged her a cup and saucer. 'Help yourself.' He turned the pot so the handle was towards her. 'Now, what can I do for you?'

Her eyebrows climbed. 'This *could* merely be a social visit, for the pleasure of your company.'

'It could,' he agreed. 'But it isn't, is it?'

'OK… you're right. Yesterday, you said you might be willing to offer me your assistance.'

'Oh?'

'Well, that's not a very reassuring reaction.'

He registered the nervous timbre of her voice. 'Why don't you tell me what kind of assistance you require, exactly? Then perhaps I can respond in a more… satisfactory manner.'

'Hm, did you know you go, not only very formal, but also ever so slightly snarky when you're put on the spot?'

'I'll make a note.'

'I said "snarky", not "sarky".'

Byron said nothing. He cut a precise square from the toast on his plate, piled it with scrambled egg, and ate, waiting.

For her part, Blake took a sip of her coffee, then put down her cup with a sigh. 'The family solicitor – Julian Rolle – is due to arrive at Claremont in about an hour.'

'Ah, to read the will?'

She gave a faint nod. 'I would very much like someone – you – to be there as an… independent observer. Just in case.'

'In case of what? I thought you expected to receive nothing from your father?'

'Oh, I know, absolutely, that I don't feature in his will.'

'Why so certain?'

The corner of her mouth lifted. 'There was a copy in the safe.'

'Which you read.' A statement, not a question.

'Of course. It would have been rude not to.'

'Of course,' he echoed. 'I'm still not clear why you need anyone else to be there. Do you suspect Rolle might do something… unethical?'

'That's the thing – I don't know. The firm is the same one my family has always used, but the old partners have long since retired. Rolle himself is well after my time.'

'Perhaps you might be better served by having your own legal representation?'

She shook her head. 'There isn't time to find someone, let alone for them to actually get here.'

'You must have known the will was about to be read. If you had any qualms about it, then why leave it until the last minute to—?'

'I was expecting it to be someone I knew I—' She broke off, although he could almost hear the unspoken end of the sentence.

'*... someone I knew I could trust...*'

'What are you afraid might happen?'

'I don't really know.' She shrugged. 'But what I *do* know is that I'd feel safer with a neutral party there. So, will you do it?'

Her words were spoken casually, but there was tension in her neck and the set of her shoulders. Either she was not used to asking anyone for anything, he considered, or it was simply that she hated having to do so.

'Yes, of course.'

'Thank you.'

She smiled again, high wattage this time. He blinked in the face of it and immediately berated himself. He might be only ten years her senior, but he was still old enough to know better. Old enough not to have his head turned by a young woman he found attractive in ways he couldn't quite discern.

And one who might – or might not – be working a con.

The outer door opened again. They both turned to see a thin figure stagger in, trying to keep a grip on the stack of bed sheets and towels she carried, as well as her handbag and paper. Byron recognised Pauline at once. As she edged through the gap, a fold of sheet caught on the latch and tugged the whole lot out of her grasp.

She swore automatically, then glanced across and saw she was the focus of their attention. Her pale face flamed. She dropped to her knees and began scrabbling the linens together.

Blake was out of her chair before Byron could move, bending to help. He took in Pauline's mortified face and realised that his assistance would make her more uncomfortable rather than less. With effort, he stayed put, but didn't miss the grateful smile Pauline gave the younger woman as they gathered together the last of her load. Something about it niggled at him but he couldn't quite put his finger on what that was. Some kind of... familiarity between Blake and Pauline, perhaps?

He caught Pauline's eye and she flushed again, dropping his gaze, just as Vera appeared from the kitchen.

'Pauline! How many times do I have to tell you to come in round the back when we've got guests?'

'The dog's loose in the yard,' Pauline mumbled. 'Always jumps up at me and gets everything all dirty again.'

'Oh, Pauline, you simply have to be firm with him and he'll listen to you, that's all…'

The door shut behind them and the rest of their conversation went with it.

Byron put aside his napkin. 'Are you ready to go?'

Blake jumped up again. As she zipped up her hoodie, a rolled newspaper almost fell out of her pocket. He went to catch it, but she beat him to it.

'Local paper,' she said. 'Thought I may as well catch up on what *else* is new and exciting around here.'

THIRTY-THREE

One of the disadvantages of living in the country, in Lily's opinion, was the lack of opportunities for dressing up. Oh, there was the trunk full of old clothes in the loft above the garage, but that was make-believe – play-acting.

It *used* to be fun. Gideon had really encouraged her ambition to act. During the Christmas holidays, she and Tom would put on their own shows, when her mother's relations provided a captive audience. Of course, Lily's brother reckoned he'd grown out of such childish games about three years ago. And now, with Gideon gone, nothing was the same.

No, she meant *proper* dressing up. A cool skirt and top, a dusting of glittery make-up across her face and neck, and shoes with actual heels that made her legs look different, not the near flats that were all her school would permit.

Gideon had been just the same about her clothes. He disapproved of make-up 'on a girl your age' – unless she was rehearsing a role, of course. When the family went out, he'd insisted she wear the kind of dresses she'd thought babyish when she was seven, with ankle socks and those doll shoes with the strap and buckle across the instep.

Just gross.

But, this morning – knowing the solicitor was coming to Claremont for the reading of Gideon's will – Lily could take advantage of a fresh audience. She put on a short, pleated skirt – over dark tights so her mother wouldn't kick up a fuss about the length – and ankle boots. Her top had a high neck but was sleeveless. When she checked out her reflection in the long mirror on the back of her wardrobe door, the effect was chic and totally cool. Or it would be – if it wasn't for the cast on her arm. Still, there wasn't much she could do about that.

She hovered upstairs, messaging her friends, until she saw a posh-looking four-by-four coming up the drive. Then she bolted downstairs and burst into the drawing room, where her mother and uncle waited.

'Mummy, I think the solicitor's here!'

'Ah, he's on time, I see. Good. Go and find your brother.'

'Oh, do I have to?'

'Yes, you do. He really ought to be here for this,' her mother said. 'And put on a cardigan – you'll catch a chill.'

She pouted. 'It will spoil my look.'

'So will goosebumps. Now do as you're told.'

By the time she'd tracked down Tom, lurking in his room, and cajoled him downstairs, the solicitor was installed in an armchair near the drawing room fire. He had a cup of tea on the side table next to him, and a large briefcase balanced on his knees.

The solicitor was a commanding presence – a big man in a sober midnight blue suit. His white shirt contrasted starkly against his dark skin. He wore thick black-framed glasses, and had a small gap between his front teeth that fascinated Lily.

'Ah, and these are your children, Mrs Fitzroy?' the solicitor asked, his voice deep and melodic. 'Tom and Lily, yes? My name is Julian Rolle. How nice to meet you both.'

Tom mumbled a greeting and slouched into a chair in the far corner. Lily perched on a sofa under one of the windows.

In the chair on the opposite side of the fireplace, Uncle Roger wriggled impatiently and glanced at his wristwatch. 'I'm sorry, but is there any chance we could... move things along?'

'Why?' Virginia staked him with a pointed stare. 'It's not as if you have anywhere more important to be, Roger. Let Mr Rolle proceed at his own pace.'

'Nevertheless, Mr Flint is quite right to request that we get to the heart of the matter – the reading of the last will and testament of Mr Gideon Fitzroy,' Mr Rolle said. He reached into the briefcase and brought out a slim folder, from which he withdrew an official-looking document. 'I had the honour of not only being Mr Fitzroy's solicitor, but also his executor. So, if we are all here, then—'

Lily straightened. 'But where's Blake? She went out not long ago. *Surely* we can't start until *she's* here, too?'

Mr Rolle looked startled. His eyes went from Virginia to Uncle Roger and back again. '*Blake*? You don't mean to say she has… *returned*? But… I thought—'

'We have yet to fully ascertain her identity,' Virginia said quickly, which had Lily blinking at her in surprise.

'Anyway, what difference does it make?' Uncle Roger demanded. 'We already *know* she doesn't get a look-in in the old man's will.'

Mr Rolle took off his glasses and put the end of one arm into his mouth, frowning. 'I'm afraid this makes a good *deal* of difference, Mr Flint. It may complicate things considerably. Oh, indeed, yes.'

He was still frowning as he opened his briefcase again, and fished about inside. He pulled out another folder. This one was considerably thicker, more battered at the corners, and tied with a piece of faded ribbon.

Movement outside the window caught Lily's eye. Another vehicle had pulled up on the gravel alongside the solicitor's four-by-four. She didn't recognise the car, but she *did* recognise the figure who climbed from the front passenger seat.

'It's Blake! She's back.'

Her mother's head snapped round, a pained look on her face. 'I suppose you'd better let her in, then,' she said, not troubling to hide her reluctance.

Lily hurried out into the hall and had the front door open before they could knock.

Alongside Blake was the serious-looking man who'd been at the funeral.

'Hi, Lily,' Blake said. 'Have they started already?'

'Not quite. Mr Rolle – that's the solicitor – was about to, but *I* said we ought to wait for you, and *he* said that may complicate things considerably. Why would it do that?'

Blake gave her a smile that didn't quite seem like she really meant it. She glanced sideways at the man. He said nothing.

Blake sighed and pushed back her shoulders. 'Well, let's go and find out, shall we?'

THIRTY-FOUR

'You were expecting this?'

Byron murmured the words quietly into Blake's ear as they followed Lily towards the drawing room.

'Expecting what? That they would try to start without me, or that my presence would complicate things?'

'Either – or both.'

She flashed him a quick smile. 'I'm afraid I was, rather, yes.'

And if her words were regretful, the way they were delivered was anything but.

Byron eyed, with some distrust, the doorway the child had disappeared through. 'Should we prepare for a high-risk entry ourselves, or simply wait until Armed Response gets here?'

Blake gave a snort and flicked his arm with the back of her hand in mild reproof.

But he saw the way she paused a second to gather herself again before stepping forwards. It intrigued him to note what this was costing her. He wondered briefly if she felt it was worth it, and if he was about to find out.

As they entered the drawing room, Byron saw the family had gathered, including Virginia's brother and son. The only stranger – besides himself – was a large black man in tortoiseshell glasses and a handmade suit. He rose at once, clutching his unlatched briefcase before its contents spilled at his feet.

'Ms *Claremont*?'

He kept his eyes on Blake – and Byron – for long enough to introduce himself as the Fitzroys' solicitor, Julian Rolle. Then his gaze moved to Virginia.

She looked, Byron saw, as if locked in an endless cycle – the consideration and rejection of unappealing possibilities.

'Mr Byron,' she said with a tight smile, 'I'm sure you won't take offence when I say this is a private, *family* occasion and—'

'I asked him to be here,' Blake interrupted, her voice entirely cool and calm. 'He stays.'

She was the interloper. As such, she should not have been able to set any conditions. But she spoke with enough command that nobody argued.

Virginia's muttered, 'Well, *really*…' was the closest thing to dissent. Then she seemed to think better of whatever she'd been about to say. Instead, she swallowed and made a vague "carry on" gesture to Rolle.

'Um, yes, of course.' He cleared his throat. 'As you know, I came here today to read to you all the last will and testament of Gideon Fitzroy. It is a very simple document, as I'm sure you are already aware, drawn up – so I understand – by Mr Fitzroy himself and lodged with my predecessor as executor. That duty now falls to me, although – had I been consulted in the matter – I would, almost certainly, have advised Mr Fitzroy to go about things somewhat differently…'

He gave a smile that was tinged with anxiety. Byron scanned the faces. Something in the solicitor's tone was affecting everyone. With the exception of Blake, they all wore the beginnings of a frown – the foreboding that something was coming they hadn't prepared for, and weren't going to like.

Rolle quickly ran through the minor bequests – sums of five thousand to each of two local charities, and to the local community association.

'The remainder of Mr Fitzroy's estate is left, in its entirety to his wife – Mrs Virginia Fitzroy.'

Byron glanced sideways at Blake. Her expression appeared neutral but he could see a muscle jumping in the side of her jaw. He noticed, for the first time, that she still carried the local newspaper she'd had at the pub. She was furling it into a tight baton, twisting the flimsy pages between her hands.

What else is going on here? he wondered. *What am I missing?*

'Just out of pure *curiosity*,' Flint said, steepling his fingers as he tried – and failed – to force a casual note into his voice, 'how much is the estate worth? Just a ballpark figure? I mean, you have a handle on the overall thing, don't you?'

'Mr Fitzroy's personal estate?' Rolle asked. 'In total, or after the bequests have been made?'

'Oh, it's always better to have the bottom line, don't you think?' Flint gave a short laugh. 'So, after.'

The solicitor pursed his lips. 'A little over… four thousand pounds.'

'*Four thousand…*' Flint echoed faintly. 'Is that… some kind of *joke*?'

'We solicitors, as a profession, are not noted for our sense of humour,' Rolle said solemnly.

'What about the rental properties? The holiday cottages? The investment portfolio?' Flint demanded, his voice rising. 'What about *this house*? Are you trying to tell me – *us* – that they're worth *nothing*?'

'Not at all. Those assets have a combined value that is considerable—'

'Exactly! So—?'

'But they did not belong to Mr Fitzroy, and so were not a part of his *personal* estate.'

'Then, to whom *do* they belong?'

It was Virginia who voiced the question, almost in a whisper. As if she didn't really want to ask, and certainly didn't want to know, but couldn't help herself.

'These assets belonged to Mr Fitzroy's first wife, Catherine. Upon her death, their *use* passed to Mr Fitzroy, along with any income derived, for the remainder of his lifetime. But, the first Mrs Fitzroy's will put her estate in trust for her daughter – should she survive her and reach majority…'

'So, are you telling us that Gideon's will is… invalid?'

'Not at all. It's perfectly valid – as far as it goes.' Rolle shook his head. 'Mr Fitzroy was, of course, quite at liberty to challenge his wife's will at the time it was executed, or at any point since. He… did not choose to do so.'

Flint lurched out of his chair, his focus on Blake. 'So *that's* why you came here? All that talk about "my father hasn't left me anything". Hah! You knew he didn't have to, you greedy little—'

'I never intended to come back!' Blake threw the words at him, each one harsh with feeling. Her eyes moved to Virginia, standing frozen to the spot. 'I never *wanted* to come back!' She threw down the newspaper, which slowly uncoiled itself at Virginia's feet. 'And I probably never *would* have done – if you hadn't tried to have me killed…'

THIRTY-FIVE

'So, are you going to tell me what that was all about?'

At least, Blake thought, he waited to ask until they were away from the house, from Flint's furious accusations and Virginia's scorn. The thing that got to her – more than she'd expected it to – was the betrayal in Lily's face. As if she'd befriended the child only to steal her favourite toy or her pet rabbit.

Almost unobtrusively, Byron had taken charge, ushering her outside, telling the solicitor that she would be in touch. He bundled her into his car without asking more than if she was all right.

Blake, sitting hunched in the passenger seat, had given him a brief nod. She wedged her hands between the heated seat and her thighs, but still her fingers felt numb with cold.

Byron drove back to the village and shepherded her into the pub by the side door rather than through the public bar. He displayed such sureness of purpose that she followed him without question. Upstairs and along a corridor, then through a door at the end.

It was only once she was there that Blake realised he'd taken her up to his room.

She had never seen the bedrooms here – never had cause to. This one was decorated with good taste, bordering on opulence. No bad thing for a guest room. There were two tub chairs, either side of a low table. Byron guided her into one of them.

She was vaguely aware that he picked up the phone by the bed and asked for a pot of tea to be brought up. The pub had never offered room service but she bet they wouldn't refuse him.

Then he took the chair opposite and asked his killer question.

'What did you mean, they tried to have you killed? When?'

'Most recently?' She gave a mirthless laugh. 'Yesterday morning. Somebody tampered with the ladder up to the hayloft at the old stables. Only it was Lily who was almost hurt, not me.'

'You think Virginia Fitzroy tried to injure her own daughter?'

'Maybe not, but somebody did, and whoever it was must have known she was up there with me.'

Blake gave him the gist of what had happened. To his credit, he didn't interrupt, but when she was done, he retrieved something from his pocket and dropped it onto the table near her. The folded-up newspaper quivered where it landed.

'What has an out-of-date copy of the local paper got to do with all this, by the way?'

'With what happened yesterday? Nothing. But look in the notices.'

He paused, as if considering whether her answer was an avoidance. She braced herself to explain but didn't need to. Byron began to scan the pages, moving quickly through the editorial until he reached the section for announcements of births, deaths, and marriages.

She watched his face as he found the right item, the stillness that came over him as he read the words and understood at once the implications.

'So, they tried to have you officially declared dead.' He sat back in his chair. 'To be honest, I'm surprised they waited so long – considering what was at stake.'

'My father had the run of the place during his lifetime, in any event. There's some kind of trust. I don't understand the legal technicalities but he probably could have challenged it if he'd really wanted to. My being dead or alive made no difference to him.'

'If Virginia didn't know about Catherine Claremont's will, why go to all that trouble?' He glanced at the page header, double-checking the paper's date. 'And less than a week after Fitzroy's death.'

Blake shrugged. 'Could've been just staking her claim?'

'Hm, did she bring the subject up before he died, do you think? It may be that Fitzroy was reluctant to accept your supposed demise, if that's any consolation to you?'

Her lips twitched involuntarily. 'Not really, but thank you for trying. If anything, I think he probably baulked at the fees involved.'

She put that one out there and let it settle, just to see what he'd do with it.

'Just out of interest, how did you find out about the notice. I assume you haven't been living inside the paper's catchment area all this time?'

'Lex,' she said shortly.

His gaze sharpened and he would have spoken but there was a timid knock on the door. He raised one eyebrow slightly, just enough to indicate he wasn't done, then rose and went to answer it.

'You asked for some tea, Mr Byron? Shall I put it—?'

Blake registered Pauline's voice at the same moment that Pauline spotted her. The woman's face betrayed her shock, then tightened into a scowl. She shoved the tray into Byron's hands, and fled.

Byron pushed the door shut behind her with his elbow and turned.

'Was it something I said?'

She struggled not to let anything show in her face, her voice. 'I doubt it. Pauline… Well, it seems she's sided with the majority of the village in their disapproval of me.'

'Oh?' He set the tray down onto the table between them, assembled cups onto saucers and lifted the lid of the teapot to inspect the contents. 'She has reason to doubt you are who you say you are?' His neutral tone gave away little of his own stance on the matter.

'No more than anyone else, but since when did that stop them forming an opinion?'

'Quite.'

He began to pour, his movements almost delicate. He had the long mobile fingers of a pianist, or a surgeon. His nails were clean and short, and had clearly never been bitten. But as she watched, she caught some slight awkwardness in his hands. She couldn't quite work it out.

In a detached way, she recognised that she found him attractive, which was fine – just as long as she kept control of it. She pulled her gaze away, but found herself looking at the bed. No help there. His next question came almost as a relief.

'Does it strike you as suspicious – that your stepmother should be quite so… single-minded in her pursuit of an inheritance?'

'No, not really. She has children. She probably felt the need to secure their future – provide for them.'

'As your mother did with you?' He handed her a filled cup. 'You knew about her will, of course.'

'Why "of course"?'

Byron lifted his own cup, took a sip. 'The money came from your mother's family. From what I can gather, the two of you were close. I imagine she would have made sure you knew.'

'Yes, I knew.'

'Hm, it makes it all the more surprising, in some ways. Not that you came back, but that you left at all.'

She blinked at his cool assessment, stung to comment, 'Money isn't everything. There's a good reason the saying that money can't buy happiness is a cliché – because so often it's true.'

'Maybe. But, if money doesn't make one happy, it certainly makes one's misery a lot less uncomfortable.'

There speaks the voice of experience, perhaps? Or are you merely fishing?

'You don't strike me as a man who's down to his last fiver, Byron.'

'Oh, I get by.'

'On more than just statutory sick pay, I bet.' She tilted her head. 'May I ask you a personal question?'

He looked momentarily surprised, or was it wary? Then it was gone and he smiled gravely. 'You may, although I can't guarantee you a personal answer.'

'Someone said you're on leave from the police force. What kind of leave – administrative?'

'It's not called a *force* any longer – we're a police *service* now, didn't you know?'

'Semantics.' She waved a hand. 'And you're stalling.'

She knew that administrative leave followed a serious incident, such as a shooting – getting the officer involved out of the way while an investigation was carried out.

'No – medical. It's not something I care to discuss.'

She gave him a slow visual inspection. He returned her stare with a quizzical slant.

'Well, you're not missing any obvious bits of your anatomy, and although there's something about your hands that means you'd never make a card sharp or a pickpocket, you don't move with any restriction, as far as I can tell, so… I'm guessing it was something psychological?'

For a split second, the pain was written clear on his face. Whatever it was, it had hurt badly, she realised. A part of her felt guilty for poking at him. But another part *needed* him off-balance enough not to start poking at her. It was that part made her add a drawling, 'Should I be alarmed?'

He put down his cup and saucer with care and leaned forwards, narrowed eyes on her face.

'Oh yes, Ms Claremont. If you've any sense, I think you should be very alarmed indeed.'

THIRTY-SIX

Lily had retreated to her usual space in the loft above the garage. She sat on the old shipping trunk that contained part of the dressing-up wardrobe, drumming the heels of her boots viciously against the side.

For the first twenty minutes or so, she had sobbed. She hated conflict, had always been upset by raised voices and slammed doors. Plenty of both had gone on, after the departure of Blake and then the solicitor, Mr Rolle.

Her mother and Uncle Roger had yelled at each other and stomped and clattered doors both to rooms and cupboards. So she had run from the house and ended up here. To begin with, she'd plonked herself down on the wooden stairs. She only realised *after* she'd climbed the rest of the way and passed the old full-length mirror covered in brown speckles, that there was now a large dirty mark on the back of her skirt.

So, of course, she couldn't really go back – not of her own accord. Her mother would go spare if she walked back in like this, even if she noticed Lily had gone in the first place. No, she would have to wait until the alarm had been raised and search parties sent out. Then, the relief of her discovery would cancel out the annoyance caused by the state of her clothes.

But she was bored, and hungry, and still upset.

Lily didn't understand exactly what had happened, because nobody had taken the time to explain the legal position to her. What she *did* know was that it was all connected to Blake. Because Blake had come back, everything that should have been theirs was now… not.

And that meant the house – Claremont. The garden and the woods and all the wild spaces where she could roam and play, without her mother wanting to know where she *was* all the time.

Which brought her back to her current problem. If her mother had been more concerned with Lily's whereabouts, she would have come to find her by now.

How could Blake have done this to them? She had seemed so *nice*, so friendly and interested. And all the while she must have known she was going to get everything.

What happens now? Will she throw us out?

Lily had lived at Claremont since she was six – half her lifetime. She could just about remember the house before, in London – the one they'd moved to after her father died. It was tiny. She and Tom hadn't had to share a room, but only because their mother had the bigger of the two bedrooms divided in half with a partition wall. They had to share the window. It had hinged from the top, with the lock on her side of the wall, and the prop on Tom's. He always wanted it open. She wanted it closed. The smell of the traffic fumes made her wheeze.

The sound of the side door to the garage opening downstairs brought her out of the memory. She screwed up her face in an attempt to refresh the tears, and was rewarded by a solitary droplet, which escaped the corner of one eye and trickled slowly down her cheek.

Slow feet on the stairs told her it was not her mother, after all, who had come in search of her. She didn't need to force the tears then.

A moment later, Tom's head appeared above the level of the floor.

'Hiya.'

She sniffed.

He gave a sigh and finished his ascent, picking through the jumble of jetsam. He pushed aside a stack of old gardening magazines from the chair opposite and sat.

'Come on, Lil. It could be worse.'

He sounded more cheerful than he had for weeks. Surprise fought with outrage in Lily's mind, so that she forgot to cry and simply glared at him.

'What do you *mean* "it could be worse"?' she wailed. 'We're going to be *homeless*.'

'Oh, don't exaggerate. We'll be OK. We're hardly going to be put out on the streets, are we?' He grinned. 'Besides, Uncle Roger said they're going to insist she takes a DNA test before anything else happens.'

'But what if she passes?'

'It's not like an exam you can swot for, dimwit. It will tell them if Gideon really was her father or not.' He sat back in the chair in a negligent sprawl. 'If *her* DNA doesn't match with his, she can't inherit. If it *does*, she gets the lot.'

He sounded deeply satisfied, either way.

Lily frowned. 'They can take DNA from hair, can't they? Does that mean they'll cut her hair?' She would hate to have her own hair short.

'They only need a tiny amount.' Tom reached across and separated maybe half-a-dozen strands of Lily's hair, to demonstrate. 'But they have to *pull* it out by the roots – like this!'

'Ow! Get off me! I bet they don't at all.'

He shrugged. 'Look it up if you don't believe me.'

She rubbed her scalp. 'And what about us?'

'If it matches, we get zilch – didn't I just say that?'

'No, I meant *we* won't be a match to Gideon. He's not our real father, so—'

Tom laughed. Normally, she hated it when he made fun of her, but it was such a relief to hear him actually laugh at all, that for once it didn't bother her.

'You don't think she *is* Blake, do you?' Lily asked. 'Is that why you're so happy?'

Tom stood. 'Come on, Lil, let's go inside. You must be freezing up here.' He reached for her hand, gave it a squeeze. 'As for if she is or isn't Blake – frankly, I don't really care.'

THIRTY-SEVEN

Jane Hudson hovered in the open doorway and rapped her knuckles on the frame. Inside the office, a plump Indian lady was eating salad out of a plastic box, clamping a phone receiver between ear and shoulder at the same time.

'Ms Devi?' Hudson asked when she looked up.

The woman beckoned her in with a plastic spork. 'Please, take a seat. I have been on hold for twenty-three minutes already. I can't decide if it would be more foolish to hang up now or to keep holding.'

Hudson sidled into the tiny space and perched on the edge of an upright chair, the seat of which was mostly taken up with a lidded archive box. Paperwork sprawled across every flat surface, dotted with Post-it notes in every hue.

Ms Devi continued to attack her lunch, occasionally tapping at her keyboard as well as keeping her ear to the phone. Hudson waited.

A minute or so later, the woman made a noise of disgust, glared at the handset and threw it down on the desk.

'After all that, they cut me off! Now, what can I do for an officer of the law?'

'Er – I'm PC Hudson. We spoke on the phone, ma'am. About a girl called Hope—?'

'Ah, of course, of course.' She pushed aside the empty lunchbox and slid a file folder out from under several others. Hudson had no idea how she knew which was the correct one, as they all appeared to be exactly the same colour. 'Hope Glennie. What do you wish to know?'

'Well, at the moment we don't know much at all about her, so anything you can tell me will be useful.'

'I had just started working for social services back then, and I remember Hope *very* well.'

After ten years? 'Oh?'

'Oh, yes. She was one of the first girls I dealt with, when I started working here.'

'What kind of a kid was she?'

'She was bright – *too* bright, in some ways. Not academically, unfortunately, but… it worried me.'

Hudson cocked her head. 'In what way?'

'You know how some people buy a dog, like an Alsatian, or a collie? A dog that should be working for a living, and they keep it cooped up in the house and don't give it enough to do? So, the dog gets bored, and before you know where you are, it has run amok and bitten somebody.'

'Aye, I know that kind of dog.'

'Well, that was sort of how I thought of Hope. I thought… if that girl didn't find a purpose, she could become… dangerous.'

She glanced at Hudson, gave a quick, almost apologetic smile. 'Let's just say that, when it came to Hope, I felt the failure with her very deeply.'

'It didn't help, then – sending her to the Allbrights' farm?'

'Yes, indeed. Working on the land, with the livestock, seemed to suit her very well. And she made a good friend there, I think.'

Hudson gazed at her in confusion. 'So…?'

'Ah, yes, I see.' Ms Devi paused, took a breath. 'Perhaps I should start again, from the beginning, yes?'

'Please.'

She grinned. Dimples appeared in both cheeks, and the stud in the side of her nose caught the light. Ms Devi wore a long embroidered tunic over plain linen trousers, with a matching long silk scarf around her neck. It did not seem robust enough an outfit for the time of year, but she showed no sign of being cold. Perhaps the amount of nervous energy she was burning had something to do with that.

'We don't know much about Hope's biological mother, except that she was thirteen years old, and nothing at *all* about her father. It is not surprising that he stayed out of the picture, perhaps, as he could have been prosecuted for statutory rape had he made himself known to us.' She glanced at Hudson as if to check for contradiction. She offered none.

'Hope was put up for adoption at birth,' Ms Devi went on. 'Everything went well until she was eight, when her adoptive parents sadly died in a car accident on the motorway. They had no living relatives, so Hope went back into the care system.'

'Poor kid,' Hudson murmured.

'Yes, indeed. She was adopted again, but it didn't work out. There were rumours of abuse of some kind – nothing was confirmed in any way. We would have dealt with *that* very severely, I can assure you. She was placed in half-a-dozen foster homes, one after another. Always trouble of some kind. Behavioural problems – temper tantrums, truanting, vandalism, petty theft.' She shook her head sadly. 'I freely admit, that by the time the charity offered her that first farm placement, I was at the end of my wits to know what to do with her.'

'And it worked for her, did it?'

Ms Devi pulled a face. 'She was a little calmer when she returned after that first visit, I think, yes. Less disruptive. But gradually she began to slip back into her old ways – so much so that the group home where she was living asked for her to be moved on again.' She shook her head in what Hudson judged to be either sadness or annoyance, or a mixture of both. 'I managed to find another home, in North London, who were willing to take her but not immediately. We persuaded the Allbrights to let her go to the farm for the month until she could move into the new home. It *seemed* an ideal solution…'

The doubt in her voice had Hudson frowning. 'What happened?'

'When she arrived at the new home she was very quiet, they said – very upset. Angry, but wouldn't say what was wrong. She stayed only until her sixteenth birthday, which was a matter of weeks, then she simply walked out one morning and… disappeared. She has not been seen since.'

THIRTY-EIGHT

When Blake cycled past the front of the pub in Brassington, on the far side of Carsington Water, she found only one of the patrons was hardy enough to be occupying an outside table. It wasn't actually raining, but the wind gusting across the stepped garden was bitterly cold, and the lone customer did not look as though he was particularly enjoying his pint.

She freewheeled into the car park alongside the pub, careful of the loose gravel. Three vehicles were parked close to the kitchen entrance, which she suspected belonged to staff members. For a country pub, out of season on a weekday mid-afternoon, it was only to be expected.

The only other vehicle was parked across the far side of the potholed area – a ten-year-old Toyota saloon in a nondescript dull silver. There was hardly a panel that didn't sport some minor scuff, scratch, or dent.

Blake propped her bicycle against the fence and circled the Toyota, blowing into her cupped hands to warm her fingers. It only took a quick look through the glass to confirm it belonged to the man she'd seen at the front. The paisley silk scarf on the back seat was probably worth more than the car.

By the time he approached, she was hunkered down in the passenger seat. He opened the driver's door and climbed in.

'Hello, kiddo,' he said. 'I do wish you'd learn to wait outside.'

'I was cold. Besides, if you'd really wanted me to do that, Lex, you shouldn't have taught me to break into cars.'

He shrugged. 'Mea culpa.'

Lex Vaganov made the interior of the Toyota seem very snug. He was a big man, with high cheekbones and deep blue eyes. He might be considered handsome, were it not for his hair, clipped so close it was as if his head had been flocked. Blake had always thought this as deliberate self-brutalisation. Or maybe it was an attempt to sidestep comparisons with an aging Hugh Grant – there was a definite resemblance. It couldn't be to avoid attention altogether, because for as long as she'd known him, he'd been a snappy dresser – today in a lilac shirt and contrasting silk tie beneath an impeccably cut Paul Smith suit. And he spoke like the former public schoolboy he'd once been.

'So, are they all convinced that you're the real McCoy?'

'I'm... not sure.'

His eyebrows shot up, then down again in a scowl. 'You're losing your touch. I thought you'd have them eating out of your hand by now.'

'Hm, I might have done, but there have been one or two... developments.' She gave him a brief outline of what had happened during her visit to the hayloft with Lily, and the reading of Fitzroy's will.

'Anything else?' When she shook her head, his lips pursed. 'Does the name Detective Superintendent John Byron ring any bells? When were you going to tell me he's been sniffing around you?'

'How did you know that?'

He gave her a sideways look of admonishment.

'OK, silly question. Who is he?'

'One of the few coppers in the Met I've made it my business to avoid. I would advise you to do the same.'

'Is he that bad?'

'No, he's that good – or he was, anyway. Any thoughts on why he's here – apart from because of your dramatic return, of course?'

'There seems to be a whisper of doubt about Fitzroy's death.' She twisted in her seat to study Vaganov. 'Did *you* kill him?'

He looked almost affronted. 'Where's the profit in that?'

It did not escape her notice that he had not actually answered the question. She said nothing.

He sighed. 'All I did was engineer his… withdrawal from public life, shall we say? He was a man who craved power – both personal and political. Taking that away from him seemed like the ultimate punishment.'

'Having him sit and rot in prison seems more like the ultimate punishment to me.'

'You know as well as I do, I couldn't achieve that without hurting those who've already suffered enough.'

'You're right, of course.'

'When am I not?' He paused. 'If this is too hard on you, there's no shame in calling it quits – live to fight another day. I could have you back in London in time for late supper at The Ivy.'

She shook her head at once. 'I've said I'll see this through, so I will. I owe her that much.'

'I know, kiddo.' He covered her hand with his own, gave it a squeeze. 'I know.'

'Besides, I've given them a sample of my DNA,' she said, picking her words carefully. 'The solicitor is getting it tested. There's a private forensics lab down near Birmingham, apparently, who can rush it through.'

Vaganov stilled. 'You've done what?'

She knew that quiet tone all too well. Despite herself, she felt her shoulders hunching as her hackles rose.

'Don't, Lex. Just don't.'

He withdrew his hand, slumped back in his seat. It creaked in protest. 'All these years, I've been *so* careful to keep you under the radar, to scrub out your official existence, so you could become anybody because you were nobody, and for what?'

'Maybe for this?'

He grunted. 'And what happens when "this" is all over, hm? What then? Have you even thought that far ahead?'

'Well, then you can scrub me out again.' She gave him a tight smile that cost her to produce. 'After all, it's not like I ever planned to stick around here.'

THIRTY-NINE

'Well, I still think it's a damned disgrace,' Roger spluttered. 'I can't believe that bloody solicitor went along with it.'

'Yes, so you've said.' Virginia's voice was weary. 'But it's not as if he had much of a choice in the matter. The wretched girl has made her claim. All Julian can do is verify or disprove it.'

'How could you *not* have known about the first wife's will – about the trust?' It wasn't the first time he'd asked that question, either. No doubt it would not be the last. 'There must be *something* we can do to contest it.'

'Well, why didn't *you* know? After all, you knew Gideon long before I did.'

'Yes, but not biblically,' he shot back. 'You're *sure* he never said anything – never even gave you a *hint*?'

'No.' All the pent-up, pissed-off tension came out in that single, clipped syllable. But then she froze, frowning. 'We may have been married, but Gideon kept me in the dark about a lot of things – why he resigned his seat, for a start.'

'Hah. He always said *you* were the one who talked him into giving it up.'

'Me? Why on earth would I want to do that?'

'Spending too much time off the leash in London?'

Virginia remained silent. There was no other dignified response.

'What?' Roger demanded.

She flicked him a quick glance. 'Nothing.'

'Oh, come on, Vee.' He shoved out of his chair, misjudged the position of the arms and staggered a little. 'I've known you my *whole* life—'

'Obviously.'

He ignored the acid interruption, plunging on, 'And I know damn well when you're lying to me. Spill it.'

She hesitated, on the verge of telling him to mind his own business, then realised there was little to be gained by it. 'You may recall, three years ago, our marriage went through a particularly rocky patch, shall we say. I suggested we separate, and Gideon told me I'd be a fool to leave him because I was his sole heir.'

'You were going to *leave* him?'

'I… considered it.'

'Why? It would have caused a scandal with the parliamentary select committee. And you had it made here, hadn't you? Life of luxury! Silver spoon up your—'

'There's no need to be vulgar, Roger.'

'On the contrary, my dear sister. I think there's *every* need.' He waved his tumbler of scotch vaguely in her direction. Unlocking the drinks cabinet, she reflected, had been a mistake. One it was too late now to rectify. ''Sides, he was only fifty-six and healthy as a horse. Well, healthy as a stallion at stud.' He snickered. 'Horny old devil.'

Were it not for the insulating layer of whisky, the look she shot in his direction would have flayed him alive. As things stood, it bounced off without leaving a mark.

'I knew, of course, that there was some kind of… restriction on the family fortune. He told me there was a sort of investment trust set up, to avoid either having to declare all his assets on the MPs' register, or paying extortionate amounts of tax.'

'And you took him at his word? You didn't ask to see the paperwork?'

'That would have been mercenary. He told me he was leaving everything to me – and the children, of course. What reason did he have to lie?'

'Reason? He was a politician. He didn't *need* a reason.' Roger snorted and took another gulp of scotch. 'Sometimes he did it just to keep his hand in.'

She flushed. 'He told me that he didn't have any living relatives. I don't understand why he was *so* convinced that his daughter was dead, if…'

Her voice trailed off as she caught the swirl of emotions that crossed her brother's face, although she couldn't quite decipher them.

Roger did his best to look innocent. 'Hey, Gid told me 'xactly same thing. Otherwise, d'you think I would've gone along with you trying to make it all official?' He sat again, enough of a slump to slosh the liquor up the sides of the glass, and gave a groan that turned into a growl, thumping his head back against the upholstery in frustration, eyes closed. 'What a bloody *mess.*'

Virginia leaned in close, her gaze sharp.

'Roger… what have you done?'

He threw back the last of the spirit in a way she recognised – somewhere halfway between devil-may-care and Dutch courage. Instead, he almost choked on it. Virginia waited while he gasped and coughed, straining to take a breath. He was her baby brother, but these days she felt more irritation for him than concern.

He tried to meet her eyes but his gaze kept sliding away. 'I *might* have been a bit rash with some… expenditure recently,' he admitted at last. 'I was expecting… Hell, you *know* what I was expecting, Vee!'

'How much?'

'Well, I was offered this—'

'How *much?*'

'Twenty grand.'

She went very still. All the air was sucked out of the room. 'From whom? Please tell me you didn't go back to that casino. You *know* who the money men are behind it. And you *know* what they threatened last time, if you didn't come up with—'

'Yes, yes, I KNOW,' he yelled. He jacked out of the armchair as if it had been suddenly plugged in to the mains. He lifted his glass on reflex, found it empty and hurled it into the fireplace. It shattered on the grate, pinging shards in all directions.

Virginia didn't flinch.

'I *know*,' he repeated, more quietly. 'They'll break my fingers first, and then my elbows, and my ankles, and then they'll kneecap me.' He swallowed. 'They go through the back of the knee joint with an electric drill and an auger bit – like they used to in Belfast during the Troubles. They told me as much last time. In *excruciating* detail.'

'So why on *earth* did you—?'

'Because I *thought* we'd be getting our hands on *money*,' he said between his teeth. '*Lots* of money.' He began to pace, too antsy to sit, and clawed his hands through his hair. 'Why the *hell* didn't you tell me it wasn't all straightforward?'

Something flared behind her eyes, but when she spoke her voice was icy. 'Why the hell didn't *you* stay away from the kinds of places that hoover the cash straight out of your pockets?'

'Oh, so this is all *my* fault now, is it?'

'And who else would you have take the blame for your own stupidity?'

She noted that the finger he pointed in warning was trembling slightly. He whirled away, clenching his fists, and moved to the window. The day was dropping fast towards early evening, the light starting to dim. Virginia fought the urge to go to him – give in to him – as she had so many times in the past. She took a breath, opened her mouth, but he whirled to face her before she could speak.

'After everything I've done for you,' he muttered, his voice bitter and sulky.

Her moment of weakness evaporated. 'Remind me – what *was* that, exactly?'

'Hah! You said it – if it wasn't for me, you and Gideon would never even have *met*. You wouldn't be living it up in a bloody mansion, like Lady Muck.'

'Get out.' Her voice was cold, her manner poised and, ironically enough, very like the lady of the manor she'd done such a good job of impersonating, these past six years.

Her brother grabbed the bottle of whisky from the side table and lurched for the door into the hallway, yanking it open. Virginia thought she caught a flicker of movement on the other side. She hoped the children hadn't heard any of this.

'I've earned every penny I'm owed,' Roger said, his voice too loud for the room. 'Working for that twisted old bastard, everything I did… No rest – not for *years*. I've bloody *earned* it!'

And with that he stumbled across the hall, flung the front door wide, and staggered out into the gathering dusk.

FORTY

Byron sat in his car, parked in a field gateway, watching the entrance to Claremont's driveway. Next to him, balanced on the centre console, was a stainless steel flask of coffee. The pub had, very kindly, provided it for him. He had told them he was off out for a night-time hike, looking for local wildlife. It was not entirely untrue. But he had omitted to explain that the wildlife he sought was likely to be on two legs rather than four. It was more of a stake-out than a work-out.

After all, he was not *supposed* to be working.

No sooner had that thought crossed his mind than his phone began to vibrate in his jacket pocket. He glanced briefly at the number before accepting the call, using his headset, so the light from the phone's screen did not illuminate the otherwise dark interior of the car.

'Evening, ma'am.'

'Byron. I got your message – about the shake-up over Fitzroy's estate,' Commander Daud said. 'Sounds like the cat is not only out of the bag but is running riot through the chicken coop.'

'Indeed.'

'Is it possible that our mystery woman, Blake, could've caused Fitzroy's accident? Driving the oncoming car that the boy mentioned, perhaps? Because, as things now stand, she has a pretty compelling motive for wanting her old man out of the way.'

Byron considered for a moment. 'There was no way she could have predicted Fitzroy's car would go off the road so completely, or that he would be killed in the crash. If he'd been wearing his seat belt, by all accounts, he might have survived. And if he *didn't* die – and he'd recognised her as the other driver, or they'd simply collided head-on – what then?'

'She might not have had to get her hands dirty – not with the kind of contacts Lex Vaganov undoubtedly has.'

'It's still a very hit-and-miss way to go about it.'

He heard a long exhale that indicated defeat. 'Yeah, you're right. It just seems so unlikely that – after everything – he'd die in a simple accident…'

'I get the impression that, if Blake *had* wanted to kill her father, she would probably have come up with something a little more foolproof. She's clearly a bright cookie.'

'Hm, interesting you should say that, because "bright" was how Hope Glennie's social worker described *her*.'

'Ah, that wouldn't be the one from the farm, would it?'

'That's the one. She and Blake Claremont were *very* cosy, back in the day, according to the social worker. Then she upped and disappeared from the group home she was sent to after she left the Allbrights' care.'

'Was that the same time Blake herself went missing?'

'About three weeks later, apparently. Your young PC, Hudson, has interviewed the couple who run the farm, and the social worker who sent the kids there. I've emailed you the reports.'

'Thank you. I'll take a look as soon as I get back.'

'Where are you?'

Just for a second, he pondered the wisdom of revealing this, but couldn't put forward a compelling reason not to. 'Keeping an eye on the Fitzroy place.'

'Oh?'

'Maybe. A… feeling, rather than anything concrete.' He took a sip of his coffee, kept his eyes on the mirrors, just in case. 'Jane

Hudson was being cagey when I last spoke to her. Is she aware we're in the loop on this?'

'No reason she should be. She's just filing her reports as normal, and I've called in a favour with her divisional superintendent to be copied-in further up the chain of command. I'm surprised she hasn't mentioned anything about the social worker to you, though. I thought you and she were supposed to be matey?'

'Ah, well, perhaps word has got out that I accompanied Blake to the reading of Fitzroy's will this morning. Jane may assume I've… taken sides.'

'Have you – taken a side, that is? And how did you wangle a ringside seat? Dropped heavy hints, or charmed your way in?'

'Actually, Blake herself asked me to be there. With hindsight, I think she was probably expecting trouble and wanted a neutral observer.'

'Ah, "neutral", are you?'

'Ma'am?'

'Don't go all coy on me, Byron. We've known each other too long for that. This young woman *interests* you. I can hear it in your voice when you talk about her.'

'She is… interesting, I'll give you that.'

'But? I definitely hear a but.'

He gave a short, self-deprecatory laugh. 'Quite apart from anything else, ma'am, there is something of an age-gap between us—'

'She's – what, twenty-five now? So, ten years. Big deal.'

'There is also the small matter of her possibly being guilty of attempted fraud, and you yourself suggested she may have had a hand in the death of her own father for monetary gain. I have no desire to sleep with one eye open.'

Daud laughed. 'Byron, if you're spending any of the time sleeping, you're doing it *all* wrong…'

FORTY-ONE

Ed Underhill stepped out of his cottage, pulling the front door shut behind him. It stuck, as it tended to with the onset of every winter, rain making the wood swell. He had to open and slam it again before he could get his key to turn in the lock.

It was turning into a miserable night, the rain coming down hard enough to bounce. Muttering a curse under his breath, he turned up the collar of his coat against the sneaky wind that blew droplets straight down the back of his neck. Half his mind was already on his first pint at the pub, and maybe a plate of whatever was the special on tonight's menu.

The other half, however, was still turning over the information Jane Hudson had given him about Hope Glennie. Hudson had called earlier, wanting to know if Underhill had remembered anything further about Hope.

Oh, he remembered her all right. She'd been trouble, as most of them were. And once she got all pally with Blake, the two of them together became even more trouble than they should have been. He could have predicted things were going to go the way they did, in the end…

Muffled beneath his coat, Underhill's mobile phone began to ring. He fumbled in his pockets until he located it. It took him long enough to wrestle it free that he rushed to answer without looking at the incoming number.

'Yes, hello?'

'Oh, Edmund, thank goodness I've got hold of you!'

Anxiety distorted the voice. That and the limitations of the phone line meant it took him a second or two to recognise the caller.

'*Virginia*? What on earth's the matter?'

'It's Roger. He was very upset – about the… situation. We had a silly argument. He ran off into the grounds and he hasn't come back. It's such a filthy night… I'm starting to worry that something might have happened to him.'

Underhill suppressed a sigh. 'Have you called Jane Hudson?'

'I rang her first, naturally,' Virginia Fitzroy said, her tone a little tart now, as if sensing Underhill's reluctance. 'She was dealing with a car accident over near Hognaston and said she would come as soon as she was able to. But…'

She didn't need to finish *that* thought. For years, Underhill had been the man to call with any local problems. He'd given a select few his personal, private mobile number, fully expecting that, when he retired, they'd forget all about it. Unfortunately, some of them hadn't taken the hint.

'How long has your brother been missing?' Underhill paused in the middle of the lane, feeling his pockets for car keys.

'Several hours now. Roger was ranting, almost,' Virginia went on. She lowered her voice. 'I'm afraid he'd been drinking…'

No change there, then.

But as the rest of her words registered, Underhill hesitated. 'Ranting about *what*, exactly?'

'To be perfectly honest, he wasn't making much sense. I thought Gideon treated him as a glorified errand boy, so quite *what* he's supposed to have done that's so important, I've no idea.'

'All right, I'm on my way. I'll be with you shortly. Try not to worry too much.' Underhill forced a false note of confidence into his voice. 'And Roger's lived at Claremont long enough to know those woods like the back of his hand. I'm sure he'll be fine…'

He ended the call and swore, curt and heartfelt, then jogged back along the lane to where his car was parked.

With his head down into the rain, he did not see the slight figure in the hooded red coat who'd been lurking in the shadows. By the time he'd climbed in and cranked the engine, she was gone.

FORTY-TWO

Flint was not, as his sister feared, soaking wet and in danger of hypothermia. Most of the time he'd been missing from the house, he'd been at the old stables through the wood, working his way through the bottle of whisky he'd taken with him.

Gideon Fitzroy had a taste for the good stuff and he didn't buy anything less than ten-year-old single malts. The old man himself would probably be rolling in his grave, Flint considered, if he could see his good whisky being swigged from a dusty plastic cup he'd found in the back of the old Land Rover.

'Well, t'hell with'im an'all,' Flint mumbled.

Every time he swallowed, he added another layer of cushioning over the anxiety threatening to crush him. He knew he shouldn't have gone back to the casino in Manchester. It wasn't as if he hadn't been there before – lost heavily there before – and owed them more than he could afford. And he was well aware of the penalties if it happened again.

He'd only got out of *that* mess unscathed by the skin of his teeth. And now he was back in the hole again. Just as deep, if not deeper. He was prepared to admit he'd been careless, in the weeks since Gideon's death, safe in the knowledge that his erstwhile boss was no longer in a position to disapprove of his habits, and with the man's money dangling in front of him.

Dangling out of reach, as it turned out.

If Flint cursed anything, it was the fact that none of them had made any moves to have Blake officially declared dead before now. Indeed, why hadn't Gideon done it himself?

He had ten years, for God's sake. It's not like he didn't know...

And when Virginia had finally set the ball rolling, the first thing they were obliged to do was put a notification of intent in the newspaper covering the area of the would-be deceased's last-known address. None of them had suspected for a moment that anyone would come forwards in response to the discreet announcement.

Or that she'd be convincing enough to get this far...

She'd even consented without a qualm to the DNA test demanded by the solicitor, which made Flint nervous. That should have been the clincher – the thing that made her run for the hills.

He couldn't quite figure it out.

After all, Blake was dead.

Definitely, *definitively*, dead.

He'd helped to bury the damned body himself.

So how the hell was she back at Claremont, sleeping in her old bedroom, and causing such mayhem?

He poured another slug of whisky, disappointed to find he was down to the dregs. He let go of the bottle, watched it drop and was mildly surprised when it rolled away across the brick floor without smashing.

'Hah, can't never catcha break – *break*, geddit?' And he giggled at his own joke, stumbling as he turned away.

As he did so, he caught a flash of movement beyond the open doorway.

Not just movement, but something red.

A figure in a red jacket, with a hood – moving fast.

His heart bounded in his chest, stuttered, then galloped on in a staccato rhythm that made him tremble with every beat.

He glanced down at the empty whisky bottle, as if that was to blame for this hallucination. But he knew it wasn't.

'Yer don' scare me *that* easily y'know!'

Flint lurched towards the opening, staggering as he tripped over the line of slightly raised bricks. He made it to the doorway and clung to the frame. As he stared out into the rain, he saw a blur of red just as it disappeared around the corner of the building.

Without thinking through the options – or outcomes – he rushed out, squinting as the droplets splashed into his face, his eyes. He reached the corner and was around it before it occurred to him that there might be an ambush waiting.

He found nothing on the other side.

Eyes straining ahead into the darkness, he had a sudden flashback to ten years ago. To another cold and rainy night, in another wood. His shiver had little to do with the weather, and everything to do with the icy fingers that clawed past his belly button and clenched tight around his guts.

Panting now, he ran on, the drink making him heavy, strides uneven and slow. He could barely see the path that led from the stables back to the rear lawn. It meandered through the trees. Every now and again, up ahead, he caught a glimpse of that red jacket, tauntingly near but far.

'I don' believe in ghosts!' he shouted. 'You're dead an' buried. Dead an' buried. Know that, don' I? *There*, wasn' I?'

His feet hit a half-submerged tree root. He flailed, arms outstretched, but couldn't keep his balance, falling heavily. His temple bounced off an embedded rock and the world crazed around him.

Flint wasn't sure how long it took for his mind to partially clear. He lay still, rolled only his eyes upwards and became aware of a figure approaching.

He called out, 'Ed? That you? You know, don'cha? *You*, 'f all people.'

Flint giggled again, blinking at the rain that was splashing up from the muddy ground. The figure was now looming over him, silently. He frowned, flapped a hand vaguely. 'Ah, giz'a hand up, eh?'

FORTY-THREE

Blake was up in her room. She absolutely refused to move out of the house until she was forced to, but she recognised that it was wise to keep away from both Virginia and her brother. Their attitude since Julian Rolle departed had been arctic.

Strangely enough, the only person who seemed remotely at ease with the revelation that she might be the sole heir to the estate was Virginia's son, Tom. She was still trying to work out why.

Her phone buzzed with an incoming text message. For a moment, Blake considered ignoring it. Only idle curiosity made her pick the phone off the bedside table and thumb open the screen. When she saw the name of the sender, she swung her legs over the side of the bed and sat up abruptly.

omg i think he's dead!

Her first instinct was to bring up the number and dial, but she hesitated. Texts could be sent and received in situations when it wasn't easy – or safe – to talk.

where r u?

It seemed to take a long time for the response to come.

bk garden

She was already thrusting her arms into her hoodie, grabbing her boots, as she sent her own reply.

meet me garage

She flitted along the corridor and hovered for a second on the landing, leaning over the rail. From the drawing room downstairs she heard the sound of two voices. The tones mingled – anxiety and calm. It didn't take much to identify Virginia's as the anxious one, a little longer to make out Anne Harding, trying to reassure her about something.

What's she doing here?

Blake hugged the wall as she moved down the staircase, hopping over the squeaky treads as she went.

In moments, she was along the back hallway, shoved her feet into her boots and was out through the back door like a shadow.

The rain was coming down harder now. She didn't bother flipping up her hood – it wouldn't have done much to keep out the rain – and ran for the garage.

As she entered, her steps slowed. She stood without speaking while her ears adjusted, while she filtered out the sound of the rain outside. A quiet slither came from the other side of the cars.

'Blake?' The voice sounded breathless and panicked.

She turned as a thin figure emerged into the light bleeding in through the still-open doorway. Blake's heart lurched at the sight of the distinctive red coat, the hood covering the face. She stepped in, pushed the hood back to reveal cheeks wet with tears not rain.

'Calm down, Pauline,' Blake said, 'and tell me what happened.'

FORTY-FOUR

Byron's curiosity was piqued when Jane Hudson's patrol car turned in to Claremont's driveway. When an ambulance followed suit, he started the Merc and drove after it.

He pulled up on the gravel outside the front door, just as the paramedics unloaded a stretcher from the rear. Oliver Harding hovered impatiently nearby.

As Byron parked up and got out of his car, Hudson came to meet him.

'Who is it?' Byron asked before the officer could speak. 'Who's hurt?'

Hudson glanced at the ambulance crew. 'Roger Flint. Head injury. Virginia called me an hour or so ago – said her brother had gone charging off in a drunken temper and she was worried he hadn't come back, but I was tied up dealing with an accident. They found him at the edge of the woods.' She eyed Byron. 'I've only just got here. What brings you?'

'The ambulance passed me and I was… concerned.' All true, if patchily so. 'It's been the kind of day when I feared emotions might spill over into conflict.'

'Aye, isn't *that* the truth,' Hudson murmured. A gust of wind blew rain into her face and she ducked her head. 'Well, now you're here, you'd best come inside, I s'pose.'

She was not keen on the idea of his involvement, Byron thought. As they stepped through the front door, shaking the rain off their coats, Hudson put a hand on his arm and said quietly, 'The lassie was caught sneaking back into the house – after Flint was found. Won't say where she'd been or what she'd been doing.'

Byron raised his eyebrows, kept his tone dispassionate. 'You suspect she was responsible?'

Hudson scowled. 'I suspect her of all kinds of things, but – at the moment – suspicion is all I've got.'

They walked into the drawing room. Virginia was on a two-seater sofa with Anne Harding's wheelchair drawn up close. Anne was holding one of Virginia's hands. Virginia clutched a handkerchief in the other. The knees of her trousers were dark with rain.

Over by the window, separated by more than distance, sat Blake. She had her arms folded tight across her chest, tucking her hands into her armpits. Her hair and clothing were damp but she seemed unaware of the fact. At first, Byron wondered if she was in shock, but she glanced up as the two of them entered. Her gaze went from one to the other, clear-eyed and calculating.

Byron gave her a brief nod. Even as he did so, he wasn't entirely sure if it was of encouragement or merely a greeting. The corner of her lips quirked upwards, then straightened, too fleeting to be considered a smile. Nobody else looked happy at Byron's arrival.

'Who is with… the patient?' he asked, preventing himself from referring to Flint as 'the victim' just in time.

'Ed Underhill.' It was Anne Harding who answered. 'He arrived a little before we did, and he and Oliver went out to search for Roger. Poor man…'

'If the ambulance is here, I should go with my brother to the hospital,' Virginia said suddenly.

'Of course, darling,' Anne said. 'I'll stay with the children.'

Byron waited a moment for Hudson to intervene. When she didn't, Byron glanced at Virginia and asked, 'You've been outside yourself this evening, Mrs Fitzroy?'

She flushed. 'Of course. You don't think I'd just sit here while my brother was missing on a night like this, do you?'

Byron looked pointedly at Hudson, who took the hint. 'I'm sorry, but I'm afraid that until Mr Flint's condition – and the circumstances surrounding his injury – have been established, I must ask everyone to stay here.'

Virginia's gaze went straight to Blake, who ignored it. 'But, *surely*—?'

'It's the standard procedure, Mrs Fitzroy – nothing against you personally,' Byron put in, his voice deceptively mild. 'I'm sure PC Hudson *will* be explaining the same thing to Mr Harding and Mr Underhill, in the event that they should wish to accompany your brother…'

He left the words hanging. Hudson hesitated, frowning, then realised the corner she'd been backed into. 'Er, yes. I'll just go and have a word.'

'Well, *really*.' Once Hudson had left, Virginia glared at Byron. 'And why don't you ask *her* where she's been, out in the grounds, hm? I hardly think it was anywhere out of concern for Roger's welfare.'

Byron turned, caught Blake's eye.

'I went only as far as the garage,' she said, her voice a little too sedate. 'I was out on the bicycle earlier – had a ride over to Carsington – and thought I might have left the lights on.'

Virginia managed to contain her disbelief to a loud snort. For once, Byron had some sympathy for the woman. He didn't like being lied to, either.

'And had you?'

'Had I what?'

'Left your lights on?'

'No, as a matter of fact. Which is why I was gone only for a few minutes. Hardly enough time to get to Roger – even if I'd known where he was – bash his head in, and get back here.'

'You *say* you were only gone a matter of minutes,' Virginia muttered, 'but as nobody saw you leave, who knows what time you actually went out.'

Blake got to her feet, crossed the room in a few strides. She covered the ground at surprising speed, while never appearing to hurry, until she had closed in on Virginia.

'Let's see your hands.'

'Excuse *me*. I don't have to—'

'No, you don't, but it will be quicker and less painful all round if you just shut up and do it.'

Virginia opened her mouth, closed it again, and held out her hands, palms downward. She wore dark red polish that hid any dirt lurking under her fingernails. Blake made a circling motion with her finger and, after a moment's continued stubbornness, Virginia turned both hands over.

Blake leaned in and pointed without making contact. 'Mud, leaf mulch, and lichen.'

'What did you expect? I was searching in the woods!'

'Searching under rocks, were you? Well, you know your brother best. But I would have thought – if he's still anything like I remember – that if anyone had it in for your brother, it would be one of the loan sharks he used to go to, in order to pay his gambling debts…'

Blake turned away from her, facing Byron now. Her stare issued a challenge. She spread her hands, showing him both sides. They were clean.

'And if anyone wanted to bash anyone else's head in, around here,' Blake continued, 'I'd have put my money on Roger having a go at me.'

FORTY-FIVE

It was well after midnight when Ed Underhill climbed into his car to drive home. Virginia Fitzroy had dragged in not only him, but also her son Tom, Kenneth from the pub, and the neighbours, Oliver and Anne Harding, to help search the grounds for Roger Flint. It had been Tom who'd eventually stumbled across him.

They'd done what they could to keep him warm and dry. Underhill was left to stand guard over Roger Flint's unconscious body, holding an oversize golf umbrella to keep the worst of the rain off both the victim and the scene. Not that there was much of a scene left to preserve, after the searchers had trampled it and the rain had done its bit.

By the time the ambulance crew turned out, negotiated their wheeled stretcher across the back lawn and along the path towards the stables, Underhill was soaked to the skin.

Virginia was appreciative enough, sitting him in front of the fire with a slug of brandy in his tea, providing him with dry clothes. Her brother was a skinny runt of a man, so Underhill ended up wearing one of her husband's Tattersall shirts and a pair of old corduroys. No doubt part of Fitzroy's country squire wardrobe.

It felt unsettling, putting on dead man's clothes, but better than sitting around sodden to his boxer shorts. Virginia hadn't offered those – and he hadn't asked – so he dressed without and trusted she wouldn't strip him before he left.

It unsettled him, also, that Byron turned up along with the paramedics. Who chased after ambulances in this neck of the woods? Which made the man's appearance seem a lot more *planned* than it might otherwise have done.

Driving into the outskirts of the village, Underhill made a mental note to ask Jane a lot more questions about her old mentor. And he recalled a mate who'd ended up in the Met. They'd lost touch over the last few years but that didn't mean Underhill couldn't make a casual phone call, re-establish contact and see what he knew about this Byron bloke.

He turned off the main street onto the lane where his cottage had stood for three hundred years, only to come to an abrupt halt.

Further along the lane, one of the houses was ablaze. The whole property was fully alight on both floors. Flames clawed at the windows as black smoke poured out from under the roof tiles. He swallowed to clear the sudden lump in his throat.

He had his window open a crack and he could smell it then – the bitter tang of ashes and ruin. In the distance came the first faint wail of sirens.

FORTY-SIX

Jane Hudson took off her cap as she walked into the pub. She'd never much liked hats, and it wasn't lost on her that she'd chosen two careers that required them to be worn as part of the uniform. Still, police regulations allowed officers to remove their headgear inside vehicles or buildings, provided it was safe to do so. She reckoned the village pub did not count as a danger zone.

She found Ed Underhill sitting over the remains of an early breakfast.

'Morning, Ed. Sorry to hear about the fire. It's lucky you weren't home in bed.'

Underhill gave a morose grunt. 'Don't think *luck* had much to do with it.'

'Oh, aye?'

Hudson kept her tone casual and friendly, but Underhill gave her a sharp look.

'Come on, lass. You must have already had a word with the fire investigator. I mean, I'm no expert, but I was a copper long enough to spot arson when I've had me nose rubbed in it.'

'I must say, it looks like *somebody's* got it in for you. No attempt to be subtle, so the bloke tells me – just petrol splashed about downstairs and a match. Any thoughts on how they gained entry?'

Underhill flushed. 'I don't have a letterbox, so I leave the kitchen window on the latch – for the postman. Plenty big enough for someone to climb through, if they'd a mind to.'

'Any ideas who might be responsible?'

For a second she thought Underhill was going to launch into a rant. But then the man seemed to deflate, his shoulders rounding as he reached for his teacup. He shook his head without speaking.

'No thoughts at all?' Hudson asked, surprised. 'I mean, was it a serious attempt, even? Or a warning of some sort that just… got out of hand?'

'Your guess is as good as mine, lass.'

But Hudson didn't miss the way Underhill shifted uneasily in his chair, as if holding his peace on the subject required actual physical effort.

'Is there… any chance the attack on your place was connected with what happened to Roger Flint?'

'Why should there be a connection?' Again, Underhill's tone was hostile enough to surprise Hudson.

Still, poor bloke's just lost his home and everything in it. Can't blame him for being prickly.

'Just the fact they both happened on the same night, that's all. You, of all people, know how quiet it is around here, Ed. Then suddenly we get two serious incidents happening at once.'

'Aye, yeah, sorry. It's just…' He shrugged, dredged up a half-hearted smile. 'I'm still trying to get my head around it, eh?'

'Of course.'

'They won't let me go in to see what's left. Said the stairs were mostly gone and the floor joists might give way at any time. Old timbers, see – the place went up like a Roman candle.'

Hudson raised her eyebrows. 'They've been on to you already, have they?'

'I was there most of the night, to be honest.'

'Well, at least the fire people were able to stop it spreading, or the whole row could have gone up. That's *one* good thing, anyway.'

'S'pose so. They've moved the neighbours out on each side, though. As a precaution – just until a structural engineer can take a look.'

'And do you have anywhere you can go, while all this is sorted out?'

Underhill nodded towards the kitchen. 'Kenneth and Vera have said I can stay here until the insurance has something sorted out.'

Almost on cue, the landlady herself swept in, coffee pot in hand.

'Oh, hello, Jane. Isn't it dreadful?' she said, with the glee reserved for disasters that occur to other people. 'Whatever's happening to this village? It's turning into a proper hotbed of scandal and vice. Would you like some coffee?'

Hudson nodded in general acceptance of all her questions. 'Ed's just told me you've invited him to stay here. That's very decent of you.'

She brushed that aside. 'Least we could do.' Underhill's table was set for two and she poured coffee into the second cup. 'But what news of Roger Flint? How is the poor man?'

'Fractured skull and borderline hypothermia. He's stable, but hasn't yet regained consciousness.'

'Well, thank goodness you all found him in time. My Kenneth came back absolutely drenched and chilled to the bone, poor thing. And poor Virginia! First her husband, then all that business with the will, and now her brother… Do you know who might have done it?'

Hudson shook her head, determinedly noncommittal. 'Still piecing together what happened.'

The outer door opened at that moment and the thin figure of Pauline appeared, weighed down with folded sheets. She came to an abrupt halt when she saw them all, muttered, 'I'll go round the back,' and fled again.

Hudson couldn't help but feel sorry for the cleaner as Vera tutted ominously and disappeared in the direction of the kitchen, no doubt on an intercept course.

She added milk to her coffee and took a sip, letting the silence stretch between them. As if reading her thoughts, Underhill glanced over briefly, then let his eyes slide away.

'Sorry about Roger,' he said gruffly. 'Meant to ask about him, but... problems of my own, you know?'

'I understand.'

'What's the prognosis?'

Hudson shrugged. 'Wait and see, basically. One of the first things they had to do when they got him to hospital was pump his stomach. He'd downed the best part of a bottle of scotch, so they reckon. It was a toss-up if that or the head injury got him first.'

'Who are they sending to lead the investigation, or is Khan going to handle it from Ashbourne?'

'Well, at the moment, Inspector Khan's in charge but anything official is on hold. The CSIs have gone over the scene but, to be honest – what with every man and his dog trampling through the woods last night during the search, plus the paramedics dealing with Flint in situ, and the rain – there's not much viable evidence they could gather. And, of course, he was so drunk that it's not out of the question to suggest he might just have fallen and hit his head. And... budgets – you know how it is.'

Underhill looked about to protest but then he simply nodded. He had, as he'd already pointed out, been a copper for a long time. Long enough to recognise the realities of the situation.

'Still, the bright side of that – if you can call it a bright side – is that I can concentrate on finding out who firebombed your house.'

'You might want to ask—'

Whatever suggestion he'd been about to make died as the outer door opened again. The young woman claiming to be Blake Claremont came through. Hudson noticed the slightest hesitation when she saw the two of them sitting together, then she nodded and closed the door behind her.

'Morning,' she said, unzipping her hoodie. 'Sorry to hear about your misfortune, Mr Underhill. Sounds like it was quite a night for upset all round.'

Underhill seemed to focus on her as the hoodie fell open and some kind of necklace – a pendant, maybe – came into view. Hudson saw his eyes widen, then narrow. He jerked to his feet and, before Hudson could react, he lunged for Blake's throat.

FORTY-SEVEN

Byron heard the noise erupt when he was halfway down the staircase. He took the remaining flight three at a time and burst through the door into the room at the front of the pub where breakfast was served.

The sight that greeted him was of Blake on the floor with Ed Underhill on top of her, his hands tugging at her neck. Byron started forwards, just as the young woman managed to reach up and get her fingernails into the soft flesh behind Underhill's ear. He let out a roar of pain as she yanked him sideways and sent him sprawling.

Underhill might have gone back for round two, but Jane Hudson dodged in then, got a grip on one arm and shoulder, keeping him down. Underhill continued to struggle.

'What the *hell* is going on here?' Byron demanded, his voice icily calm.

Both froze in automated response. Blake took advantage of their immobility to jack to her feet. She stood, tense – ready to fight rather than run.

Byron had spent the early hours reading the reports the commander had sent through on Hope Glennie. He remembered the social worker's impression that she might become dangerous. At that moment, he was inclined to agree.

Regardless of who she really is…

He stepped deliberately between the young woman and Underhill, forcing her gaze to shift onto him.

'Are you all right?'

She shook herself, little more than a twitch. 'Yes, I think so…'

But as she spoke, her hands went to her throat, patting the collar of her shirt as if checking for something no longer there. Byron just had time to glimpse the panic in her eyes as she rounded on Underhill.

'Where is it?' she demanded.

'Where's what?' Underhill's jaw jutted. 'Not yours, anyhow.'

'It belonged to my mother, and now it's mine,' she said, voice gritted with fury. 'Give. It. *Back*.'

Byron's eyes flicked from one to the other, then landed on the officer still restraining Underhill. Hudson, perhaps in answer to Byron's unspoken question, tightened the lock she had on Underhill's arm. Underhill held out a few seconds longer, then capitulated with a grunt, the fingers of his left hand opening almost against their will. An oval locket on a broken chain dropped to the floor with a clatter.

Blake sprang for it but Byron was closer. He picked up the locket, felt the weight and the age of it. He glanced at the man on the floor, one eyebrow raised.

'I don't suppose you'd care to explain your behaviour, Mr Underhill?'

Underhill took a breath, his face contorted. Then he seemed to wilt. Sensing all the resistance had gone out of him, Hudson manhandled him up into a chair and released her hold. Byron waited a beat. No one spoke.

He flicked open the locket's catch with his thumb. As he did so, he noted out of the corner of his eye that Blake gave a twitch of protest but she, too, said nothing.

Inside the locket was a small black-and-white photograph of a young woman. She was laughing, her head thrown back. The style of dress suggested the picture had been taken maybe thirty years previously. He studied the features, but it was hard to see from the angle if there was any family resemblance he should be able to spot.

Byron snapped the locket shut again and held it up. 'Not quite your style, I wouldn't have thought, Mr Underhill. So…?'

'It's mine,' Blake said tightly. She stepped forwards a pace. 'And I'd like it back, please.'

'Nicked it, more like,' Underhill muttered.

'Oh? From whom?'

'Well…' Underhill's gaze flitted between them. He shrugged a sullen shoulder. 'Stands to reason, don't it?'

'Am I to assume that you… recognise this item?'

Underhill cleared his throat. 'Yeah, it's… it's part of a haul reported taken during a robbery – a few years back – by the looks of it.'

'In that case, what's in it?'

His mouth opened, closed again. He scowled. 'Why don't you ask *her* that?'

'Because if she arrived here wearing this locket, it would be reasonable to assume that Ms Claremont is already well aware of what it contains. If you're going to accuse her of theft, then the least you could do would be to accurately describe what's inside, don't you think?'

'Could've changed it, couldn't she?'

Byron sighed. 'Even if you were still wearing the uniform, Mr Underhill, you know as well as I do that you can't simply confiscate personal property on so flimsy a pretext.' He glanced pointedly to Hudson. 'Or is that how modern policing works in Derbyshire?'

'Absolutely not,' she said quickly.

Byron nodded. He held out the locket towards Blake. She reached for it almost tentatively, as if expecting him to snatch it away again at any moment.

'Thank you,' she murmured.

'Good. Unless there's anything else, I think I'd rather like my breakfast now – preferably without a side order of drama.'

FORTY-EIGHT

Hudson hustled Underhill outside before the older man wrenched his arm free.

'What on earth was that all about, Ed?' she demanded.

He rounded on her. 'Never mind about that. What's the story with Byron?' he demanded. 'I mean, I know the lads from the Met all think they're something special, but he takes pushy to a whole new level.'

Hudson opened her mouth and closed it again. 'Mr Byron wasn't being pushy, Ed – even you have to admit you were completely out of order in there.'

Underhill scowled, admitting nothing. 'What's he doing still hanging around, anyway?'

'If he wants to spend a few days away from London, you can't blame him for that. He's supposed to be off sick, after all.'

That earned her a sharp glance. 'What d'you mean "supposed to be"?'

'Well, as far as I know, he is.' She tried to shrug it off, eyeing the man who'd become her friend with concern. 'But what were you on about with that locket? I thought I'd looked through all the outstanding local cases and I don't remember any lockets being taken.'

'It's…'

Hudson waited, but even as he began, Underhill seemed to run out of steam.

'It's what?'

Underhill rubbed a tired hand across his face. He'd been loaned a change of clothes and showered, Hudson noted, but a faint whiff of smoke still clung to him.

'I'm dead on my feet, Jane,' he admitted. 'Probably not thinking clearly. I'm… sorry. For being a pain in the backside, eh.'

'No problem, mate. You've been through a hell of an ordeal. Be enough to make anybody go off the rails a bit.'

'Yeah. Thanks for understanding.'

But as she turned away, Hudson said, 'It might be an idea to apologise to Blake, though. You'll be lucky if she doesn't press charges.'

Underhill swung back, eyes narrowed. 'Not a chance in hell.'

FORTY-NINE

Byron ordered his usual breakfast. He invited Blake to join him, but she asked merely for coffee, then sat in silence while he ate, staring into her cup without drinking.

'I thought one was supposed to use tea leaves to foretell the future,' he said.

She lifted her head, frowning. 'Hm?'

Byron put down his knife and fork, neatly together on his empty plate. 'Do you want to talk about it?'

'Not particularly.'

He inclined his head in acknowledgement. 'In that case, you're doomed to listen whilst *I* talk.'

That raised a half-hearted smile. 'Ah. A fate worse than death.'

He rested his elbows on the tabletop and regarded her over the rim of his own cup.

'For what it's worth, I don't believe you fractured Roger Flint's skull with a rock. Not that I think you aren't more than capable of it, mind you.'

'Thank you – I think.' She pulled a face. 'And what makes you so sure I didn't do it?'

'The evidence. For one thing, your clothes last night were spotted with rain rather than wet through – consistent with your story of going only as far as the garage, without a coat.'

'I told you—'

'On the other hand, that tale about thinking you might have left your bicycle lights on was laughable.'

That threw her, just for a second. 'I would have said "feasible" at least.'

'Then we must agree to differ,' he said briskly. 'So, are you going to tell me what it was about your appearance here this morning that provoked Ed Underhill into attacking you, by the way?' He put down his cup, his eyes on her face for tells. She would have made a good poker player, he decided. It was determinedly blank. 'And whilst I am… dubious, shall we say, of his claims about your locket being swag from an old robbery, there was certainly *something* about it that disturbed him. So, what was that, hm?'

'Who uses the word "swag" anymore? Are you certain you're a policeman?'

'Stop deflecting,' he said sternly, but couldn't help a smile.

She made pretence of contrition. 'Sorry. But I'm not entirely sure *why* he reacted so strongly to…'

But from the way her voice trailed off and she suddenly stilled, Byron knew she had indeed thought of a reason. One which, unless he read her wrongly, she was not about to share.

'Blake—'

'All finished, are we?' Vera came bustling in, her eyes darting between them, alight with curiosity. 'Can I get either of you anything else?'

'Not for me, thank you.'

'I'm fine.'

The landlady chattered as she began clearing the tables, filled with all the gossip about the fire and Roger Flint's misfortune, so further conversation was impossible. They both stood, silently, moving out of her way.

As Vera swept from the room with her first armload of cutlery and crockery, Byron cocked his head and said quietly, 'If you'd care to come upstairs, I may have something of interest to show you…'

Her eyebrows went up in faux shock, lips curving. 'Is this, by any chance, a variation on "come up and look at my etchings"?'

'And who uses the word "etchings" anymore?'

She was still grinning when he unlocked the door to his room and ushered her inside. Then, as if shrugging off a costume, she turned to face him, all business.

'So, what do you have for me?'

'Before we get to that,' he said, closing the door behind them, 'I suppose I have to ask… Did you firebomb Ed Underhill's cottage?'

All the air seemed to suck out of the room. She was silent for a moment, holding his gaze straight and level. 'If you really do have to ask, then you're hardly going to believe me when I say that no, I did not. Are you?'

Byron considered her answer. 'Perhaps.'

'OK, in that case, *I* have a question for *you*. Do you believe I am who I say I am?'

He considered that, too. And then said, again, 'Perhaps.'

'You don't believe me,' she said flatly, 'so why would you trust me?'

'I could say that the same applies. *You* don't trust *me*, either.'

'Trust has to be earned!'

'And therein lies the problem. Clearly, you've learned that lesson the hard way. You've been let down – betrayed, even. So now you trust no one and are proud of your own self-reliance, yes?' His voice became clipped as he detached himself from his own words.

She gave a cautious nod, obviously wary of being lured into a position she might not be able to defend – or get out of.

'The trouble with that is, by definition, no one can ever trust you, either. If the only person you trust is yourself, then that's the only person you look out for. Everyone else is of no importance.'

'I—'

Byron knew he should shut up but at the same time he wanted – no, needed – to make her jump the rails of the line she was taking. He wasn't sure why it was suddenly imperative to convince her. Maybe that was something he needed to examine, but not now.

'And when you do, finally, find someone who might just be worth trusting, you make them work *twice* as hard to prove themselves, and you run the risk they're going to decide you're a lost cause after all, and bail out on you. Thus completing another cycle of your own self-fulfilling prophecy.'

Blake stared at him with something very like distress in her eyes, her face, her hands. As he watched, she fumbled into one of the nearby chairs and sat, her movements devoid of certainty and grace.

'Is that what you wanted to show me?' she asked then, her voice shaky. 'To hold up a mirror to all my deficiencies of character?'

'Deficiencies? Good God, no. I think you're probably one of the strongest people I've ever met.'

'So, why—?'

'I'm merely trying to make you see that, whatever you're trying to achieve here – maybe I could… help.'

She blinked at him, then gave a raw laugh. 'Damn it, Byron, if that's how you go about offering a favour, I'd hate to see you make a threat.'

He took the chair opposite, sitting forwards, intent, with his knees only inches from hers. 'You seem to forget that I have already trusted you with my reasons for being here in the first place. You could have disseminated that information and shut me down in an instant. But you didn't.'

She favoured him with a cool assessing eye. 'It might not have suited my purpose to do so… yet.'

'Quite. So, in an attempt to persuade you that I am more use as an ally than a sacrifice, I'm going to share the latest intel.' He paused, as if giving himself a final chance to back out. Then he said, 'What can you remember about a girl called Hope Glennie?'

FIFTY

When Pauline pushed open the door into the ladies' toilets, half an hour later, her arms filled with cleaning products, Blake was waiting for her. She had been leaning on the cast iron radiator under the window, listening to it tick and gurgle, as if the pub's ancient heating system was trying to send out a message in Morse code.

'Flippin' 'eck!' Pauline yelped, letting slip her mop and bucket with a clatter. She gave a quick, nervy smile. 'You nearly gave me a heart attack.'

'We need to talk.'

Pauline glanced automatically over her shoulder. 'What – here?'

'Uh-huh.'

'Is this about… last night? I told you I didn't actually do anything, like. You said Roger Flint was the weakest link and I just wanted to shake him up a bit, y'know? Give him a push—'

'This is nothing to do with Flint. This is about Ed Underhill. Or – more particularly – his cottage.'

Pauline wouldn't meet her eyes. 'Oh.'

'"Oh." Is that all you can say?' Blake turned away, fisting both hands into her hair in frustration. She took a couple of quick strides and spun back. 'For heaven's *sake*, Pauline. Burning down the man's house was not part of the plan!'

Not yet, anyway…

'He deserves it – and the rest...' Pauline took in an uneven breath, pressed her lips together to stop them quivering. 'You didn't hear him.'

'Underhill?'

'No – Roger. I mean, he was rambling, not making much sense, but he was shouting about how he knew "she" was dead – "dead and buried" – because he was *there*. And then he called Ed's name.' She started to tremble, wrapping her thin arms around her waist. 'How could I just do nothing, after that?'

Blake's anger collapsed like a punctured balloon. She put her arms around the woman's bony shoulders, pulled her tight and held on. For a few moments they stood like that, rocking.

'Well, at least now we know what happened to her,' Blake said, her voice drier than dust. She disengaged gently. 'But *knowing* isn't enough, is it? If we're going to find out the rest of it, we *have* to stick to the plan.'

'Yeah.' Pauline hung her head, sniffed. 'Yeah, I'm sorry.'

'And you're sure you didn't see who it was – who got to Flint?'

Pauline shook her head. 'Like I told you, I had me head down and was running by that time. Scared stiff of getting caught.' She frowned, bit her lip. 'Maybe I should've hung about, like, tried to see—'

'No. You're taking more than enough risks in all this. You did the right thing by getting away.'

Or there might be two of you in Intensive Care right now.

'I can't say I'm sorry about the fire.' Pauline's chin firmed, her mouth a thin line. 'But I am sorry if it's caused you more trouble. Vera said Ed had a right go at you, just before. It gave me such a fright when I came in this morning and saw him sitting there. It were like he was waiting for me. And then Vera said he tried to strangle you!'

'That wasn't about the fire – not as such.' Blake reached into her pocket, brought out the locket on its broken chain. 'He saw me wearing this, and went ballistic.'

Pauline paled as she reached for the locket, then recognised it and pulled her hand back, as if afraid to touch. Afraid of what it signified.

'I don't understand... Why?'

Blake turned the locket over in her hand, smoothing her thumb across the engraved pattern. 'We both had one. It made us feel... connected.' She gave a sad smile. 'Like we were sisters, in every way that mattered.'

Pauline put her hand on Blake's arm. 'Ed Underhill must have seen the other locket – maybe even on the night when...' She swallowed. 'That night.'

'I wondered about that earlier. Why would he react the way he did, unless...?' Blake held up the locket. 'Unless he thinks there's only *one* locket, and this is it.'

'So he thinks... what? That you found it? That you found *her*...?'

Blake frowned. 'He must know that's not the case, or something else would have happened – he would have been arrested. No, I think he might have kept it as some kind of sick memento.'

'Ah, yeah. I saw a programme on the telly, a while ago – about some serial killer in America,' Pauline said suddenly. 'They never caught him while he was alive. But, after he died, his daughters were cleaning out his house and they found a box of odd trinkets – a single earring, a charm off a bracelet, stuff like that. One of his daughters, she takes the box to the police, and it turns out all these bits of jewellery, they're trophies from his victims. Some of them go back years.'

In her mind's eye, Blake replayed the scene with Underhill, his attack on her, his reactions afterwards. 'Yeah, I think he didn't just *see* the locket that night,' she murmured, more firmly now. 'He *took* it. And he's kept it, all these years.'

'And now he'll dump it, won't he? Because of what I did.' Pauline's face crumpled. 'Oh, I'm an idiot! I'm so sorry.'

'Don't be. Don't you see? He must have had it at the cottage. And now, thanks to you, he can't go back in there – the fire people won't let him. It's not safe.' Blake flashed her a huge smile. 'So, what you've actually done, my lovely, non-idiotic friend, is buy us a couple of days.'

Pauline smiled with her but it quickly died away. 'Supposing that's not it at all? Supposing, what I've really done, is destroy any evidence that linked Ed Underhill to murder…?'

'What's done is done. We've got to work with what we have. And, for the moment, what we have is Underhill believing we took this locket from somewhere inside his house, before we burned it. Otherwise, why would he be so desperate to get it back he actually physically attacked me?'

She watched Pauline chew it over, didn't try to hurry the process. At last, the older woman looked up with a little bit of courage in her features.

Blake hated to take it away again. She sighed.

'There's one more thing. PC Hudson is on the trail of… of Hope Glennie. She's been out to the Allbrights' farm, talked to the social worker. It's only a matter of time before she pulls on that thread hard enough to unravel it.'

Pauline swore softly. 'We always knew they *would* get there, I s'pose. Just didn't think it would be this quick…' Her head jerked up suddenly. 'You don't think they'll find anything out…? I mean, those old records are all sealed, aren't they?'

'If it was just Hudson, I'd say no,' she admitted, 'but it's this Byron who worries me.'

'He sees too much,' Pauline said dully. 'And you're right – he knows stuff he shouldn't…'

Blake nodded. 'Yeah, he does have that knack.' She didn't add that Byron's worst attribute, as far as they were concerned, was the fact the man seemed far too aware of what he didn't know.

He could somehow divine where his knowledge was lacking, and exactly what steps he needed to take in order to fill the gaps.

After all, from what she'd learned of John Byron, he'd become a detective superintendent before he turned thirty-five. That kind of senior rank couldn't be attained by nepotism or riding on the backs of others.

No, it took the kind of luck you made yourself by possessing single-minded determination, but – more than that – it took the kind of outstanding natural talent that came along once in a generation. She'd encountered enough coppers to know that Byron was by far the biggest threat she'd ever faced.

What scared her more was the pull she felt towards him, like a moth to the flame that will scorch its wings. And much as her instincts were screaming at her to get as far away as possible, before he uncovered all her darkest secrets, she knew that wasn't going to be possible. The only way she stood even the remotest chance of achieving what she'd come here to do was by getting as close to him as she dared.

FIFTY-ONE

It was past noon before Hudson made it back to her desk in the station at Ashbourne. She'd called in to see a farmer over near Callow, who'd had some machinery stolen. Then a member of a village hall committee on the other side of Winster, where they were having a problem with local kids breaking in to use the place as a drinking den. And so, the morning disappeared.

Ed Underhill's behaviour had been bothering her, on and off, since she'd left the pub. Now she had a chance to sit and think about it, it bothered her even more.

'What *is* it about the lassie that infuriates everyone she meets until they want to smack her one?' she wondered out loud.

'You do know that talking to yourself is supposed to be the first sign of madness, don't you?'

Inspector Khan's voice made her jump. Hudson flashed her superior a sheepish smile.

'Sometimes I find it's the only way to get a sensible conversation.'

Khan laughed, much to Hudson's relief. She didn't yet know the inspector well enough to predict how he was going to react, and there were times when the man's sense of humour had been known to fail him.

'What's the latest on Roger Flint's condition?' Khan asked.

'I spoke to one of his doctors on the way back here, boss. Still unconscious. No change. They've said they'll call me when he comes round.'

Khan's long face grew pensive for a moment. Hudson didn't have to be a mind reader to know what he was thinking.

If *Flint comes round...*

'And the fire at Ed Underhill's home?'

'Definitely arson, according to the fire investigator. He's waiting for a couple of lab tests on the accelerant and then he'll let us have his report. I went door to door with the neighbours, but it was a rotten night, so most of them were indoors with the curtains shut and the telly on.'

'See no evil, hear no evil, eh?'

'That seems to be the size of it, aye.'

Khan shook his head. 'I assume you spoke to Ed himself when you were over there this morning. Can *he* shed any light on who might be responsible?'

Hudson hesitated, thinking of Underhill's attack on Blake Claremont. If she said nothing, and it turned out the fire was the reason he'd attacked her, Khan was bound to ask some awkward questions. Hudson didn't believe for a moment the story about the locket – it sounded a little too much like a hastily thought-up excuse.

But Underhill had become more than just her predecessor, since Hudson had moved to Derbyshire. He was advisor, mentor, even something of a mate. And sometimes you had to overlook slightly odd behaviour, when your mates were involved, and trust that they'd level with you before the situation reached the official stage.

So, she shook her head and said, with a note of frustration she didn't have to feign, 'Not really. And he's fairly easy-going, from what I know of him – not the type to get into daft feuds with his neighbours, is he?'

This attempt at levity at least produced a fractional smile. 'No, he was a good officer to have around. Er, as are you, Jane, of course.'

'Thanks, boss.'

Khan nodded, as if – having dispensed his quota of compliments for the day – his duty was done. He started to turn away, then paused.

'Oh, one last thing. That DNA test we fast-tracked on the Claremont girl. Any sign of the results yet?'

'Not as far as I'm aware, although I've only just got back in myself.' She shuffled through her overflowing in tray, more in hope than expectation.

'Hm, well, chase it up, would you? No point in us paying through the nose for rush-processing if we're not going to be prompt about collection.'

Hudson thought that Virginia Fitzroy had offered to pay for the test but wisely kept that to herself. 'Yes, sir.'

'I'm sure one of the Valentino Rossi lads on a Traffic bike could be there and back in less than ninety minutes, if he put his mind to it.'

Hudson followed MotoGP motorcycle racing just enough to know who Valentino Rossi was. She smiled, and murmured her assent.

Khan left with the air of a man who had more important places to be. Hudson began to sort through her messages. She was almost at the bottom of the stack when she came across a return call from the adoption agency who had originally dealt with Hope Glennie. She pushed the other notes aside and dialled the number.

'Mr McDonald? My name is PC Jane Hudson from Derbyshire Constabulary, sir.' She pushed a cheerful note into her voice. 'I think we've been playing telephone tag.'

But McDonald, she quickly discovered, was not of cheerful disposition himself. In fact, by the end of their twenty-minute conversation, she'd decided the man was definitely one of life's drains rather than radiators.

She put the phone down feeling exhausted. The gist of what she'd learned was that, even if McDonald had been personally willing to provide the information Hudson sought, there were any one of half a dozen other – mostly bureaucratic – reasons why she couldn't have it. She got the feeling he'd been through the same spiel many times before.

Hudson swore quietly under her breath, scraped both hands over her face. Her eyes felt gritty, as if some of Underhill's smoke had found its way in.

'Jane Hudson?' asked a voice from the doorway.

Her head jerked up to see a tall woman in full motorcycle leathers, with the usual fluorescent police jacket over the top. She wore a white flip-face helmet with the front panel raised. Because of her height, the visor came perilously close to hitting the door frame.

'Er, aye, that's me,' she said belatedly. She searched her memory furiously. There weren't many female bike coppers in Derbyshire. 'Greta, isn't it?'

'It is,' she said, ducking into the office. 'Got a rush DNA test for you. Sign here, if you wouldn't mind?'

Hudson scrawled her signature across the required paperwork to preserve chain of custody.

'There you go. And thanks for getting this back so quickly.'

Greta grinned. 'No problem. It's not often I get to thrash the Yamaha flat out along the A38, so the pleasure's all mine.'

When the woman had gone, Hudson opened the packet and read the results, flipping to the summary rather than wading through the technical detail.

When she was done, she went back and read through it again.

Then she pushed back her chair and hurried to Inspector Khan's office. Yes, she'd struck out on one line of enquiry, but the paperwork in her hands might just make it a moot point anyway.

Khan's office door was propped open and the inspector himself was on the phone when Hudson appeared in the doorway. Khan looked up and beckoned her in while he wound up the call.

'Now then, Jane, what do you have?'

'Well, boss, I wasn't able to get anywhere on Hope Glennie's biological parents. Ran into a bit of a brick wall with the adoption people, I'm sad to say. If we want to progress it any further, I think it's going to take authorisation in writing and in triplicate.'

'Hm, I think we might hold off on that for the moment. At least until we can rule out our Blake Claremont as the genuine article.'

'The DNA test has just this minute come in.'

'And?'

Hudson handed across the lab report. 'See for yourself.'

FIFTY-TWO

Lily sighed. However much she wriggled, she couldn't stop the hard plastic hospital chair from digging into the backs of her thighs. And the temperature in the waiting room was so high it was putting her to sleep. She'd already shed her coat and scarf, and her woolly jumper. That left her in only a long-sleeve blouse, thick tights, and a knee-length skirt. There wasn't much further she could go.

Besides, she wasn't even sure there was any point in her being there in the first place. Of course her *mother* had wanted to be near Uncle Roger, after what happened, but Lily didn't see why she and Tom had to go, too.

Not until Uncle Roger came round, at any rate.

It wasn't even as if they were allowed to sit around his bedside. At the insistence of the police, the hospital had moved him into a private room. It was one right by the nurses' station, and nobody was allowed in without their say-so.

Her mother had, at one time, read a lot of medical romance novels where young, idealistic nurses swooned over tall, dark, handsome, but usually very rude and bad-tempered surgeons. Until recently, Lily had thought of the nursing profession as being filled with gentle creatures whose soft hands were designed for the mopping of fevered brows.

When she'd been taken to hospital after her stepfather's car crash, however, she had revised her opinion. The nurses had not been particularly young, nor startlingly pretty. They were kind enough in a brisk, no-nonsense sort of way, but always in a hurry, and tired. As she watched the staff now from her vantage point, she saw nothing to revise that view.

Tom told her that the reason they weren't allowed in to see Uncle Roger was because the police thought one of them – someone in the family – was responsible for bashing half his brains in. And if they were allowed near him, this person might try to finish him off.

Lily didn't quite believe him. After all, what earthly reason could she, or Tom – or their mother, for that matter – have to wish him harm? It was typical of Tom to come out with something like that. He was always making up the worst possible scenarios for any situation. Sometimes she thought he did it just to wind her up.

In fact, the only time he *hadn't* done that was over Gideon's accident. Now she thought about it, he hadn't come up with a single conspiracy theory about how or why their stepfather's car should have gone off the road so dramatically. Lily scowled in concentration. She wished she could remember more about that night, but much to her annoyance and frustration, it was still hazy.

She scratched absently at the skin of her forearm where it disappeared inside her cast. It itched almost constantly now and her skin was horrible, dry and flaky. Idly, she wondered if it was too early for them to take the cast off, and if perhaps she could get it done while she was here.

'Leave it *alone*, Lily,' her mother said automatically, her voice distracted. 'It will never get better if you keep worrying at it.'

'It *is* better. If it itches, that means it's mended. Honestly – I googled it.'

Tom said, 'Oh, well, if you read it on Google, it *must* be right then…'

She gave him a daggered glance. He managed to roll his eyes without shifting his attention from the screen of his phone. Lily had already used up her data allowance for the month so her own phone sat uselessly in her pocket.

Lily slumped and looked around her again, desperate for something – *anything* – to relieve the boredom. As if the fates were actually *listening* for once, she noticed a figure walking along the corridor towards them.

'Oh, look. It's PC Hudson. Is she here to see us?'

Her mother snapped upright in her chair, as if bracing herself. Hudson stopped a metre or so away. She looked unusually discomfited.

'Mrs Fitzroy,' she greeted, her voice cautious. 'Any news on Mr Flint?'

'Not as far as I know – but as well as being prevented from sitting at my brother's bedside, they're telling me very little about his condition. Is *that* on your instructions, too?'

Her voice had that icy note Lily often tried to emulate when she was navigating the politics at school of who was in and who was out. It was just as effective there as here.

PC Hudson flushed in the face of her disdain. She had her bowler cap clutched nervously between her fingers and had begun to sweat, although Lily wasn't reading too much into *that*. So had everyone else.

'Mrs Fitzroy, you must know that our first priority is to protect your brother. We'd be failing in our duty if we didn't take every precaution to keep him safe until we can talk to him about what happened.'

Her mother gave a long sigh, sounding as tired as the nurses. 'Yes. Yes, I *do* know that – and I *do* appreciate it. Please excuse my bad manners. It's been a particularly stressful few days, what with the funeral and everything. And then this girl…' Her voice trailed off and she glanced at the policewoman with quickening attention. 'Is *that* why you wanted to see me? The DNA test?'

'It is, ma'am.'

She hesitated and Lily's mother gave a tsk of irritation, her voice turning brittle. 'Oh, *please* – just get it over with!'

'Virginia, are you all right?'

Lily swivelled in her chair. With the drama unfolding in front of her, she hadn't noticed the Hardings' approach until Anne spoke.

Virginia stared at her friend without – it seemed to Lily – really seeing her, and answered, 'To be quite honest, Anne, I'm not sure…'

Anne wheeled forwards and took one of Virginia's hands in hers. Lily, not to be outdone, edged closer to her mother and gripped the cuff of her sleeve.

'Why are you here?' Lily asked, since it seemed nobody else was going to.

It was Oliver who smiled at her and lifted the cardboard tray he held, which contained three disposable coffee cups. In his other hand, he held two cans of Coke. 'Thought you might need something to drink – these places always make me thirsty.'

He handed the cans of Coke to Lily and Tom. They were straight out of a chiller cabinet, condensation forming around them. Lily opened hers gratefully and took a long swig, immediately giving herself hiccups.

Oliver dispensed two of the coffees to Virginia and Anne. The final one, he held out towards PC Hudson, although Lily knew he must have bought it for himself. Hudson shook her head.

'Thank you, sir, but I need to be on my way shortly.'

'I'm so sorry,' Anne said. 'We interrupted you, but I thought Virginia might like some company, and that perhaps we could take Tom and Lily home with us and give them some tea?'

'Yes, please,' Tom said instantly. He was at an age when he was always hungry. Lily's mother blamed it on his hormones.

'You were going to tell me about the girl,' Virginia said. 'About the results of the test…'

'It's a match,' Hudson blurted out, face reddening. 'The lassie is Mr Fitzroy's daughter. So, it would seem that she *is* Blake.'

Virginia's face went blank and she murmured, 'She is…?'

Oliver Harding said, 'Are they absolutely sure?'

Anne said, 'Well, it's obvious, isn't it, when you look at her…'

Lily said, 'Oh, wow. I have a sister!'

She looked at Tom – the only one who hadn't spoken – just in time to see a myriad of expressions flit across his face, from anger to relief, happiness to shame.

'Tom…?'

'"Sister."' He threw her a quick, contemptuous glance. 'Don't kid yourself.'

'Stop being mean!'

'I'm not.' He laughed. 'All that – for what? You haven't *gained* a sister. We'll be evicted before you know what's hit you. She's not going to want *you* around. She's not going to want *any* of us.'

FIFTY-THREE

Later the same afternoon, Ed Underhill was shopping in Belper town centre when his mobile rang. He juggled a fistful of bags from one hand into the other and dragged the phone out of his pocket. It was a London number, but not one he recognised, so he answered cautiously.

'Ed! It's Dan Lambert, mate. You left me a message to call you. How're you doing?'

'Oh, hi, Dan. I've been better, to be honest. How's life in the Met treating you?'

'Not getting any younger. Otherwise I can't complain. But what's up at your end?'

Underhill tucked himself into an empty shop doorway, out of the flow of foot traffic on the pavement. He explained about the fire. Lambert made all the right noises of shock and dismay.

'Have the Red Cross been round yet with your parcel of goodies?'

'Yeah, they have, thanks.' Underhill couldn't quite keep the bitter note out of his voice. Oh, he was grateful enough for a toothbrush and a few essentials, but being on the receiving end of charity – however well meaning – stuck in his craw.

Hence the fact he was in town now, shopping for new clothes. He'd keep his fingers crossed that the insurance reimbursed him before the next credit card payment was due.

'So, I assume you didn't call me up to reminisce about the good old days.' Lambert's voice turned businesslike. 'What can I do for you?'

'Well, I was hoping you might be able to fill me in with a bit of info on a detective superintendent from down your way?'

Lambert gave a snort. 'You do realise there are more than thirty thousand coppers in the Met, don't you? It's not like it is up there in the sticks – we don't all know each other personally.'

Underhill suppressed a sigh of both irritation and disappointment. 'Ah well, it was just on the off chance.'

'Hold on, hold on. Who is this bloke you're after?'

'A guy called Byron. I understand he—'

'Wait – not *John* Byron? Or maybe I should say, *the* John Byron?'

'That's him – why? Do you know him?'

'Know *of* him, mate. Of course I do. Bravest man in the service – poor bastard.'

'But… I'd never *heard* of him, before he turned up here.'

'Ah, that's not surprising. They hushed it up – stuck a D-notice on it, or something, so there was nothing in the media. But a couple of the guys I work with were there that day, and they saw it all go down…'

FIFTY-FOUR

Unaware that he was the subject of conversation, at that precise moment Byron himself was knocking on the front door of Claremont. He was not altogether surprised when there was no answer.

Nevertheless, he stepped out from under the portico and took his time staring up at the windows, including the one where he'd caught his first glimpse of Blake.

This time, there was no flicker of movement, no sign of life.

He had just admitted defeat and turned back towards his car, parked at the edge of the gravel, when his phone rang.

'I hear it's all got very exciting up there in Derbyshire,' Commander Daud said as he answered the call.

Almost on cue, Byron heard shotgun blasts in the middle distance. Yet another pheasant shoot. He paused a moment.

'You could say that, ma'am, yes.'

'Ever the understatement with you.' Her voice turned brisk. 'So, you got my email about the DNA results on Blake Claremont?'

'I did, thank you.'

'You don't sound surprised.'

'Well, either she knew it was going to be a match, or she should be making a fortune playing professional poker. I didn't pick up a single indication from her that she was worried about the test.'

'So, you're thinking she had no reason to lamp Roger Flint over the head, then?'

'I could envisage that anyone who was forced to spend time with the man might want to do that,' Byron said drily. 'But no, I don't think so.'

'Perhaps Flint was the one who tampered with the ladder to the hayloft, and she found out? It could have been tit for tat?'

He paused, staring out across the lawn towards the edge of the trees. 'Perhaps,' he allowed. 'Although, we could be approaching this from entirely the wrong angle. It could be that someone is targeting the whole family for whatever reason – starting with Fitzroy, then his stepdaughter, and now his brother-in-law.'

'We have more questions than answers, either way,' Daud muttered. 'What's it all got to do with Blake's reappearance, apart from the fact that it leaves Virginia Fitzroy financially out in the cold?'

'I don't know, but I think her return has been the catalyst, for whatever it is that's happening here.'

'Yeah, I got your email about Underhill jumping on her this morning. What was *that* all about? I don't buy his story about that locket being part of a robbery haul, any more than you did.'

'Hm, I get the feeling there's more to this than simply the money, as far as Blake is concerned. I just haven't quite got to the bottom of what that is yet.'

'Well, you watch your back. Just in case it's you poking about that's tipped someone into arson and attempted murder.'

'I will continue to sleep with one eye open,' he promised.

There was another pause, longer this time. Byron tried not to brace for the next question. It came anyway.

'All joking aside, Byron… *Are* you managing to sleep?'

'Some,' he lied.

'Hm, thought not. I can hear it in your voice. You don't sleep when you're onto something. That wasn't my intention, in sending you up there. I know what you went through and I never want to put you in a position where… Well, you know.'

'I do know.' He took a breath. 'If that's all, ma'am—?'

'Hang on, sunshine. I'm not done yet.'

'Oh?'

'You asked me to find out what I could about Hope Glennie. And – in particular – the details about her biological parents.'

'Which you've now done,' he guessed, allowing the admiration to trickle through his voice.

'Which I have now done,' Daud agreed. 'And it could give a bit of a new perspective on things, I can tell you.'

FIFTY-FIVE

Blake had cycled into Wirksworth at lunchtime. Partly this was to get away from the atmosphere in the village. Without anything actually being said out loud, she could sense that blame for the fire at Underhill's cottage was being pointed in her direction.

In some ways, she could see the logic. After all this time away, she was a stranger here, and people usually prefer to believe that unpleasant acts are carried out by strangers rather than friends, neighbours, or people they see every day.

Virginia Fitzroy and her children were at the hospital in Derby, waiting for news on her brother's condition. It was clear that Virginia had not been happy about leaving Blake in the house on her own. Nor did she particularly want to take her along – not that Blake herself wanted to go.

On *that* point, at least, they were in agreement.

She had thought that she might spend some time with the Hardings, but there was no reply when she arrived at their house and knocked on the door. The pickup was in the driveway, but the minivan was not. Belatedly, she realised that they, too, were likely to be at the hospital.

She thought of seeking out Byron, but shied away from the temptation.

Because that's exactly what it was – a temptation. A desire to take him up on his offer of alliance, made precisely at a moment she was feeling at her most vulnerable.

At her most alone.

It had genuinely shocked her, what Pauline had done to Underhill's cottage the night before. Shocked, but not surprised. Pauline had held in so much, for so long, that Blake could not be taken aback when some of it came festering to the surface now, just as the end was within their grasp. The last thread to snap always lasted longer than you expected it to, then went without warning.

Not long to go now. Just keep your head, and it will all be OK…

She kept those words going to herself, round in a continuous loop.

So she had looked for something to keep herself busy and distracted. When Byron had driven her through Wirksworth two days before, she recalled seeing a small jeweller's shop on the main street. Taking advantage of a break in the dreary rain, she cycled the two or three miles, only to find it was early closing day. She had a coffee in one of the cafés, enjoying the anonymity, before pedalling back.

As she climbed the long hill, standing up to lean into the grade, she could hear the occasional blast of shotguns across the fields. She cycled past the church and started up the main street, then was overcome with curiosity. She cut off to the left, into one of the narrow lanes that led past Ed Underhill's cottage.

Initially, the damage didn't look too bad. The structure was still standing, its roof intact. But when she got closer, she saw the blackened stonework around the windows on both floors. Sodden curtaining still clung to what was left of the frames. A scattering of burned and broken furniture had been piled up on the opposite side of the road. The acrid tang of smoke hung in the air like a bad mood.

Blake heard a door slam and caught movement further along the lane. One of the neighbours had come out into his tiny front garden and stood there, making no secret of watching her, his arms folded as if expecting trouble. Not wishing to provoke any, she pushed off quickly and didn't ease up until she was heading out of the village again.

The lane was narrow, bordered by high hedges and she kept one ear out for other traffic. The noise of the guns was fainter now and, if she was any judge, further to the south of the village. She dismissed it from her mind.

Right up until the deafening discharge of a shotgun sent her wheeling into the dirt.

FIFTY-SIX

The noise of the shotgun was close enough to make Byron start. Even as his hands clenched around the steering wheel of his Mercedes, he berated himself for being way too jumpy. Sometimes, it was hard to remind himself what was considered normal and what was not.

Wary of meeting oncoming traffic, he was driving at little more than a walking pace, heading back from Claremont towards the village and the pub.

If he'd been going faster when he rounded the next blind corner and came upon the bicycle lying on its side in the middle of the road, he probably would have run over it.

He braked instantly, sat motionless for a moment while his eyes raked the scene and his thought processes accelerated. The road surface glistened with viscous mud and rain so that – if there was blood around the fallen bike – it was impossible to spot.

But, over to the right the hedge dipped back into a gateway that led to a ramshackle yard. The entrance had been laid with limestone chipping, packed down by heavy machinery. And there, across the pale stone, he saw a smear of red.

To the other side of the road was a metal gate into a field. He nosed the car forwards another couple of feet, opened his door and slid out, keeping below the level of the glass. He glanced towards the bicycle again.

This time, he recognised it. He ought to – he had lifted it into the rear of the Mercedes only a couple of days before.

'Blake?' he called. 'Are you all right?'

For a second or two there was silence, then her voice shouted back, 'More or less.'

She was somewhere in the muddy yard to his right. He scanned the gateway. Saw another smudge of blood, then cautious movement amid the foliage.

'What happened?'

'Call yourself a detective? Some bastard took a potshot at me, that's what.'

'Can you move?'

'Yes.'

'Good. Wait.'

He edged forwards, using the body of the Mercedes as a shield. Stretching out an arm, he managed to get his fingers onto the front wheel of the bicycle, dragging it out of the road and into the gateway. It grated across the tarmac, the end of one pedal and handlebar scraping the surface.

Byron scuttled backwards and pulled open the rear door on the driver's side.

'Blake?'

'Yeah?'

'Get in. Stay low.'

'You may have cause to regret that.'

'What?'

'You have cream upholstery.'

He let his breath out slowly, tried to keep the frustration out of his voice. 'Do I look like I give a *damn* about the leather? Just shut up and get in the car.'

There came a brief pause in which he could almost feel her bristling against the brusque order, then he heard her scuffle forwards out of the gateway. He waited until she had scrambled into the back seat, although his view of her was blocked by the door, before slamming it shut and hauling himself back behind the wheel. As he shifted the car into gear and put his foot down, he was aware, gratefully, that nobody fired at them.

He didn't stop to look back at her until they were almost into the outskirts of the village. Blake lay sprawled across the rear seat and did not appear to be noticeably injured.

'Do you need a hospital? A doctor?'

'No. A stiff drink will probably do it,' she said, but without the certainty he'd come to expect. She shifted, gave a wince. 'And if you have a first aid kit, I can sort myself out.'

He didn't reply to that as he moved off, more sedately this time. Shortly afterwards, he pulled up next to the pub. Blake was now upright in the back seat. He opened her door as he got out but she ignored the hand he offered, clambering stiffly out unaided.

'Here,' he said, passing her his room key. 'I have a medical kit in the boot. I'll meet you up there.'

She hesitated a moment before taking the key, as if doing so would commit her to something, then took it anyway.

'Thanks.'

She limped only slightly on her way to the door. Byron watched her go with narrowed eyes, aware of a rising anger. Both for her and for himself. He could feel his heart punching against his breastbone, knew that if he stretched out his fingers in front of him, they would be trembling.

He grabbed the kit from the spare wheel well under the boot floor, then followed her inside. As Byron climbed the stairs, he formulated and rejected excuses for her to be there, deciding the truth would probably raise the least objections. In the event, he met no one.

Blake had left the room door on the latch. When he pushed inside, he saw her jeans thrown over the back of a chair, and her hoodie on the end of the bed, boots on the floor next to it. The light shone from under the bathroom door. He tapped on it cautiously.

'Want some help?'

'I can manage,' she said, but it was an automatic response and she sounded weary.

'I'm well aware of that,' he said, speaking through the still-closed door. 'But I didn't ask if you *needed* help – it's obvious that you are quite capable. I asked if you *wanted* it.'

'In that case… Yes, please…'

He pushed the door open. Inside, Blake sat on the edge of the bath, stripped down to a skinny T-shirt and underwear. The outside of her right leg and arm was peppered with small bleeding wounds. She had filled the sink with water and was wiping the blood away with a washcloth.

Byron regarded her for a moment, kept his voice expressionless as he commented, 'You were lucky.'

'Doesn't feel like it from where I'm sitting. If I was "lucky", he would have missed altogether.'

'"He?"'

She shrugged. 'Figure of speech. Could just as easily have been "she".' Blake chucked the washcloth back into the sink and nodded to the medical kit. 'Do you have some antiseptic and a pair of tweezers in there?'

Byron unzipped the kit and opened it out.

'That looks very comprehensive,' Blake said as he rolled up his sleeves to scrub his hands. 'Do you always travel so well-prepared for trouble?'

Byron glanced at her. 'My wife was a doctor.'

'Oh… I didn't know you were married. I mean, there's no reason why you shouldn't be, of course, but—'

'She died.'

'Oh,' she said again. 'Oh, I'm… sorry. There are times when life really does suck, doesn't it?'

'Yes.' He wanted to say more, to expand, to explain, but found he couldn't quite bring himself to do so. Instead, he pulled a pair of needle-nosed tweezers out of the kit. 'Where would you care to start?'

'Take your pick.'

'Leg, then, I think.' He crouched in front of her, ran a careful hand up the outside of her right calf. The shot had only just penetrated the skin and lay close to the surface, from which he gathered it had been fired from some distance. 'You didn't see who did this, I assume?'

'No. Wasn't accidental, though.'

His turn to say, 'Oh?' as he stretched the skin tight and dug for the first pellet. It popped out with surprising ease, followed by a small trickle of blood. Byron dropped it into the spare water glass and searched for the next.

Blake's voice was only a little strained as she said, 'Whenever they used to hold shoots around here, there were beaters, a dozen other guns, warning signs on the field gates, and lumbering great four-by-fours blocking the lanes.'

'Could simply have been a farmer after rabbits, perhaps?' He deposited the next pellet into the glass and paused to hand her a tube of antiseptic cream. 'Here, follow me with some of this.'

'Farmers don't usually shoot someone off a bicycle and run away afterwards.'

Byron raised an eyebrow but didn't reply. A couple of pieces of shot had landed close to the side of her knee, where there was little flesh to cushion their extraction. She hissed in a breath but made no other sign of complaint as he dug for them.

He worked on in silence, removing pellets from her thigh, hip and upper arm – even a couple from the inside of her left leg, where the shot had passed through the bicycle's frame. There were a dozen in total.

Byron checked her over one last time, then rose with a nod. 'I think that's as much as I can do for you here. I'll bring your clothes and leave you to get dressed.'

'Thank you,' she said. 'Just one last question, if I may ask?'

'What's that?'

'What happened to your hands?'

FIFTY-SEVEN

The silence that followed her question had Blake regretting her impulse to ask it in the first place. The air disappeared out of the room, all at once, like the de-pressurisation of an airliner at altitude. She suddenly found it hard to breathe.

But it had been impossible not to notice.

Oh, his touch had been impersonal enough. She'd come across actual doctors who were more handsy. But his palms did not match the cultivated appearance of his nails and fingers. His palms were ridged and callused, oddly rough, as if he'd spent another lifetime engaged in hard manual labour.

He brought her jeans and hoodie into the bathroom, leaving again without speaking. She thought for a moment that – not only did he *not* want to answer – but the very act of putting the question had caused offence or upset. It seemed extraordinarily ungrateful of her, in the circumstances. Maybe the stinging left behind by the shot was affecting her judgement.

As she shimmied into her jeans, as carefully as she was able to, she heard the tinkle of the tweezers landing in a coffee cup. He flicked on the electric kettle. By the time she emerged, he was tipping a little boiling water onto the tweezers to sterilise them.

'Have a seat. Can I offer you a tea or coffee? Only bag or instant, I'm afraid.'

'A teabag sounds great about now, thank you.'

She watched him prepare their drinks without further conversation. It was only as he put a cup down on the table next to her, and lowered himself into the chair opposite, that she dared to look him straight in the eye.

'If you don't want to tell me, that's fine.' But she heard the challenge in her tone, and knew he did, too.

It's all very well to speak of trust, and then to demonstrate a lack of it.

Byron sighed. 'It's not a pretty tale,' he said. 'Nor a pretty result.'

He held out both hands in front of him, palms upwards, but initially with fingers folded over them. He seemed to take a deep breath, then uncurled his fingers.

Blake had primed herself not to react, to whatever it was, but she couldn't stifle a quiet gasp.

Both of his hands were criss-crossed in scar tissue. She didn't need to ask the cause. She'd been in enough places with enough people who had been attacked – usually by a partner – wielding a sharp blade. Defence wounds usually occurred on the palms of the hands and the forearms, as the victim fought for their life. A desperate attempt to ward off a killing blow.

Leaning forwards, she took both his hands in hers, as if about to tell his fortune, smoothing her thumbs across the uneven ripple of his skin. His lifelines were in ribbons, bisected, disrupted. She imagined his life had been through the same.

'I'm sorry.'

He didn't ask what for, and she wasn't sure she could have answered him. But sorry she was – for the pain writ large in those scars, for the months of rehabilitation narrated by the depth of them, and for the fear conveyed by their number.

His quiet, 'Thank you,' told her that he understood.

She realised she was still holding his hands. 'Is this why…? You said you're on medical leave?'

'Among other reasons, yes.' He cleared his throat. 'You may recall, there was an… incident, near Covent Garden, almost a year ago now. A teenager who'd been radicalised. He… ran amok, stabbing people…'

'I remember. Eleven, wasn't it? Is that…?' She broke off, started again – with a statement, this time, not a question. 'You were there.'

'Yes.' He shut his eyes for a moment, opened them again, his voice matter-of-fact and entirely devoid of emotion. 'Nobody tells you how extraordinarily difficult it is to disarm somebody who has a knife taped to each hand…'

He shrugged, withdrew his hands and rose abruptly. 'I'll go and retrieve your bicycle before the light goes. May I suggest you stay here – rest up – just until I get back?'

She shouldn't agree, she knew. If she'd any sense, she'd get out now, while she still could – run and keep on running. And yet, at the same time, she was reminded of her doubts and fears about Byron. About needing to know what made him tick. She'd just found out some of it, and it had blown up every expectation, destroyed every preconceived idea.

What else was there?

'Stay, Blake,' he said again. 'Please.'

'Yes, I… All right, yes.'

FIFTY-EIGHT

Pauline was making herself a sandwich when the feeble chime of the doorbell brought her up short.

She froze, poised with the jam knife hovering over the two rounds of a cheap white sliced loaf. As she did so, a blob of blackberry jam fell from the blade onto the work surface. Tutting, she grabbed a sheet of paper towel and carefully wiped up the spill before hurrying along the hallway to the front door.

Through the frosted glass panel, she could see the outline of a figure. Smallish, not heavily built, it did not seem to present much of a threat.

There was a pile of laundry in a bag by the door, neatly ironed and folded. She had told the customer she'd drop it in later, but sometimes people got impatient. Pauline grabbed the handles as she went past, pulling the door open with excuses for not delivering it sooner already on her lips.

'*Oh.*'

'Hello, Pauline. I'm sorry to trouble you at home. It's John Byron. Do you think we could have a quick chat?'

Pauline almost shrank back. 'Er, well, er, actually, I was just about to… to go out!' She grasped for inspiration, hefting the bag of laundry. 'Er, to deliver this.'

'Well, I won't keep you long. I wouldn't ask if it wasn't a matter of some importance,' the man said politely. 'If you're reluctant to invite a stranger into your home – which I can quite understand, by the way – I'm happy to talk out here.'

But as Pauline glanced around she saw the neighbours' curtains already twitching. Besides, it wasn't as if he was some harmless-looking old feller. He wasn't *old* at all – thirties, maybe, slender, dark-haired, dark-eyed, with an intensity about him. She'd noticed *that* the first time she'd seen him, at the pub. When he looked at you, you knew he wasn't looking at anything else. She had to admit that it flustered her.

'Come in, then,' she muttered, backing away from him down the hallway, still clutching the bag of laundry in front of her, like a shield.

He stepped inside, wiping his feet. Pauline retreated to the kitchen, finally putting the bag down on the Formica-topped kitchen table. The makings of her abandoned jam sandwich were in full view on the worktop, giving additional lie to her story of just being on her way out. She flushed. He made a point of not noticing, although she was sure he did.

He was the type of man who noticed everything.

'What d'you want me for?'

'Hope Glennie,' the man called Byron said, his voice still calm, almost gentle. 'You remember her staying at the Allbrights' farm, ten years ago?'

She lifted one shoulder, pulled a "maybe, maybe not" face, and tried not to let it show that her pulse had bolted. 'What about her?'

'Did you know, before or after she first came here, that she was your daughter?'

Pauline blinked at him, the blood falling from her face in out-right shock. Her vision tunnelled down, blackening at the edges.

The next thing she knew, she was slumped into one of the kitchen chairs and he was pressing a glass of water into her hands. She took a gulp, needing both hands to hold the glass steady.

Even so, some of the contents sloshed over the sides, dripping onto her knees.

'How did you…?' she began, then shook her head. 'No, it don't matter.' There was a bitter taste in her mouth, at the back of her throat.

'I am sorry,' he said, sounding as if he meant it. 'I realise I've taken you somewhat by surprise, but we don't have the luxury of time here.'

'What…?'

'Tell me about Hope,' he insisted. 'I know you were… *very* young, when you had her – a child yourself. I can't imagine what you went through.'

She gave a brief nod, fumbled a piece of tissue out of her sleeve and blew her nose, saying nothing.

'Even so, it must have been so hard for you to give her up.'

'No chance they'd 'ave given me custody, anyway, was there?'

He said nothing. Somehow, she respected him more for not trying to tell her she was wrong.

'It must have been harder still when she came to stay at the farm?'

She shook her head. 'I pestered Mrs Allbright to let me help out, like, so I could be *near* Hope – just for a bit,' she admitted. Her face crumpled. 'I never thought it would…'

'Never thought it would what, Pauline?'

She flicked her eyes towards him, ran her tongue over lips suddenly cracked dry. Then she whispered, 'I never thought it would put her near *him*…'

'"Him?"'

'*Fitzroy*.' She spat the name out, putting all her loathing, fear and pain into it.

He stilled, head tilted as he watched her. 'Was Gideon Fitzroy…? Was he Hope's father?'

She nodded, letting her head hang. The tears ran freely now, dripping from her nose, her chin.

'I'm so sorry,' he said softly. 'Why didn't you… tell anyone?'

That brought her head up. 'Tell who? Who would've listened to the likes of me?'

'You were under age – only thirteen. Surely, the local police—?'

'Local police – hah! *He* was in Fitzroy's pocket.'

'Ed Underhill?'

'The bloke before him – PC Lowther, 'is name was. And when the cancer got him, and Ed Underhill first came, I tried to tell him, an' all. He promised to "look into the matter" and then told me to keep my mouth shut, if I knew what was good for me.' She sniffed. The bit of tissue was a sodden lump between her fingers. She wiped her nose on the back of her hand, limp with exhaustion. 'Thought the new lass might be different, but she's just as bad.'

'Oh?'

'It was Fitzroy hit my car – week before he drove off the road and killed his'self. Hudson was right there. She practically saw it all happen. *His* fault, but does she make him pay for the damage? No. "Knock for knock", she says, so he gets away scot-free, like always.'

Byron was silent for a moment, then said, 'I know it couldn't have been Blake who set fire to Underhill's place. So… was it you?'

Her eyes filled again. 'Will they send me to prison?'

'Not if I can help it.' He leaned down, making sure he had eye contact. 'Listen, Pauline, I need you to go to my room at the pub—'

'What?' She reared back, almost scrabbling off the far side of the chair in her haste to get away from him.

'No! Not like that!' he said quickly. 'Blake is there.'

Something in his voice got through. The nature of her alarm changed. 'What's happened?'

His gaze narrowed and he hesitated, as if choosing his next words with great care. 'Someone took a shot at her.'

'*What*? When?'

'Maybe an hour ago.'

'Oh my Lord. Is she all right?' She tried to put the glass down and missed the table. Byron's hand shot out, caught it before it fell.

'I've patched her up, but it was a close-run thing. Which is why,' he added, 'like it or not, you're going to have to come clean with me about Blake, and about Hope – where they are now and how they fit into all this, OK?'

FIFTY-NINE

Blake's first instinct, when someone tapped on the door to Byron's room, was to ignore them and hope they went away.

Then Pauline's voice called, 'You in there, duck?'

Blake hopped off the bed – or tried to. She hobbled a little as she crossed to the door and opened it. Pauline slipped through the gap. Blake locked it again and hugged her tightly.

'You all right?' Pauline asked.

'Just about. What are you doing here?'

'Your Mr Byron came to see me. He—'

'He did *what*?'

Pauline stopped, her mouth opening and closing again. 'You mean… you didn't send him?' she asked faintly. 'You didn't *know*?'

'Of course not! I wouldn't tell him anything about you – not without talking to *you* first… Oh, Pauline,' she groaned, seeing the woman's face, 'what have you said to him?'

'I-I… Nothing he didn't know already! About Hope, about who I am…' Her shoulders drooped. 'I thought he'd got it from you. I thought *you'd* told him…'

Blake swore under her breath.

'What do we do now?' Pauline asked in a small voice. 'We could leave – just go. Get out of here.'

Blake shook her head. 'We set this in motion for a reason. I'm not going anywhere until it's done.'

'But…'

'We've come this far, Pauline. Don't lose faith now.'

The other woman took a shaky breath, gave her a wobbly smile. 'Yes… OK. So, what do we do – about Byron?'

But Blake's mind was scrambling back over their last conversation, here. About everything she'd let him see – not body, but soul. And just as she began to cringe away from her own foolishness, she remembered what *he'd* shown her, too.

The scars on his hands – which he managed to hide with such dexterity, so that nobody noticed he was hiding anything at all. But he'd also given her just a hint of his other scars – the ones on the inside. The ones, she was almost certain, he never showed to anyone.

So, why did he show them to me?

'We tell him what he wants to know.'

SIXTY

The police-liveried motorcycle pulled up with something of a flourish in the lay-by behind Byron's Mercedes. He climbed out to meet the new arrival, a sealed evidence bag already in his hand.

The rider set the bike on its stand and dismounted, flipping up the front of her helmet. 'You Mr Byron?' she asked, not without a hint of suspicion.

'I am indeed.'

He handed over the clear bag. It was one of a bunch he'd had left over and now kept in the car for emergencies. She took it with a frown, glancing at the contents. 'Another rush job, is it?'

'Quick as they can, please. The lab does know this is on its way.'

'Er, and does my inspector know about this, sir?'

'Probably not, but your divisional superintendent certainly does,' Byron said mildly, and he hoped that Daud's assurances on that front were true. 'If you've any qualms, please give him a call, by all means.'

The bike officer nodded. 'Good enough for me. Just wanted to make sure my arse was covered. I've already made one land-speed record attempt down the A38 today.'

Byron watched her tuck the bag into one of the bike's rear side panniers. 'Well, I always understood you had to do two runs to make it official.'

She flashed him a quick grin. 'In that case, sir, I'll see if I can beat my previous personal best.'

Flipping down the front of her helmet, she threw her leg over the bike and roared off. Byron watched her picking up speed, then checked his watch and got back behind the wheel. He still had to collect Blake's abandoned bicycle, and he had the distinct feeling that leaving the two co-conspirators alone together for any longer than necessary was asking for trouble.

SIXTY-ONE

Sitting in Byron's room, with Blake dozing off the effects of adrenaline and shock, Pauline had little else to do but wait, and remember.

When she thought back to her childhood, she had only hazy memories of the time before her mother died. Before her father faded away, first into a withered greyscale version of himself, and then into cheap vodka, a half-litre bottle at a time. And before Pauline's life became a tiptoe challenge to stay out of his sight, out of his way.

Her first meeting with Gideon Fitzroy, by comparison, was like an explosion of Technicolor. She was ten or eleven. He presented the prizes at her school. She received one for a project she'd been part of on local wildlife – the return of red kites, hen harriers, and other raptors to the Derbyshire hills.

Fitzroy was still in politics then, something of a local celebrity. When he talked to Pauline, he wasn't looking over her shoulder, or straight through her. He saw, right from the start, how starved she was of affection and attention, and what he could get her to do for just a little of both.

It was, after all, not his first time.

Pauline had always been small for her age, slim, boyish even. She looked younger than she was.

That suited him, too.

Now, she knew, it was called 'grooming'. An expression she hated for the way it understated her experience. Fitzroy had flattered her, encouraged her, taken her under his wing and into his home – first as wait-staff when he had dinner parties. And if anyone expressed their doubts, or pointed out how young she was, he mentioned her dead mother, her psychologically absent – and physically barely present – father. Who would deny such a disadvantaged child the patronage of such a worthy local philanthropist?

And nobody could argue that she hadn't blossomed, that first year.

Now, she knew, that what they did was called 'unlawful sexual intercourse' – consensual or not. Because, by the time he finished seducing her, she was willing to the point of desperation. For the first time she could ever remember, she felt treasured.

And when he invited her to his *special* parties – the ones he held only when his wife, Catherine, was away – then she felt doubly prized.

In fact, looking back, the worst thing he did was to make her enjoy it.

The shame she still felt, all these years later, made her want to crawl inside herself, block out the world and scream into the void.

As she approached her thirteenth birthday, she began to fill out a little. She took some ribbing at school for getting fat. Terrified that it might cause Fitzroy to reject her, she took to a starvation diet. Inevitably, perhaps, having gone alone on the bus one Saturday into Derby, she fainted in the shopping centre. One of the security guards called an ambulance.

By the time it arrived, she was bleeding.

They took her to the Royal Infirmary. Shortly after arrival – and to her utter astonishment – she delivered a three-and-a-half-pound baby girl. They estimated she was probably around thirty-two weeks gone.

It had never entered Pauline's head that she might be pregnant.

They kept her in for a week, but wouldn't let her see or hold the baby – who, they told her, had some issues and needed to be put into an incubator. To Pauline's ears, it made her sound like an egg from a chicken.

She was too dazed, too shocked, to talk to the social worker who came and hovered at her bedside. Besides, PC Lowther – Ed Underhill's predecessor back then – had dropped by with 'advice' not to say much of anything to anyone, or he'd see to it she was locked away.

So she stayed mute, turning her head from all the questions until, eventually, they simply went away. But not before telling her that the baby was going to be put up for adoption, which would be 'better for everyone'.

Nobody asked what Pauline herself wanted. It didn't occur to her that she might have any say in the matter.

Her father never came to visit her at all.

When she got home, the story had already been put about of a sudden illness to cover her absence – meningitis. She received wide-eyed sympathy from her classmates, leeway on her grades from the teachers. The Fitzroys came to see her – Catherine as well as Gideon, which made any kind of *private* conversation impossible – bearing flowers and sweets and good wishes for a speedy recovery. After they'd gone, she discovered that Catherine had just given birth herself, to a daughter.

And she wondered, for a while.

Until she saw little Blake for the first time, in her pram by the village shop. And one glance was enough to tell her, instinctively, that the child was not hers.

Her father never mentioned the baby that had been stolen from her.

That was the end of her time at Claremont, at Gideon's invitation, anyway. His wife still called her when they needed extra help for parties. Never *those* sort of parties, of course. She was even asked to babysit, as if her own pregnancy had never happened. Sometimes, she wondered if it was all in her imagination.

Throughout her teenage years, she swung between rage and despair at the injustice of her unacknowledged loss. Her moods left her largely friendless, although for some strange reason Blake seemed to gravitate towards her, regardless of Pauline's attempts to shoo the child away.

Unqualified and aimless, in her twenties Pauline drifted into whatever work she could get. Mostly cleaning for the richer incomers to the village, looking after holiday cottages, acting as the chambermaid when there were B&B guests at the pub, or waiting-on in the bar.

Despite her apparent apathy, when Pauline was working, she worked like a demon. Perhaps it was a way of channelling all that anger. Her reputation ensured she was always in demand. Better than spending time at home with her father, who'd slipped from taciturn into dementia with little change to their relationship.

When there *were* lulls, she signed on with a cleaning agency in Derby who provided gangs to nightly scour and scrub the office blocks of the city. Working twelve-hour shifts for sub-minimum wage. Again, her efficiency saw her sent to tackle jobs alone and unsupervised, where normally a crew of two or three would be required. And was often, she suspected, charged for.

That was how she found herself, working alone, with the run of the floor that housed the adoption agency offices, from seven at night until seven in the morning, two nights a week. It took her a couple of shifts to get into the filing cabinets that held the records, and another to narrow down her search. The only information she had to go on was the date and place of her daughter's birth, and her weight.

But it was enough. Enough to learn that her little girl had been adopted by a Worcestershire couple named Glennie. They had called her Hope, and sent their contact at the agency photographs of birthdays, Christmases, and special occasions.

Pauline drank in these pictures. She studied every line of her daughter's face until she could be certain she would recognise her anywhere. And she searched the backgrounds for clues to the Glennies, and how they might be treating the precious gift they had been given, at such cost.

Which was when she discovered that Mr and Mrs Glennie had been killed in a traffic accident. Hope, who survived unscathed, was eight years old. Neither parent had any living relatives, so the child went back into the system. Pauline read between the lines of the carefully worded reports that followed, divining behaviour problems towards a string of temporary foster carers as abuse, and friction with fellow inmates of various group homes as bullying, or worse. Hope's all-too-frequent visits to hospital were put down to sports' injuries, but she played no sports.

She already knew that the Allbrights had some agreement with a charity to take in delinquent girls for a kind of work experience on their farm. You couldn't live locally and *not* know. But it was still a shock when a note appeared in Hope's file about the possibility of sending her on such a placement. Four different farms were mentioned, from Somerset to Cumbria. The Allbrights were third on the list.

Pauline prayed for the right choice – even wondered if she could somehow engineer it, but didn't know where to start. She was overjoyed when the Allbrights' farm was chosen.

The next day she made a point of bumping into Xuan Allbright outside the village shop, gave her a sob story about her father getting worse and how she needed the work. Xuan was not a soft touch but she was kindly. By the time Hope's stay was confirmed, Pauline had a regular cleaning spot at the farm, every Friday afternoon.

And so, when Hope was fourteen, Pauline finally got to meet her daughter.

She never had the courage to tell her who she was.

But, for a few exhilarating hours, Pauline got to simply be around the girl, to watch and listen to her – to talk to her, even. And when Hope and Blake met, and clicked together in that way that teenage girls do, as if somehow recognising the unique bond they shared, Pauline went home and sat on the sofa, alone in her little housing association bungalow on the edge of the village, and hugged a pillow against her chest, and wept.

And then *he* saw her.

Fitzroy.

Pauline supposed, when she thought about it, it was inevitable that he would, sooner or later. Blake's mother was long dead by that time, and although Blake was far more inclined to cycle about the vicinity rather than allow her father to drive her, occasionally he would still turn up to collect her from the farm, regardless of her wishes.

Pauline was there, taking bed sheets off the clothes line along-side the farmhouse, when he climbed out of his car and spotted his daughter – his *daughters* – laughing together. She recognised the change in him immediately, from irritation to a predatory awareness.

Perhaps it was his own self-absorption that made him attracted to Hope. He saw an echo of his own features in hers and could not resist. Pauline found herself suddenly on her knees beneath the washing, retching onto the grass.

Knowing she could not tell Hope the truth, Pauline gathered her courage and went to see Fitzroy himself, to warn him off. She thought if she told him it would be incest if he laid a hand on Hope, it might be enough to dissuade him.

Instead, he'd laughed in her face.

When both Blake and Hope went missing, within weeks of each other, Pauline prayed that it meant they'd run away to find a life together, away from harm. Not hearing anything of either girl for the past ten years had been both agony and relief. She almost began to believe that they'd done what she never could – escaped the life they seemed destined for.

Then a man called Lex Vaganov had turned up, out of the blue, to tell her things she had never wanted to hear.

The sound of the key in the lock brought Pauline out of her reverie with a startled gasp. The door opened.

Byron stepped into the room.

Pauline took one look at the grim expression on his face, and her first thought was to flee.

SIXTY-TWO

'I'm not entirely sure where to start.'

As Blake spoke, Byron glanced at her. She had pulled on her hoodie again, but she was barefoot. Perhaps it was that, together with the note of uncertainty in her tone, that made her appear uncharacteristically vulnerable.

She and Pauline sat near the small table. They had dragged the chairs out so they both faced him. Byron leaned against the wall by the window, far enough not to crowd them.

He folded his arms, saw by the flicker of her eyes that Blake had caught the gesture. She thought he was hiding his hands, he realised. Maybe he was. Such actions had become too second nature to tell.

'Before we start, perhaps I ought to return this to you,' he said, glad of an excuse to unfold his arms. Reaching into his jacket, he pulled out the locket containing the photograph of Catherine Claremont.

Blake took in a sharp breath, her hand going automatically to her throat, a reflex action, before memory kicked in and she dipped into the pocket of her hoodie.

He crossed just close enough to drop the locket into her outstretched palm, then retook his position by the window.

She stared down at it. 'Where…? Where did you find it?'

'In the gateway, near the bicycle,' he said. 'Which is now stowed in the boot of my car, by the way. The chain had come off, but otherwise I think it's still rideable.'

'What about the chain? The one for the locket, I mean. It was broken but…'

He shook his head. 'Just the locket itself. We can go back and look, if you like? You know exactly where you hid, so may stand a better chance of finding it.'

'Yes…' But she frowned and her tone was guarded, even as she repeated, 'Yes, OK.'

'As for where you start, I think we had better clarify exactly who you are,' he went on, his voice dry. 'It seems DNA confirmation that you are indeed Gideon Fitzroy's daughter does not narrow things down quite as much as was first thought.'

'I—'

'She's Hope!' Pauline blurted out. And when the younger woman gave her a sharp look, she went on, 'Oh, come on, duck, what's the use of it? He knows anyway, don't he…?'

Byron was aware of that stab of disappointment again, more acute this time. 'Is that true?'

The young woman looked set to argue, then her shoulders drooped and she wouldn't meet his eyes. 'I'm sorry.'

He kept his expression bland and said, 'If that is the case, what happened to the real Blake?'

'She's dead,' Pauline said harshly.

They glanced at each other and the young woman added, 'At least, we think so…'

Pauline said, 'Well, what other explanation is there?'

Byron held up a hand. 'Tell me what happened, ten years ago.'

'We were best friends,' the young woman said. 'Almost from the moment we met. Maybe it was because, in a strange way, we each recognised something familiar about the other.'

'You're talking about your shared parentage.'

'No, I'm talking about being survivors!'

Her vehemence at once surprised him and yet was totally in character.

'Fitzroy had been abusing Blake since her mother died,' Pauline said. 'He couldn't stand not being able to influence Catherine's cancer, see? In his eyes, it killed her just to spite him. Maybe that was even what started him off.'

'When you say he was abusing Blake – you mean sexually?'

It was the young woman who shook her head. 'No. It might have been easier to bear if he had… No, he controlled her life. Utterly. Everything she did. What she wore. When she slept. If she was allowed to eat—'

'And yet he still permitted Blake to spend time at the Allbrights' farm. Wasn't he taking a risk?' Byron raised an eyebrow. 'That she might… tell someone? Ask for help?'

'By then, disobeying him was… well, it never entered her head. He'd got her so browbeaten – so brainwashed – she not only didn't dare, but she wasn't even sure what he was making her do was wrong.' She pulled a face. 'Plus the pickings at the farm were too rich for him to ignore, you see.'

Byron was aware of a bad taste in his mouth. 'You mean… the girls?'

She nodded. 'What better way to lure them to his disgusting parties than by using his own daughter to do it? By making her his accessory?'

'She was clearly under coercive control.' He kept his tone carefully neutral. 'Any jury—'

'Oh, come on, we're talking years ago! Coercive control was hardly a valid defence back then. Besides, he had her convinced that he'd make damned sure she took all the blame.'

'It were mental cruelty, that's what it were,' Pauline put in. 'That "psychological warfare" – torture by any other name.'

'So, what changed for Blake when Hope… when *you* arrived?'

There was a pause, then the young woman said, 'The Allbrights' farm was one place he allowed Blake to go alone, outside of school. No boys – he thought there'd be nobody to be a bad influence.' She flashed Byron a sudden, wicked smile. 'Hadn't counted on me. We planned to run away together. Easier to gather your courage and make a break for it when there's someone else to watch your back. But… we needed money – to get us started.'

'And you thought perhaps you could get that from Fitzroy,' Byron said.

She nodded, had the grace to look faintly embarrassed. 'He was still a backbench MP, then, but he had his eye on a cabinet post. We knew he couldn't afford any whiff of scandal.'

'You threatened him with what, exactly?'

'He started sniffing around, the first day I got there,' she said, disdainful. 'I played along. Nothing I hadn't done before, after all.' And though she strove for bravado, Byron caught a glimpse of what lay beneath. 'We thought we could record him, doing or saying something incriminating, and it would be enough… We thought, if we both stood up and accused him, it would be more convincing than either one of us…'

'Be enough for what?'

'A decent pay-out.' She shrugged. 'People like him don't end up in jail, do they?'

Byron glanced at Pauline. 'Surely, if the three of you had joined forces and tackled him together, Fitzroy wouldn't have had a leg to stand on? Accusations are one thing, DNA evidence of a highly inappropriate sexual relationship, which resulted in pregnancy, would have sent him to prison, without a doubt. Where,' he added with dark satisfaction, 'he would not have fared well, trust me.'

Pauline took a shaky breath. 'Hope didn't know – back then. That she was mine, I mean. I-I still hadn't… If *only* I *had*…'

'How *did* you find out about Pauline, by the way?'

'Lex.' The young woman reached across and squeezed Pauline's hand, offering a gentle smile. 'It wasn't your fault, Pauline. After everything Fitzroy did to you...'

Byron cleared his throat. 'So, what happened – before you left?'

'I went to see him—'

'Alone? Or you and Blake together?'

'Just me. Blake was in pieces, terrified that he'd still somehow force her to stay.' She gave a sad smile. 'With hindsight, going to see him at all was a huge mistake. I'd no idea how to go about blackmailing someone. He laughed in my face, told me we wouldn't make it a mile – he'd make sure of that. We decided to run, regardless. They were moving me from the group home I was in to another down south. It was then or never. We were supposed to rendezvous that night, but she never showed.'

'The night she disappeared?'

'Yeah. We think Fitzroy killed her and hid the body.'

'Why would he do that?'

The young woman shrugged again. 'Because she'd finally found the courage to leave? Because of what she might say about him? Who knows what went on in that twisted brain.'

'He would've had help,' Pauline said, almost blurting it out. 'Roger Flint, definitely. And Ed Underhill.'

'Why those two?'

'Flint because he did whatever Fitzroy told him to do, and because of the way he's reacted since I came back. He has guilt written all over him. I think that's why he got bashed over the head – because he's a liability. And because he's desperate. He's a gambler. You might want to look into that.'

'And Underhill?'

'I was in the woods, the night Flint was attacked,' Pauline admitted. 'Went to put the wind up him, didn't I? I heard Flint shouting to Underhill about him being there when they'd buried her.'

'Plus, Fitzroy had been reeling Underhill in for years. I think he rather liked having the local copper well and truly under his thumb,' the young woman said. 'And also because of the way Underhill reacted to this.' She brought the locket out again, smoothing her thumb across the surface. 'We both had one, but nobody else knew – that there were two of them. We think Underhill saw Blake's locket when they were getting rid of the body.'

'We think he took it,' Pauline said. 'Probably kept it hidden in his cottage somewhere. Only, now – because of the fire – he can't go and look for it, see?'

'From his reaction this morning, he thinks I took the locket and set fire to his house,' the young woman said. 'Which I did not, by the way.'

'I know.' Byron stared out of the window, frowning. The afternoon was fading rapidly into evening. At last, he turned back, asked, 'Why are you doing this? After all, Fitzroy's dead. What do you hope to achieve?'

'We want to find her body – give her a proper burial. I owe her that much. And we know he didn't act alone. There are others who've never paid for what they did.'

'So, why the subterfuge? Or was that part of it purely about the inheritance?'

'It was *never* about that.' The young woman flushed. 'Blake was the daughter of local bigwigs – Hope was a nobody. If I'd come back as Hope, there was no way anyone would have taken me seriously. Now, they'll be falling over themselves trying to find the body, if only to stop *me* getting my hands on the money.'

SIXTY-THREE

The following morning – after a largely sleepless night – Pauline was jumpy enough to hear the sound of a car pulling into the Close. She took a quick look out through the sitting room window, she was already in the hall with the front door open when Byron climbed out and walked towards her.

'What d'you want?'

'Good morning, Pauline.' He ignored her prickly greeting. 'I'm looking for… Hope. I understand she spent last night here?'

Pauline couldn't help the hitch in her breath at the sound of her daughter's name on his lips. Just for a moment, she thought about refusing him entry, then bowed to common sense. She forced her mouth into an unforgiving thin line and jerked her head in grudging invitation.

He followed her in. The young woman was in the kitchen, sitting at the table with both hands wrapped around a mug of coffee. He took the chair opposite. Pauline moved to lean against the stainless steel sink, where she could watch them both.

'Mr Byron,' the young woman said. 'To what do I owe the pleasure?'

He didn't answer right away. Pauline's eyes flitted between the two of them as they sat and stared at one another across the table, like it was some kind of competition that neither wanted to lose.

'I'm just on my way over to Claremont. You might like to come with me.'

Oh, he spoke politely enough, the way he always did, but Pauline heard the steel underlying his tone. It made the words definitely not a question, and not quite a suggestion. More like an order.

The young woman's eyes narrowed in response and she said softly, 'Now, why would I want to do a thing like that?'

'It might just dissuade Mrs Fitzroy from pressing charges against you.'

'Hm. Oh, yes, I can just see her wanting all this dirty linen washed in public. Can't you?'

He raised an eyebrow. 'Well, in that case, to apologise, perhaps. To explain.'

'You will excuse me if I decline your… invitation. I don't feel I owe my father's second wife any such courtesy.'

'Who said anything about Mrs Fitzroy?'

'No?'

'I was thinking of your step-siblings – and in particular of your stepsister, Lily. Of all of them, I believe she will find your… motives the least fathomable, and therefore, your… betrayal the most disturbing.'

She flinched at that. Pauline caught the slightest twitch of her fingers, saw the way they tightened momentarily around the mug and knew the dart had hit home. She took a breath to launch into her own defence but the young woman silenced her with a flicker of her eyes.

Instead, she swallowed the last of her coffee, and rose. 'All right,' she said. 'Shall we?'

Byron inclined his head and got to his feet. He was surprised, Pauline thought, that she hadn't put up more of a fight. Indeed, Pauline was surprised herself. Mentioning Lily was a low blow, though – after everything they'd all gone through as children.

'Don't you let him bully you into anything, duck,' she warned.

The young woman paused at the kitchen doorway to smile at her, but there was little heart in it. 'Don't worry. I won't.'

They went out. Pauline heard the front door slam behind them, rattling the letterbox. Automatically, she picked up the empty coffee mug, washed it at the sink, dried it and put it away in the cupboard.

It was only as she did so that she noticed, on the shelf above, that one of her drinking glasses was missing. The unevenness bothered her. Thinking perhaps that the young woman had taken a drink of water to bed with her, she did a quick circuit of the rooms, without success.

Frowning, she searched her mind back. The last time she'd used such a glass, she recalled, had been when she'd almost fainted the day before. It was Byron who had sat her down and made her drink. She made a mental note to ask him, when he returned, what he'd done with the glass.

SIXTY-FOUR

Lily was in the loft above the garage, lost in a world of her own devising. Initially, she ignored the sound of the car pulling up, having just reached a dramatic high point in her narrative.

It was about ten minutes later when she peered down onto the gravel and recognised the Mercedes belonging to Mr Byron. A yelp escaped her, because where *he* was, Blake often seemed to be as well.

She hastily tossed her costume back into the trunk and ran for the stairs, but as she left the garage by the side door, she was overcome with caution. Something had happened last night – she wasn't quite sure what – but, this morning at breakfast, when Lily asked where Blake was, her mother had almost exploded.

Blake was *not* Blake, she'd been told, firmly.

She was an imposter.

It had all been a monstrous practical joke – one in very poor taste.

The best thing any of them could do would be to forget all about Blake Claremont altogether.

Which was easier said than done. Lily found she was more bereft at the idea of not seeing her stepsister again – if indeed she *was* her stepsister – than she was at the prospect of having to move away from Claremont. After all, that had only been brought up as a faint possibility that hadn't actually happened yet.

Blake, on the other hand, had been right here.

And now she was gone.

Lily skirted the house to the back door and let herself in, tiptoeing along the passageway to the main hall. She listened carefully, even holding her breath, to determine which room they were in. It didn't take long to identify the study.

Lily slunk in close and pressed her ear to the thinnest part of the panelling. The voices came through quite distinctly, hardly muffled at all.

'—apology doesn't even *begin* to make up for the malicious disruption you've caused – and that can have been your only *possible* aim,' her mother was saying, stress making her voice shrill. 'I shall *personally* see to it that you are prosecuted to the *fullest* extent of the law.'

'Your choice, of course,' said the young woman Lily could only think of as Blake. Her voice, by contrast, was surprisingly relaxed. 'If you think you're prepared for the fallout?'

'What fallout? What is this latest ridiculous scheme you've cooked up? I don't have to listen to this nonsense—'

'No, you don't,' agreed a man's voice, slightly clipped. Byron himself. 'But you really should.'

'What on earth is *that* supposed to mean?'

'We already know that a DNA sample from Hope was a match to your husband,' Byron went on. 'We have now also identified Hope's biological mother.'

'I don't see what that has to do with—'

'She was just thirteen years old when Hope was born.'

Lily felt her eyes widen as the weight of the words dropped like stones into a pool of sudden silence.

After a long pause, she just made out her mother's voice, 'But, that's...' There was a cough, a clearing of the throat. Then, an attempt at confidence that was only partially successful. 'Some girls are very... advanced for their age. Perhaps she was—'

'She was a child,' Byron said. 'As your husband well knew at the time.'

'He was not… We weren't… *married* then. And if you think I would have, knowingly, involved myself with someone who… I have a *daughter* that age, for heaven's sake.'

Perhaps because all she had to go on was her mother's disembodied voice, with none of the familiar facial expressions or gestures to distract her, Lily was more aware of the tone and timbre. And something about the way her mother spoke did not sound entirely convincing to her ears.

'Yeah, and if I were you, I'd be talking to Lily very closely about things my father might have said – or done – when they were alone together.'

Lily heard her mother gasp. And this time, her question came out subdued. 'What are you talking about?'

'He's very clever. Charming them, seducing them, so by the time things get really twisted, he can do what he likes to them. And he does, believe me. But the worst part is that he convinces them they want it, too…'

'It's called "grooming", Mother. Surely you know what that is?'

Tom's voice this time, surprisingly deep and resonant, like a cello. She could almost hear him rolling his eyes as he spoke.

Lily held her breath again. They'd been shown a video about grooming at school, but it was very superficial and she'd been so busy giggling with her friends over something unintentionally risqué their form mistress had said at the start of it, that she didn't pay quite as much attention as she ought. Anyway, wasn't it something that happened online? Old men in dirty string vests, posing as teenagers on social media, who tried to get you to send them nude photos and then meet with them in seedy, out-of-the-way motels or motorway service stations.

Her relationship with her stepfather had been *nothing* like that. Gideon had been… attentive and affectionate with her – with both of them. He hadn't crowded her, or creeped her out, or tried to touch her anywhere she didn't want him to…

Well, he *had* touched her, but not like that. So it wasn't like he was doing anything he shouldn't – not really. They'd been acting. He knew she loved to act, and he'd suggested scenes from plays and movies she could learn and then perform for him, and he'd encouraged her, coached her, given advice. He'd just been playing the part of director, that's all.

And while those were times she hadn't told her mother about, because she would have found some way to spoil them, or interfere, there was nothing like *that* going on.

Was there…?

She'd struggled to explain this to Tom, one time he'd come looking for her in the loft above the garage. He found her in full make-up and a wig and evening frock from the dressing-up trunk, gazing into Gideon's eyes and delivering an impassioned speech from *The English Patient*.

Tom had not been satisfied initially with her explanation. Gideon ignored him, and told Lily to run through the scene again, with suggestions on her delivery and technique. She felt embarrassed to be doing so in front of her brother, but at least it seemed to put a stop to his suspicious questions.

From what he had just said, though, it had clearly not put an end to them altogether.

Lily flushed, realised that in her distraction she'd missed the next part of the conversation. And then she heard another car arriving and knew that the occupants of the study would hear it at any moment, too.

She dashed across the hallway into the drawing room and leapt for the sofa near the window, craning forwards to peer out through the glass. A marked police car had just pulled up next to Byron's Mercedes. The uniformed inspector, Khan – the one they'd met at the police station in Ashbourne on the day of Gideon's funeral – had just climbed out, and was settling his peaked cap into place.

And, from the serious look on his face, her mother was not going to like whatever it was he'd come to say.

SIXTY-FIVE

'A dramatic reconstruction?'

Byron heard the disgust in Virginia Fitzroy's voice. For once he was inclined to agree with her.

'Whatever else it might have done, the return of Ms Glennie has highlighted the fact that Blake Claremont disappeared, apparently into thin air, ten years ago,' Inspector Khan said. 'And that she went, possibly not of her own free will, and possibly as the victim of foul play.'

Virginia opened her mouth, then closed it again. She glanced at Lily, sitting on the sofa by the window, scuffing her shoes on the carpet but following the conversation with rapt attention. Byron could almost see the realisation hitting the woman of what might happen to her own daughter, and how she might feel. Byron had thought her a cold fish on first meeting, but it seemed even she had a well-hidden heart in there somewhere.

'I assume you didn't come for my permission, Inspector, so…?'

She left the question hanging. Khan, sitting in one of the wingback chairs that framed the fireplace, picked an imaginary piece of lint from the cap resting on his knee before he spoke.

'Not your permission, no. But perhaps your… support? Besides, as far as we can ascertain, Blake left here on the day she disappeared. We would like to replicate that journey, as far as we're able to.'

Virginia frowned. It was clear to Byron that she would prefer to refuse. And equally clear that she could not come up with a good enough reason for doing so.

'Do you honestly think anything useful will come of this, a *decade* after the event?'

'Reconstructions have been known to produce worthwhile results.' Khan's response was cagey. He sighed. 'Because nobody reported Blake's disappearance at the time – and the reasons behind that decision require further examination, in my opinion – we have no contemporaneous evidence. No tyre tracks, no blood, hair, or DNA. At the moment, we don't even have a probable crime scene. And no witness statements, either. Nothing. This might give the investigation team a place to start.'

'You wanted to prove me dead,' the young woman said, reinforcing her as Blake in Byron's mind. 'Now's your chance to do so.'

The brief look Virginia flicked in her direction was more troubled than defiant. She returned her attention to Khan.

'I can take it, then, that you will also be reconstructing the events surrounding my brother's assault?'

'The circumstances are somewhat different in the case of Mr Flint, but I'm sure we would not rule out any reasonable investigative method that might produce a result,' Khan said smoothly.

'Just out of interest,' Byron said, 'who did you have in mind to play the part of Blake?'

'I could do it!' Lily said at once.

'Don't be ridiculous,' Virginia said, her tone crushing. 'Quite apart from anything else, you're far too young.'

Khan's eyes slid sideways until they rested on the young woman standing next to Byron. 'Well, we rather thought, given the family resemblance—'

'*No.*' The word was out of his mouth before it had finished forming in his brain.

'Back off, Byron,' Blake snapped. 'You have no rights over me, and you certainly don't speak for me.'

Byron ignored her protest. He was focused on the inspector instead. 'Someone has already made attempts on her life – the latest of which was only yesterday. And now you're asking her to act as bait – alone?'

'What attempts?'

'Byron!' Her voice was sharper this time. 'It was nothing – I very much doubt it was a serious effort.'

'Hm. It's curious how you weren't saying that when I was picking lead shot out of you.'

'*What?*' Khan's shout cut across the pair of them. He took it down several notches. 'Are you seriously telling me that somebody shot you? Why wasn't this reported?'

She shrugged. 'Like I said – not a serious go, or I'd be in hospital now.'

'Nevertheless, this changes—'

'It changes nothing. I want to know what happened to my friend,' she said with a deadly calm. 'After the lengths I've gone to, just to get this far, do you think I'd let something so trivial stop me?'

Khan grimaced. 'If you call getting shot "trivial", then I hate to think what might classify as a serious attempt.'

'It's all subjective.'

'The normal procedure is to use one of your own people,' Byron said. 'Why deviate in this case?'

'I'm willing to do it, so why waste resources better utilised elsewhere?' the young woman countered with infuriating logic. 'Investigating Roger Flint's attack, for instance.'

'The publicity is likely to be more widespread if Ms Glennie takes part,' Khan pointed out.

Byron sighed. He could admit when he was outmanoeuvred. 'When is this going to happen?'

'As soon as it can be arranged,' Khan said. He nodded, accepting Byron's defeat, and rose, as if glad of the opportunity to make his escape before a more convincing argument could be put forwards. 'We'll be in touch.'

Blake got to her feet, also, following the inspector. By the time they reached the front portico, Virginia and her children had joined them. Khan paused to shake Virginia's hand and thank her for her cooperation.

Lily tucked in alongside the young woman, slipped her hand into hers, and asked in a small voice, 'Would you like to see my box of costumes now?' as if desperate for reasons to get her to stay, just a little longer. 'You *did* promise.'

Watching the young woman's conflicted face, Byron thought she might refuse, but Lily's pleading eyes got to her. She would have needed to be chipped from stone for them to do otherwise.

And, if she was so hard-hearted, she would never have come back here in the first place.

'All right, but only five minutes. Then I have to go.'

'OK,' Lily said brightly, and dragged her across the gravel towards the garage.

Tom stood protectively at his mother's shoulder, moving back inside with her and closing the door firmly behind them, leaving the two men in no doubt that they'd worn out their welcome.

'I have something for you,' Khan said then, and the congenial face he'd been putting on was no longer in evidence. He jerked his head towards the patrol car, strode around to the boot.

Byron let the man lead, watching as he opened the boot lid and reached in for a padded envelope. Khan thrust it into his hands. Byron peeled open the top and peered in. Inside was a clear evidence bag he recognised at once.

'Most forensics labs are open to private work these days,' Khan said tightly. 'Might I suggest that, in future, you operate on your own account, rather than taking advantage of Derbyshire

Constabulary's? Not to mention using our highly trained personnel as your own personal courier service.'

'My apologies – for overstepping,' Byron said immediately. 'It won't happen again.'

Khan's eyes narrowed as though he suspected mockery, although there was only sincerity in Byron's tone.

'Hm,' the inspector said, slamming the boot lid again with more force than was necessary. 'See that it doesn't.'

He pushed past to climb into the driver's seat, then fired the engine and pulled away along the drive with commendable restraint.

Byron, also with self-control of which he was proud, waited until the police car was out of sight before he slipped the accompanying report out of the envelope and scanned the contents. Having picked up the gist of it, he began again, reading it more carefully on the second pass. The conclusions were the same.

'What are you scowling about, or shouldn't I ask?'

He looked up to see the young woman approaching across the forecourt, hands in the pockets of her hoodie and attitude in every line of her.

'Oh, just having a theory confirmed.' He refolded the report and shoved it into the jiffy bag. 'Shall I run you back to Pauline's?'

The young woman hesitated. He already knew that she had well-honed survival instincts and, right now, they were telling her to approach with caution – if not run like hell.

He took a breath and tried to let go of his annoyance as he exhaled. He opened the passenger door of the Merc with a rueful smile. 'Come on. We can chat on the way.'

SIXTY-SIX

'So, what did the good inspector have to say that's wound *you* up so much?' she asked when they were back out onto the lane.

'Khan? Nothing beyond a mild slap on the wrist for… interfering.'

She turned to study his features but they gave nothing away. He kept his eyes on the road. Before she could make another gentle probe into his mood, he said, 'It was good of you to go with Lily to admire her toys. I have the feeling she doesn't get much attention – of the right kind, I should say.'

'No, I don't think she does,' she agreed, making an effort to relax. 'But it wasn't toys. She has a trunk of old clothes for dressing up and family plays. Most of them belonged to… Catherine. I found it hard to look.'

In fact, she'd fled with a mumbled apology the moment Lily opened the lid.

He did glance at her then, just a brief flicker, but he said nothing for the rest of the short journey.

When he pulled up outside Pauline's house, she forced a smile. 'So much for that chat, huh?'

'Perhaps I could come in – speak with you both.'

'Pauline won't be there. She's working at the pub this morning.'

'Ah, where does that leave you?'

'I have her spare key, if that's what you mean. Don't worry, I won't be forced onto the streets.'

She tried to keep her tone light but the look he gave her then suggested he'd taken her words far too literally.

'So, what *are* you going to do – when all this is over?'

She unclipped her seat belt and got out, hedged rather than lying. 'I think that rather depends on the outcome, don't you?'

It was only when she slid the key into the lock and pushed open Pauline's front door that she glanced over her shoulder and noticed Byron was carrying the padded envelope he'd had outside Claremont.

'What's that?'

He didn't answer, just stepped past her into the hall. She had to turn sideways to avoid him brushing up against her, and she told herself it was proximity rather than premonition that made the hairs riffle on her arms and at the back of her neck. She followed him into the kitchen, forcing a smile into her voice.

'Come on, Byron. Level with me. What's going on?'

He spun then, crowding her. They were much the same height, so how did he suddenly manage to loom? She swallowed, knew he'd caught the gesture.

'Why would I level with you, hm?' he asked. 'When you have not afforded me the same courtesy?'

Not trusting herself to speak, she raised an eyebrow.

With a quick grimace of disgust – at himself or her, she wasn't sure which – he reached into the envelope and pulled out the contents, placing it on the kitchen countertop. It only took her a second to recognise the glass as one from Pauline's set, to take in the evidence bag with the scrawled signature on it that clearly belonged to a lab technician, and to understand the implications.

'Oh.'

'Yes, "oh",' he echoed. 'So, first you're Blake Claremont, and then you're Hope Glennie. Tell me, does Pauline know you're not really her long-lost daughter, or are you conning her too?'

She recoiled. 'No! I wouldn't… She knows.'

He nodded, eyes scanning her face. 'And what about me?'

She opted for levity – a natural defence mechanism. 'Oh, I think she knows you're not her daughter, either—'

A mistake.

The rage flared in his eyes, fast and vicious, then it was gone, snuffed out as if it never existed. Even so, she took an instinctive step back, tensed to flee.

A distant memory unfolded inside her head. A news report, after the terrorist incident he'd mentioned – the one where eleven people had died. The perpetrator, she recalled, had been 'neutralised by police at the scene'.

Such a nicely sanitised way of putting it.

Rightly or wrongly, with so many civilian casualties, nobody batted an eyelid. The culprit's picture had been all over the news media. Survivors mentioned his size, his speed and strength. There were no cries for a public inquiry into anything other than how the young radical had slipped through the security services' net in the first place. The identities of the officer – or officers – involved remained unknown.

But she remembered Byron's classic understatement, when he'd explained his scarring.

'Nobody tells you how extraordinarily difficult it is to disarm somebody who has a knife taped to each hand...'

And in that moment she knew beyond doubt that it was Byron who'd killed the man, alone and unaided. The wording of the news report suggested a clean, surgical strike. She suspected it had been hand-to-hand – an up-close, desperate, brutal, bloody sprawling mess of kill-or-be-killed.

She put out a hand. 'Byron...'

He flinched away from her show of sympathy. 'The tests confirm you are Fitzroy's daughter, and that you are *not* Pauline's. As yet, we do not have a match on file for your matrilineal DNA. So, who are you?'

'I'm… I am Blake,' she admitted. 'It was a mistake to try to pretend otherwise with you, and for that I'm sorry.'

She waited but he said nothing.

Bastard.

'You knew anyway, didn't you?' she murmured. 'Why else would you go to all that trouble – the glass, the test – if you didn't at least suspect…?'

He nodded then, little more than a slight incline of his head.

'How?'

'Give me some credit – I am a detective superintendent, after all.'

'Yeah, one who's supposed to be medically unfit for duty.'

'Just think what I could do if I was on form.' His turn to speak with a lightness that was forced.

The silence stretched between them. The compressor in the fridge-freezer cycled and began to hum quietly in the background. Outside, a tractor and trailer rattled past on its way out of the village.

'Why?' he demanded at last. 'Why pretend?'

'I already told you why! Because I know – in my heart, in my bones – that Hope died that night, and my father was at least partly responsible. But we've no idea what they did with her body. My father might be dead – the others involved are still out there.'

He nodded slowly, almost reluctantly – understanding the logic without having to approve of it. 'They know that all they have to do is sit tight—'

'And we can't prove a damn thing,' she finished for him. 'Unless—'

'*Unless* somebody is pushed into making a mistake.'

'Yes. It was Pauline's idea – that I swap from me to Hope – but I went along with it, so I'm as much to blame as she is. We were worried initially that nobody would take Hope seriously – either as a possible witness or a possible victim.'

'And now you have everyone fired up, trying to prove exactly who you are, because of the inheritance.'

'Fired up enough to have a couple of goes at getting rid of me, anyway. And maybe enough to stove in Roger's skull because he was visibly losing his nerve.'

He looked impressed almost in spite of himself. 'Everyone agrees that both you and Hope were bright girls.' He was standing too close to her, eyeing her with cool regard, but she found herself unable, or unwilling, to move away. 'Even so, why did you allow Hope to go and confront your father, alone, on the day you disappeared? From what I've gathered, he was a cunning man with the skills of a parliamentarian and the instincts of a shark. You must have known he would run rings around her.'

She took a shaky breath, not bothering to deny it. What was the point, when it was true?

'Because I was too scared!' she cried. 'He'd had three years to work on me by then, to strip my confidence and grind me down. If you've never lived through it, you can't begin to understand what it's like, or how long it's taken me to get past that – to try to undo some of the damage he did. Now? If he wasn't dead already, I would have stuck a knife in his guts with a song in my heart. But back then?' She bit her lip, let her chin drop so she no longer had to meet his eyes. They saw far too much.

Byron put his hands on her upper arms. 'Don't, Blake. To all intents and purposes, you were still a child. Even attempting to get away from the situation you were in took enormous courage. You must know that.'

'If ever I've felt like giving up, I have only to think about what she sacrificed… for me.'

A muscle jumped in the side of his jaw. 'Don't build her up into some kind of saint. I doubt it was the case that Hope willingly gave up her life for yours.'

Stung, she pulled away from him, said roughly, 'You don't know a thing about it!'

'No, but I've come across more than my share of victims – survivors. Enough to know that sometimes living on – with the guilt – is a lot harder than dying.'

SIXTY-SEVEN

Lily was lurking in the orchard that lay just beyond the pub's beer garden and car park. She had slipped away not long after everyone finished dropping bombshells on her family back at Claremont.

The more she thought about it, the angrier she became about the things they'd said – about what her stepfather was up to. It was absurd. Of course he hadn't been doing something as sleazy as *grooming* her.

That would have been horrific.

It would have meant he intended to…

He wasn't. He couldn't have been. He wasn't like *that.*

Grabbing her bicycle from the garage, she had pedalled furiously along the lane into the village, determined to confront Blake-Hope – or whatever her name was – and *make* her take it all back.

It was only when Lily reached the main street that she realised she had no idea where to start looking for her.

She stopped outside the village shop, staring at the pub with indecisive eyes. Lily knew Blake-Hope hadn't slept at Claremont, the night before. And she also knew that, when people came to stay in the village, the only hotel of sorts was the pub.

Therefore, logic dictated that was where she would be.

Unfortunately, Lily was aware that she was not allowed in the pub without an adult, and Vera, the landlady, tended to be annoyingly strict on this point.

Nevertheless, the *outside* of the pub was fair game, as far as Lily was concerned. So, she rode into the car park at the side of the building and did a quick circuit, looking for the Mercedes Mr Byron had driven out to the house.

It wasn't there.

That threw her. It should have taken them far less time to drive than it had taken her to cycle, which meant they hadn't come straight here.

If they were coming here at all.

Lily bit her lip, then dragged out her smartphone and checked the time.

I'll wait for twenty minutes.

Decision made, she dismounted and wheeled the bicycle into the old walled orchard, leaned it against one of the gnarled apple trees, and positioned herself near the gateway to keep watch. She shivered, wishing she'd put on another jumper under her coat.

In the end, she had to wait only ten minutes before the Mercedes turned in from the road to park. Her victory grin lasted until she realised that Mr Byron got out alone. She almost went to ask him where Blake-Hope was, until she spotted his glowering expression.

So she stayed out of sight and let him walk inside without interruption.

Lily was just contemplating her next move when the back door opened and Pauline came out with a bag of rubbish to take to the wheelie bin across the yard.

That seemed like a far better option. Pauline cleaned at the pub, and made up the guest rooms. She was bound to know who was staying there.

Lily ducked out of cover and jogged across to intercept Pauline before she could disappear back inside.

She rushed through her enquiry, not missing the woman's uneasy surprise.

'Oh no, duck, she's not staying here.' But just as Lily's dismay blossomed, she added, 'She's round at my place…'

Retrieving her bicycle from the orchard, Lily rode into the housing association cul-de-sac only a minute or two later. In her haste to get to the front door, she dumped her bike onto the small patch of moss and dandelions that passed for Pauline's front lawn.

'Lil, wait up!'

The cry made her spin, almost tripping over her own feet. Tom leaned his own bicycle against the stone wall that marked the entrance to the close, and hurried across to join her.

'Tom, what are you doing here?'

'Following *you* – what do you think?'

'But… Why?'

He let out an exaggerated sigh. 'Because I'm worried about you, of course, dummy.'

She stared at him blankly, but before she could question this extraordinary statement, the front door swung open and Blake-Hope appeared in the gap.

'Hello,' she said, cautious rather than hostile. 'What can I do for you two?'

'Nothing,' Tom said quickly. 'We were just leaving—'

But Lily elbowed him in the ribs, hard enough to shut him up, then glared at her stepsister. 'Why did you say all those horrible things about Gideon, when he wasn't like that at *all*? He was so lovely to me, and he listened to me, and he was the only one who paid me any attention—'

'Oh, I paid plenty of attention,' Tom muttered. 'Trust me…'

Lily ignored him and ploughed on, fists on her hips in an effort not to cry. 'Just because *you* don't have any good memories of Gideon, that doesn't mean you get to take away mine.'

Blake-Hope was silent for long enough to make Lily twitchy. Then she jerked her head. 'You better come in.'

Lily marched inside, leaving Tom to shut the door behind them.

Blake-Hope led them into the tiny sitting room. There was just enough space for a two-seater sofa and a single armchair, squeezing the TV, side table and lamp into the corners. Lily plonked herself on the sofa, arms crossed defiantly. Tom perched beside her with all the enthusiasm of someone unexpectedly defusing their first landmine.

'I—' Lily began.

Blake-Hope held up a silencing hand. 'No, my turn. You've made your accusations. Shall I tell you what I think has been going on?' And without waiting for Lily's agreement, she launched straight in, describing the sudden attention Gideon started to pay Lily, how he assumed a far more active role in her life, gave her little gifts, flattered her, became more involved in her studies and hobbies. How he slipped her money whenever she asked – and sometimes even when she didn't. How he began to suggest what kind of clothes he'd most like her to wear. And how much she, in turn, then wanted to please him.

Lily listened with growing dismay, feeling something contract inside her chest. Pauline must have the central heating turned up too high. No other reason she felt suddenly dizzy and far too hot.

'But… how do you *know* all this…?'

'How do you think?' She spoke gently, sinking into the armchair and reaching for Lily's hand. 'Because he did it to… to me – and to others. Men like Gideon Fitzroy… it's like they have a playbook, and they follow it to the letter.'

'He deserved to die,' Tom said quietly.

Lily's eyes snapped to her brother. He sat immobile alongside her, hunched forwards, staring a hole in the rug. His forearms rested on his thighs, his hands clasped so tight together she expected his fingers to crack.

'No,' she whispered. 'Please, Tom, you knew him. Tell her. It wasn't *like* that…'

'I'm sorry, Lil, but it was – *he* was. It was exactly like that.' He threw her a quick glance, and she was amazed to see his eyes welling up. 'Otherwise I wouldn't have…'

Silence fell heavily between them.

Blake-Hope cleared her throat. 'Wouldn't have what, Tom? Grabbed the wheel?' Her voice was soft, almost tender. 'There was no oncoming car to make him swerve, was there?'

'No.'

She nodded. 'Unclipping his seat belt first was a nice touch.'

Lily gave a little moan. She clamped a hand to her mouth, suddenly afraid she might throw up.

Her brother continued as if she wasn't there, remote, disconnected. 'We had a road safety talk at school. They said you're twice as likely to die in a car accident if you aren't wearing your seat belt.'

'You're just lucky you didn't also kill the person you were trying so hard to save. Not to mention yourself.'

Tom's head came up, as if he'd just woken from a daze. He stared at Blake-Hope, his face streaked with tears, like Lily's own.

'What happens now?'

SIXTY-EIGHT

When Byron opened his room door and saw Blake waiting outside, his first instinct was to ask if she'd come for a rematch. But he took in her face and that changed everything. He stepped back without speaking. She moved past him.

He closed the door and turned to study her. She was strung so tight she almost quivered.

'Are you all right?'

She let out her breath on a shaky laugh. 'Not really, no.'

'Tell me.'

Her gaze shot to his face, searching. 'If I do, will you listen as a human being, not as a detective superintendent?'

'I can't promise, but I'll do my best.' He gestured to a chair. 'Sit.'

She narrowed her eyes. 'If you tell me to roll over as well, I may bite your ankles.'

'I'm sorry. Please, take a seat.'

She did so as if her knees were about to fold anyway. 'You came up here to find out what happened to my father, yes? And, beyond that, why he gave up his career for no apparent reason?'

He nodded, took the other chair, and waited.

'And, I get the feeling that you won't give up until you find something…'

He said nothing, which she seemed to take as an answer in itself.

'So… when I first got to London, all those years ago, I wanted nothing more than to put the past behind me. It took me a long time to tell anyone what had happened to me – even part of it. And when I finally did, it didn't occur to me that person might try to… right any wrongs on my behalf.'

'You're talking about Vaganov.'

'Yes. I should have realised, of course, that once I'd given Lex something to get his teeth into, however scanty, he wouldn't let it go – like someone else I know.' She flicked her eyes in his direction, took a deep breath. 'He was the one who found the connection between Pauline, and Hope, and Fitzroy.'

Byron's brain zipped ahead, making connections of his own. 'He confronted him.'

Blake didn't even look surprised. 'Yes. But he thought Fitzroy had got rid of Hope because she was living proof of his crime. All it needed was couple of DNA tests and he would have been ruined. So, without my knowledge, Lex went to see him in the guise of a potential party donor – wangled an invite for tea on the terrace of the Houses of Parliament. And he learned two things.'

'Which were?'

'One, that my father totally got off on the power of being in government. And secondly, that he had no idea Hope was dead.'

'Surely Fitzroy would have cottoned on?'

'You seriously underestimate Lex's ability to cold-read people and improvise on the fly.'

'If he passed on half those skills to you, then no, I don't.'

The tiniest of smiles tugged at the corner of her mouth. 'By the time tea was over, Lex had Fitzroy convinced he had Hope stashed away somewhere and was prepared to use her against him if he didn't pay the price.'

'Which was to give up his seat,' Byron said, unable to keep a hint of admiration from his voice.

'For a man like Fitzroy,' she agreed, 'it was a fate worse than debt.'

His lips twitched at the pun. 'OK, but there's nothing here that particularly offends my detective sensibilities. Impossible to prove any of it, I would have thought. One could argue that Vaganov did nothing more than appeal to Fitzroy's better nature – particularly if no money changed hands.'

'Ah, well, now we come to the other half of the story.'

'Why do I get the feeling I'm really not going to like this?'

'Because you have good instincts.' Her smile slipped into sadness. 'And because, unfortunately, Lex's actions had unforeseen consequences.'

'For whom?'

'Well, suddenly, my father found himself back in Derbyshire full time, with nothing to occupy his Machiavellian impulses, and his attention turned to his rather lovely – and very young – stepdaughter.'

'Lily.' Byron was aware of a cold prickle that ran across his scalp and pooled at the base of his skull. 'He began to groom her.'

She nodded. 'I believe so.'

'Did Vaganov kill him?'

'It might have been easier if he had. But no… I suppose, I should have realised something was off because, of all the people who felt threatened by me turning up – by the possibility of me taking away what they saw as theirs – the only one who *didn't* seem to care was… Tom.'

'Tom?' Byron echoed.

She nodded. 'He actually said he felt better if his mother failed to inherit the estate, because then he – Tom, that is – could be sure he'd acted for the right reasons, not for financial gain.'

Byron got up then, too restless to sit. 'I think you better tell me the rest, don't you?'

By the time she finished, he was leaning against the wall near the window, staring out over the main street.

'May I ask, what you expect me to do with this information?'

'Well, you told me to trust you… So, what do I want you to do? Nothing. Fitzroy's death has already been ruled an accident. Leave it at that and go home satisfied. I want you to remember you're a human being first and a copper second. We're talking about a scared kid who was trying only to protect his sister from a monster.'

'It's not as easy as that.'

'Of course it is! We both know Fitzroy had a hand in killing Hope.'

'Do we? I thought you just told me he had no idea Hope was dead.'

She set her jaw, stubborn. 'He killed her, all the same.'

'Who was it who said, "The only thing necessary for the triumph of evil is for good men to do nothing"?'

'I think it was Edmund Burke, but don't give me that.' She swatted as if at an annoying insect. 'How many of those "good men" did nothing while Fitzroy was on his quiet rampage? If Tom hadn't acted, my father would have ruined Lily's life.'

'You don't know that.'

'You only have to look at his track record – Pauline, me, Hope. Do you think we were the only ones?'

'No.'

'So?'

He shook his head. 'It's not my call to make.' Even to his own ears it sounded like an excuse.

She lurched to her feet. 'Bollocks, Detective Superintendent. Absolute bollocks. If not you, then who else? It *is* your call and you're being too stubborn to do the right thing.'

'Since when is agreeing to cover up a murder doing the right thing?'

'It is in this case, and you know it.'

They were toe-to-toe but he didn't recall moving. She grabbed his hand, turned it over and jabbed a finger at the scars transecting his palm.

'I'm sure the proper procedure told you to run and hide, not go and take on a maniac, but you didn't have a problem doing the "right thing" then, did you?'

Byron felt himself shut down, hoped against hope that he'd managed to do so without letting her see the pain she'd inflicted, the weakness she'd uncovered – however unknowingly. He jerked his hand free and stepped away, in every sense.

'So then, further down the line, I'll get a tap on the shoulder from your mate Vaganov, saying, "I have a small favour to ask…" Is that how this works?'

The blood dropped out of her face. Her eyes flashed briefly and turned blank.

'"Trust me," you said. I never would have taken you for a hypocrite, Byron.'

'Me a hypocrite? One minute you're telling me I should care about a girl who died a decade ago, and the next you're asking me to ignore a murder that happened a month ago.'

He cursed his own choice of words as she recoiled. 'You "should" care? You mean you *don't*?'

'That wasn't what I meant.'

'Oh, save it.' She whirled away, threw a final lethal shot over her shoulder. 'I should have known better with you than to forget my own maxim – sooner or later, everybody screws you over.'

And the door slammed with utter finality behind her.

SIXTY-NINE

Byron knew he'd been in the village too long when, a day or so later, he walked into the pub and the lunchtime regulars greeted him with friendly nods rather than suspicious silence.

Vera stood behind the bar with, unusually, the local radio station playing in the background.

'Hello, Mr Byron. I hope you don't mind the news. I put it on to see if they mentioned the re-enactment thing for Blake. It is today, isn't it?'

'By all means, leave it,' Byron answered. 'And as far as I'm aware, yes, it's today, although I'm somewhat out of the loop, I'm afraid.'

'Oh.' She sounded disappointed not to have the inside story. 'Will you have lunch? We've a very nice Stilton and broccoli in puff pastry as the special. And the guest beer is Dusty Gibbon IPA. We only serve that in an eight-ounce glass, though – it's stronger than it looks.'

He said yes to the food but declined the beer, plumping for coffee instead. Vera went to the kitchen with his order, leaving him to the tender mercies of Bruce Springsteen, then Kylie Minogue while he waited at the bar. Byron, who preferred his music either thirty years younger or three hundred years older, mentally tuned it out.

Around him, murmured conversation flowed. Even so, he heard the latch on the outer door behind him. When all voices stopped at the same moment, he already had half an idea who he would see when he turned around.

'Byron,' Blake said, nodding to him. She was poised in the open doorway as if not sure whether to stay or go. Her uncertainty surprised him, but not as much as the fact her hair had gone from ash blonde to brunette in the day and a half since he saw her last.

'Hello.' He deliberately did not use her name in public – either of them. 'I'm just about to have lunch. Will you join me?'

The mundane question seemed to break the spell. Conversation slowly started up again. She crossed to join him at the bar. He raised an eyebrow at her hair. It completely altered the way she looked.

'I know,' she said ruefully, catching his stare. 'I've grown rather used to being blonde, but this is more… authentic to the period, as it were. And it will wash out.'

'I see. So, you still intend to go ahead today then?'

Her jaw tightened. 'Of course.'

He clamped down on the uneasy feeling in his gut, and the objections he'd promised himself not to voice. He didn't get the opportunity, in any case.

Vera bustled out of the kitchen at that moment, with a sheet of paper in her hand. 'There you go, Mr Byron – you asked for a receipt for your room. You'll just need to settle up for your lunch at the bar. I hope everything was all right for you. Do come back and see us again, won't you?'

Blake waited until Vera had disappeared again before she spoke, moving in so they would not be overheard. Her voice was flat. 'You're leaving.'

'Yes… Unfortunately, my boss has ordered me back to London.'

'How convenient. I thought you were on extended medical leave.'

'So did I.' Byron gave a short grimace, recalling the awkward exchange he'd had with Daud. Being able to confirm to the commander that Fitzroy's murder was nothing to do with the rumour she'd started was one thing. Not being able to tell her why he was so certain was another. It led to one of the most difficult – and combative – conversations they'd ever had. 'Turns out the extension was at their discretion.'

'So that's it, huh? I help you solve your little problem, but then… What about mine?'

'I'm sorry. I—'

'You're sorry? Well, that makes two of us.' She leaned closer, speaking fast and low. 'You never had any intention of helping me find where they put her, or catching the others, did you? You got what you were after and I'm all right, Jack. You coppers are all the same, and more fool me for actually trusting one.'

'Oh, come on!' he snapped, keeping his own voice down to a savage whisper. 'It's not as if your motivation for coming here is so pure. There's the small matter of the fortune you're about to inherit, after all.'

She straightened and took a step back, much as he had done during their last encounter. He watched the shutters come down, one by one. She held out her hand.

'Goodbye, Mr Byron,' she said at normal volume as they shook. 'Good luck.'

As he watched her turn to stride out of the pub, he wondered which of them would need it more.

SEVENTY

Ten years ago

Blake stepped out through the back door and pulled it shut very quietly behind her, clutching her coat and a small duffel bag. On the terrace, she paused, staring up at the windows. Her father slept on this side of the house, his rooms overlooking the lawns, but the curtains were still firmly closed, the material hanging motionless.

Moving on the balls of her feet, so her boots didn't echo on the paving, she darted across onto the grass. Then she put her head down and ran for the woods.

At the edge of the trees, she stopped and looked back. She wasn't very fit and the short sprint had her breathing hard, heart thudding in her chest. The house remained apparently undisturbed.

She stayed a moment longer, taking in what might well be her last view of Claremont. Pressing her lips together, she turned away, shrugging her arms awkwardly into her coat. It was a red duvet jacket with a hood. She would have preferred something less bright, but this was the warmest she owned. It would have to do.

Soon, it wouldn't matter much anyway.

She hurried along the path that led to the old stables. There had been no horses there for years – not since her mother was a child.

But, in the old lofts above, there were still bales of hay and straw stacked up to the rafters – mouldering and musty now.

Blake paused in the overgrown courtyard, glanced about her, but all seemed quiet. She slipped into the carriage house and stood under the hatch in the high ceiling.

'Hope!'

Silence greeted her. Her heart, which had finally settled, began to pound again. It took another couple of increasingly frantic, whispered shouts before she heard a thump of boots landing on the wooden boards above, then footsteps. The hatch lifted and the ladder slid out and down, scattering dust and seeds and stalks. Hope's face appeared in the gap.

Blake scrambled up the ladder, her duffel bag bumping awkwardly against her legs. Once she was up, Hope pulled the ladder up after her and shut the hatch. The two girls embraced.

'You're here,' Hope said, looking happy and sad at the same time. 'We're *really* doing this…'

'What – you thought I'd let you go alone?' Blake asked, trying to cover the tremor in her voice. 'Never!'

Hope led her to the far side of the loft, where the hay was stored. They climbed up onto the stack, clambering over one of the rough oak beams. She had made a nest up there, Blake saw, with her sleeping bag and her torch, a bottle of cola, and some protein bar wrappers.

'Were you OK here, all night?' Blake asked.

Hope shrugged. 'It was fine – not too cold. Really snug, actually. And I found an old electric kettle in the harness room down below. Looked like it came out of the Ark, but it worked, so I could have a wash and everything this morning.'

Blake knew why it was important to her to be clean today – not to feel at a disadvantage. She squeezed Hope's hand.

'I got you something,' she said, reaching into her pocket for the flat plastic box. She'd risked her father's wrath to go into Derby, found a little artisan jeweller who was just starting out and was keen enough for the work to copy an old piece. Shyly, she handed it over. 'Here.'

'What's this – a proposal?' Hope's tone was jokey, but there was a catch in it they both heard.

Blake waited, tense, while Hope opened the box, undid the draw-string on the little velvet pouch and slid out the silver locket. For a few moments she sat there, as if frozen, then she flicked the clasp open to see the tiny photograph of Catherine Claremont inside.

'You never knew your mother – your *real* mother, that is – so I thought we could, maybe, I don't know, share mine? If you want to, that is…?' Her voice trailed away. It had seemed exactly the right thing to do, when she'd had the copy made, but now she began to have doubts. Sweat prickled along her hairline, under her arms. 'I mean, if you hate it, or whatever, it doesn't matter. I just—'

'Oh, Blake,' Hope said. She launched herself across the gap that separated them and hugged her until she thought her ribs would crack. 'I love it! I absolutely love it. What a beautiful thing to do.'

Blake went limp with relief.

'Oh! That's… good. Hey, I made us some sandwiches.' Embarrassed now, she dug into the duffel bag, came out with chunks of bread filled with cheese and pickle, bound together in cling film.

Hope dived in as if starving. 'First thing we do, when we get to London, is go for a slap-up meal – just the two of us – to celebrate our freedom. Somewhere really posh, eh? The Savoy, maybe? Or The Ritz! We'll be able to afford it, after all.'

Blake frowned, tried not to let the knot in her belly tighten into real pain. 'Hope, are you sure about this…? About asking my father for money?'

Hope snorted, licked a piece of chutney from her fingers. 'Trust me, B, I won't be politely "asking". I'll be telling him. Either he pays us off, or we go to the press and he can kiss goodbye to his dreams of high office, that's for sure.'

'I know, but what if—?'

'"What if", nothing. He won't have a choice. Besides, he *owes* you, after everything he's done…'

Blake nodded, dropping her chin so her hair fell forwards over her face.

Hope nudged her arm. 'Come on, you and me against the world, B, remember?'

'Yeah, I know,' she mumbled, reluctant to admit just how scared she was.

Hope flipped her hair back over her shoulder, then looped the locket's chain around her neck and tucked it away beneath her T-shirt.

'Cheer up, B. Look, I got something to show you.' She dragged her backpack closer and pulled a mini tape recorder from one of the side pockets. Blake recognised the device – the kind she'd seen her father use to dictate letters, or when he was out in the car and had an idea for one of his speeches.

'Voice activated, so all I do is switch it on before I get to the door, and let it record him digging himself into the mud. Easy.'

Blake frowned. Whenever she tried to argue anything with her father, he tied her in knots, turned it all around so that it was always her fault. Until the only option left to her was rage. It had been a long time since she'd allowed herself to feel that. The price was usually more than she was willing to pay.

'Please, Hope, promise me you'll be careful.'

'Of course.' But she didn't sound careful. She sounded cocky and confident. The ache was back in Blake's belly. It reached up into her chest and gripped her heart, her lungs, with icy fingers.

She followed Hope down off the stack and over to the hatch, watching mutely as the other girl slid the ladder down to the floor below. As she started her descent, Hope paused to grin at her. 'Don't look so worried, B. I'll be back before you know it.'

SEVENTY-ONE

Now

At Ashbourne police station, Inspector Khan was fighting a losing battle against the pile of paperwork on the corner of his desk. He'd spent all morning wrestling with it, but would swear it had not reduced in size. When one of the admin staff knocked on his open door, he rolled stiff shoulders as he sat back.

'I hope that's not for me?' He nodded to the documents in her hand. 'Just as I begin to think there's light at the end of the tunnel…'

'In my experience, sir,' the woman said drily, 'any light at the end of the tunnel is usually somebody with a torch, bringing more work.'

Khan gave her a wan smile. 'True enough. What d'you have there?'

'Well, it's an invoice from the forensics lab, with a copy report for a DNA test, but I can't find a note of it on file, so there's no case number I can attach it to.'

'Strange. Isn't there a reference number on the invoice?'

'That's just it – there's no number, just a name. Byron.'

Khan scowled and held out a hand. 'Ah, I know what this is about and I've already had words with Detective Superintendent Byron. Leave it with me and I'll deal with it.'

Once the woman had departed, Khan found himself flipping through the pages. It took only a few moments before he recognised what he was looking at.

And a few more before he realised the significance. Still reading, he shoved his chair back and rose. By the time he'd reached the doorway, the scowl was back in full force.

'Hudson!' he yelled. 'My office. *Now.*'

SEVENTY-TWO

Ten years ago

The waiting was almost unbearable.

Stuck up in the hayloft, Blake wished she'd brought a book or a magazine. Anything to take her mind off the time passing and distract her imagination from the scene taking place in Gideon Fitzroy's study, up at the house.

Not that she would have been able to concentrate on reading.

She fixated on the possible outcomes. They'd done their sums – they knew London wasn't cheap. But they'd projected, with anywhere from a few hundred to several thousand, they could at least get a toehold into a new life.

She huddled into her coat, on top of the hay, staring up through the dirty skylight at the clouds, and wishing the time away until Hope's return.

There had been little sun in the day and now it began to rain. Big splotches of water landing on the glass above and sliding down. It seemed appropriate, somehow, that it should rain on her last day.

When Hope *did* come back, Blake found herself strangely unprepared. She heard the voice, urgently calling to her from the carriage house below. She almost tripped over her own feet in her haste to climb down from the hay, to open the hatch and let down the ladder.

She could tell simply by the way Hope climbed, stamping onto each rung, that it had not gone as she'd anticipated. But Blake was not prepared to see her friend's eyes raw with tears.

As soon as they'd hauled up the ladder and closed the hatch, she stepped in and took Hope's face in her hands, forcing their eyes to meet.

'What happened? What did you say? What did *he* say? How much did he give you?'

Hope's eyes bubbled over again and her mouth quivered. 'He laughed at me,' she admitted. 'I told him what we wanted – and what we'd do – and he just stood there and… *laughed* at me. It was horrible…'

Blake, a hollow dread gripping her chest, reached for her friend and wordlessly they clung to one another.

Eventually, Hope pulled back, sniffing. Blake could tell there was something more. Her father was not the kind of man to resist twisting the knife once he had it in your flesh.

'What else?' she asked quietly. 'What else did he say?'

Hope took a deep, unsteady breath. 'He told me you'd lose your nerve. That you'd back out at the last minute and leave me high and dry,' she said flatly. 'He told me he'd got you too well-trained to do something as stupid as try to run.'

Blake flinched.

'So, I told him he didn't know you like he thought he did, and you were finally gonna prove him wrong.'

'W-what did he say to that?'

Hope shrugged. It didn't take the sting out of her answer: 'Just that he'd make sure you regretted it…'

Panic flooded down over Blake in a cold wash, leaving goose-bumps all over her skin. She didn't need to explain that one to Hope – they'd told each other everything.

'Did you manage to record him saying… any of that?'

Hope hung her head. 'First thing he did was check if I was wired, didn't he? Smashed it, right in front of me.'

'What are we going to do?'

Hope swallowed, her voice firming. 'I'm going anyway – there's nothing else for it. We can still do this, B. Even without his money. As long as we've got each other.'

She bit her lip. 'What if we get caught? You're due at that new group place at the end of the week. Surely they'll raise the alarm when you don't turn up?'

'We've been through this. They won't send the dogs out until next Monday, if then. I can be far away by then – we can *both* be far away.'

Still, Blake hesitated. 'I—'

Hope spun back, grabbed her arms. 'Don't let him keep doing this to you, or you'll be a prisoner here forever. You won't get away until one of you is dead. Is that what you want?'

SEVENTY-THREE

Now

Jane Hudson pushed open the door to the pub and looked around more in hope than expectation. It was just after normal lunchtime, and the only occupant of the small front bar was Ed Underhill, sitting reading the local paper at a table near the fire. He looked up as she entered.

'Now then, lass. What brings you here?'

She hesitated a moment then said, 'I was trying to find Mr Byron. His phone goes straight to voicemail.'

'Ah, you've not long missed him,' Underhill said. 'Packed up and gone back to London.'

The way he said the name of the city made it sound like the outer reaches of the solar system.

'Oh. That was… sudden.'

Too sudden even to say goodbye.

'Aye. I got the impression he'd been summoned from on high.' He took a swig of his pint and sucked the foam from his top lip. 'And you don't get to his rank, at his age, by failing to jump when they say so, do you?'

Hudson said nothing.

'So, what's going on?'

'Hope Glennie.'

'What about her?' Despite his best efforts, Hudson heard the sour note that crept into his voice. 'You on your way to do that reconstruction – this afternoon, isn't it?'

'It was supposed to be, aye.'

'Oh yeah?'

'Turns out, she isn't Glennie after all.'

Underhill froze for a second. 'So… who is she?'

'Well, that's the thing. Apparently, Mr Byron tracked down the biological mother – don't ask me how – and got a DNA sample from her. He put it through our lab and it's not a match. So, she's Mr Fitzroy's child, all right, but she's not Hope Glennie. Unless Fitzroy went round sleeping with half the county, I suppose that means she might well be Blake, after all.'

'But, what…?' Underhill began. He stopped, and started again. 'I mean, why would you…?'

'Search me. I'm only the oily rag, not the engine driver. Inspector Khan's livid.'

'I'll bet.'

'It's why he's called off the reconstruction, which is embarrassing all round, what with the local media taking an interest.'

'What does your Mr Byron have to say for himself, then?'

'That's what the inspector wants to know. Personally, I've no idea what Byron's playing at. He knew a couple of days ago that she couldn't be Hope, and he said nothing about it.'

Underhill looked contemplative. 'I couldn't help thinking there was something just a tad sneaky about the bloke, when you first introduced him.'

Hudson hesitated, felt obligated to go to Byron's defence. 'He's a bit of a legend within the Met.'

'Well, don't believe everything you hear. You know what these stories are like. People are made out to be heroes. But, when you get right down to the nitty-gritty, it usually turns out that what they really did wasn't very heroic after all, eh?'

SEVENTY-FOUR

Ten years ago

Hope had bought a couple of large tins of spray-on hair colour – a kind of burgundy red to hide Blake's naturally dark hair, and a coffee brown to cover her own blonde. Between the two of them, they managed to apply their disguise without making their hands, clothes, and faces look like a bad art project.

Without a mirror, Blake couldn't really judge if the red colour suited her. On Hope, the dark brown, without any colour variation for authenticity, made her hair look like a wig. She had a sudden snapshot image of her mother during the depths of her chemo sessions, when her hair was long gone. She'd had some beautiful wigs.

'It'll do,' Hope said, with more confidence than Blake felt. 'It's supposed to last about ten washes, so at least the rain won't affect it before we're free and clear.' She picked up the empty tins. 'What should we do with these, d'you reckon? Leave them here?'

Blake shook her head. 'They might search. And, if they find them, they'll know what description to put out.'

'Oh, yeah. I'll take them both, then. We can ditch them later.'

'Why don't we each take the one we've used?' Blake suggested. 'Then, if one of us is caught, they won't know what the other looks like.'

Hope stared at her for a few moments. 'You're amazing.'

Blake shrugged, flustered. She let her head drop, hiding her face, mumbled in response, 'No more than you.'

'No, don't do that!' Hope's sharp tone had her head snapping up again. 'Don't do yourself down, B. You're really smart, in a dead practical kind of way, as well as a books-smart kind of way.'

'Yeah, if I'm so smart, why has it taken me so long to get away from him?'

'Don't do that, either! If people around you – people you're supposed to be able to trust – chip away at you, day after day, it's only natural you get to believe everything they're telling you. About how useless it is to try and leave, or tell anyone, and how this is the best you're going to get because it's all you deserve.' She reached out, tucked a strand of Blake's new bright hair behind her ear. 'Sometimes you don't need bars on the windows to make it a prison, B.'

'Blake! Come on out. We know you're in there! Don't make this worse for yourself.'

The voice – male, harsh – bellowed up from the courtyard outside. Both girls jumped. Blake pressed both hands over her mouth so she didn't scream.

Hope put a finger to her lips and jerked her head. They both tiptoed to the wooden doors at the front of the building. When it was still in use, the doors swung inwards to allow each load of hay to be thrown off the wagon straight onto the upper floor. There was even a wooden beam that swung outwards with rope and pulleys attached. It hadn't been used in years. The rope had rotted and the doors were nailed shut.

Blake put her eye to the gap at one side and peered down. Rain blew in gusts, flattening the weeds that sprouted between the bricks of the yard. She could see the back of a man, facing away from them, a waxed cotton hat covering his head from view. Even so, she recognised his voice.

'It's Roger Flint,' she whispered to Hope. 'Oh God, what do we do?'

Hope shushed her. 'If he really knew we were here, he'd be facing the other way…'

Blake held her breath. The man turned a slow circle, squinting at each window and doorway in turn, looking for movement. The girls froze in place like rabbits, too scared to run.

Below them, they heard the scrape of footsteps and the clatter of doors being opened, possible hiding places poked and prodded.

After an agonising few minutes, Blake saw Ed Underhill join Flint in the courtyard below. He was in uniform and carrying a big torch as if ready to beat someone with it. That scared her all the more. The two conferred briefly, then moved off, pausing every so often to yell her name and to repeat their hazy threat.

Eventually, their voices faded into the trees.

Blake turned her back to the stone wall and slid to the floor, hugging her knees. Tears sprang from her eyes. She shivered so hard her body kept going into spasm.

Hope knelt in front of her, took her hands. 'Look at me, come on. We can do this.'

'H-how?'

Hope was silent for a moment, then she shrugged out of her jacket, a dark blue nylon parka with fake fur around the hood.

'Give me your jacket and we'll swap. We'll wait another hour or so – just until the light's starting to go. You head across the fields and take the footpath around the reservoir, and I'll walk along the road. If they see that coat, and the dark hair, they'll come after me and I'll string them along, play for time.'

'But—?'

Hope waved her objections aside. 'If it comes to it, you meet the guys with the minibus at the Visitor Centre and leave with them, as planned, and I'll follow on when I can, OK?'

Hope had coaxed seats on the bus out of the leader of an outward bound group who'd been camping near Carsington Water while they learned to windsurf and sail dinghies. They were due to leave by six.

'No, I can't ask you to act as bait for me, Hope. What if they catch you?'

But Hope grinned at her. 'That's the beauty of real friends, B – you don't *have* to ask. They may have given up searching by then, anyway. And even if they haven't – even if they *do* catch up with me – I'm not the one they're after. So, what are they going to do?'

SEVENTY-FIVE

Now

Since the accident, Lily had not enjoyed being in a car, but especially not in heavy rain on twisting country lanes, at dusk. The sky still had light and colour in it, but at road level, the verges, walls, and hedges all amalgamated into one gloomy morass.

After Gideon's accident, she worried about it more. She was always looking for suicidal wildlife about to leap into their path, loose livestock, unlit cyclists, or stupid walkers in dark clothing. She had seen all these during the time they'd lived in Derbyshire.

They had just been to the hospital to visit Uncle Roger. She and Tom had squabbled over who got the front seat for the ride home, until their mother snapped and consigned them both to the rear. They'd hardly spoken a word – to her or each other – since then.

Lily was sitting directly behind Virginia, and could see the tension in her mother by the hunch of her shoulders. When the phone rang, loudly, through the Range Rover's speakers on hands-free, Virginia's hands twitched violently on the wheel. Either that, or they hit a really deep pothole.

'Are you all right, Mummy?' Lily asked. 'Are you getting one of your headaches?'

'I'm *fine*,' Virginia said firmly, but her tone twanged with tension as she answered the call. 'Yes, hello?'

'Virginia, is that you?'

'Who's this?'

'It's Ed Underhill.'

To Lily's ears, he sounded miffed that their mother hadn't known him at once. He was somewhere outside – Lily could hear the rustle of wind across the microphone.

'I apologise. We're just on our way back from visiting my brother in the hospital and the conditions on the road are terrible.'

'Ah – how is he?' Underhill asked.

'Still unconscious.'

'Well, I'm very sorry to hear it.'

She unbent enough to say a stiff, 'Thank you, Edmund. Was that all?'

'No, it wasn't, as it happens. I… wondered if you'd heard the latest about Blake?'

Lily held her breath at the mention of the name.

'I assume you mean this Hope Glennie?' Virginia couldn't help saying the name with a hint of disdain.

'No, I don't – because she isn't Hope. I don't know all the details, but that's definite, apparently. I thought you might appreciate a heads-up.'

Beside her, Lily heard Tom give a quiet gasp. She shoved her head between the front seats to demand, 'Ooh! Does that mean she *is* Blake, after all?'

'Lily, sit up properly and put your seat belt back on!'

She sighed loudly. 'It *is* on, Mummy.'

But Underhill answered her anyway. 'It looks like she might be. She's got this locket that used to belong to Blake, which might serve as some kind of proof, I suppose.' He sniffed. 'Although, where she got it from is another matter.'

At last, they were turning into the driveway at Claremont. Almost home – while it *was* still their home, at any rate.

Lily could feel Tom almost vibrating with rage alongside her. Worried, she glanced at him, at the way his fists clenched in his lap.

'She lied,' he muttered. 'She lied… just to get me to…'

As soon as they pulled up near the front portico, he had the door open and was away across the gravel, ignoring his mother's shout.

After only a moment's hesitation, Lily darted after him.

She ignored their mother's shout, too.

Tom was stronger and faster than she was, and his legs were way longer. By the time she reached the corner of the house, he was already halfway across the back lawn, heading for the path through the wood to the old stables. In the gathering darkness, she could hardly make him out.

Lily wasn't scared of the dark, exactly, but since their uncle's attack, she'd certainly been more careful not to be out alone in it.

I'm not alone – Tom's here.

Squinting into the lash of rain, she put her head down and ran. At the start of the black hole into the trees, she faltered.

'T-Tom?'

He didn't answer, and she couldn't see him ahead of her any longer. Her heart was racing and her chest felt tight, and fear coiled and slithered in her tummy.

She started forwards again, more cautiously now. After only half a dozen paces, she heard noise in the trees to her left. She prayed it was just a badger, or a fox.

It wasn't.

A moment later, an arm snaked around her body, trapping her own arms to her sides. Her feet were lifted clear of the ground, kicking as she tried to flee. Another hand clamped across her mouth, cutting short her squeal of sheer fright.

SEVENTY-SIX

'I wish you'd stay, duck,' Pauline said, sounding close to tears. 'I mean, we still don't know where… But we're so *close*. I just know we are.'

Blake's hands were occupied packing the few items she'd brought with her into her backpack, which lay zipped open on the spare bed.

'The cops have called off the reconstruction,' she said, glancing up to give the older woman a brief, reassuring smile. 'But this is a tactical withdrawal, not a full-scale retreat. I'll be back – soon. Lex and I will come up with another plan. It won't do any harm to let them think they've got away with it.'

'They have,' Pauline muttered. There was a hint of sulkiness in her tone.

'For now, yes.'

And that's bloody Byron's fault. Too clever for his own good, that one.

'How long—?' The sudden ring of Pauline's mobile phone interrupted whatever she'd been about to ask. She dragged it out of her pocket and stared at the screen.

'Who is it?'

'Dunno – it just says "private number".'

'Put it on speaker.'

Pauline did so. 'Yes, who is it?'

'That doesn't matter,' said a heavily disguised voice. Blake recognised the mechanical undertone. She had an app on her own mobile that produced an identical effect.

'Tell Blake to go to the crossroads near the old plantation.'

'You can tell me yourself,' she said. 'What do you want?'

'Go to the crossroads,' the caller repeated. 'On foot, alone. Bring the locket and tell no one. Understand?'

'No. Why would I want to do something like that?'

'You've got thirty minutes,' the voice said, ignoring her question. Then the line went dead.

Pauline looked at her, dumbfounded. 'What was *that* all about?'

'I don't know,' Blake murmured, just as her own mobile buzzed to signify an incoming text message. The incoming number was Lily's phone, so she thumbed it open, and stilled. 'Oh my God…'

'What? What is it?'

Blake showed her the phone. On the screen was a photograph of Lily, clearly bound. Her eyes were wide and terrified above the duct tape across her mouth. Underneath the image was a caption:

at least your friend was dead before we buried her…

SEVENTY-SEVEN

The Hardings were sitting down to a late dinner when the phone started to ring. Oliver wiped his mouth on his napkin as he rose.

'Can't you leave it, darling?' Anne asked. 'We are eating, and you've been rushing about all day.'

'Ah, but one never knows…' He was already crossing to the handset, lying on the counter that separated the kitchen from the living area. He picked it up and glanced at the incoming number. 'It's Virginia.'

'Oh! About Roger, do you think?'

Harding thumbed the receive button. 'Virginia. How are you? What news?' He paused, frowning, and shook his head to his wife. 'Tom and Lily? No, they aren't here. We haven't seen them. Why, what's wrong? What? Really? How extraordinary…'

To Anne's irritation, he walked towards the hallway, so she was unable to overhear even his half of the conversation. But, a moment later he was back, shrugging awkwardly into his Barbour jacket while still trying to keep the phone close to his ear.

'Yes, I'm on my way. Try not to worry, Virginia, I'm sure they'll be fine. No, no. And Tom's a sensible lad. Don't distress yourself. Yes, I'll be with you directly. Bye-bye.'

'What's happened?'

'Another upset for poor Virginia concerning Blake.'

'I thought it was something to do with the children. And don't you mean Hope?'

'That's just it. Another DNA test has proved she can't be Hope, apparently.'

'I don't understand. Are we back to her being Blake again?'

'Who knows? After all, if Gideon fathered one illegitimate child, there may be more out there.'

Anne frowned. 'What does that have to do with Lily and Tom?'

Oliver picked up his car keys and a flat cap, absently patting his pockets. 'Well, Virginia wasn't being very clear, but it would seem she was in the car with the children when she got the news about Blake not being Hope, so of course they heard it, too. She said as soon as they got home the pair of them bolted from the car and are now nowhere to be found. That was more than an hour ago. Naturally – after what happened to Roger – she's in a complete panic.'

SEVENTY-EIGHT

Ten years ago

Hope was late.

Blake stood on the downwind side of the minibus, mostly out of the rain, staring across the car park of Carsington Visitor Centre towards the entrance from the road. The wind blew the rain in flurries across the exposed tarmac, and her teeth chattered in the cold. She hunkered down a little deeper into the parka. When she checked her watch, only another five minutes had crept past.

'Is she coming, your mate, or what?' one of the outward bound kids asked. His name was Jason and he'd said he was one of the team leaders, but was only a teenager himself. Maybe that's why he felt the need to be aggressive, just to keep order.

Blake had stolen through the wood and across the fields with the last of the light, glad of Hope's darker coat as she shadowed the hedges. She'd taken the footpath around the bottom end of the reservoir and along the top of the grassy embankment that formed the dam wall. Her heart was in her mouth for most of the journey, and by the time she arrived she was sweating as much from fear as exertion.

The closer she got to the car park at the Visitor Centre, the more nervous she became. The prospect of being caught when she was almost at her destination seemed doubly cruel. But her father, she knew, delighted in toying with his prey.

Hope had told her which group had promised them the ride, so she knew who to approach. The guy Hope dealt with was called Mikey. But when Blake did finally arrive, breathless, she was told Mikey had already left. One of the kids was sick. Mikey had taken him home early, seeing as he'd brought his own car, leaving this guy, Jason, in charge.

'He told me to expect you, though,' Jason had said. 'And as long as your mate gets here around six-ish, that should be fine. We packed up early because of this weather, so we're aiming to leave then.' And almost as an afterthought, he'd added, 'You're Hope, yeah?'

He was already turning away before Blake's wits caught up with his parting words. She took a step, opened her mouth to correct him, but he was striding back to his group, shouting to them about tents, or sleeping bags, or something. The moment passed, and then it was too late to correct him.

Now, Jason appeared, pointedly checking his own watch. 'Sorry, Hope, but we really need to go, yeah? These kids have got parents meeting them at the other end.' He followed her gaze to the entrance – or what they could see of it. 'Looks like your friend has stood you up. So, you coming or staying? Your choice, but you need to make your mind up.'

SEVENTY-NINE

Now

'What do you mean, you've called it off?' Byron snapped into his phone. 'At this notice? Have you even told her?'

'I hardly think that concerns you, Byron,' Inspector Khan returned with heat. 'If you had passed on the information about the DNA test – which *we* paid for, I might add – we would all have been aware of the facts days ago.'

Byron was on the ring road skirting the north side of Derby, heading for the motorway. But as he'd begun to listen to the inspector, he'd instinctively lifted off the throttle and looked for somewhere to pull over.

'What "facts" are those? A vulnerable teenage girl went missing ten years ago – most probably the victim of foul play – and you have a chance to apprehend those responsible. What else do you need to know?'

'You have no authority here. Once again, I find myself appalled by your cavalier attitude towards those of us who do. You're way off your patch, Byron, and even your own superiors consider you currently unfit for duty, which makes you practically a civilian. I'd thank you to remember that I can have you charged with obstructing an investigation just as easily as the next man.'

What investigation? From where I'm sitting, you're investigating nothing.

Byron flexed his gloved hands around the rim of the steering wheel. He had the wipers on full speed and they were barely keeping up with the rain lashing the windscreen. He wondered if the filthy weather had anything to do with Khan's decision. Still, he felt he had to have one last try.

'You're putting her at risk, and you're allowing a possible murder to go unscrutinised.'

He heard Khan take a breath at the other end clearly wrestling with his temper, or his conscience. 'She lied to us – as did you, for that matter. You must understand that we can't base any investigation on the uncorroborated word of a witness who has already proved totally unreliable.'

'You don't get it, do you? You don't see what she's been doing.'

'Which is what, exactly?'

'Drawing them out, man. Messing with their heads until they're fighting one another because they're coming apart at the seams. Whatever happened ten years ago – whatever her father did – she knows he didn't act alone. And whoever his accomplices were, they're still out there, and they're getting desperate. And now you've publicly washed your hands of her, and by doing so have all but called open season.'

There was a second's pause while the implications penetrated, then Khan spoke again. His voice was hollow.

'I'll get a car over there, just to be on the safe side. If necessary, we can take her into protective custody.'

An exit came up on his left. Byron floored the accelerator, dived across two lanes and onto the slip road. He threw the Merc into the roundabout, re-emerging seconds later onto the opposite carriageway, heading back the way he'd come.

'I'd send more than one. And tell them to hurry.'

EIGHTY

Blake hurried along the narrow lane towards the crossroads bordered by the old plantation, head down into the rain. It was almost dark now, heavy with cloud cover.

She checked the time again on her phone. They must have known she was at Pauline's, because they'd given her just enough time to get here – but only if she set off immediately. No time to delay.

No time to plan anything, either, or seek help from any quarter. *Not that there's anyone I can ask.*

She had refused to let Pauline come with her. It was too dangerous, for one thing, although she didn't say so out loud. That would not have deterred Pauline.

But, if it all went bad, Blake needed someone on the outside who knew what had happened and could tell the tale. She'd told Pauline she was relying on her to raise the alarm.

As back-up plans went, it was not exactly reassuring, but it was the best she could come up with in the time she had.

She half-wondered, had Byron not run out on her, if she might have gone to him for help. She had a feeling he would have tried to take over – too used to doing things his way.

It hardly mattered now.

In the pocket of the red coat she'd borrowed from Pauline, she heard the muffled ring tone of her mobile. She dug it out and tucked it against her ear, inside the hood.

'Wait! I'm almost there.'

'Blake? It's Byron.' Not who she was expecting. 'Where are you?'

His voice had that slight echo of hands-free, and she caught the tick-tock of an indicator in the background.

Just for a moment, a mixture of hope and relief flared in her chest, followed by the crushing memory of his betrayal.

I don't need your help. Or want your interference.

'Why are you calling? You made your position perfectly clear.'

'That was before someone grabbed Lily.'

'How—?' She stopped the question as the answer came to her, added bitterly, 'Pauline, huh?'

'I went there first, looking for you,' he said. 'She's scared for you – for both of you.'

'If you've just come from Pauline's, then you'll know I was told to come *alone*.'

'You're being stubborn. You need my help – for Lily's sake if not for your own.'

'That's a low blow, Byron. I'd rather play this my own way, thanks all the same. Turn around and go home.'

A flash of headlights against the hedgerow ahead caught her eye and made her turn. There was a car coming down the hill towards her, travelling fast. She swore under her breath and stepped off the road onto the narrow verge, her boots sinking into the sodden ground.

'Blake? What's the matter?'

'Is that you coming now?' she asked.

As if in answer, the car went up onto high beam for a moment, blinding her.

'Byron?'

'I don't see anyone. Where are you?'

'On the verge to the right of you, just ahead. You better slow down, though, or…'

Distantly, she heard Byron's voice shout, 'Blake, I can't see you… Blake!'

Then she was turning, running for the nearest gateway, for the nearest escape route. She could hear the rev of the engine now, even above the sound of the rain drumming onto the road. And she knew, however fast she ran, it wasn't going to be fast enough.

The vehicle hit her left side. She was aware of a solid thump, a blaze of pain, the momentary feeling of weightlessness and the tearing tangle as she cartwheeled into the hedge and slammed down into the unforgiving earth.

Then blackness.

EIGHTY-ONE

At Byron's end of the call, the sound effects came through loud and unmistakable. First, the phone tumbling onto the road surface, then the skitter of tyres locking up on the loose gravel near the verge, the sharp, chopped-off cry of impact, and the thump of something solid, landing hard.

He could visualise the scene as clearly as if he was there.

'Blake. Talk to me!'

Through the car's speakers, he heard the slam of a car door. He was sure the footsteps that followed were in his imagination but he would have sworn he heard them, too. Then a hefty crunch as, no doubt, a boot was stamped down onto the fallen phone. The speakers relayed its last distorted squawk.

And then all Byron could hear was the eerie silence of a lost signal, a disconnected line.

He slapped his palms against the steering wheel in frustration, ignoring the pain in his hands, and pressed the accelerator. The Mercedes' automatic gearbox kicked down and the car surged forwards.

Byron tried to reassure himself that driving at speed on lanes so narrow and twisting was safer at night. At least oncoming head-lights allowed a few seconds' notice of other traffic. Unfortunately, that warning did nothing to prepare him for the blinding flare of light that hit him head on.

The driver of the vehicle coming the other way made no attempt to slow down, move over, or dip the headlights. Byron shut his eyes instinctively and yanked the steering wheel to the left.

He felt the passenger-side front wheel drop down suddenly, heard the graunching sound of the Merc's undercarriage scraping across the edge of the road. The nose lurched downwards into the ditch and the whole car began to veer off sideways, heading for the trees.

Byron let go of the steering wheel – useless now, anyway – and clamped his arms tight to his body so they didn't flail around if the car rolled. A nightmare vision of the lethal flight path taken by Gideon Fitzroy's vehicle flashed into his head. He shut it out.

With an almighty bang, the Merc hit the trunk of a large tree and stopped dead. The seat belt yanked at his shoulder and the airbag deployed, hitting Byron in the face and chest with the force of a swung sandbag. The pressure increase inside the cabin made his ears pop.

In front of him, the headlights still blazed. In their beams, he could see steam rising from the busted radiator. Automatically, he reached down to switch off the engine, which was – remarkably enough – still running.

He unclipped his seat belt and, expecting the driver's door to have stuck, got his shoulder behind it, only for it to open at once, almost spilling him out into the mud. The sound of an approaching engine and the strobe of headlights through the trees hurried him into scrambling out. They were coming from behind him – the direction the aggressive vehicle had taken. He still couldn't be sure if it was accident or malicious intent, and did not plan to find out the hard way.

But this vehicle slowed as soon as it came into view, the nose dipping sharply as the driver stood on the brakes at once. Byron held up a hand to shield his eyes. He heard the heavy tick of a diesel motor, guessed at a four-by-four by the overall bulk, but could see nothing beyond the lights. A door opened.

'Mr Byron?' Oliver Harding's voice. 'My goodness. Are you all right?'

'More or less.'

'My dear chap… What happened?'

'Some idiot ran me off the road. They were heading your way. I'm amazed they didn't do the same to you.'

'Ah, I've just had to avoid someone driving like a lunatic. If there hadn't been a gateway for me to swerve into, you and I would likely be in much the same boat.'

Byron was already at the passenger door of Harding's vehicle, an old Toyota pickup. 'We need to get to Blake – I think she's injured.'

Harding got back behind the wheel without argument, put the pickup into gear and started rolling. 'Where is she?'

'Along here somewhere. We were talking and then… I rather think someone deliberately ran her down.'

Byron put a hand against the dashboard to brace himself as the pickup bounded through the ruts. He risked a sideways glance at Harding's face, just visible in the instrument lights.

'Clearly, you already know – that she *is* the real Blake.'

'Yes,' Harding said at last. 'Virginia called us. The children are missing. Tom took the news of Blake's duplicity rather badly, it seems. He ran off and Lily went after him. Now they're nowhere to be found. That's why I'm out on such a night.'

Byron caught sight of something lying to the side of the lane and flung out an arm. 'Stop. There, look.'

Harding braked hard and the Toyota pitched to a halt. Byron jumped down, realising as he did so that he'd wrenched his shoulder when he crashed.

Almost on the verge lay the smashed remains of a smartphone that he recognised. He went further along the road, checked the hedges on both sides, and found one section where the smaller branches gleamed pale in the headlights where they'd been snapped off.

Of Blake herself, there was no sign.

Byron took out a handkerchief and used it to pick up the smartphone. It was quite dead. Harding had got out by this time and stood with his collar up against the rain. His face was grim as he regarded the shattered phone.

'Is that…?'

Byron nodded. 'Tell me, I realise Tom is only fifteen, but can he drive?'

EIGHTY-TWO

Roger Flint surfaced slowly from the depths of unconsciousness. Snatches of conversation were the first things to emerge, a few words here and there that made little sense to him. Then patches of light and shade, and smells – antiseptic, and the kind of cooking odour that he associated with school dinners, a long time ago.

But when he finally woke, everything came back at once, like the switching on of a light. He opened his eyes and – this time – they stayed open. He was aware of a dull, throbbing ache in his head, and tubes sticking out of everywhere. He paddled at them weakly, heard a distant alarm sound, then footsteps.

A nurse loomed into his field of vision, her hand cool on his shoulder.

'Roger, can you hear me? Just nod, if you can. Don't try to speak. Doctor's on her way.'

She fussed around him until the doctor arrived – a young Indian woman who looked barely old enough to drive. Some of the tubes were removed and she checked his blood pressure and pulse, shone a penlight into his eyes. The nurse brought him a few ice chips to soothe his raw throat.

'How long…?' His voice was a raspy croak.

'You've been here for three and a half days – you're at the Derby Royal,' the doctor told him. 'Where is the last place you remember?'

'Woods – near the old stables.'

'And you were drinking.'

He closed his eyes briefly to escape the censure in her face, her voice. 'Yes.'

'What happened?'

'Running.' Every word seemed to tear his throat. He swallowed, ran his tongue over parched lips. The nurse fed him another few ice chips. They melted almost instantly in his mouth. 'Tripped, fell.'

'That's it – just a fall?'

There was something in her voice. His eyes slid across to her, standing over him. The action triggered a memory, of another figure approaching until they towered above him, of something heavy in their hands, raised up.

He flinched instinctively, squeezing his eyes shut, tried to scoot over to the far side of the bed to get away from the threat.

'It's all right, Roger,' the doctor said, catching his arm. 'Calm down. You're safe here.'

As the nurse helped him resettle, she was watching him intently. 'The police have been here, off and on, and they wanted to know – did you see whoever it was? Did you see who tried to kill you?'

EIGHTY-THREE

Blake came round to find someone was shaking her like a dog with a rat in its jaws.

Her eyes snapped open. Darkness and noise greeted her. It took her a second or two to realise she was inside the boot of a car, and moving fast enough to throw her around.

She was lying on her side, facing backwards, with both arms behind her. There was a painful tightness in her hands. She flexed them, found they'd been bound together at the wrist.

Blake swore softly under her breath. She had no idea how long she'd been out, or how far her attacker might be taking her, but she knew she couldn't do much about it – not like this.

She heaved herself up onto the point of her shoulder and tucked in tight, forcing her hands under her backside. The bulky coat made it harder, but she'd made a point of staying agile.

With a last effort, she managed to jerk her hands so they were now down behind her legs, then fed each foot through in turn. Bringing her hands up to her face, she tried the bindings with her teeth, discovering ribbed plastic with a thin tail at each wrist.

Zip ties. He came prepared – whoever he is.

She swallowed, tasted her own blood.

The car slowed. Blake held her breath, let it go when they turned without stopping and sped up again.

Working quickly now, fumbling in the dark, she stretched down and untied the laces of her boots. She threaded the ends awkwardly between her hands and re-tied them, then began to pump her feet like she was running up a flight of steps, tensing the muscles in her arms to heave in the opposite direction. The friction of the laces sliding over the zip ties created enough heat to melt through the plastic.

It gave way suddenly, causing her feet to thud against the inside of the boot. She held her breath, but the driver didn't react.

Moving as quickly as she could, she refastened her laces. She scrabbled her fingers at the edges of the boot carpet beneath her until it peeled up at one side. Underneath was the well for the spare wheel. Her hands dived into it, tracing the shape of the spare itself, and the usual tools for jacking the car up and removing the wheel nuts.

They slowed again, engine note dropping. Her fingers touched on the object she was after but the car took a swerve to the right. It thudded into something, rebounding with a shudder, throwing her off balance.

They came to a sudden stop. The engine died. She strained harder, grasped the wheel brace and tugged it free. She heard the driver's door open and then close. Kept listening but no other doors opened.

Good, there's only one.

She scuffed the carpet straight again, tucked both hands behind her and closed her eyes not quite all the way, just as the boot lid swung upwards. The interior light came on. For a moment, the figure stood and stared down at her. She couldn't see past the light to get a look at his face.

She didn't need to.

As he leaned into the boot to lift her, she brought the wheel brace round from behind her back and struck out, aiming for his head.

EIGHTY-FOUR

Harding did a multiple-point turn in the next gateway. They headed back in the direction they'd come, slowing only to squeeze past the tail of Byron's crashed Mercedes, which stuck out partially into the road.

'Where would he have taken her?' Byron wondered aloud.

'I do think you're wrong about Tom,' Harding said. 'I know Blake was coming between his mother and inheriting Gideon's estate but, even so… Running her down and kidnapping her – especially in such a violent manner – is a little extreme, don't you think?'

Had Blake been wrong about her stepbrother, Byron wondered? He thought back to her assurances that Tom was relieved not to benefit from his own actions. Had the boy fooled her? Somehow, he doubted it.

'I've known people do things far more extreme, with far less at stake.'

'He always struck me as a rather gentle boy – protective of his sister, respectful to his mother – quiet, studious.'

Byron produced a grim smile. 'It's always the quiet ones.'

'I daresay you have rather more experience than I do of this kind of thing, but still…' Harding did not look convinced.

'So, all that aside, where would he go? Where would he take her?'

'Well, both he and Lily were always drawn to the old stables at Claremont – as was Blake, as I recall. It was her place of refuge…

after Catherine's death. Anne and I tried to do what we could, of course but—'

'*Stop.*'

The Toyota twitched as Harding's hands jerked on the steering wheel. He braked hard enough for the nearside wheels to lock in the gravel of the verge.

'What? Good grief, man, you almost gave me a heart attack. What is it?'

But Byron was already opening his door and jumping down. He picked his way back down the lane. Harding had been going slowly, but they'd travelled maybe two or three vehicle lengths in the time it had taken them to stop.

'Do you have a torch?' Byron asked.

'Yes, of course. I always keep one in the glovebox… Here you go.'

The torch was new, a modern ultra-bright LED. He got his bearings and pointed it towards an open gateway that led to a track into the woods. Fresh tyre tracks were visible in the mud.

The gate itself was galvanised metal, but the gateposts were old-fashioned chunks of solid stone. The hinge post was intact, but the latch post had been split about a third of the way up. The upper two-thirds now lay partly across the opening.

Harding joined him, as Byron played the torch around the stone.

'You can see tyre tracks, look. Somebody came through here at speed, travelling in the same direction we are, and side-swiped the gatepost.'

'Hm, to be honest, I'm not sure if it was like that before. The local farmers around here don't tend to be too assiduous about repairs and maintenance on their land, in my experience. If they'd keep the drainage ditches clear, for instance, we would have half the amount of flooding on the roads.'

Byron highlighted the stump. 'It's a clean break, and hardly wet. I'd say this hasn't been down long.'

'Well… you may be right. What do we do?'

Byron reached into his pocket for his phone. It wasn't there. He'd last used it in the car, he realised with an inward curse. It could have been on the passenger seat or the centre console when he went off the road. Either way, he'd made the mistake of not searching for it.

'Do you have a mobile phone on you?'

'Yes, only an old thing, but it works. I keep it in the truck, for emergencies.'

'Call the police, and if you wouldn't mind waiting here for them to arrive? I'll see if I can pick up the trail.'

He began to turn away, when Harding stopped him. 'But surely I ought to come with you. I know the boy—'

'Thank you, but I'd rather you stayed safe. Just explain the situation and point them in the right direction.'

'Yes… all right.'

Byron stepped over the fallen gatepost and headed into the trees. He took one last look back, saw Harding fumbling with an old-fashioned mobile phone, its keypad lit up as it went through its ungainly start-up routine.

Help, Byron considered, might be a while coming.

EIGHTY-FIVE

'Stay on your feet and walk, dammit, or I'll break your other arm!'

Blake staggered under the weight of the man dragging her downwards. She was pretty sure she hadn't hit him *that* hard, but he was still groggy and sluggish.

How much of it was real, and how much of it was a delaying tactic, she wasn't entirely certain. But she was in no mood to give him the benefit of the doubt.

When she'd climbed out of the car boot – still clutching her improvised weapon – it was not much of a surprise to find Ed Underhill sprawled in the mud.

Blake staggered to the driver's side in search of something to handcuff him, and found more zip ties in the door pocket. Unfortunately, he started to come round as she was applying them. He made a grab for her and she lashed out with her boot. It was partly luck that she caught his elbow. She heard the bone fracture, even as he screamed.

It didn't stop her finishing the job of fastening his wrists tight together, as hers had been. He continued to roar and writhe, until she gave him an open-handed slap to the face, hard enough to make her palm sting.

That quietened him into snivelling sobs. She grabbed his good arm and heaved, ignoring his shriek as one arm pulled on the other.

'Where's Lily? If you've hurt her…?'

'I don't know where she is.'

Blake gripped the elbow she'd kicked and dug her thumb in deep.

He screamed.

'I don't! I swear.' He was gabbling. 'But she's OK. She's nearby. Will be here.'

'If you're lying to me…' she growled. 'Come on, Ed – up!'

'I can't! Get off me, for—'

She pushed her face in close, saw him flinch. 'If I have to leave you here, I'll make damn sure you can't run away, even if I have to hobble you. Your choice.'

And suddenly he found it in him to get to his feet. Patting him down produced a mobile phone, torch, and the keys to the car. She pocketed the lot.

With the torch switched on, she looked around. She could see nothing but the track they came in on, and trees.

'Why here, Ed? And where *is* here? Where are we?'

He was breathing hard, as if practising for labour, or going into it. 'One of… old plantations… Gravel pit…'

'Why here?'

He didn't answer, but she knew anyway.

'Is this where you buried Hope? Planning to dig another hole for *me*, were you?'

'Just wanted the locket… One you took from the cottage, before… fire. How did you know…?'

She shook her head. 'I didn't know you had the locket, and I didn't start the fire, you idiot. There were *two* lockets.'

Underhill closed his eyes and let out a low moan.

'If you've hurt Lily because of this…'

His face screwed up. 'Look… I never wanted—'

'What happened to you, Ed? You were a copper. How did my father get you to do his dirty work in the first place?'

'He reels you in… don't realise it. Until, one day, I woke up and he… owned me. He was a bloody master at that. Did it to you, didn't he?'

'Oh, save your breath. Let's go.'

She gave him a shove. He moved off slowly, stumbling over brambles and fallen branches, the leaf litter slick with rain underfoot.

The dizziness and nausea drenched down over her then, as the adrenaline hangover began to kick in. She realised one hip burned like the devil, and her head ached. When she touched her fingers to her temple, they came away greasy with blood.

And her only hope was that she could stay on her feet long enough to see this through.

EIGHTY-SIX

Jane Hudson pulled off the road and tucked the patrol car into the gateway, nose-to-nose with the Toyota Hilux already parked there. She climbed out, leaving the engine running and the lights on.

The driver of the pickup was standing in the rear load bed and gave her a brief wave. She recognised Oliver Harding.

'That's good timing – I was just trying to call you,' Harding said, leaning on the side of the bed. 'Mobile phones are a bit outside my remit, I'm afraid.'

'Why the call?' Hudson asked. 'Is it about Blake Claremont? Have you seen her?'

'Blake? My word, no. Virginia Fitzroy called me because her children are missing. I've been driving around half the county trying to find them. Some idiot in a Mercedes almost ran me off the road back there, though. And by the looks of it'—he gestured to the fallen gatepost—'they passed through this way.'

'Is this part of your property, Mr Harding?'

'No, no, but I do know the owner, and he'll be concerned that trespassers can trespass against him, as it were. I thought I'd see if I could get the gate shut, at least.'

'Right, I'm sure he'll be grateful to you for that,' Hudson said. 'Do you need a hand?'

'Not at all. I have some tools with me, so I'll jury-rig something for tonight and come back to it tomorrow. You're looking for Blake, did you say?'

'Yes, if you'd keep an eye out?'

'And likewise, if you spot Tom and Lily on your travels, please call Virginia at once. She's worried to death about them.'

'Will do, sir.'

Hudson climbed back into the patrol car and closed the door, glad to be out of the rain. She backed out of the confines of the gateway and rumbled down the bumpy lane.

Less than a mile further on, she found the crashed Mercedes. After Harding's warning, it did not come as much of a surprise. But when she started to punch in the registration number to bring up the owner's details, she realised she already knew both the car and its owner.

Byron.

She climbed out, frowning, reached for her phone and dialled Byron's number.

Somewhere inside the Merc, she heard it ringing.

She pulled out a torch and looked for the driver, but it was clear the vehicle had been abandoned.

Why?

Hudson headed back to the patrol car and lifted her radio to call the control room when her mobile began to ring. She answered at once, with half an idea it might somehow be Byron with explanations and apologies. It wasn't.

'PC Hudson? It's Derby Royal Infirmary here. You left a card, if you recall, and asked us to notify you as soon as Roger Flint regained consciousness.'

'Right, yes. He has, I assume?'

'He started to come round a little while ago. The neurological consultant has called by to see him on the ward, and has given permission for Mr Flint to be interviewed.'

'Can he remember anything? About who attacked him?'

'Oh, yes,' the nurse said blithely. 'He was very clear on that, remarkably enough.'

Hudson took a breath, trying not to snap. 'Did he say who?'

'Yes, indeed. He was anxious we didn't allow the gentleman to visit him, in case he tried to finish what he'd started. A chap by the name of Oliver Harding, he said. Does that mean anything to you?'

'Oh, yes,' Hudson echoed faintly.

She made her excuses to get off the line as fast as she could, turned the car round and roared back up the lane, on the radio as she did so.

When she reached the gateway, the pickup was still there. But of its owner, there was no sign.

EIGHTY-SEVEN

'This is it,' Underhill said. 'Near as I remember…'

Blake gave him a prod in the back. 'Then let's have you on your knees.'

He threw her a quick glance over his shoulder. She caught it in the beam of the torch, recognised a swirl of fear, and anger, and resignation as he slowly complied.

'So, where's Lily?'

'She'll be here – soon, OK?'

They'd struggled deep into the plantation. It was neglected enough for saplings to take hold between the crop spruce and pine, making the going hard. The rain was in their faces, despite the tree cover. Thin branches whipped at their limbs.

Underhill had brought her to the rim of an old gravel pit, long since disused and now clawed back by the forest.

'Why here?' she asked.

He managed to produce a shrug. 'Dunno.'

She stared him down. He avoided her gaze, shuffled uneasily. His knees squelched in the mud.

'Why kill Hope at all?'

'I didn't!'

She jerked forwards and he cringed, tucking in his chin like a boxer expecting a knockout punch.

'For every lie you tell me, I will break another bone. Is that understood?'

He mumbled a reply, eyes on the wheel brace still clenched in her hand.

'So, why did you kill her? She was just a kid – fifteen.'

'I didn't,' he repeated, sullen. She shifted her weight and he added quickly, 'It wasn't me, all right? Buried her? Yeah – OK, you got me. Killed her? No way.'

She'd been expecting that – suspected it might even be true. Suspected it enough not to carry out her threat.

For the moment.

'Then who did?'

'Your dad.'

Blake experienced a fast burst of rage. As if, by describing him as *her* father, Underhill was somehow shifting the blame onto her. As if she wouldn't know who he was talking about if he simply said: Gideon Fitzroy.

As if I don't have enough guilt to carry already over what happened to Hope.

'Lying by omission is as bad as lying outright.'

'You've changed.' Underhill shook his head. 'Fire in your belly now, isn't there?'

'I grew up. Get over it.' She put her head on one side. 'Why did Gideon kill her? What was it – couldn't stand the thought of someone running around, outside his control, knowing his secrets?'

'Said it was an accident. He and Flint were out in that old Land Rover of his – looking for the pair of you. Saw a girl walking along the side of the road – your coat, your hair. And she started to run when she saw them. He said they was just trying to get in front of her – stop her. I… I don't know exactly what happened. I wasn't there.'

'He ran her down, didn't he?' Blake spoke through her teeth. 'Nothing "accidental" about it.'

'He *swore* it was an accident.' He took a breath. 'But *I* don't know because I. Wasn't. There. For God's sake…'

'As soon as they stopped to pick up the… body, they must have realised it wasn't me they'd hit.'

Underhill swallowed. She saw his Adam's apple bounce convulsively in his throat. 'She landed… badly. Her face…'

Blake forced herself not to let the implications of that show. She took a couple of steps away from him, so she wouldn't be tempted to lash out. Instead, with remarkable calm, she said, 'So you saw what you wanted to see.'

'Fitzroy said he'd talked to the other girl, only a few hours before. How was we supposed to know she'd changed her hair, her clothes—?'

She spun back. '*Hope*. Her name was Hope.'

'Yeah, OK, OK. Hope. Later that night, we brought her here. Fitzroy had dug a hole by then, and we put her – Hope – into it.'

'Was that when you stole her necklace – with the locket?'

'Hardly stealing…'

'What else would you call it, Underhill – looting? Grave robbing? You were the copper. You tell me.'

'It wasn't like that. I—'

But the denial died in his throat when Blake suddenly brought the beam of the torch up onto his face. He screwed his eyes up.

'What do you mean, "Fitzroy had dug a hole"?' she demanded, backtracking. 'Dug it how, exactly?'

Underhill opened his eyes again cautiously as she let the beam drop. 'A JCB, of course. What – you thought he'd put his back into it with a shovel?'

She moved towards him then, purposeful and intent. 'You're lying, Ed. I warned you what would happen if you lied to me…'

'I'm not! I didn't—'

'Even on a good day, Gideon Fitzroy was a terrible driver. He struggled enough with an automatic, so there's no way in hell he could have operated a JCB.' She paused, muttered almost to herself. 'But I know who *does* have those skills…'

Behind them, in the woods, came the unmistakable sound of twigs breaking underfoot. Blake twisted on the balls of her feet, just in time to see a man emerge out of the trees. She couldn't quite see who, but there was no mistaking the object he held.

A double-barrelled shotgun.

EIGHTY-EIGHT

Byron, standing silent in the darkness nearby, had been waiting and listening while Blake interrogated Underhill. He'd noticed Oliver Harding arrive – that he, too, had lingered in the shadows for a time before moving into view. It disturbed Byron that he had not picked up any inkling of the older man's intention to follow him into the forest.

Nor that he would bring a shotgun with him.

That, Byron recognised, had been a mistake.

Where did he get the damn gun in the first place?

Even as the thought formed, he remembered the padlocked tool chest running full width across the pickup bed, just behind the cab. A large box that could very easily have doubled as a gun cabinet.

As Harding moved closer to where Blake stood with Underhill – still on his knees, hands tied – Byron entertained the faint possibility that the old man was simply going to intervene. To keep everyone contained until the police came.

Then Harding turned and seemed to look directly into his place of concealment.

'Would you care to join us, Mr Byron?'

He saw Blake's head twist, as if searching for him. He couldn't read her expression.

If I give myself away now, I'm no use to her…

'Oh, please – don't make me do anything you might have cause to regret.'

With reluctance, Byron stepped out of cover, switching on the torch to ensure he didn't trip in the last few yards.

Blake ignored Harding, despite the shotgun. Her gaze was on Byron.

'How long have you been out there?'

'Long enough. You're bleeding. Are you all right?'

She nodded, but some of the fight seemed to go out of her. She touched a hand to the side of her head. Scalp wounds always looked bad. Sometimes it was hard to judge how serious they really were, but her eyes looked clear, her stance steady.

'Shame they didn't go ahead with that reconstruction,' she said. 'It would have been very realistic.'

'Well, I don't quite know what's going on,' Harding said, his voice brisk, 'but now we're all here, I'm sure we can sort this out in a civilised manner.'

He shifted his grip on the shotgun so it lay through the crook of his arm, which was the conventional way to carry it. But he had not broken the barrels, Byron noted. And he had positioned himself close enough to threaten, but not so close he was within easy reach.

Clever. All we need to do is keep him calm and play along…

But then Blake said, 'Oh, I can be civilised… providing you brought Lily with you and she's not in some hole in the ground, as you threatened.'

Byron's gaze snapped to Harding, then to Blake. 'Him?'

'They sent me a picture – of Lily, bound and gagged. Told me they would bury her alive if I didn't meet them. What did you *think* I was doing out tonight?'

'My dear girl, that's nothing to do with me,' Harding said, his voice kindly – everybody's favourite uncle. 'I'm simply one of the search party, looking for both Lily and Tom. Indeed, it may be that this is something they've cooked up between them, to ensure their mother inherits.'

She gave a short, harsh laugh. 'That would have been so much more believable, had Underhill not just run me down… The same way my father ran down Hope.'

'Did he? My word.'

'And you have a JCB, don't you, Oliver? You landscaped the garden for Anne.' Her focus was on the old man's face, rather than the gun in his hands. 'Was it you, that night, who helped them get rid of Hope's body?'

'Of course not. Why would I do a thing like that? And, actually, Gideon *could* operate a JCB. I know because I taught him myself.'

'Really.' Sarcasm drawled through her voice. 'When?'

'Before I started on the pond, so… the summer you turned fourteen, I think it was. He asked me to show him how it was done, and I was happy to oblige. Naturally, I never thought for a moment he'd use that knowledge to do anything like you suggest.'

'Oh, *naturally*,' she echoed. 'But if you're so innocent, Oliver, what are you doing here?'

'Well, I could hardly let Mr Byron come alone, could I?'

Byron cleared his throat. The time for appeasement was over.

'That doesn't explain the shotgun. Is that the same one you used to take a shot at Blake, by the way?' Harding said nothing. He nodded. 'You might want to consider a heavier load, if you're attempting to bring down prey larger than a pheasant.'

'Thank you. I'll bear that in mind.'

'Was it you who rigged the ladder to the hayloft, also?'

'That could easily have been Roger,' Harding hedged.

Byron turned slightly. 'Mr Underhill?'

Underhill had stayed on his knees and silent. He no doubt realised that keeping as low a profile as possible was his best option. Even now, his only response was to shrug.

Harding said, 'It would seem, Mr Byron, that you are not quite as off your game as you have led us to believe.'

Before Byron could answer, one way or another, they saw the beam of a powerful torch moving jerkily through the trees, and heard the crackle of twigs and branches. They all twisted to watch. Harding, Byron saw, improved his grip on the shotgun. He risked a step closer, but the old man's head jerked in his direction, bringing the gun round.

Then, a moment later, a figure burst out of the trees.

'Oliver Harding, hold it right there,' came the unmistakable sound of PC Hudson's voice. 'I'm arresting you for—'

Harding didn't wait to hear the charges.

He swung the shotgun to meet the new threat, and pulled the trigger.

EIGHTY-NINE

Blake half-expected the blast to take Hudson off her feet and toss her backwards into the trees. Her only previous experience with shotgun injuries – not counting her own minor brush – had been on TV or at the movies.

Instead, the woman just seemed to crumple with a chopped-off shout. She dropped the torch. It rolled slightly into the under-growth, producing a shrouded beam that shivered through the fronds of ferns and bracken.

Instinctively, Blake started forwards. Harding shifted the barrels of the gun in her direction. The one on the right let out a wisp of smoke, just visible in the gloom. It was a stark reminder that he still had another cartridge loaded and ready to go on the second trigger.

'Ah-ah, Blake. Leave her, my dear. Not much you could do for her anyway.'

Blake glanced at Hudson, a dark outline on the ground, hard to make out beyond the glare of the dropped torch. The police were issued with stab vests, Blake knew. But how much protection they afforded against lead shot was another matter. Hudson did not seem to be moving.

Her eyes slid to Byron, who was nearer to where Hudson lay. Could he tell if she was still alive? But Byron's face was shuttered, his expression grim.

Blake was not reassured.

'I think I'll have the pair of you together, if you don't mind?' Harding said, gesturing her to move across, closer to where Byron stood. 'Where I can keep an eye on you.'

Blake looked back at him, saw the face of a man she'd known since childhood. The face of a man she didn't recognise.

'No.'

He'd already begun to turn away, taking her compliance for granted. He stopped, irritation in his face. 'What?'

'I think I'll stay where I am, thanks,' she said, pushing insubordination into it. 'Why should I make it easy for you?'

On the far side of Harding, she saw Byron give a twitch of an approving smile. As she watched, he took a small step sideways, so they were directly opposite each other with Harding dead centre between them.

'Give it up, man,' Byron said. 'It doesn't matter which of us you shoot first, you won't have time to reload before the other takes you down.'

Harding hesitated. After a moment, he edged the muzzle towards Byron. 'I think I can handle her – she's a little slip of a thing.'

'Don't kid yourself, mate,' Underhill said suddenly. 'She broke my bloody arm.'

'Luck,' Harding said, his tone dismissive.

Blake smiled, devil-may-care. 'Oh, you keep telling yourself that, by all means…'

Underhill laughed, a coarse rasp of sound. 'And don't expect *him* to jump in and save you, lass. Only thinks of himself, does Mr Byron, eh?'

Blake looked to him, but Byron said nothing.

'Glory boy, this one. Ran chasing after a maniac, looking to get himself a medal – and *left his own wife to die in the street.*'

Something cold washed down the back of Blake's neck that had nothing to do with the rain.

Byron had told her about the terrorist attack in which he'd been injured. And he'd told her that his wife, who'd been a doctor, was dead.

As if the two things were completely separate.

But that his wife had died in the very same terrorist incident was something he had absolutely failed to mention.

Underhill was watching her face, saw the shock, and the realisation as it took hold. His voice was a sneer. 'What was it you said to me before? "Lies of omission are still lies." Was that it?'

'Close enough…'

'If you think Blake is going to believe—'

'So, tell her it's not true, then. Go on!' Underhill taunted, spittle flying. 'See? He *can't*.'

Byron met her eyes. For an elongated moment of time, they stared at each other.

'She either trusts me, or she doesn't,' he said, 'but I'm not going to work *twice* as hard to prove it…'

She heard the emphasis. It triggered a memory – of a conversation about trust, and those who were worthy of it. The rest of it unfurled in her mind, smooth and fast.

Then Byron said, 'Now, Jane!'

Blake hadn't seen her moving, but realised that Byron must have done. At his order, Hudson rolled, grabbed the torch and pointed the powerful beam directly into Harding's eyes. He flinched back, shutting them against the glare.

But at the same time, he brought the shotgun up, his hands tightening. This close, he hardly needed to aim.

Without thinking about it, Blake rushed him. She sensed Byron doing the same from the other side. Byron grabbed the barrels of the shotgun, forcing them harmlessly upwards.

Blake ducked under their grappling arms, and brought her knee straight up into Harding's balls.

He released his grip on the shotgun and dropped like an old sack of spuds.

Byron thrust the gun into Blake's hands. 'Here. Keep an eye on them both.'

He went to Hudson, helped her sit. They spoke in murmured undertones, but she could hear the pain leaching through in Hudson's voice.

'Is she all right?' Blake asked when he returned.

'She will be. The vest bore the brunt. She was lucky.'

Blake let out a breath. She turned, bringing the butt of the shotgun up into her shoulder. The muzzle was centred on Under-hill's chest as he knelt in the mud.

'OK, Ed, very last time of asking – *where's Lily?*'

NINETY

Lily woke in the dark, trapped inside a long box that was barely bigger than she was.

A coffin.

She tried to scream, but there was heavy tape across her mouth. Her wrists and ankles were taped, too.

The last thing she recalled clearly was following Tom when he ran from the car towards the old stables.

What happened after that?

She'd got as far as the woods when someone had grabbed her. They held a cloth over her nose and mouth that smelled both sweet and bitter at the same time.

After that was either a blank or a blur. She remembered the flash of a camera, the sound of an engine, of being bumped and bounced around and now…

Silence.

Darkness.

Cold.

In total panic, she began to thrash wildly. Nothing loosened, and her knees and elbows throbbed from hitting them against the sides of the box. Where her hands banged against one side, it ran with damp and clanged dully – metal, not wood.

Tears leaked from her eyes, sliding sideways across the bridge of her nose and into her hair. It tickled. She shook her head like a horse shaking off flies.

She suddenly remembered standing over Gideon's grave, watching his coffin being lowered into the earth and wondering what it must be like to wake up in your own grave.

She screamed again.

This time, she managed to produce a squeak of sound. What little spit was in her mouth had leaked under the adhesive on the tape and lifted it at one side. She rubbed her tongue against her teeth in an effort to produce more. It felt disgusting, slithering across her face.

But the next time she screamed, it was louder again.

Suddenly, she froze.

Was that a voice?

She sucked in a deep breath, then hesitated. Supposing it was her kidnapper? Supposing, if they heard her, they would hurt her? Maybe even… kill her?

Anything's better than being buried alive…

She screamed, so loud this time it stung her ears, as she writhed and twisted, feeling the box sway.

Something clanged and juddered. She heard more voices, closer now but still muffled. Banging, the squeal of rusty hinges, then the lid of the box was wrenched open and water splattered in on her.

Hands grabbing her, lifting her out.

It was almost as dark out of the box as it had been inside. They were by the edge of a wood, she saw, and the box had been in the bed of a pickup truck.

The road was crowded with vehicles, some of them with blue lights flashing. And people with torches that hurt her eyes.

But most confusing of all, it was Blake, who'd rescued her, was holding her, and peeling the tape from her mouth.

'It's OK, Lily. It's all OK,' Blake said. 'I've got you. It's all over.'

NINETY-ONE

The camera was mounted high in one corner of the room. It looked down over the shoulders of the two interviewing detectives, across the table and into the face of Oliver Harding, sitting alongside his solicitor.

'Of course, I didn't set out intending to kill Roger,' Harding said, his tone almost conversational. 'But the man was coming apart at the seams. Wanted to confess about the girl – about all of them. A complete liability. Naturally, he had to go. I saw my opportunity and took it, that's all.'

To Byron's eyes, observing the interview via video feed from another room, Harding's solicitor looked pained.

Harding himself seemed older from this angle, his shoulders more stooped, and the top of his bald head dotted with liver spots. Altogether, a lot less substantial than he had in the forest, a few days before, with a shotgun in his hands.

'Not making things easy on himself, is he?' Commander Daud remarked. 'His type never does.'

'"His type"?' Byron echoed.

Daud snorted. 'White, upper-middle-class men of a certain age. Entitled, arrogant. The type who think they can do what they like to women, or young girls, because – I mean, seriously – what else are they there for?'

She was leaning on the back of a chair, too restless to sit, in a denim jacket over a chic black dress. Even out of uniform, she did not look like a woman to be trifled with.

On the monitor, the detectives had moved on to the subject of Gideon Fitzroy and the girls he'd abused.

'What I'm struggling to understand, Mr Harding, is what you got out of it,' the senior detective said. They'd brought in a specialist team to handle the questioning. 'Help me out here. What was in it for you?'

Harding cleared his throat. 'My wife, as I'm sure you are aware, is confined to a wheelchair, and has been for many years. Prior to that, our sex life was extremely… active and satisfying, for both of us. But I have particular… tastes, which she can no longer fulfil. I was forced to seek… other alternatives.'

'What alternatives were those?' the detective asked, without inflection.

'She encouraged me to seek sexual encounters outside our marriage and then relate them to her, in detail. Sexual pleasure for women is a largely brain-mediated response, after all.' Harding spoke in a remote, matter-of-fact tone, without embarrassment. But Byron noted that the solicitor's head was bowed. He appeared to be utterly absorbed in his note taking. A dull red flush crept up the sides of his neck, and the tips of his ears were practically glowing.

Byron glanced sideways at Daud. She was watching with frank interest.

'So, not merely entitled, but a full-blown narcissist,' Byron murmured. 'No wonder he and Fitzroy got along so well.'

'After some experimentation, we found that a very particular kind of erotic scenario worked for her,' Harding was saying.

'What kind of scenario, Mr Harding?'

'An older man, sophisticated and worldly, seducing and then initiating a young girl—'

'A *child.*' The younger of the two detectives spoke for the first time, his voice flat.

Harding glared at him, silent.

In the observation room, Daud sucked in a breath. 'He's blown it. Never let your disgust show – no matter what they've done – or they'll clam up on you. You've gotta flatter them, stroke their ego, make 'em boast.'

'I think Harding wants to put his side of it,' Byron said. 'In his own mind, he's convinced this is the truth.'

Daud threw him a doubtful glance, but refrained from comment.

Eventually, Harding shifted in his seat. Then he frowned, picking up the thread.

'Gideon would hold parties with a very select guest list – when his family was away, naturally. There were enough rooms in the house to ensure an appropriate level of privacy for the activities.'

'Was Mr Fitzroy recording these… activities?' the senior detective asked.

Harding shook his head. 'Oh no, that wouldn't have been wise.'

'Whereas sexually assaulting underage girls is perfectly sensible,' Daud muttered.

'Hush,' Byron said. 'He's been given the rope and he's busy hanging himself. Let him get on with it.'

And Harding did, listing dates that Byron knew would be checked against Fitzroy's known location – the times when he was in parliament and those when he was in the country. Byron had little doubt that they would line up. Harding named girls, too. Not just Hope, but many others, going back years.

Those girls, Byron considered, might be harder to trace.

Finally, the detectives moved on to the night of Blake and Hope's disappearance. Harding admitted that he – not Fitzroy – had been the one operating the digger. Fitzroy, meanwhile, had scuttled home to make an entirely unnecessary phone call to one of his old political cronies. Someone to vouch for his whereabouts, should that ever be required. Apart from that, Harding's story matched statements already taken from Ed Underhill and Roger Flint.

They had all assumed it was Blake they were burying – right up until the day she came back from the dead.

NINETY-TWO

Daud let Byron drive her to the same pub in the village where he'd stayed, for lunch. He was using a hire car while his own was being repaired. She had travelled from London by train to Derby – a direct run from St Pancras – where he'd collected her.

'Whilst I'm well aware that perversion is not entirely the province of able-bodied males, do you think his wife really did encourage him to get involved?' she asked over home-made chicken and mushroom pie. 'After all, according to the reports, she was the one who first brought up the girls at the farm, when it would have been in her best interests to keep shtum.'

Byron was aware that she was being discreet in case of eaves-droppers – and equally aware that they had the back room and an open fire to themselves. It had been a while since he'd discussed a gory crime scene or a stomach-turning confession over a meal. Not an aspect of being a copper he'd missed.

He shook his head. 'Not necessarily. It could be a clever ploy. Knowing *someone* would mention them, sooner or later, she might have decided to get out in front. Having met her, though, I don't think she has the stomach for that kind of exploitation of minors, quite apart from anything else,' he said. 'But, he's a very convincing liar. I'm sure he'll argue in court that people have all kinds of strange fantasies on which they never normally have recourse to act.'

'Really?' Daud's eyes widened, mocking. 'Care to share any of yours?'

'I don't think so, ma'am.'

'Spoilsport.'

*

Over dessert, Daud said, 'The techs found blood and tissue trace under the paint on that old Land Rover of Fitzroy's, did you know?'

Byron shook his head. 'No, but I didn't expect to be kept informed.'

'In that case, you won't have heard that the search teams uncovered human remains near the gravel pit.'

'Hope?'

'And at least two others, so far, who've been there longer. They identified Hope pretty sharpish.' She gave him a sideways glance. 'Seeing as some clever-dick had already obtained a DNA profile from the girl's mother.'

'Hm. Has Inspector Khan withdrawn his complaint about me making free with his resources, then?'

'Initially, he said he would… providing the Met agreed to foot the bill.'

'Ah. And what was your response to that?'

'Told him I'd arm-wrestle him for it – best of three.'

Byron put down his spoon and raised an eyebrow. 'The result?'

She grinned. 'No charge.'

*

At least, Byron considered, Daud waited until the coffee had been served before she cut to the heart of the matter. Not quite surgical precision with a scalpel, as a rampage with a chainsaw.

'So, this elephant in the room,' she said, leaning forwards with her elbows propped on the table. 'It's got its arse in the fireplace and its trunk in the sugar. Are you going to bring it up or do I have to?'

He thought she was talking about Blake, felt compelled to stall. 'Elephant, ma'am?'

'When are you coming back to work?'

'Ah… I thought my discretional leave was over, in any case?'

'It was.' She pulled a face. 'Then I remembered how stubborn you are, and I told them if they try to force your hand, you'll damn well resign, just to prove a point.'

He took a sip of his coffee. 'Indeed.'

The thought of being entirely out of police work – for good this time – did not sit comfortably with him.

But…

'To be honest, I'm not sure I'm ready to return to the kind of full active-duty role where I might have to deal with a similar… incident,' he admitted.

'Not yet.'

'If ever.'

'Well, in that case, what I have to say may very well be right up your street.'

If he didn't know better, he'd say the commander appeared almost smug.

'Oh?'

'Yeah. The IOPC are looking for an investigator.'

'No.' He was shaking his head before she finished speaking. 'Digging up dirt on other coppers is not how I envisage spending what remains of my career.'

'Hear me out. They're looking for a kind of unofficial advance guard.'

Byron raised an eyebrow, took another sip of his coffee, and said nothing.

Daud sighed. 'Look, we both know that the reputation of the police is at an all-time low with the public. They don't trust us, and – more particularly – they don't trust us to clean our own house either.'

'And the solution?'

'That they utilise someone like you to look into cases of possible wrongdoing, misconduct, or corruption, *before* the investigation goes public.'

'The point of that being?'

'Don't play dumb, Byron.' She rolled her eyes. 'So they know the probable outcome before they begin, that's why. No further damage to public confidence, or to police morale, by chasing cases that will never go anywhere.'

He met her gaze, keeping his expression bland as he put down his empty cup. 'And to sweep things under the carpet, if it looks like they *are* going somewhere?'

Her turn to shake her head, as emphatically as he had done. 'Uh-uh. Definitely not. First question I asked, because I knew you'd say no, if there was any hint of that about the job.'

'Who would I be reporting to?' He knew he'd implied too much interest when he saw a hint of triumph in her eyes. 'Hypothetically speaking.'

'Liaising with the IOPC, but ultimately responsible to the Home Secretary.'

'London based?'

'Largely, although I understand it's something of a roving brief.' She studied him, her gaze calculating. 'Shall I email you the details?'

He shrugged. 'Perhaps.'

'I would advise you – both as your senior officer and as your friend – to give this some serious consideration. Pressure's on to find someone suitable for the role and, at the moment, you're it. Why do you think I've been able to give you so much help behind the scenes with this one?' Daud leaned forwards in her chair, a note of urgency slipping into her tone. 'If you don't take it, Byron, they'll put you out to grass. And if they do that, I know you – you'll die of boredom inside a year.'

NINETY-THREE

The funeral for Hope Glennie – when it finally took place – was held in the village church on a bitter clear winter's day. Pauline was her only remaining family. But Byron was heartened that the Allbrights turned out, as did Hope's social worker, Ms Devi. And what seemed to be half the village residents crowded inside the sturdy Norman walls to line the pews.

On this occasion, Byron planned his journey better from London. He arrived in plenty of time to hear the eulogy, read by Blake Claremont, looking unrecognisable in an immaculate, masculine black suit and tie. Her hair was back to blonde again – perhaps as a tribute to Hope.

She was accompanied by a big man in his late forties. He dressed like a Hollywood star but stayed close enough to be bodyguard rather than boyfriend. Byron looked beyond the skinhead haircut and the sharp suit, and saw a ruthless intelligence in those cold blue eyes.

Commander Daud, sidling into place alongside Byron just as the service started, whispered in his ear that this was the infamous Lex Vaganov. Either antiques dealer or conman, depending who you talked to.

Inspector Khan and PC Hudson attended. They both wore their No1 dress uniforms, as did Daud, who outshone the pair of them. Byron had on his usual suit under a wool overcoat, aiming to blend.

As he watched the mourners follow the coffin to the grave, he could not help but remember his last visit. His last funeral. He noted those who were absent as much as those who were present. The three men who'd conspired to hide Hope's death – no surprises there. They were all in jail.

But he was disappointed that Virginia Fitzroy and her children stayed away. He'd kept his word to Blake that Tom's confession would go no further, so could only assume that perhaps Virginia had not wanted to remind Lily of her own near-burial.

Perhaps there's hope for her maternal instinct, after all.

He stayed back during the ritual of lowering Hope's bones into the earth. Vaganov's bulk proved useful for keeping Pauline on her feet towards the end of it, steadying her. Byron frowned as she unwrapped a familiar silver locket, dropping it onto the lid of the coffin with the first handfuls of dirt.

'Don't worry, that's not the locket recovered from Underhill's cottage,' Daud murmured, at his elbow. '*That* one's evidence for the trial. I understand Blake gave her own locket to Pauline for this.'

'You're staying well-informed.'

'I've made a point of it. Anne Harding has denied all knowledge of her husband's activities, by the way – no surprises there.'

'And do you believe her?'

'Ah, that will be one for the jury to decide…'

At the grave, Blake dropped in an assortment of flowers and stepped aside.

He realised that Daud had finished speaking, was expecting an answer to a question he hadn't heard. Turning, he found she'd followed his gaze and was watching Blake.

'You haven't called her, have you?' Daud said quietly. Her voice held a mix of accusation and disappointment.

He tilted his head in the direction of Vaganov. 'Well, I don't think she's been lonely.'

'Hardly the point.' She rolled her eyes. 'What are you going to do about her?'

'Why would I want to do anything about her?'

'You're playing dumb again, Byron. I can hear it in your voice – every time you mention her. Something about her gets to you, and I think you ought to find out exactly what that is.'

He sighed, clasped his gloved hands in front of him. 'I… admire the way her mind works,' he allowed at last.

'Her *mind*?' Daud repeated. 'Sod that, what about the rest of her? Come on, this is the first female who's shown even a glimmer of being able to melt that block of ice you keep in your chest, and all you'll say is that you "admire her mind"?'

Byron couldn't prevent a twitch of a smile at her outrage. 'Yes.'

Daud slouched, clenched her fists and gave a growl of frustration that was not entirely feigned.

He relented.

'All right, yes, I find her attractive… and intriguing—'

'Ah-ha.'

'*But*, at the same time, she can lie without apparent compunction. She seems to have spent the last ten years consorting with conmen and criminals. She has breaking-and-entering skills… I don't even want to think about where she got them. And she probably cannot be trusted not to make off with the family silver, given half a chance.'

'Just the type to keep you on your toes then.'

'Indeed.'

But Daud was not about to let it go. 'If not her criminal tendencies, what is it about her that so intrigues you?'

They began to walk. It did not escape Byron's notice that they took the same gravel path he and Hudson had followed, the day he'd first met Blake.

'When we were out there in the forest – with Harding between us, brandishing that shotgun – I didn't have to spell out what was needed. All I had to do was catch her eye, and she… *knew*. She just knew… And, at the same time, I knew I could rely on her to get the job done.'

'Even you have to admit, that kind of connection is rare.'

'It is. But, it feels… disloyal to have any kind of connection.'

Daud halted and turned towards him, her gaze intent as she touched his arm briefly. 'Isobel wouldn't have wanted you to turn into a monk, Byron. You know that, right?'

'With all due respect, ma'am, stop matchmaking.' He glanced at Daud's face. She had looked away, back across the churchyard, but he could see the corner of her mouth curving upwards.

Blake had tucked one hand through Vaganov's crooked elbow to cross the grass and gravel towards where he and Daud stood, near the garden of remembrance. In tall-heeled boots, Blake's walk took on a slow, sensuous sway. A far cry from the Doc Martens of their last encounter.

'Now's your chance,' Daud murmured. 'I'll run interference.'

Blake paused when she reached them, forcing Vaganov to pause as well.

'Mr Byron,' she said, her voice remote. 'Thank you for coming.'

He nodded, noticing for the first time that she still held one flower of the bunch she'd dropped into the grave. Realisation landed softly. 'For your mother?'

Her turn to nod mutely.

Daud turned to Vaganov.

'I understand there's a local pub with some very good guest beers, just up the main street, Mr Vaganov. How about I buy you a drink?'

He regarded her, stone faced. 'I don't think so, Commander Daud,' he said finally, then cracked a smile. 'Not unless, first, I buy *you* a drink…'

NINETY-FOUR

As Blake laid the single white lily on Catherine Claremont's grave marker, she was acutely aware of the man standing a pace or two behind her. She was shivering, partly from the cold but also from nerves, she realised. Byron was still difficult to read, even in the light of shared experience.

He'd unsettled her the first time she'd laid eyes on him, right here in this churchyard.

He still unsettled her now.

She straightened, wiping her hands and nodded in the direction of the main gate – the direction in which Daud and Vaganov had disappeared. 'Do you think those two will be all right on their own together?'

'I doubt they'll have time to do each other any real damage.' Byron flicked her a sideways glance. 'What will you do now, by the way?'

She blinked at the sudden change of subject. 'Go back to London – back to my life.'

'What about Claremont?'

'What about it?' Her eyes went to her mother's grave marker and her mouth twisted. 'I always knew, by bringing Hope's body to light – and her parentage – that meant I'd have to let go of Claremont.'

He stilled. 'Oh?'

'I've shown that, just because Gideon Fitzroy was my father, it doesn't follow that Catherine was my mother. Virginia could fight me to the last brick.'

'And you're not prepared to do that?'

She gave a half-hearted shrug. 'Legal battles inevitably cost a lot of money.'

'Well, I couldn't help noticing that you arrived in a very nice Bentley Continental,' he said, his voice dry. 'The antiques business must be booming.'

'Lex has fingers in a lot of pies.'

'So I understand.'

'I told you – he's just a friend, Byron.'

He raised an eyebrow. 'I thought we were talking about business, not where he might have his fingers…'

She turned her head, bit her lip in an effort not to laugh, and quickly sobered. 'Anyway, I already told you – it was never about the inheritance.'

'Yes, you did,' he murmured. His gaze followed hers to Catherine Claremont's stone in the grass. 'You could always… have her exhumed.'

Blake shook her head. 'She was cremated. No viable DNA in ashes.'

'Ah. That's why she's in this part of the churchyard, isn't it?' he said slowly. 'But I thought there had been Claremonts in the village for generations. Don't you have a family plot?'

'It was what she wanted. She planned it all ahead of time – even picked out her own stone.' She took a breath, hoping to force the sadness out of her voice. 'And when the cancer spread, and she knew she would lose all her beautiful hair, she grew it longer so she could have it all cut off and turned into a wig when she started the chemo—'

'Wait. The wig she had – it was real hair? Her *own* hair?'

'Yes, of course. She—'

'Then we need it.' He took her arm, began to hurry her towards the side gate into the lane, where his car was parked.

'Byron, slow down. It's *cut* hair – no use at all. Even I know the roots still need to be attached.'

'Ah, but you need only the hair shaft to extract mitochondrial DNA, which is inherited *only* from your maternal line,' he said, pressing the key fob to unlock the car doors. 'Now trust me, and get in.'

NINETY-FIVE

Lily wept for all the things she'd lost.

The most important of which, it seemed to her, was her innocence.

Oh, physically she was unharmed. Untouched.

But mentally, that was another matter.

She'd thought herself fairly sophisticated – for her age. Some of the girls at school were just so gullible it wasn't true.

It had been a shock to find out that, when it came to her step-father, she was no more worldly-wise than the greenest of them.

So, very careful to show no outward sign of tantrum, she took down the photographs of actors from her bedroom walls. She removed each photo from its frame, then rehung the empty frames, as a reminder.

She could hardly bring herself to spend time in the loft above the garage, let alone open the trunk of costumes she'd used for all those scenes she'd performed for Gideon, when they were alone together.

When her brother came to find her there, she was struggling to drag the trunk across the wooden boards towards the staircase.

'What are you doing, Lil?' Tom asked as he climbed up.

'What does it look like?' she demanded, breathless. 'Getting rid of stuff I don't want to *be* here anymore.'

She thought he'd question that, but he simply nodded, like he understood. 'Need a hand?'

That was one good thing to come of all this, she reckoned. She and Tom had managed to regain something of the closeness of their earlier years. She ought to have been horrified by what he'd done to protect her from their stepfather. Actually, she was in awe of his bravery.

And grateful.

She only found out afterwards that the night she'd been kidnapped, Tom had seen Oliver Harding bundle her into his pickup. He'd tried to intervene, but Mr Harding had threatened to hurt her.

I can still hardly believe it. He always seemed so nice.

Tom was eventually found, locked in one of the old stables, and frantic with worry over her. It was lovely to know how much he cared.

Now, they managed between them to bump the loaded trunk down the wooden stairs. Tom fetched a wheelbarrow to transport it across the rear lawn to the rusting brazier near the trees, used for burning the leaves of autumn.

They were not quite out of sight of the house, but their mother was likely to be in one of the rooms at the front. By the time she noticed what they were doing, it would be too late.

They scrunched up some old newspapers and piled on twigs and sticks for kindling. Tom even jogged down to the stables for some of the stale petrol that had been drained out of the Land Rover into a selection of empty glass bottles.

Once the fire was going, she opened the lid of the trunk and began pulling out clothes. They might be old, but they were still lovely.

'Are you sure you want to do this, Lil?' Tom's hands faltered over the silk and satin. 'I mean, really, they belong to Blake, don't they?'

Lily forced her heart to harden. 'She tricked you into confessing.'

'And then she saved *you*.'

Lily scowled to hide her indecision, and dropped the first piece of clothing into the brazier. It swamped the flame for a moment, then caught. She fed in an embroidered evening dress, then a lace shawl.

Watched it all burn.

She picked up the wig of long chestnut hair. It was gorgeous, both in colour and quality. No cheap party wig, this was made from real hair, she could tell. It felt silky and soft as she ran her fingers through its strands.

Everything must go.

She bunched the wig in her hands, preparing to toss it into the brazier.

'Besides,' Tom said then, almost diffident, 'Mr Byron called me… It was not in the public interest to pursue, he said. So it rather seems like I… got away with it.'

He was poking at the fire with a stick. Lily turned, clutched his arm until he stopped and looked at her.

'Better *you* getting away with it, than our stepfather,' she said.

He froze for a second, then gave a jerky nod.

From the corner of the house, she saw two people come into view. A man and a woman. She recognised Mr Byron at once – he was dressed as she'd first seen him, in a dark suit. Recognising the woman took a moment longer. Lily had never seen her in anything other than ripped jeans.

'Oh! It's Blake.'

Then she realised the picture they painted, standing next to the burning brazier, with the trunk open, still in the wheelbarrow, and clothes spilled out onto the grass. She glanced down at the wig in her hands.

Do I stop, or keep going?

As if sensing her thoughts, across the lawn towards them, Blake and Byron began to run.

A LETTER FROM ZOË

Dear Reader,

Thank you so much for choosing to jump into Blake and Byron's world in *The Last Time She Died*. If you enjoyed this novel and want to keep up to date with future instalments, just sign up at the following link. Your email address will never be shared and you can unsubscribe at any time.

www.bookouture.com/zoe-sharp

I had so much fun creating the very different characters of Blake and Byron in *The Last Time She Died*, and feel I've only just begun to explore their underlying story. This is just the beginning of what I think will be a very interesting partnership between the con artist and the copper, each bringing their own unique skills to the pursuit of justice. I see plenty of trouble ahead!

I really hope you loved *The Last Time She Died*, and if you did I would be so grateful if you would write a review. Just a few heartfelt sentences make such a difference helping new readers to discover one of my books for the first time – be that Blake and Byron, the award-winning Charlie Fox series, Lakes crime thrillers, standalones, or short stories.

I always love hearing from my readers. You can get in touch via my website, on my Facebook page, through Twitter, Instagram, or Goodreads.

Thank you again – a satisfied reader is always a writer's best friend. Zoë

ZoeSharpAuthor

@AuthorZoeSharp

@AuthorZoeSharp

AuthorZoeSharp

www.ZoeSharp.com

ACKNOWLEDGEMENTS

Alex Holmes

Brian Price

Celine Kelly

Claire Rushbrook

Daniel Macintosh

David Penny

Derek Harrison

Jane Eastgate

Jane Hudson

Jill Harrison

John Lawton

Lewis Hancock

Lucy Dauman

Noelle Holten

Peta Nightingale

Pippa White

Rachel Amphlett

Ruth Tross

Sarah Harrison

Tim Winfield

Printed in Great Britain
by Amazon